Desert Runner

By
Joseph Swicegood

PublishAmerica

Baltimore

First printing

ISBN: 1-59129-911-X
PUBLISHED BY PUBLISHAMERICA BOOK PUBLISHERS
www.publishamerica.com
Baltimore

Printed in the United States of America

ACKNOWLEDGMENTS

A SPECIAL THANK YOU TO:

My son, Ron, whose ideas contributed greatly to the story line. Ron also designed the book cover.

My 89 year old brother, John, whose experiences riding the rails as a hobo during the thirties, looking for work, provided details I couldn't have known about.

My 97 year old sister, Fanny, for her encouragement while anxiously awaiting another chapter of *Desert Runner*. During the thirties her husband, Tom, built their family a one room log house out of cottonwood trees. He cut and hauled them up from the banks of the South Canadian River with his team of mules.

Victoria, my Diablo Valley teacher, who from day one, insisted I could become a writer.

Barbara, my always loving wife, who always read the first draft of each chapter, giving both praise and criticism where due.

My always loving daughter, Linda, who diligently poured over every word, crossing out some parts and rephrasing others.

Also thanks to my many friends, neighbors, and kinfolks for their inspiration, sense of humor, enthusiasm, encouragement and assistance, which helped to make this book happen.

Alice	Beverly	B.J.
Bob	Craig	Don
Doris	Gene	Jeff
Jim	Kitty	Lindsay
Lloyd	Lori	Mary
Rachel	Ray	Rick
Ruth	Adrienne	Virginia

CHAPTER 1
1938
MUTTERED INSULT

Most of the flesh was missing from the face of the withered corpse where hooked-beak scavengers had torn it away. Yellow and brown stains showed on the tattered dusty pants where escaping body fluids had dried in the blistering heat of the desert.

After the last mule plodded in and the iron gate clanged shut, the lead guard dismounted and cut the dirty cotton rope. He stepped back and watched as the prisoner's body slid off the mule's back and hit the ground, shooting out a spray of dust. A trace of amusement tugged at the corners of the sergeant's mouth. Even though the body was impossible to recognize, all of the assembled prisoners knew, without question, who the buzzards had found.

A sickening stench drifted to where John Reece stood near the stone wall. He swallowed hard, choking back the vomit welling up in his throat and spread his feet to steady himself. None of his 114 days in this squalid Mexican hell-hole had prepared him for the sight of Thompson's bloated, sun-blackened remains.

It had been Thompson who came to Reece's rescue the first week he was brought into the prison when two men had tried to rape him. Thompson had easily been the toughest of the *gringo* prisoners. All of the *americanos* and many of the Mexican inmates had looked to him for protection. If there had been a prison uprising, Thompson would have been the leader.

Rodriguez, the tall captain of the guard, stood with a sneer, looking out over the prisoners. He slowly walked back and forth -- a strutting pea cock in his spotless uniform, the brass buttons glistening in the noonday sun. His polished boots came up to just below his knees. He didn't say a word, obviously savoring the vivid proof of his oft repeated warnings about trying to escape.

The tired tracking dogs lay panting, stretched along the sliver of shade at the base of the prison wall. The best of the dogs, a shy older bitch named Blue, with darkened, sagging teats, got up and scratched a deeper furrow in the ribbon of shade by the stone wall. She raised her head briefly, sniffed towards

Thompson's body, and lay back down.

Saddle horses and pack mules stood with lowered heads, eyes closed against the flies that sucked at the bits of moisture on their muzzles and in the corners of their eyes.

The captain's boot heels scraped the sandstone entry of the prison compound as he paraded back and forth. He repeatedly whacked a leather riding crop sharply against the top of his highly polished boots, a habit he exhibited when extremely pleased with himself.

"This is all such a shameful tragedy, *un frasco* -- but after all, he did try to escape," said Rodriguez softly, with a touch of mock sympathy in his voice. The captain paused. Stroking his mustache and looking off into the distance, he gave the appearance of a man who would like to be considered both thoughtful and compassionate. "I'm quite sure that an offer from a generous relative would have resulted in a reconsideration and possible forgiveness by those wronged by this man. The judge is a reasonable person. Perhaps some of you other *americanos* have relatives who are not so stubborn as this man's were."

"That blood sucking pimp has a price for everything," muttered Al Limesand, a former salesman from San Diego who was standing in the row behind Reece. On some days Limesand acted a little crazy. There were rumors that he'd been caught carrying drugs across the border.

Rodriguez whirled around and stared directly at Reece. Reece felt his rectum draw up tight and his mouth immediately lost its saliva. Everyone knew the rules. You learned them the first day. You'd better.

"So. Our newest *gringo* hasn't learned any manners, *es muy tosco.*" Rodriguez continued his pacing, stroking his chin and smoothing his mustache. He had two main obsessions: Impeccable personal attire and absolute control over all prisoners and guards.

"Bring Reece over here."

The lead guard, sergeant Sanchez, stepped up on a stone ledge by the end of the heavy iron gate post and surveyed the group before him. He grinned and moved directly toward Reece, shoving men out of his way as he went. The burly guard thoroughly enjoyed his responsibilities. Reece knew that he did not dare explain that Rodriguez had made a mistake. There was nothing he could do to stop the act of retaliation that the muttered insult was about to bring down upon him.

"Yes, bring him over here by his good friend and let him have a real close look at his face -- or what's left of it," said Rodriguez.

Sanchez, laughing loudly, grabbed Reece around the neck with one of his hairy, muscular arms, choking and dragging him over to Thompson's grisly remains. He shoved Reece's face within inches of the eyeless sockets, holding him there with an iron grip on his neck.

After long minutes passed, Reece was allowed to stagger back to his assigned place, vomiting down the front of his shirt as he went. He was barely able to stand, his legs shaking uncontrollably. The muscles in his neck throbbed and he could hardly breathe.

Sanchez stepped over to Rodriguez and spoke to him privately, then pointed to Thompson's body. Rodriguez smiled and nodded.

"You're all going to line up and file past this stinking corpse," snarled Rodriguez, his mood suddenly changing. "Look closely at the hands and knees. The skin and flesh are ripped down to the bone. I have to give this *gringo* credit, he was one tough man, *un hombre muy doro.* Many of you had never known a hard day's work -- that is, before you came here." Rodriguez turned to Sanchez, who had led the search, giving him a slight nod of approval.

Sanchez, who was in charge of all work assignments, beamed, enjoying this rare moment of praise.

The vomit on Reece's shirt began to dry in the broiling sun. It would be a week until he'd have an opportunity to wash his clothes. Until then, the smell would only add slightly to the overwhelming stench of the room he slept in.

Rodriguez nodded toward a canteen hanging on the saddle horn of the nearest horse. Sanchez moved quickly for the water. Rodriguez took out a neatly folded white handkerchief, wiping his forehead, under his chin, and the inside of his hat band.

Reece glanced at the canteen, still tasting the vomit in his mouth. What he wouldn't do for a drink of that water, he thought. Better yet, a beer.

It had been over four months since Reece had even seen a beer. He had never needed a drink more in his life, not even the time he was beaten up and left unconscious behind a bar in Flagstaff. Just the thought of a nice cold drink was intoxicating in itself. Right now it would help to steady his trembling legs.

Now Sanchez spoke up. "Like I told you, we don't got to chase you if you try to run away. No more than two, maybe three days pass before we ride out and watch for buzzards circling over your body." Sanchez made circling motions with his right arm over his head. "They're just waiting for you to swell up and get ripe and stinking. That's the way they like you best." Sanchez broke into a belly laugh.

Rodriguez stood relaxed, obviously enjoying the dejection and misery reflected in the faces of his captive audience. As usual, they stood, almost to a man with downcast eyes. He appeared smug and confident, toying with his charges. When standing before a group, he seldom passed up an opportunity to demonstrate his authority and rigid control.

The captain's reference to Thompson's toughness reminded Reece of what his own condition had been when he'd first entered the stone-walled compound. Of all the inmates, he had been one of the least prepared for the rigors and dangers of prison life. He'd been terrified, until Thompson came to his aid. He had lost twenty or more pounds; there was no way to tell for sure except that his clothes were getting loose and baggy. And on his next birthday, if he lived that long, he would be 48 years old. He hoped he was in condition to at least try to defend himself if he had to. Now that Thompson was dead, he'd better be.

CHAPTER 2

NACOZARI

Three days after Thompson's body was brought in from the desert the prisoners were assembled again -- this time for an announcement by the warden who'd been in poor health for over a year. Rodriguez helped the aging man up the steps near the main gate where the stone landing provided an elevated view. Although he hadn't been seen at the prison for several weeks, the warden cleared his throat and put on his glasses. He spoke slowly, his voice raspy but forceful. "Two hundred of you are going to be transferred within the week. You'll be sent north to begin work on a telegraph line that will run from," he paused for a moment and continued, "somewhere near the border down to Durango." Rodriguez handed the warden a glass of water when he paused again and looked at his notes. A murmur spread through the anxious prisoners, hearing the news for the first time.

After sipping the water slowly the warden continued, "Your previous work experiences and your attitudes have been taken into consideration in making these assignments. It'll be a tough job, out in the open, with plenty of dust and flies and your work days will be long and hard. It's important that this project be completed as soon as possible. Those of you who can stand the pace will be well fed for your efforts. The others will be sent back here. It's up to each of you to make the most of this assignment."

While Rodriguez helped the warden down the steps the level of excited voices increased.

On the following day Reece learned that he was selected because of his previous experience as a cook. He'd cooked for men in hunting camps in the Rocky Mountains and for road construction crews building sections of Route 66, the main link between Chicago and Santa Monica, California. Cooking over an open fire would be nothing new for him. When work was scarce he'd cooked his food in tin cans in hobo jungles.

After four days of preparation and three days of riding in the back of a truck, Reece arrived at the first camp where the line construction would begin.

Off to the north a train whistled. Reece stopped in mid-stride and looked off into the distance from the elevated slope where he was gathering firewood. His skin tingled and he felt a lump in his throat as the familiar mournful sound floated up over the stunted sage and mesquite on the sparsely covered mountainside. In earlier times, when he was a hobo, he'd ridden freights on most of the major lines.

Straining to see through the haze, Reece could make out a column of smoke trailing behind the dark form of an engine. As if being moved along by an invisible hand, the blackened locomotive slowly drew a dark line southwest across the valley floor. When his eyes adjusted to the distance, he could see that the engine was pulling a long load of freight cars through a pass on the horizon.

At the southern end of the valley he could see the gray forms of buildings clustered around an area where the ground appeared terraced up the hillsides in giant steps. Dust hung in a pall over the entire area, obscuring any detail of the individual structures.

Reece glanced around furtively as he carried the armload of dead mesquite branches over to the cooking tent that was being set up by other prisoners. He didn't want anyone to notice that he'd even become aware of the freight crossing the valley -- especially the moody Sergeant Sanchez. Sanchez was keeping a watchful eye on all the prisoners setting up the first base camp. Reece dropped the wood on the growing pile near the campfire, then knelt and carefully placed some of the finger-sized sticks on the blazing kindling.

Reece stared into the fire for a moment, thinking of the warden's announcement. He'd now learned the telegraph line would be built down across the eastern slopes of the Sierra Madre Occidental range. The surprising news had thrilled the prisoners. There had been little talk of anything else among the men who'd been, at least temporarily, freed of the stone walls and stinking cells. At a later date, additional lines were planned. They would be strung to towns lying east and west of the main line that would connect Durango with Nogales, Arizona. It was apparent that the warden didn't want any prisoners to know their exact location. Some might make the foolish mistake of believing they could escape to the States. The brief remarks by Captain Rodriguez on the day they lined up to climb into the trucks for the trip north had made one thing clear when he said. "Anyone caught trying to escape will be shot and left to rot in the desert. No notification will be sent to any dead man's family."

Reece remembered the chilling effect of Rodriguez's warning and the smile that had played on his face when an audible murmur spread through the prisoners.

The base camp they were now setting up would be the first phase of the communication link that would be constructed by prisoners. Trucks and stock trailers loaded with additional prisoners and animals were scheduled to arrive before sunset. An American contractor would furnish the necessary supplies and equipment, and Mexican prisons would furnish men for the backbreaking labor: digging holes along the rocky slopes, carrying and setting pine poles in place, stringing copper wires overhead, fastening them to glass insulators on wooden crossarms.

Reece recalled that after the men were loaded onto the trucks the warden had made another brief appearance. He emphasized again that time was the most important factor. The warmongers in Europe were making the entire continent nervous. The warden had stressed that the ability to communicate quickly in times of danger would be vital to survival.

Moving down now into a sandy swale, breaking dead branches from a mesquite, Reece became aware that someone was quietly moving up behind him. His body tensed, but he tried to continue gathering wood as if unaware of any intruder. He broke one of the limbs off into a length that could be used as a club. He held it along his side in a tight grip while his heart raced wildly, he casually turned and tried to see whoever was approaching from the rear.

"I want to talk to you--"

"Stay away from me!" Reece cautioned through clenched teeth, as he held the club in view. It was the first time he'd seen the salesman since the day the guards brought in Thompson's body. Reece was disgusted when he now realized they'd been assigned to the same work detail. "You damn near got me choked to death."

"I didn't mean you any harm. It's just that sometimes I can't control myself. I say things that just pop into my head, especially when I'm scared." The man hesitated for a moment. Glancing warily at the club in Reece's hand, he continued. "When I was a pharmaceutical salesman I took too many –" The tall prisoner's voice trailed off and he lowered his head and kicked his shoe idly against a mound of dirt.

Reece glanced over his shoulder, then continued gathering wood for the cooking fires. He relaxed and began breathing more slowly. "You're Limesand, aren't you? I hear you're from Los Angeles."

"Yeah, near there. I'm Al Limesand. Could -- could we shake hands? I'm really sorry that I got you into so much trouble." Limesand extended his hand but Reece turned his back and continued gathering wood.

"You better start picking up some sticks or we're both going to be in trouble this time. If Sanchez stands up he can see us both and we better not be shaking hands. He won't like that neither."

Limesand dejectedly began breaking off pieces of dark weathered branches and throwing them into a pile. They'd each carried a couple of loads and dropped them onto the growing mound of fuel before there were any further attempts at conversation. Reece thought about this man admitting being too scared to control himself. When Reece noticed the sergeant move his seat around to the other side of the tent he asked, "What was that you said you sold again, farm supplies or something like that?"

Limesand laughed and his eyes crinkled at the corners "Pharmaceutical. Drugs. You know, like you buy at a drugstore. Medicine, like you take when you're sick."

"Oh, I see," Reece said, feeling foolish and embarrassed at his lack of education. Limesand obviously had been to college but he didn't seem to think it made him any better than anyone else. Reece liked that. He liked the man's voice and the way he expressed himself -- simply and directly.

"I saw you freeze when you heard that freight train whistle -- like it might mean something special to you. You ever ridden one?"

"Yeah, a few times," Reece answered, disturbed that Limesand had been able to guess something about his background.

Limesand nodded in the direction of the cluster of buildings, barely visible now that the sun had dropped to the horizon. "Any idea where we are?"

"Nope."

"You're looking at the big copper mine at Nacozari. If you look closely you can see the train stopped there. It's the end of the line. It runs down from Nogales. There's a telegraph line right beside it."

"Nogales, huh. About how far would you reckon?" Reece bit his lower lip when he realized what he was saying. Limesand could be nothing but a stool pigeon for Rodriguez.

Limesand looked at Reece for a moment, raised his eyebrows in mock concern and asked, "Say old man, you're not thinking of making a run for it, are you? You look a little out of shape for that."

"I wasn't thinking nothin' like that," Reece lied. He knew that every man in the prison thought about it day and night from the first moment the steel doors slammed shut behind them.

"I was just kidding. But in answer to your question, it's not quite a hundred miles straight north to the border. Nogales is actually northwest of here," he said, nodding in the general direction of the border town. "If you look over to the north you can make out where another rail line runs due north of where we're standing. It goes through that cut in the hills. The one that just stopped at Nacozari came down that line."

"I hadn't noticed that before," Reece said, still unsure of making conversation about the camp's location.

"They haul the copper ore to the smelters in Bisbee and Douglas, just over the border into Arizona. Other shipments are sent east to the big smelter at El Paso"

"What are they going to do with all that copper?" Reece asked, wondering how Limesand knew so much about northern Mexico and the copper mines.

"There's a drive on to build power lines in the rural areas of the States. It's good for business. It doesn't cost much to build lines when land is cheap and so many people are looking for work," Limesand said soberly.

Reece could see the advantages of being educated and apparently having widely traveled on something besides freight trains. He felt a twinge of jealousy. If only he'd been given the opportunities this man obviously had.

"We better get busy before one of the other guards notices us," Reece cautioned.

By the time they'd each gathered another load a guard walked over and shouted. "That's enough wood, Reece. Get up here and start cooking. *¡Ahoro mismo!*"

Reece raised his hand. "Be right there, *Señor*."

The guard turned and walked back out of sight.

"Say, how come you know so much about so many places?" Reece asked, hoping his question wouldn't seem rude.

"Remember, I told you I used to be a pharmaceut -- I mean a drug salesman."

Both men laughed. It was the first time Reece had laughed since he'd been given a ten-year prison sentence.

"I had a big territory and traveled a lot. I had a lot of customers, many down here in Sonora and some over in Chihuahua." Reece noticed Limesand frown before he added, "It's still hard for me to talk about it..."

There was an awkward pause as both men stepped toward each other.

"Call me Al," said the salesman, sticking out his hand, his smiling blue eyes suddenly filling with tears.

"I'm John."

They shook hands and for the first time since he'd been in prison, Reece knew he had made a friend. Having a friend would take away some of the loneliness of being a prisoner in a foreign land.

Limesand's eyes cleared and serious concern showed on his face when he glanced up to the ridge behind Reece.

Reece turned and saw six dark figures sitting in a row on top of a rocky ledge a half-mile or so away.

"Yaquis!" Al exclaimed. "Keep an eye out for them -- they're the most vicious tribe in all of Mexico. Even the Apaches leave them alone. For the first hundred and fifty miles, they'll be watching us day and night."

CHAPTER 3

THE CONTRACTOR

Reece looked up from the cooking fire where he squatted, frying two more slabs of ham for the still hungry Sanchez. Wiping his hot sweaty face on the sleeve of his shirt, he glanced up at a sudden movement that caught his eye.

Overhead, a dozen or so small brown bats darted in zigzag patterns, twittering their barely audible high-pitched squeaking sounds. They were beginning their nightly quest, gorging themselves on the insects swarming above in the diffused twilight of early evening.

The six dark forms, still sitting on the rocky outcropping at the top of the ridge, were now barely visible. Silhouetted by a sliver of a new moon rising behind them, the menacing shadowy figures would serve as an unspoken warning. Reece began to ponder what Limesand had said. If he was right only a fool would try to escape through the lands of the vengeful Yaquis.

Reece would feel relieved when they got farther southeast to the state of Chihuahua. The line was to be built through an area that had once been the ancestral home of the Tarahumara Indians. Stories of their feats of running hundreds of miles across the desert had fascinated Reece when he'd heard them in prison. Even though the stories seemed impossible and some thought they were just made up legends, he preferred to believe them.

Limesand had said that as they progressed southeastward there would be stretches of country that would be inaccessible to all trucks and that supplies would have to be brought in by pack mule. He'd also told him that the Tarahumara would be hired to cut and carry pine poles for supporting the overhead lines. In some places they would carry the 200-pound logs on their backs for twenty miles or more. "They'll be paid little more than pennies a day," he'd said.

Reece was surprised that the well-educated Limesand, who appeared to have lived a life of privilege, would concern himself with the fate of a people whose existence seemed of little consequence to anyone else. He could hardly wait to reach the eastern slopes of the Sierra and see the runners for himself.

Over thirty years before, when he was a lanky boy in his early teens, he'd considered himself a promising runner, even though there had been no organized running in his community. He'd been too skinny to participate in any of the contact sports at the small school he'd attended, and, looking down at his now ample waistline, it was hard for him to believe that his body was once lean and hard.

It was then he noticed that the crew of guards and prisoners were all standing and looking in the direction of Nacozari.

The American contractor, who would act as superintendent of the construction project, had been scheduled to arrive earlier in the day. Three days before, when the trucks left the prison, Captain Rodriguez had left on the train for El Paso. From there he was scheduled to take the train west to Nogales to meet the superintendent and help him with the trucks, horses and pack mules, and getting loads of construction supplies through the Mexican custom officials.

In the distance a droning whine of motors sounded as if they were laboring in low gear. In the gathering darkness Reece could see scattered lights that he assumed were coming from houses near the mines. When he got up and stepped over to get more wood for the fire he saw a line of headlights midway to Nacozari. The beams of light moved slowly toward them. The lights on the lead vehicle turned abruptly and proceeded on a downward course. One by one the trailing lights changed course at the same location and followed. Shortly, the lead vehicle disappeared from sight. The others, in turn, soon vanished in the growing darkness.

Only one set of lights was still visible when another came into view. It was much closer and both headlights on the truck first in line were now distinct. The trucks that had been due a few hours earlier were traversing the foothills and arroyos in the darkness. Reece saw the silhouette of a man on foot, walking in front of the headlights of the darkened, looming form of the lead truck. With a flashlight, he directed the driver around the boulders that lay scattered across the steepening grade.

"That's them!" yelled Sanchez, alerting the other guards to look sharp. "The *capitán* and the *americano, Señor* Neilson, are here. I thought they would have stayed in Nacozari until morning. That Neilson must be…" the sergeant said, his voice becoming indistinct as he turned his head and spoke to the guards standing behind him. There was a low chuckle that broke off abruptly when a sudden light illuminated the area around the cooking fire.

Reece stepped back and jerked the skillet from the glowing coals. Flames had flashed over the skillet's sides and engulfed the hot grease. When the flames shot over his arm, Reece lost his grip and the skillet plopped back down onto the outer rim of the hot embers, spilling the meat into the dirt.

The flare of sudden light was reflected on the faces of the men standing nearby. The heavy-jowled features of the glowering Sanchez made his appearance even more sinister in the flashing yellowed light of the burning grease -- the acrid stench quickly replacing the aroma of frying pork.

"And you call yourself a cook, *un cocinero,*" Sanchez snarled. There was a long pause and the men behind the sergeant began to laugh. They stopped abruptly when Sanchez looked behind him.

"You're just another dumb *gringo*, Reece--maybe the dumbest one we've had yet."

Reece swallowed hard. The hulking form of the sergeant was not like a foreman on a road construction job. Sanchez held the power of life or death in his hands.

"I'm very sorry, *Señor* Sanchez," Reece stammered, both embarrassed and disappointed that his first opportunity to impress the sergeant had been wasted in such a careless manner. The freedom he'd felt a few moments before while watching the diving, darting bats in the cooling evening breeze had vanished. -

"I can do much better, *Señor* Sanchez," Reece added, hoping his words sounded sincere. "I'll work hard an' show you I'm a good cook. You'll like the special desserts I can make for you -- things I'm sure you've never tasted. I'll make you some tonight."

The sergeant's fondness for sweets was well known and the mention of special desserts seemed to pacify Sanchez's agitation.

"All right, Reece. You get one more chance, *un solamente una más oportunidad.* If you can't do the job you'll be the first sent back to prison. And I'll send along some special instructions on what's to be done with you. Do you understand?" the snarling sergeant asked in a voice loud enough for all to hear.

"*Gracias, gracias, Señor,* I won't disappoint you again," Reece added, convinced that Sanchez would now be even harder to please.

The sergeant's attention was diverted by the arrival of the lead truck, slowly climbing the last 100 yards of the slope. Dust from the spinning tires drifted over the campsite, covering the tables and cooking utensils with a fine layer of grit as the truck rolled to a stop.

Two men got out of the cab and approached the fire. Captain Rodriguez nodded to Sanchez and stiffly introduced the man who had stopped alongside him. It appeared there had been some kind of a disagreement. Neither man seemed comfortable with the situation, or glad to be arriving at the campsite after dark.

"This is *Señor* Neilson, and this is *Señor* Sanchez." Rodriguez said, motioning toward the muscular uniformed man who stepped forward and nodded at the *americano*.

The burly man glanced up and down the frame of Sanchez but made no comment. He slowly looked around, surveying the camp with a look of disdain before nodding in the direction of the sergeant. "I prefer to be called Swede."

Both the captain and the Swede stepped over by the cooking fire, obviously tired and hungry, their faces lined, their mouths still set in a defiant expression.

They both seemed to notice the blackened skillet at the same time. Smoke was curling up from the charred pieces of meat lying in the dirt at the edge of the embers.

The Swede slowly drew his finger tips across the top of the nearest table, then rubbed them against his thumb and the heel of his hand.

"Should have brought my own cook," he said in a detached voice.

Reece could see by the light of the fire that the man wore a starched khaki shirt and pants that were sharply creased. His belt was expensively tooled. The field boots that reached his mid-calf were highly polished. A gold watch was on his thick hairy wrist and a gleaming gold matched pen and pencil set showed in his left shirt pocket, clipped to a leather liner protecting the fabric. The reddish-blond hair above the man's shirt collar was neatly trimmed. He wore a massive gold ring with a dark stone on his right hand. The man appeared to be equal to the captain when it came to impeccable clothing.

If the proud captain and the arrogant Swede could find a way to work together, the telegraph line would be built. The first few days would be critical. If their egos clashed, the project could be doomed since the use of prison labor was on a test basis. Word had spread among the prisoners that the Swede had preferred to bring his own crew from the States.

Reece was determined to do everything in his power to make both men as comfortable as possible. He would be their humble servant in all outward appearances.

CHAPTER 4

UNSIGNED MAIL

This was the second campsite they'd moved to, and the eighth day since the line construction began. Reece lifted the bucket of boiling water from the grate over the campfire and poured it slowly over the stack of pots and pans sitting in a rack on a nearby table. Turning his face to the side, he avoided the cloud of steam that shot up when the scalding water splashed over the metal utensils.

It was still early morning and the sun was just breaking through a thin layer of clouds on the horizon. A warm current of air was already moving up from the wide desolate plain to the east. It would be another hot one.

Less than half an hour before, the campsite had been bustling with activity. Men assigned to dig the holes for the telegraph poles were filling their canteens, each in turn taking his digging tools from the pole railings where they had been stored the evening before. Before noon a mounted guard would lead a string of pack mules up along the line to refill the canteens and hand out food to the sweating diggers.

Each day had been long and tiring for Reece, after rising at 4:00 a.m. to build a fire and begin preparing the food for breakfast. At the end of the day, when he collapsed on his blanket, it was usually near midnight.

While glancing at the long column of prisoners climbing the slope to his right, Reece stretched a sheet of red-checkered oilcloth over the top of the steaming pots and pans. He placed rocks on each corner of the covering. If the wind came up, the rock weights would hold the oilcloth in place, keeping the dust and flies away.

Limesand knelt in an area of coarse sand below a rock ledge, scouring the last of 30 cast-iron dutch ovens. The coarse grit quickly cleaned the particles of food stuck to the inner surfaces. Now Reece could wash and scald them.

Limesand looked around and checked the captain's tent. The flap was still closed. He carried two of the ovens over and set them on an empty table behind Reece.

"I was out past the corral last night and I overheard two of the guards," Al whispered. "They walked out and started talking not more than ten feet away from where I was squatting behind a bush. Once or twice they looked in my direction but they couldn't see me. Must've smelled me though -- but neither one said anything. Each of them probably thought the other one farted." Al laughed quietly at his own little joke, then looked around and became serious.

"Sanchez had a real hard-on for Thompson. Couldn't stand him. He knew Thompson could take him in a fair fight and he wasn't about to let that happen. He was afraid to push Thompson around like he does everyone else -- afraid Thompson would kick the shit out him without even stopping to think."

"An' he would've too."

"Damn right he would!" Limesand emphasized the point with a short jab of his left fist.

"I saw them staring hard at each other once." Reece said. "Sanchez finally walked away first, pretending nothin' had happened, but he sure looked nervous."

Al nodded. "I'd seen that too a couple of times." He checked the captain's tent again before he continued. "Both guards lowered their voices and I couldn't hear everything they said -- but I heard enough. They said Sanchez got the captain to set Thompson up. He convinced the captain it would teach the goddam *gringos* a lesson and make sure that we'd all think twice about trying to escape."

"It didn't make no sense to me, Thompson trying to run away like he did -- didn't have a snowball's chance in hell of making it."

"First they stopped all of Thompson's mail. Threw the letters from his wife into the fire. A couple of weeks later the unsigned letter Thompson got in the mail about his wife moving in with his neighbor was just a ruse."

"What's a ruse?" Reece asked.

Al chuckled and his mischievious eyes showed his amusement at Reece's question. "It's when someone pulls a fast one on you. Plays you for a fool."

"Oh. I see --"

The canvas flap of the captain's tent suddenly flew back.

"Bring me some hot water. I'm ready to shave," the captain ordered.

"Be right there, Captain," Limesand responded immediately and hurried over with the teakettle that had been left steaming on the back of the grate as the captain had instructed them on the first morning at the camp near Nacozari.

While watching the salesman walk briskly to the captain's tent, Reece wondered if what Limesand had overheard was true. It made a lot of sense.

In some ways it even explained Thompson's senseless behavior. It simply didn't pay to defy the sergeant openly. The life of any prisoner didn't mean that much to Sanchez.

Looking at the dwindling pile of firewood, Reece almost envied the men building the line. Their day was not nearly as long as his. Now silhouetted against the skyline, they made an odd-looking procession, walking in single file with two of the guards riding along on horseback behind them, their rifles strapped to their backs, the barrels jutting above their heads. They worked hard, but at sundown they could relax for a couple of hours.

The crew they were following were the men assigned to dig holes for the long slender pine logs that would support the telegraph lines. Reece could see the large twelve-foot-long digging spoons that the men carried over their shoulders. From this distance a hostile force moving across the mountainside could hardly appear more sinister.

Al returned with the kettle and placed it back on the grate. "I better get back to work. The captain didn't sleep too good. He's in a nasty mood this morning. He really doesn't like living out here in the wilderness, as he calls it."

"Ain't that too bad," Reece said in a low voice.

Al nodded and carried the remaining ovens over to the table where he began peeling potatoes for the evening meal. While Reece washed and scalded the dutch ovens, Al worked on the sack of potatoes. As Reece was dipping more water from a wooden barrel and refilling the kettle, Limesand got up from the bench and started walking away.

"I'll be right back. I'm going to get another sack of spuds off the truck."

"While you're up see if you can find me another armload of wood. I've got to cook the captain's breakfast."

"Well, Mr Reece, I shore-nuff will, but I can't help wondering who carried the wood for you when you used to be a hobo!"

Limesand laughed and gave Reece a mock salute. He wasn't offended that Limesand made fun of his country way of talking. The former salesman seldom missed any chance to make a joke or tell a funny story.

Standing at the end of the table, Reece could look in the Swede's direction without being obvious. The well-organized and disciplined man sat at his writing table, some thirty yards away. A stack of black loose-leaf binders stood in one corner. Three long leather cylindrical tubes that contained his maps stood upright in a rack.

Neilson appeared to be looking at a line of ragged peaks that ran across the middle of a wide valley to the south. Earlier, Reece had seen him peering through the lens on the transit mounted near the table, then writing in one of the binders and unrolling one of the maps. Smoke curled upward from the intricately carved pipe he cradled in his left hand. Without even looking in Reece's direction, the Swede rapped his coffee cup twice on the top of the table. Reece grabbed the pot from where it sat warming on the edge of the grate, hurried to the Swede's table and refilled the heavy mug with the gold rim. He stepped back and stood silently while the Swede carefully measured out two level teaspoons of brown sugar from his own personal tin. He stuck the stem of his pipe back in his mouth and without looking up, motioned Reece back toward his duties with a casual wave of his hand.

Reece sucked in a quick breath and held it. He clamped his jaws hard and felt a surge of anger tighten the cords in his neck before he could turn and walk away. He had decided to act every bit the lackey, but it was more difficult than he thought it would be.

"Get a move on, Reece. Get over here. I'm starved."

The captain had finished shaving and was now sitting at the table reserved for the guards. As Reece approached, he took deep breaths and tried to hide his contempt for the Swede's haughty manner. He felt a knot in the pit of his stomach. At least the moody captain looked at him and knew his name.

"Good morning, Captain. What can I fix you for breakfast?"

CHAPTER 5

CUNNINGHAM

The day had been long and hot and now it was almost midnight. A cooling breeze came from the west. Reece lay down on his blanket and looked up at the stars, their brilliance contrasted against the blackness of the moonless sky. He was exhausted but happy to be assigned to the construction crew. Sometime he would ask Limesand if he could teach him how to tell time by the position of the stars. Some people said it could be done, and if anyone would know it would be Limesand. Reece listened to the crickets and somewhere a coyote yelped with a high-pitched warbling yodel. Farther up the mountain another one answered. He reckoned it must be its mate.

Reece rubbed his aching legs and ran his hands up his sides to his armpits. He could now easily count his ribs. The layers of fat that had covered them for so many years were gradually disappearing.

"You awake, John?" whispered Limesand from his bed a short distance away.

"Hell yes. How could anyone sleep with them damn coyotes carryin' on? They been gettin' bolder every night. Past two mornin's, tracks showed in the sand just behind the corral." Reece turned over on his side and pulled the corner of his blanket up over his shoulder, cushioning his head on his forearm as relief from the hard-packed ground.

"Probably been drinking out of the horse troughs and looking for scraps. They can live just about anyplace -- eat anything, living or dead. Don't care which. We had a lot of them in the hills when I lived out near San Diego."

"Sounds like a whole bunch of 'em this time." Reece was only vaguely aware of the towns in southern California. He'd heard of San Diego and he knew it was somewhere on the Pacific Ocean. Mostly he'd heard of Hollywood, but really didn't know just where that was either.

"Two or three can sound like a dozen when they really get to wailing and making babies." Limesand stifled a quiet chuckle.

Reece could see Limesand's silhouette. His head was propped up with his elbow. "If they wake up the captain again tonight he's gonna make us bury or burn every scrap of food 'fore we go to bed. This still beats that stinking prison life," Limesand said. "The only thing is, nobody can see any of their family way out here. In the last letter my mother wrote me, she promised to bring the kids down to see me."

"You must miss 'em terribly."

"I sure do. I think about them, especially at night when it gets dark and quiet. It's a long trip for my mother, her health's not so good. When the newspapers printed the story about my arrest and sentencing she had to be given sedatives, phenobarbital, for nearly a year."

Reece heard Limesand sniffle, then blow his nose. It was hard to know what to say to a grown-up blubbering man, so lonesome for his family, especially his children. The friendly face with the deep blue eyes and big grin showed a sunny disposition. It was there every morning for all to see. Inside, however, there was a deeply troubled soul. The good life he'd enjoyed was gone. But, strangely, he never complained about the long hours of toil or the heat and dust or the endless clouds of insects.

It had been so different for Reece. His family had seldom known anything but a meager subsistence. His folks had moved from the Deep South out to Oklahoma, nearly all of them, aunts, uncles and cousins, too. They'd arrived too late. All of the Indian lands the government opened to eager white settlers had been grabbed up several years before by those who got there first. So, just like on the places his folks had come from, they wound up being sharecroppers. He'd grown up hearing endless stories about the old home places -- places he'd never been to: Chickamauga, Chattanooga, and the historic Lookout Mountain and the battles in the Civil War that had raged around them. There too, except for one grandfather who'd fought for the North, his family had been on the side of the losers.

It was hard for Reece to tell who was worse off -- those who'd had a prosperous life and lost it, or those who had little more than the clothes they wore on their backs.

Limesand seldom made any attempt to hide his feelings, but it was different in Reece's family. He'd been raised mostly to keep to himself and avoid showing how he felt or offer his opinions.

"I told you about my family but you've never said a word about yours," Limesand said. When Reece didn't respond, he added, "You do have a family somewhere, don't you?"

The question had caught Reece off guard, and he hesitated before answering. A coyote close by let out a long plaintive cry, then ended the wail with a staccato of crisp yelps. It gave Reece a few moments to think of a reply.

"Not really. Just some distant cousins -- never was very close to but one of 'em. My folks been dead for a long time now. I got a sister but I got no idea where she's at."

"No wife or kids?"

"Oh, I was married once for a short time, but it didn't last. We separated after a few months and went different ways. Last I heard she'd moved back to Amarillo with her folks. I was on the road looking for work most of the time."

"How was it that you ended up at this prison?"

"It's somethin' that's hard to talk about an' I try to put it out of my mind when I can."

After a long pause, Limesand asked, "Did you kill somebody?"

"Well, no. But I hurt somebody pretty bad -- but not on purpose." Reece lay there in the dark, once again running the events of the fateful day through his head.

"Tell me about it, John."

"I was out of work an' just bummin' around Tucson, tryin' to get any kind of work there was. This fella' asked me if I'd drive a pickup truck loaded with some tractor parts down to Dublan -- said one of his best customers, a Mormon farmer, needed them right away."

"So, you did?"

"Yeah, it was a 1929 Model A pickup an' everything went just fine for a spell an' then…" Reece could feel his hands begin to sweat and he couldn't seem to take a real deep breath.

"And then what?"

"There was this boy herdin' goats along the dirt road an' one of the little ones played like it was fightin' another one an' it jumped right out in front of the pickup." Reece knew that the sudden vision of the kid goat, bouncing right out in front of the pickup, would be forever fixed in his mind.

"Did you run over the boy and the little goats?"

"No. I turned the steering wheel as hard as I could an' ran into the side of a school bus. I hurt two of the kids pretty bad."

"Then what happened?"

"The police came an' arrested me. Found an' empty wine bottle in the back. I didn't even know it was there."

"You hadn't been drinking?"

"No. I hadn't had a drink for over a month. I barely had any money for grub."

"You shouldn't feel guilty, John. It was just an accident. What some people would call an act of God."

"Well not exactly. I told the man who hired me that I had a driver's license. I lied. I'd never even driven a car before."

There was another long pause. For once Limesand didn't seem to know what to say. After several minutes Reece thought Limesand had finally gone back to sleep. Then he asked, "What did folks back home think about your arrest? Did they put it in your hometown newspaper?"

"Are you kiddin'? Hometown newspaper, that's almost funny."

"What's the name of the town you're from? It must have been pretty small if it didn't have a paper."

"We called it Scheluter's Branch. It was just a bunch of old farm houses an' one little store. The houses were mostly surrounded by wild plum thickets an' willow trees that growed along the banks of the South Canadian River."

"You were on the road a lot?"

"You could say that. It was good work when we were building old number 66. When there was no work I mostly went back to hoboin'. It's not an easy life though, the bulls watch the yards real close -- beat the shit out of you if they catch you, too. They get paid for it but some of them assholes would gladly do it for free. But once you learn your way around the yards, you can usually keep away from 'em. I could run real good when I was a little younger --'fore I got so fat."

"I've noticed that you've lost a lot of weight in the last few weeks. Your clothes hang on you like an old burlap sack. What's the matter, can't stand your own cooking?" Al laughed.

"Nothin' wrong with my cookin'. Even the Swede likes it. Course he'll never admit it, the miserable son-of-a bitch. It's just that they're damn near workin' us to death."

"Tell me more about your days of hoboing."

"Once two of the bulls chased me an' my cousin, J.H., when we jumped off the Rock Island when it was rolling into the freight yards in El Reno."

"El Reno, where's that?"

"Just west of Oklahoma City. We were gonna' catch another freight there an' go north up through Kansas to work in the wheat harvest. When it was finished we were goin' on to Nebraska. J. H. jumped off one side of the train an' I jumped off the other. I squatted down an' watched under the boxcars as the train kept slowly rollin' into the station. The bulls caught J. H. an' really beat

him sumpin' bad. I could hear that poor bastard screamin' but there was nothin'
I could do."

"They beat him like that just for riding on a freight car?"

"Sure did. They cut willow limbs about eight feet long an' whittle 'em
down. They leave only three or four forks cut short, makin' a hard nub that'll
tear the hide right off you. One lash can rip an eyeball right out of the socket."

"God, it's hard to believe people are treated like that." There was a period
of silence before Limesand continued. "It's just not right. It's not right that a
human being should be beaten when he's just out looking for work."

Reece lay in the darkness thinking about his days of riding the freights and
the nights when it was freezing cold and him and J. H. had to find shelter.

"You've certainly been down some different roads than I have, John.
You've seen a different side of life than most people ever will. I almost envy
you for it -- just going out there and not knowing what you're going to find, one
day to the next -- taking life as it comes and doing your best to hang on. It's
got to give you a certain amount of satisfaction after you've done it -- a feeling
you couldn't get any other way."

"Satisfaction, hah." Reece couldn't understand why Limesand would
want to even think about living the life of a hobo -- even for a day. There was
another long silence and Reece hoped Limesand would go to sleep this time.

Then he asked, "What ever happened to your cousin?"

Between the coyotes and Limesand's questions, Reece knew he had little
chance for sleep, but he hesitated to offend the only friend he had by asking
him to keep quiet.

"I lost track of him. Often think of him though, when I hear a train whistle
in the night." Reece had told Limesand more about his family than he'd told
anyone for the last ten years. He hoped his friend would drop the subject. It
really wasn't something he cared to discuss. It was another area where he felt
like a failure. In fact, if Limesand would just shut up and the coyotes would
move on, they could both get a little more rest. A faint light showed on the
mountains to the east. Morning would be here all too soon.

"Did the bulls ever catch you, John?"

It was useless. The salesman liked to talk and he was now wide awake.
Reece took several deep breaths, recalling a sober experience on a bitter cold
evening. "Well, not exactly. Like I told you, 25 years or so ago I was a pretty
good runner. We had a game when I was just a boy in school called Blackman.
It was the only game I was ever any good at. Boys would line up, usually at
a fence or wall, an' then try to run to the opposite fence or building. A couple

of the fastest runners would stay in the middle of the field an' try to chase down anyone who tried to make it across. I don't want to brag but few ever got by me once I'd chose 'em as my target."

"What do you mean, target?"

"Sometimes five or six would spread out an' all take off at once. You had a couple of seconds to pick the one you wanted an' drift over toward 'em an' then really give it everything you had. I always went for the one I knowed was the fastest."

"What did you mean when said you didn't exactly get caught when you were hoboing?"

"We was comin' into Chicago, just before dark. It was hard to tell where we was at when we jumped off the train. It's a big place. Two bulls spotted me -- big burly guys carryin' them long willow whips. I got mixed up an' ran toward the back of the yard. I didn't know they'd built a high bob-wire fence to keep the hobos out. The bulls yelled an' three others saw me an' cut me off. I told you I was pretty fast but you oughta see me run when I'm really scared. That fence was 12 feet high an' I went over it like a turpentined tomcat. Well, all of me didn't exactly get over but most of me did. Damn near tore off all of my clothes an' several pieces of my hide."

Limesand laughed. "John, you sure have a funny way of saying things. Sounds like you were almost as fast as that famous runner, Cunningham."

"Who?"

"Cunningham. Glenn Cunningham, who set the world record in the mile a couple of years ago. Don't tell me you never heard of him? The whole world's heard of him. Don't you ever read a newspaper or listen to a radio? He also won the silver medal for the 1500 meters in the Olympics. I saw a newsreel of him. Watching him start his run you wouldn't think he could ever even finish, much less win. He wobbles and looks like he's going to fall with every step until his muscles and tendons get warmed up."

"He wobbles when he runs?"

"Yeah, he wobbles all right but he set such a blistering pace around that big oval at the University of Kansas that the best runners couldn't stay with him -- running each lap in just a whisper over 60 seconds."

"I've seen runners puke after running real hard." Reece couldn't imagine how it must feel to be a world champion and know that no one else had ever run that fast.

"I've seen a lot of University half-milers collapse after two laps when they weren't even close to running 60 second laps," Limesand agreed. "But imagine keeping that pace up for four laps, against the best runners in the world and then finding yourself all alone at the finish. Even with his jerky gait he never slows up."

"What's the matter with him that he runs so funny?"

"Well, when he was eight years old he and his older brother got trapped in a schoolhouse fire. After a few days his older brother died and the doctors told Glenn's mother that the muscles and tendons in his legs were so badly burned he would never walk again."

Reece felt the muscles in his chest tighten as he pictured the two frightened little boys trying to escape from the burning schoolhouse. "You aren't telling me a whopper, are you?" Reece couldn't picture such a badly injured child ever becoming a world champion runner.

"Somewhere in his mind he must have had a picture; seeing himself walking again, maybe. Who knows? The mind is a funny thing."

"Do you know anything more about him, Al? Why do you suppose he wanted to run so bad?"

"That's about all I know. At the university I took some classes in psychology like I told you. That's the study of how the mind works -- or at least how some people think it does. It seems that most of the men in history who accomplished the impossible did it because they wanted to impress somebody, usually a woman. It's about as simple as that."

"Then this boy really wanted to impress somebody?" Reece was sure he knew just how the boy must have felt.

"I think it might have been his mother. Little doubt she was there when he took his first step. Who knows, it could have been a little girl from his Sunday school class. We'll never know. But it doesn't matter. It's one of the greatest athletic accomplishments in the history of the entire world."

"That's the best story I've ever heard."

There was a period of quiet when neither man spoke. Now that Reece was awake he became convinced that Limesand had gone back to sleep.

"I don't mean to pry, John, but I couldn't help noticing that you never get any mail."

Reece realized that there was no way he was going to get any more sleep this morning.

"It's my own fault. I don't write so good. I'd write to my sister, but, like I said, I don't even know where she lives. Maybe it's just as well that she don't know I'm in prison. It would break her heart. She'd pray for me though -- I know that for sure 'cause she always reads her Bible every night 'fore she goes to bed."

"If I get out of here before you do John, I'll write to you."

"Really? You'd do that?"

"Sure I would."

Reece immediately felt his eyes water. It had been years since he felt such emotion. He'd almost believed he was past the point of feeling deeply about anything or anyone ever again. He swallowed and lay silent, considering Limesand's remarks. He swallowed again and then replied. "I-I 'preciate that more'n you could ever know." Quickly changing the subject, he asked, "Say, 'bout how many days you reckon we been out here now?"

"It's either 22 or 23, I'm not sure."

"How far do you think we've come?"

"When I saw the Swede rolling up his maps two days ago, I heard him tell the captain we'd come about sixty miles. They seem to be getting along better. They're at least talking to each other. But the Swede's really getting impatient. He insist that we have to more than double our speed and average 8-10 miles a day. Says he only calculated one week to train and condition the prisoners for building the line. He claims smaller crews in the states building the lines across the continent averaged 15 miles a day. What do you think of that?"

"He can claim anything he wants, but I don't believe him. Wasn't across no stretch of hell like this place. Shoot, even if they did make 15 miles they was probably diggin' in sand an' drinkin' ice-cold lemonade. I figured him to be a real slave-driver, who really doesn't give a rat's-ass about anyone."

"The Swede told Rodriguez that's what we'd have to do," Limesand replied.

"Ten miles a day and we'll kill them mules. Two trips out and back to the end of the line, carryin' them heavy loads of water'll be forty miles. In this heat we'll run 'em all to death. I sure as hell know a lot more about mules than he does."

"I don't doubt that, but the Swede said the corporation'll abandon the project if at the end of the first one hundred miles the cost per mile is running too high."

"I'll bet that's another one of his lies. They can't be payin' much for crossin' this blowed-away land. Hell, it wouldn't even sprout beans as folks say back home. An' just where did his corporation ever build a line with labor that cost as cheap as us? Ten miles a day! What a bunch of horseshit!"

"We'd have to hump our asses near day and night to cover that much ground. It would hardly even pay to go to bed," Limesand readily agreed. "And we're going to have some climb going over those mountains in the east -- the ones with the little bit of snow on the peaks. That's the Continental Divide."

"Where do we go then?" Reece asked, still disgusted that the smart-assed Swede was turning out to be a cold-hearted bastard just like he had figured.

"We'll cross them in another week or maybe less. Then we swing a little bit south and head toward Juarez. It's a small, mostly Mormon community about 40 miles east of the divide. I used to have a Mormon customer there who bought supplies from me. He had a small drugstore…"

"An' I bet he bought some of that pharma -- stuff like you told me about…"

"Right, John, pharmaceutical," Limesand interrupted and then added, "Over on the eastern slopes we'll start seeing the runners you like to hear about."

"You mean the Tarahumara?"

"I guarantee it."

Reece grew silent. He wondered why his favorite stories had always been about men who'd tried to do the impossible -- and did it. He didn't understand why he felt that way. He'd certainly never been like that himself. Maybe that's what made him like the stories so much. He envied the courage of that kind of man, especially the Cunningham boy in Limesand's story.

"I did hear the Swede tell Rodriguez that he was going to use runners to cut and carry poles for the line when we got across mountains. You can bet that cheap bastard will find some way to cheat 'em--listen! Did you hear something?" Limesand whispered.

Reece and Limesand sat up and looked down the slope in the opposite direction from where the coyotes had been wailing.

"It's the guard makin' his rounds. I saw sparks fly when the horse's shoe hit a rock. He's comin' pretty fast."

"Shh--" Limesand interrupted. "Notice anything different?"

"Yeah. I don't hear the coyotes no more. The guard must be drunk if he thinks he can run them down on horseback. He'll break his fool neck."

"What the hell's happening?" Limesand asked as the guard's horse galloped past no more than ten feet from their beds, two of the dogs racing ahead of him.

Suddenly there were sounds of squealing horses and the coarse, agitated braying of frightened mules, followed by rapid hoofbeats.

Angry shouts from the Mexican guard included a few words that Reece could understand, mulas and caballos, and then one word that tied it all together: "Yaquis!" Six shots rang out as the sounds of running hoofbeats quickly faded down through the mesquite and into the darkness.

For a moment there was a stunned silence, followed immediately by complete bedlam in the camp. Shouting curses, a dozen men were up and running toward the corral.

CHAPTER 6

YAQUIS

Reece hastily scraped away the hot ash and exposed the glowing coals from the evening before. He added kindling and built up the fire while nervously listening to shouts and heated accusations coming from the direction of the corral. The leftover coffee began simmering in the pot which he'd shoved directly into the hot coals. He placed a thin aluminum sheet on the edge of the cooking grate and spread the remains of the peach cobbler from a still warm dutch oven.

The Swede's voice was clear and emphatic. "You got twenty- three armed guards and yet the tracks show that no more than six Yaquis sneaked into the corral and stole all of the horses and mules -- and to top it off, two of the little bastards were barefoot! The only horse left is the one your lazy guard was riding and he was probably off sleeping somewhere. With a little luck they might have gotten that one too," the Swede snarled as he and the captain came striding back toward the campfire.

Reece watched as both men stopped abruptly and stood face to face. The captain didn't seem to be the least bit intimidated by the construction superintendent's damning accusations or combative stance. Although unable to hear the captain's response, Reece knew this was the most critical moment yet -- the showdown he'd expected since hearing the fading hoofbeats of the running stock. If either of the men did something foolish, their actions could shut the project down until the Swede's company could negotiate a new contract with the Mexican officials.

He shuddered at the thought of returning to prison and pushed the pot further into the flames. He had momentary thoughts of slipping away. It might be possible to elude only one mounted guard. No more than a mile to the north he'd seen where the sloping terrain changed unexpectedly -- uncountable fissures dropped abruptly, splaying out into arroyos cut into solid rock. If he made it to the rim of the drop-off, where overhanging slabs jutted over the arroyo's upper flanks, there would be a thousand places to hide. He looked over at Blue, the tracking dog. After the commotion she had returned to her favorite spot under the captain's table.

The shy mongrel bitch's scruffy hair was shades of gray and black, half hidden under a layer of yellowed dust. Eluding her relentless search, however, would require him fleeing over a different type of terrain. Blue's sleeping form brought back the memory of Thompson's body sliding off the mule's back and hitting the dirt. Any immediate thoughts of trying to escape disappeared.

Thompson had failed. The cocky prisoner hadn't had a carefully thought-out plan. Reece wasn't going to make the same mistake.

The boiling pot was bubbling. Black coffee was running over the sides and noisily hissing where it seeped into the coals and ash. "Gimme a hand, Al, an' grab a couple of clean cups, a couple of bowls an' some spoons," Reece said, hurrying to the upright wooden cabinet and getting the Swede's personal tin of brown sugar and spices.

The Swede stood with his feet spread, his left foot a half-step ahead of the other. His meaty hands were in position to deliver a brutal blow to the captain's midsection if he stepped forward with either foot. The long-armed Captain Rodriguez faced the Swede with a look of disdain, unconcerned that he wouldn't be the victor if the argument escalated into a fistfight. His reputation as light-heavyweight boxing champion at the military academy was well known.

With both men squared off in a fighting stance, the one that backed down now would definitely lose face. The large audience expected a fight and it was obvious to Reece that they wanted one, too. Many of the men, prisoners and guards alike, were winking and nodding and holding up fingers, apparently betting as to the outcome. Like a flock of curious sheep, they inched forward, eyes riveted on the quarrelsome pair as if expecting a bloody battle.

Reece would have been glad to see the two men beat each other senseless, however, he'd been running some ideas through his head for several days. So far, all of his plans were little more than fantasies but none of them included a return to the prison.

Sanchez and the Swede's assistant, Jess Harper, stood off to the side, talking quietly. The puzzled expressions on their faces made it clear neither had any ideas for a resolving the confrontation they were watching. Their job was to attend to the supervision of the prisoners and daily work assignments. Resolving the animosity between the two men in charge was another matter.

Reece measured the brown sugar exactly as he'd been instructed the first morning the Swede was in camp. "Come on Al, you bring the cobbler an' I'll take the coffee. We can't let them fight over something that couldn't be helped, anyhow."

Limesand hurried ahead while Reece tried to keep from spilling the hot coffee onto his bare feet.

"Here you are, gentlemen. My medical training at the University always emphasized that one shouldn't fight on an empty stomach." Both men turned to face him. He leaned forward, lowered his voice slightly as if in complete confidence, and added, "It can make your balls fall off and that wouldn't be such a pretty sight, now would it, watching them rolling off down the mountainside?"

While Limesand, smiling broadly, held both bowls of cobbler toward the two men, Reece offered them each a steaming cup of coffee. The action and Limesand's questionable attempt at humor seemed to catch both the Swede and the captain off guard. An incredulous expression spread across each man's face and almost simultaneously they both somewhat appeared to relax. After a few tense moments the two key men responsible for the line's completion seemed to have weighed the consequences of their impulsive behavior. Both muttered apologies and after an awkward pause, shook hands, and reached for the coffee and leftover cobbler.

There was a barely audible groan of disappointment from the assembled spectators.

"Hurry up and fix these men something to eat," Rodriguez ordered. "There's plenty of work to do."

Soon the aroma of frying potatoes and onions mixed with an extra ration of salt pork, ordered by the Swede, wafted across the campground. The cooling night air was now warming and drifting back up the slopes to the higher elevations. Smoke rising from the cooking fires showed the direction of an early morning breeze.

Rodriguez and the Swede sat at one of the tables, studying the maps of the terrain to the east. Reece and Limesand served breakfast, first to the two men reviewing the maps and then to the guards. As he neared the table, John tried to overhear their conversation and get a closer look at the maps.

Each of the men seemed to realize that they'd better settle the matter of the Yaquis' raid as quickly as possible. Rodriguez's face was partly hidden under his hat and it was hard for Reece to see if his anger had subsided. The Swede's glowering face, however, still showed some of his earlier animosity. His company had lost valuable assets. But even more critically, the loss would definitely slow the line's completion.

Limesand was frying ham when Reece returned to put more wood on the fire.

"You have saved the day, John, distracting them with the coffee and cobbler. It gave them both a chance to back down gracefully -- and it kept us out of that stinking prison," Limesand said, smiling.

"You're the one who came up with the fancy words."

Reece was impressed with the salesman's funny comments and his ability to grasp things so quickly. He'd never before felt comfortable around any other well-educated person.

"Hey, my friend, we're quite a team." Limesand reached over and shook Reece's hand and added, "Actually, both of them know they've got to get along -- they're really still a little bit mad but they'll get over it."

"Why do you say that?" Although Limesand was usually right, Reece feared he wasn't this time. The two men were accustomed to having their own way.

"Watch them. After two men with their kind of backgrounds have come so close to a fight, they'll usually turn their hatred onto someone else. You'll see."

Returning with a skillet of sizzling ham, Reece heard the captain say, "-- no use trying to chase them on foot, we wouldn't have a chance. And one man on horseback wouldn't make any difference either. Like you said, they'd probably figure a way to grab that one too."

"Then there's nothing we can do?"

"No. Some of the horses were branded, but I don't think we'll ever see any of them again."

"What do you think the thieving bastards will do with them, sell them to some farmers?"

"Probably eat them."

"The mules too?" the Swede asked.

"The ones living back in these mountains are pretty wild--little more than savages. They'll eat anything," Rodriguez explained. "Back when the surveys were being made to build the railroad down to Hermosillo, some of the crews had their mules stolen and eaten."

"Goddam miserable beggars, running off our stock. The Mexican government ought to get rid of all of them. They're little more than wild animals," the Swede said, rapping his coffee mug twice on the table top. "The company paid a hundred dollars apiece for those mules."

When Reece hurried over with the pot, the Swede casually picked up his cup and slowly drained the last of the coffee. Reece stood and waited for the contractor to set the cup back down, finally realizing this was just a game the arrogant bastard was playing. Reece hated the way the Swede acted as if didn't know Reece's name --or perhaps didn't even know he had one.

"Jess, get me my scale, I need to make some calculations, then rig yourself up a backpack. You're going on a trip over those mountains," the Swede said, pointing to the crest of the Sierra Madre, where the early morning light streaked through narrow pink strands of clouds, layered above the peaks. "The captain says you can take Limesand and head for Juarez. It's about twenty miles southwest of Casas Grandes. There's a Mormon community there. I want you to buy some more horses and mules. The farmers are switching over to tractors and don't really need their mules. Keep that in mind while you're bargaining for the best price."

"Yes sir." Harper nodded his head, listening for any further instructions.

Rodriguez leaned over the map. "You'd better take two canteens a piece. You won't find water until you get to the Rio Papigochic -- about fifteen miles from here -- could be twenty -- hard to tell from the maps. Two guards will to go with you," Rodriguez added. "You'll have a tough climb crossing the divide but the rest of the trip shouldn't be too hard. We can't go any higher here with the trucks, it's too steep and rocky. Straight through to Juarez shouldn't be more than fifty or sixty miles. It'll be a lot faster than going back around with a couple of the trucks."

"I'll expect you back in no more than five days. And I'll also expect you to be bringing some very fine animals." The Swede looked squarely at Harper and cocked his head at an angle, fixing his assistant with a hard stare, as if for added emphasis.

Harper appeared uncomfortable and looked down at the ground. It was another one of the Swede's mannerisms that Reece hated.

Stuffing some extra clothes and his blanket into a burlap feed sack together with some of the leftover food, Limesand turned to Reece and asked, "You going to be all right without me here to do all of the work?" He smirked and made a face, pulling the corners of his mouth down with his fingers in a show of mock sadness.

"That's why they're sending you instead of me. You don't do enough aroun' here to earn your keep." Reece felt pleased that he'd finally thought of a quick response to his friend's incessant joking.

"Well now. I do believe you can handle the cooking without me here to show you how to do it." Limesand looked around and added, "Seriously, John, keep your eyes open. That Swede's a more treacherous son-of-a-bitch than Rodriguez. Remember I told you about my studies in psychology--"

"Get over here, Limesand," Neilson barked.

"I heard you say you know some of the merchants in Juarez."

"A few."

"Ask around and see if they know any farmers who've recently bought tractors. If they have, Harper may be able to drive a better bargain with someone who has either horses or mules with nothing for them to do but stand around and eat."

"Oh, another thing, Harper," Rodriguez interrupted. "Have the switchboard operator in Juarez call the prison as soon as you get into town. I'm expecting a letter from a certain lady. Tell the operator to have Lieutenant Juarez bring up all of our mail. By the time you're ready to leave he should have it there. If he doesn't tell him I'm going to whip his ass," he added, chuckling.

Reece could see the Swede beginning to relax. He grinned slightly at the captain's comments. It was hard to tell whether it was the comment about the certain lady or the one about whipping Juarez's ass. But determining a definite course of action to cope with the new problem was, no doubt, at least partly the cause of relieving some of his tension. Reece had seen men like him before. They thrived on making decisions that became the responsibilities for others to carry out. Their control over men of a lower rank seemed to give them pleasure. And, like both Rodriguez and the Swede, they often wore an air of disgusting smugness.

Limesand had been right again. Both men had been laughing and talking quietly since breakfast. While Reece heated water and washed the dishes and pots and pans, he wondered how far Limesand and the other men had gotten. The sun was now almost straight overhead. They'd been gone for about five hours and Reece was already missing his friend.

"Let me show you something," he heard the Swede say when Rodriguez got up and stretched and then walked over toward his tent.

Reece kept busy working. There was plenty for him to do. Some of the guards had earlier gone off up the mountain with the prisoners. Most of them were carrying some type of axe or grubbing hoe to cut brush and scrub trees from beneath the path of the overhead lines. Their range would be limited to the distance they could carry a sufficient amount of water for the day.

The Swede came walking back carrying two long, sturdy wooden boxes.

"Hey hobo, come here. Drag this table over into the shade of that acacia," the Swede ordered, nodding toward the largest of the stunted trees in the area serving as the temporary base camp.

Reece felt a sudden rush of blood in his neck. His jaws clenched but he nodded slightly and did as he was told.

"Bet you never saw anything like this before," the Swede said as he opened the latches and turned to Rodriguez. He took a leather thong from inside his shirt and pulled it over his head. With a brass key he turned the lock and laid back the lid of the nearest box.

The captain stood with his mouth agape, his eyes riveted on the gleaming barrel and shining rifle stock inlaid with the ivory figure of a bull elk.

"It's a 300 H & H made by Griffin and Howe. Won the Wimbledon Cup Matches three years ago. The target was at 1000 yards."

"Magnificent! Just magnificent!" The captain shook his head in disbelief. "You're right. I've never seen anything like this." He rubbed his fingers across the grain of the gleaming walnut stock and felt the intricate carved ivory inlays of the elk's antlers. "When you asked if you could bring a couple of rifles with you I didn't expect anything like this. What's in the other box?"

"Another one just like it except the inlays are different. They're each one of a kind," the Swede answered, smiling as he unlocked the box and laid back the lid. "Pushes a 150-grain bullet out of the muzzle at over three thousand feet per second."

"That's damn near unbelievable," Rodriguez said, shaking his head in wonder.

Reece could tell the Swede was eyeing him, wanting to see if he was equally impressed. Reece said nothing, not even acknowledging that he'd noticed the weapons. He had no intention of giving the son-of-a-bitch the satisfaction. It was his turn to ignore Neilson.

Walking back over to his work table, he poured a burlap sack of potatoes into a large wooden basket. With a paring knife, he began peeling and slicing them into a big aluminum pot for the evening meal. He'd seen expensive rifles the year before when he cooked for a bighorn sheep-hunting camp near Gunnison, Colorado. Those were much better days, he realized with a heavy-hearted sigh. He knew now that no price was too much to pay for one's freedom.

"Get your ass over here, hobo! We've got some work for you to do." The Swede's grating voice reverberated in John's head. He closed his eyes and bit his lip until he realized he must be careful and patient. Even one foolish mistake could seal his chances.

"Yes sir, Mister Neilson. What can I do for you?"

CHAPTER 7

GLASS TARGETS

It was late afternoon. Reece put four more empty one-gallon food jars in a line as the Swede instructed and ran back to crouch between the nearest boulders. The distance was 300 yards from the line of glass targets to the table where Rodriguez and the Swede sat with loaded rifles. Reece had been instructed to measure the length to the exact foot with the coiled 50-yard cloth tape the Swede handed him.

Peering around the side of the boulder, Reece squinted at the two men sitting in the shade of the acacia. The scorching sun bore down into the crevice where Reece hunkered in an attempt to avoid the flying shards of glass and ricocheting bullets. A dozen or more times -- he'd lost count -- he had been told to run and get more jars. Each round trip of 600 yards had left him exhausted, his poorly conditioned lungs gulping hungrily for air. His chest ached and he was unable to clearly focus his eyes. The two shaded forms sitting at the table were little more than a blur.

For the first two hours the Swede had never missed a target.

The captain, however, was clearly out-matched. He was obviously unaccustomed to the jolting recoil from a rifle loaded with magnum cartridges, specially designed for long-range accuracy.

The carved ivory forends of the rifle's wooden stocks were cradled on sacks of sand the Swede positioned on the table. For even an experienced marksman the supporting bags insured an extra margin of accuracy.

The jarring blast from the big-bore rifles reverberated off the rock cliffs behind Reece as both men continued to fire at their selected targets. The natural rock basin amplified the sounds. Reece wondered what the Yaquis might be thinking about the loud blasts from the magnum rifles.

After another rapid-fire salvo, all of the food jars were blasted into slivers.

This would be the last trip, Reece knew, as he hurried for more targets. Only three empty jars remained. When he neared the table where the two men sat in the shade he noticed that the bottle of brandy they'd opened earlier was almost empty. That explained why the Swede was now missing almost half the targets with his first shot.

"I'll lay you three to one on my next shot," Reece heard the Swede say, his voice slowed and his pronunciation more deliberate.

"I'll take that bet," Rodriguez offered, laying his money on the table. "Make it for five."

The Swede glanced at Reece with a look of amusement. He took his time selecting one of the shiny brass cartridges laying in a tray at the side of the table. After carefully looking them over the Swede selected one and made a show of kissing the lead tip then winking at the captain, before slowly pushing it into the rifle breech. Sliding the bolt forward, he securely locked the action and sat back with a satisfied look on his face.

Rodriguez nodded in the direction of the target area and yelled. "Hurry up, Reece, I'm about to win some easy money."

"Please, Captain, can I get a drink, first?" Reece's lips were dried and cracking.

Both half-drunk men looked at him and started laughing. They'd both now reached a state of intoxication where everything was extremely funny. When they finally stopped laughing the Swede turned surly and glared at Reece. "Get a move on, hobo. I'm going to give the captain a demonstration of some really fancy shooting and you're holding up the show." The Swede's words were beginning to slur. He bent forward in another fit of laughter.

Reece turned and ran to set the three jars in place. The sooner the miserable drunken bastards finished their little contest, the sooner he would get a drink of water. He was winded and out of breath when he reached the ledge where countless glass shards lay scattered among the weeds.

After setting the first two jars on a rock ledge, a couple of feet apart, Reece grasped the threaded top rim of the last one and reached across the first two to set it on a slightly higher ledge. When the bottom of the glass container was only inches from its intended location a sudden blinding force drove upwards into his face, stinging his nose and ears. Instinctively, he dropped to the ground as the force of the rifle's blast reverberated around him. Flattening his body against the glass littered surface, he shook uncontrollably with fear as the drunken men roared with laughter. His nose and earlobes dripped blood onto the slick weathered rock.

A cold conclusion swept across his mind. One of the drunken bastards had deliberately shot the glass jar out of his hand and there was no question as to which drunken bastard had fired the near-deadly shot.

Through the sparse stand of weeds, Reece could now see both men get up from the table and shake hands. Apparently their little game was over for now. They left the two remaining targets for another time. Once again, Limesand had been right. Neilson, in spite of his fancy airs, was the most treacherous son-of-a-bitch Reece had ever seen.

Reece's life meant little to either man. There was no longer any question -- his only hope was to concentrate on escape. The pain that gripped him now brought back a memory of a painful childhood accident.

Reece was no more than five years old, still wearing short pants that came only to his knees. He'd watched while his mother canned peaches. The day was hot and the kitchen was filled with steam. When his mother removed the big shiny cooker from the top of the stove it slipped out of her hands and crashed to the floor. The heated jars flew out and slid into the side of the wood box. He remembered screaming when scalding juices and yellow peach slices splashed against his legs, raising large blisters from his knees down to his bare feet. His mother had poured cool water on his legs to ease the pain -- cool water she'd run and drawn from the well.

He remembered the summer when he was eight. It was early morning. He and his father had been on their way in the wagon to the cotton field. They needed to chop the weeds from between the cotton stalks in the long rows of the dark green leafy plants. It was his first day to wield a heavy hoe and help his father cultivate the plants.

When they'd first arrived at the field his father had taken two large glass jars, each sewn in burlap, from beneath the wagon's wooden seat. Near the end of one of the rows of cotton he took his hoe and dug a hole in the sandy earth, burying both jars of drinking water.

Reece had noticed his father's scarred hands as he'd taken a rag from the back pocket of his bib overalls and tied it to the cotton stalk directly above the buried jars. The moist ground, his father had explained, would keep the water cool until they needed a drink, and the rag would show them where to find it.

As Reece lay in the weeds he blinked and counted his good fortune. None of the glass shards had struck him in the eyes. The cuts he'd received appeared to be minor. He watched as the two men stood by the table, drinking from a bottle they passed back and forth between them. If they passed out from drinking, that would be even better. The wracking thirst that made his mouth feel like cotton would be quickly eased if even one of the shattered jars lying in useless shards among the rocks and weeds were instead unbroken and filled with water.

His mind raced. His chances for escape would be much better if he had a source of water… buried water. The very thought of it became intoxicating. He was now as lightheaded and happy as the two drunken men who had been firing wildly at the glass jars. The sharp image of the piece of rag tied to the cotton stalk so many years before burned into his consciousness. Buried water that couldn't be found would be more useless than a hundred tons of gold buried under a mountain of solid rock. But buried water that could be found….

The euphoria that raced through his every fiber was not limited by his body's present state of exhaustion. As the guard's cook he had a source of hundreds of empty food jars -- jars that had been filled with beans and pickles and peanut butter and yellow mustard. There would be no shortage of jars if those two crazy bastards with their custom-made rifles didn't blow them all to pieces.

Now he would work on a plan to fill jars with water and bury them and mark their hiding places.

"Hey you goddam hobo, get your ass up here!" the Swede was yelling, his speech now even more slurred from the second bottle of brandy.

Up to his left John heard the sound of footsteps. The crews were coming down the mountainside, walking in single file. One mounted guard bringing up the rear was silhouetted against the pink and red striated bluff behind him.

It would be long after dark before he'd have the food cooked and served to the drunken men slouched at the table and the guards and prisoners nearing camp. Some of them would be abusive when they had to wait for their supper, but it wouldn't matter. He could take it. He thought again of the boy, Glen Cunningham, whose legs were burned. He could take anything now.

Reece walked toward the camp with a new spring in his step. He breathed deeply and the ache and exhaustion in his legs suddenly vanished. A new resolve and determination replaced his earlier fears. It was his only sensible choice. Jars. Buried jars full of water.

He would watch for any opportunity and make the most of every chance he got.

CHAPTER 8

NEW MULES

It was shortly before sundown on the sixth day since Limesand and the other three men had left for Juarez. Narrow leaves on a palo verde filtered the sun's fading light into dappled shadows, creeping across the table's checkered oilcloth. Reece gazed in wonder at the starkness of the dark timbered slopes to the east that climbed abruptly to the sunlit backbone of the Sierra. He remembered Limesand's description of the country on the other side where the slopes fell away gradually onto a high desert plateau.

The rolling foothills climbed up through a blue haze to the flanks of the distant mountains. Rodriguez and the Swede sat on a sandstone shelf, looking through binoculars for any sign of mounted riders leading a pack-string. Brushing away the flies from the festering cuts on his face, Reece prepared for the evening meal.

"They're a day late now. What the hell could be keeping them?" The Swede asked. The captain kept scanning the vast sweep of hills and arroyos.

It appeared to Reece that the hard-driving Swede was growing increasingly annoyed with both the line's delay and the lack of any meaningful activity.

The captain, however, was quite at ease. He had one advantage the Swede didn't. He didn't have to keep a daily log of his activities. If the guards and prisoners did their job and there were no escapes, Rodriguez would be considered successful.

"Maybe I should have sent more than two guards. They could have been ambushed in the canyons where they'd have to cross the river." The captain's voice was flat, still questioning his earlier decision.

The Swede took a sip from the bottle sitting between them and wiped his mouth with his shirt sleeve. It was hard to predict how the men would act when they were drinking. The captain would sometimes be boisterous and hilariously vulgar. At other times he could be just the opposite, moody and irritable. When drinking, the Swede had shown a dark, mean side and a tendency to be suspicious.

They had returned late the previous evening from a three-day trip to Nacozari. They'd taken five of the trucks and seven guards with them. They'd brought back enough supplies to last until they crossed the divide and started southward along the westernmost slopes of Chihuahua's high desert.

While working at his chores, Reece tried to overhear fragments of the men's conversation. So far, he'd learned nothing of significance. The ledge they sat on was too far from the tables. For awhile, they entertained themselves picking up pieces of sandstone and throwing them at a large lizard trying to climb down from a ledge where it had been sunning. After it escaped into a crevice they briefly looked through the binoculars at the mountains to the east.

A period of silence followed and Reece heard the Swede chuckle at something Rodriguez said. The captain was telling jokes about a Mexican whore. It was unusual to hear the Swede laugh out loud. He seldom found many subjects amusing. As the drinking continued, however, both men found more things to laugh about.

Reece became aware that they'd lowered their voices and kept glancing in his direction. He looked again and saw them watching him and grinning. The captain held the empty whiskey bottle at arm's length and the Swede closed his hand with index finger extended. He pointed at the bottle and yelled "boom!" The empty bottle dropped, shattering as it struck the jagged face of the sandstone rock formation, scattering glass slivers down to the base. Both men roared with laughter. Still chuckling, they turned toward the divide, brought the field glasses up and scanned the vast expanse. Within a minute both men erupted into another fit of laughter. Although Reece was watching them they were no longer even looking in his direction.

His insides churned with a feeling of disgust. He placed his hands flat on the table top to steady himself and gain some control over his seething emotions.

After a couple of minutes his breathing became more controlled. He turned slightly to a position where he could watch them out of the corner of his eye, and tried to look busy. He hoped someday to get even with both the mean bastards.

This was just a little game for them. Someone had to be the butt of their jokes. He'd seen men like them before while cooking for a road crew in Arizona. The worst he'd seen was when they built the section of Route 66 between Flagstaff and Kingman -- a hot, desolate, godforsaken land that stretched in all directions.

There were two men, one named Atkins and another Wheeler, who had repeatedly taunted a man with a bad lisp. He'd tried his best to avoid them when he could and had never offered any direct retaliation to either man, but when they each found a rattlesnake in their bed on the same evening, the abuse abruptly stopped.

It was like Limesand said. Rodriguez and the Swede would always turn their anger and frustrations onto someone else. Reece knew he had to ignore it and concentrate on his plans. Having an idea for escape in his head, that he could study on while he worked, would help him keep his sanity.

Off to the northeast, Reece spotted a trace of dust rising above a cleft in the rolling greasewood and creosote-covered foothills.

The two men got up and started back to the table, their field glasses hanging around their necks by leather thongs. Neither man had eaten much and both appeared tired from the jaunt into town. Upon their return from Nacozari, Reece noticed lipstick on the Swede's shirt collar and the captain's handkerchief had a bright red smudge across one corner.

"What are you looking at, Reece?" the captain asked in a weary voice, idly glancing back over his shoulder. The Swede turned toward Reece, his mouth half open as if he was going to say something but instead waited for Reece to answer the captain's question.

"I think they're coming through them hills yonder Captain."

"You think you can see something we can't see when we're using binoculars?" He turned and raised the magnifying lenses to his eyes. "And just what do you think you can see, hobo?"

Reece could tell by the alignment of the binoculars that the hungover bastard was looking in the wrong direction. The faint cloud was more to the northeast. It could have been nothing more than a fading beam of sunlight. It was hard to tell.

"I thought I saw something," Reece replied to the Swede, who was now trying to tell just what direction Reece had been looking in.

"If they run into a party of Yaquis, two armed guards might not be enough to get them through," Rodriguez said, showing an increasing concern for the success of the venture to Juarez.

"I'll feel a lot better when I know they're all right," the Swede replied, adjusting the focus of the binoculars.

While the Swede and the captain both scanned the slopes, Reece saw the beginning of a faint darkening line. It was moving toward them through a cleft that had been folded into a sharp crease in a stratum of rock millions of years before. The returning men and animals were still another eight or ten miles away.

Reece continued his preparations for the guards' supper. He could see that the two men were still anxious and irritable. They were in no mood to tolerate a prisoner they might even suspect of being a smart-aleck.

"When they left they went through them hills over yonder. Maybe they'll come back that way."

The impatient Swede sat down on the bench, steadied his elbows on the table-top and studied the rolling hills through the binoculars. "I've spotted them, Captain. They're coming through a cut between those hills to the north -- must be forty or more of them, moving along in single file," he said, pointing in the direction of the place where Reece had first seen the faint cloud of dust.

Reece squinted. "Must be a long ways off. I can't see 'em yet." It was best to let the construction superintendent think that he was the first to see the returning crew and animals. Reece wanted to appear friendly and cooperative. It was best that they continue to think of him only as a meek and obedient cook. Being the oldest prisoner working on the line would also work to his advantage. He'd be the last one anyone would suspect of planning an escape.

While Rodriguez rapidly swept his field glasses back and forth across the distant slopes, the Swede eyed Reece suspiciously.

"Them binoculars must be like magic," Reece said, "lettin' you see so far. How many miles you reckon to where you can see 'em?"

The Swede ignored Reece and put the field glasses back into their hard leather case. It was difficult to tell whether the Swede was convinced that he was the first to see the returning crew. Reece feared the Swede might suspect he was being played for a fool. If he wasn't more careful he'd have worse than a face cut by flying glass.

Walking over to the woodpile, he got more sticks for the fire. He'd killed, scalded and plucked every feather from the whole crate of chickens brought back from Nacozari. He stirred the dumplings and the pieces of chicken, simmering in the stewing pots. Quickly dumping a sack of dried apples into a large pan, Reece began preparing three cobblers for the guards, still, he figured, some two hours from camp. He'd added extra cinnamon. Limesand liked it that way. When no one was looking, Reece would sneak some cobbler out and hide it. They could both have a treat to help celebrate Limesand's return.

The sounds of rocks tumbling downslope meant the party was climbing the last few hundred yards. Scrambling for footing in the darkness, the horses and mules knocked pieces of sandstone loose. Men stood in the light of the campfire and the hanging coal-oil lanterns, awaiting the arrival of the riders and animals.

The lead horse came into view bearing a rider with a light-colored hat. "That you, Harper?" the Swede called out.

"Yessir, Mr. Neilson." Riding up closer, he stopped his horse. "We left the crest of the divide two hours before daylight like you said. We pushed hard all day -- We didn't want to have to spend another night out--"

"Did you see any Yaquis?"

"Yes, Mr Neilson, we did see a few. They stayed about a mile behind us. Followed us ever since about noon. A couple of them were riding the horses they stole the other night--"

"Thievin' worthless bastards," the Swede snarled.

"Want us to bring the stock over there or take them straight on to the corral?"

"Bring them over here near the light and let's see what you got."

Harper's horse shied away from walking directly up to the men standing in the shadows of the hanging lanterns, moving sideways instead as Harper spurred him and urged him forward. The other mounted riders cursed at the nervous horses and balky mules strung out behind, stretching their lead ropes taut. The whites of the eyes of the first mules showed their fear of the shadowy forms clustered in the mountain campsite.

Reece could see the mules were young and would take time to break to the conditions of packing heavy loads on steep mountain slopes where there were no trails. He sighed with relief when he spotted Limesand walking behind and cracking a whip, keeping the stragglers at the rear bunched together, in an attempt to drive them forward.

"Take them on to the corral and fasten the gates tight -- and make sure you don't let them get away. We can see them better in the morning." The relief in the Swede's voice was noticeable, obviously glad Harper had made it through and brought back a healthy-looking pack-string.

"Sergeant, put four men on guard," the captain said to Sanchez. "It'll be your ass if any of the stock's not there in the morning. Who's got the mail sack?"

"Right here, *Capitán*," Felipe, the guard mounted on a horse behind Harper answered, dismounting and carrying the bag over to Rodriguez.

Holding up the sack for all to see, the captain said, "You'll all get your mail in the morning when it's light enough to read it. I'll keep it safe in my tent tonight." He laughed and added, "I'm going to take a lantern and all of the letters that have been sprinkled with perfume, I'll read myself."

Mock groans and laughter followed Rodriguez's spicy promise.

"I'll bet you're an expert at sticking your nose in places that have been sprinkled with all kinds of perfume, *Capitán*," a voice from the back of the assembled mass called out. An immediate hush fell over the gathering.

A brief moment of silence was immediately followed by the captain's laughter. "Who told you that?" the captain asked in false irritation. "Your wife or your sister?" The group's nervous relief was evidenced by a burst of loud and prolonged laughter. When it died away the captain said, "Hurry up and get the stock put away. It's time to eat."

Reece was pleased at the captain's light-hearted jesting. He reckoned that both the captain and the Swede must have felt a great deal of tension until they knew the replacement animals had been purchased and safely delivered.

Reece and Limesand barely had time to say hello while they served the guards their supper.

"What's wrong with your face? Looks like you tangled with a wildcat," Al asked, frowning, when they both were at the cooking table refilling the serving bowls. The light from the lantern, hanging on a wire hook from a scrub oak limb, cast a dim yellow glow on the surroundings. "You got some nasty-looking cuts on your nose and ears. What happened?"

"I'll tell you later," he answered quietly, nodding in the direction of Neilson, who was sitting at the second table over.

"Didn't I tell you to watch out for him? Remember me telling you that?" Limesand whispered.

"Later. We'll talk about it later. I saved us some dessert."

"I'm going to slip out while the guards are all watching the corral. There's a stand of spikenard just down the slope. I'll dig some roots and in a couple of days that old battered face of yours'll look as good as new."

Limesand was still sound asleep, worn out from the trip. He'd briefly told Reece of the trip's main events after Reece told him of the day the Swede shot the jar out of his hand. They'd agreed there wasn't much they could do about it. This was a Mexican prison and they were there to serve their sentences. The only choice they had was to make each day as good as it could be.

When the birds started chirping in the nearby thickets, Reece rolled over and pushed himself up into a sitting position. He started the fire and began preparing the biscuit dough. The Swede would be up soon and ready for his coffee.

In the meantime Reece walked over near the corral for an armload of wood. When the guard saw that Reece was already busy with his chores he continued sharpening his knife on a whetstone. Reece had learned a valuable lesson. People who like to eat regular meals leave the cook alone as long as he looks busy.

Holding the wood, he sidled over to the corral and sized up the animals Harper had purchased. The horses appeared quite calm, considering they'd been brought into new surroundings after dark. The mules, however, paced the pole corral fences, nervous and wary of Reece's presence. He could see immediately that whoever was assigned to break them for carrying heavy loads of water would have to keep clear of their deadly rear hooves. One in particular was clearly the leader. The others gave way when he whirled and laid back his ears in a defiant warning. He was tall and honey-colored with a dark stripe down his back, and his lower legs were black -- no doubt out of a big-boned buckskin mare bred to a Missouri Jack. He'd be the toughest and most dangerous to break to the heavy loads.

When Reece noticed the guard watching him he hurried back to the fire. He was surprised when he saw that most of the men were already up, milling around and glancing toward the captain's tent. He tried to appear unconcerned when he saw Al coming in his direction, rubbing his eyes and yawning. "Say Al, what's going on?" Reece asked, puzzled by the men's early behavior.

"They're waiting for the captain to get up and give them their mail. I'm as ready as they are."

"Oh yeah, I remember. I hope you get a bunch of letters from your family. It's been, what now, about a month since anyone got mail?"

"Yeah." Limesand's brow wrinkled and his lips pursed as he stared straight ahead with moist eyes.

Watching his friend's anxiety, Reece realized there were some disadvantages for prisoners who waited for mail and visits from close family members. At least he didn't have those problems, too.

When the captain stepped from his tent holding the mail sack, there were audible sighs of relief from the two hundred prisoners and the guards. Rodriguez nodded and began calling out the names listed on the letters at the top of the first bundle he untied. Even with the mail, all prisoner's records were kept in alphabetical order.

"Abando, Jose!"

"Aburto, Felipe!"

"Acosta, Tony!"

"Adams, Robert!"

"Arriola, Luis!"

Reece took two large pails and went to the truck with the barrels of water. With everyone up already he'd have to hurry to have breakfast ready. He could see Al moving pots and pans around, trying to look busy while staying near the captain.

It was sometime later while he was slicing potatoes that he heard the captain call out, "Limesand, Allen!"

Reece felt his chest tighten and a lump knotted in his throat when he saw his friend kiss the top envelope, addressed crudely in blue crayon. Moving discreetly away, Reece distanced himself so that Al could be alone with the mail from the family that he missed so much.

While he was out by the corral getting more wood he thought he heard the captain calling but he wasn't sure. Then he heard it plainly.

"Where the hell did Reece go?"

Reece hurried back, concerned that he'd done something to offend the captain.

"What's the matter with you Reece? Don't you want your goddam mail? If not, just say so." The captain's jovial bantering of the previous evening was over.

Reece hesitantly approached the captain. Was this some kind of joke? He tentatively took the envelope from the captain's outstretched hand, avoiding Rodriguez's puzzled stare.

"*Gracias*," he mumbled and backed away. He looked at the name in the upper left corner. It was one he didn't recognize. There appeared to be some mix-up: It was a letter from someone whose name was Reese -- with an "s" instead of a "c." The first name was lightly smudged but he finally made it out: "Eula Mae."

With trembling hands, John carefully tore open the letter. In capital letters across the top it said:

MILWAUKEE NURSING COLLEGE
842 Arnold Drive
MILWAUKEE, WISCONSIN
June 27, 1938
Dear Mr. Reece
I hardly know how to start this letter but I think you might be my papa...

CHAPTER 9

THE LETTER

Reece closed his eyes, unable to fully grasp the meaning of the words: I think you might be my papa… His mind in a state of confusion and disbelief, he barely heard the droning of the captain's voice or the joshing of those who had received mail.

A thousand times, Reece had fantasized about someday having a family, but he knew he'd wasted too much time. Lately he'd just figured that time had cruelly passed him by. He'd never gotten a single piece of mail since he'd been in prison, and now this -- Reece spelled with a "s" and not an "c."

Could this be another one of the captain's jokes?

The captain's voice grew louder and Reece became aware that Rodriguez was now holding up the last piece of the mail. "Ybarra, Amando!"

Folding the envelope, Reece slipped it into his pocket and glanced in the Swede's direction. Reece didn't want them to see his disappointment if this was nothing but a hoax.

The Swede was sitting at his table, carefully refilling his pipe with tobacco from a red tin of Prince Albert, a dozen or more letters stacked neatly alongside two rolls of maps. The captain selected a letter from a spread of about twenty at his table, some of which he'd already opened. He held it up to his nose and breathed deeply, a broad smile crinkling the skin under his eyes.

Neither man looked at Reece. How long would it be before the two men led the crew in a fit of laughter?

Reece could be sure of at least one thing: Al wouldn't join in any of their mean little tricks. When Reece became aware that he was breathing rapidly, he forced himself to take longer and slower breaths. If this was a sham it would hurt far more than the cuts from the glass slivers.

Limesand looked over at Reece and grinned. Was he in on it, too? No. Limesand opened another letter, his face radiating the joy of receiving his long-awaited mail. A feeling of embarrassment swept over Reece that he'd mistrusted his only friend.

52

Several of the men looked downcast and sad. They moved off, quietly and singly, away from the others reading their mail. A few walked in the general direction of the corrals.

Could it actually be that the letter from Eula Mae Reese was for real? Reece took two buckets and headed back toward the trucks.

After filling one of the buckets with water, Reece slipped around behind the truck's tall sideboards and pulled the letter from his pocket. Milwaukee, Wisconsin was printed in the circular stamp along with the date, June 28, 1938.

"This is no hoax," John mumbled to himself. He tried to hold the two typewritten pages steady while he reread the first sentence. When he got to the word papa, he stopped and swallowed hard, looking up to the crest of the divide just as the morning sun touched the highest peak. It was a day he knew he would never forget. Nothing in his forty-seven years had prepared him for such an overwhelming feeling.

After a long pause he braced his arm against the sideboards just above the truck's bed and began reading:

I hardly know how to start this letter but I think you might be my papa. I hope so.

Even though our names are spelled differently, there could be a reason for that.

I was born on August 23, 1917 in Albuquerque, New Mexico. My mama's name was Clara Mae Reece but according to my great aunt Jennie Kirk, mama was so mad she deliberately misspelled my father's name on the birth certificate. Aunt Jennie said Mama didn't know she was in a family way when she left you -- I mean, in case it really was you.

If you were ever married to a Clara Mae Reece who had an aunt named Jennie Kirk then you must be my papa. I once saw a picture of my mama and papa, taken on their wedding day when I visited my Aunt Jennie. She is a switch-board operator in McAlester, Oklahoma. A friend of hers saw a newspaper article about a man named John Charles Reece from Scheluter's Branch, Oklahoma being sentenced to serve ten years in a Mexican prison.

I am in my third year of nursing college in Milwaukee, Wisconsin. If you are my papa please write to me at the address at the top of this letter. All of my life I have dreamed of someday meeting my papa.

Hopefully, I am your loving daughter
Eula Mae Reese

As hard as it was to believe, there was no longer any doubt. Eula Mae Reese was his daughter. Reece sat down on the truck's running board, afraid that he was going to faint. A warm rush of blood surged through his entire body, pounding into his eardrums, leaving a tingling sensation crawling across his skin and his heart pounding wildly.

"Where's the cook?" It sounded like Sanchez's voice, coarse and deep. Quickly stuffing the letter into his pocket, Reece hurried from behind the truck and filled the other bucket.

"Right here, Sergeant, I -- I'm getting more water."

"Then get it and get back over here where you belong. Mr. Neilson wants more coffee."

Reece hurried to get the coffee for the Swede and in his bewildered state of mind knocked the pot over, spilling most of the contents into the fire. Grabbing the steaming pot with his bare hands, he was able to save just enough for a half-cup for the Swede.

As ashes billowed upward through the steaming mesh grate, several of the prisoners looked at Reece and then toward the captain. Fortunately, both the captain and Sanchez were busy reading their mail and hadn't noticed Reece's erratic behavior. After stoking the fire, Reece refilled the coffee pot and then began preparing to scramble the crate of eggs Rodriguez had brought back from Nacozari.

"What's wrong, John? I know you got a letter but you look like you've seen a ghost. Did someone die or what?" Limesand asked as he walked up alongside Reece.

"Why do you say that?" Reece asked, turning his face to the side.

"Look what you just did. You cracked the eggs and threw the shells into the skillet and dropped the whites and yolks into the garbage bucket."

"Oh, I -- I," John stammered, "I'm all mixed up. Uh--"

The two guards sitting on a bench looked at each other and shook their heads in disbelief, but neither, it appeared, wanted to interrupt the captain.

"Look at me, John. What's bothering you?"

Reece got a spoon and scooped the eggshells out of the skillet and threw them into the galvanized pail where he'd inadvertently dropped their contents. He was seized with anxiety. He desperately wanted to tell Limesand about the letter but he was uncertain how to start.

"I can't hardly believe it," Reece whispered, pausing to catch his breath and collect his muddled thoughts.

"What can't you believe? You can tell me," Limesand answered, lowering his voice and putting his hand on Reece's shoulder. "Say, your whole body's shaking. Just slow down and speak slowly."

"Well you remember that I told you that I--I don't have a family --"

"Yes, except for a sister and you'd lost track of her."

"Well, maybe I do have some family. I got this letter here an' it says I could be a papa." Reece turned his face away from Limesand when he felt his eyes flood with tears.

"What do you mean, you could be a papa? Either you are or you're not. There's no in between," Limesand said softly. "Did you get some girl pregnant?"

"You remember that I told you that I was married for a few months? Well, it seems that my wife was…" After a long pause Reece continued, "My wife was in the family way when we split up. We didn't know it. Ain't that somethin'?" Reece looked at Al, forced a happy grin and sniffled.

"I'll say. Who wrote to you?"

"Hey, you two, get busy. Just because you got some mail doesn't make this some kind of holiday," the captain barked. "I want my breakfast and I want it now. How about you, Swede?"

The Swede peered over the top of his glasses at Rodriguez and nodded, knocking the charred tobacco from the bowl of his pipe.

"Let me explain it to him." Al winked at Reece. "Yes sir, Captain, we'll get right on it. We didn't want to cook the eggs until you finished your mail. Wanted them to be sizzling hot an' serve them to you right out of the skillet. We know that's the way you like them best."

"You're a crazy bastard, Limesand. You sure you weren't sent to prison for selling bullshit instead of drugs?"

Limesand laughed loudly and lowered his voice again. "He's in a good mood. Must have been something in that letter he was sniffing besides perfume. Now tell me about your letter."

"It's from a young woman named Eula Mae Reese, but the last name is spelled different from mine." Reece paused. "But there's an explanation for that. An' you know what else?" Reece asked, sniffling twice as his chest swelled with pride, "She thinks she's my daughter an' I do too."

"Hey, that's great!"

Glancing over at his friend, Reece could see Al's eyes shining. "There's nothing like having kids." Al held up the packet of letters he'd just received and shook them for emphasis. The one addressed with a blue crayon, he'd kept on top.

Reece beamed. "This one's no kid. She's twenty-one years old. An' guess what? She's in college. Gonna' be a nurse. None of my family ever went past the eighth grade, an' most of 'em never even went that far."

"A nurse, huh? Then she's taking most of the same subjects I took to become a pharmacist," Al said, nudging Reece with his elbow and nodding in the direction of the captain.

Turning to get more eggs, Reece looked across the table where Rodriguez sat and saw the captain frowning with an obvious look of impatience.

"Better move two of those skillets over so I can slide a couple more in an' get the ham frying," Reece said. "We'd better warm some biscuits an' make plenty of gravy."

It was noon before Rodriguez and the Swede returned from watching the wrangler work the new stock. While the captain and the Swede dozed in the shade, Reece slipped out to the corral with a small sack of salt. He waited behind one of the water trucks and watched as Puente worked the young mules. An earlier roping accident had left the slim wrangler's left hand folded back at the wrist. His fingers still worked but he couldn't extend his hand. Reece knew the limitation could prove to be a serious handicap in handling young stock.

Sanchez had given Limesand the job of shining the dress boots for the captain and the guards, a job that seemed pointless since the boots would be covered with dust after a couple of steps.

It was best that Reece couldn't talk to his friend for a while. He could use the time alone to figure things out. Learning that he had a daughter could totally change his plans.

Reece was now gripped by mixed emotions. His earlier decision to escape was based on having nothing to lose. But things were different now. A feeling of guilt swept over him, leaving a resolve to someday make up for the many years that his child had missed having a father. He owed her that. And to do that, he'd have to find a way to escape. He'd have to be even more disciplined and determined in his plans. Seeing his daughter someday would require him staying alive.

He wouldn't be brought in from the desert, his stinking corpse slung over the back of a mule like Thompson's was. But then, self-discipline had been more difficult for a man like Thompson. Big tough men often grew up having things their own way. He'd perished because of his belief in his superior strength and toughness. The hostile conditions in the desert had taken his life.

His strength had ultimately become his greatest weakness.

Reece himself, in earlier years, had been the kind of man who sometimes acted on impulse. Getting older had changed that. This was an advantage that Thompson didn't have.

Reece weighed his chances of dying in the desert. With over nine years remaining on his prison sentence, there was a chance he'd never even live out half his full sentence. Either way the odds were stacked against him.

As Reece watched, the wrangler took a long whip and nervously moved the mules in circles, then reversed them in the opposite direction. The honey-colored mule was clearly the leader. The wrangler was competent with well-broken stock, but he'd obviously never been around untrained animals. Reece knew he had the edge on the man there.

Twenty years before, Reece had worked as a field-hand for a man named Pitts who'd had a tall mule named Jake with one white front foot. Jake would be his name for the one leading the circling mules.

After considering his earlier schemes for escape, Reece decided to stay with his first plan and make adjustments later as needed. He stayed out of sight until the wrangler shut the gate and left.

Several flat slabs of sandstone protruded from the upper slope of the pole enclosure. The wary mules watched as Reece crawled between the poles and slowly approached the nearest slab. Any sudden motion on his part would startle the fearful animals. He poured a thin layer of salt across the lower edges of the slabs and moved away. He watched until the curious mules finally approached the salt and licked it. When all the salt had disappeared, the mules continued to lick the porous rock for any trace of the vital substance. After looking around to make sure no one was watching, Reece eased over near Jake. From his pocket, he took a handful of the Swede's brown sugar and placed it in plain sight of Jake. A coal-black mule with a white muzzle was the first to approach the slab. She stretched her slender neck and sniffed. With her nostrils flared, she rolled her eyes until the whites showed, keeping Reece in constant sight. Her long ears rotated in an attempt to hear any sounds of danger.

Reece waited to see the mule's reaction to the Swede's favorite blend of spices and sugar. When the young mule finally licked the sugar Reece was pleased by the thought of how furious the Swede would be if he caught any prisoner, especially Reece, in such an act of defiance. The mule's long tongue waggled in and out of her rubbery lips until she was suddenly pushed aside. Jake had been content to let another herd member take the risk. Seeing there was no danger, he wanted to have the sweet-smelling offering for himself.

This was another part of Reece's plan. If he could somehow get to be Puente's helper he would have more freedom and he might get a chance to work out along the telegraph line. He'd slip out early every morning and bring the guard on duty a cup of coffee. When the guard wasn't looking he'd leave a couple of lumps of cane sugar for Jake. Before long he'd have the defiant mule eating out of his hand.

It was dusk when Al finished cleaning and polishing the guards' boots. Reece looked up as Al walked over to help him wash the cooking and serving utensils. Reece pointed down into the valley back toward Nacozari.

"Look Al, someone's lit a long row of giant candles. Must be the Yaquis in some kind of celebration."

The Swede grabbed his binoculars and hurried over toward where Reece was standing. Rodriguez came out of his tent to join them.

"They lit something all right. It's just like when they kept burning the railroad trestles south of here and kept one of the rail lines shut down for eleven years," Al replied. "It's their land, you know."

"What are you talking about, Limesand?" the Swede snapped, fumbling with the focusing adjustment on the lens.

With a sideways glance Reece saw the Swede's hands begin to shake, his heavy squared jowls locked in a grimace.

"They're burning the telegraph poles. I'm not surprised. I've been expecting something like this for the last few days. We're not far from their eastern boundary and it's their way of saying you forgot to pay us for using our land," Al added.

"Their land! It's the Mexican government's land and we paid for the rights to build the line here!" Neilson blurted, spraying spittle as he yelled at Al.

"They obviously don't agree," Al calmly replied.

"Who the hell are you to say it's their land?" Rodriguez asked, his face only inches from Al's.

Reece knew that Al was not the kind of man who relied on physical ability. He relied on what he'd learned from reading so many books. Al was very smart -- and Reece had a fleeting but proud thought that he had a daughter that was going to be smart just like Al.

"No captain, I didn't say I thought it was their land," Limesand replied without backing up an inch or even blinking. "What I think is of no consequence to anyone, especially the Yaquis. It's what they think that's causing them to burn the poles."

Rodriguez looked back toward the line of flaming torches lighting the evening sky.

The Swede continued to peer through his binoculars, fine-tuning the adjustments for the greatest clarity in the diminishing light. "The dumb bastards must have some superstition about the number three. They're only burning every third one."

"Not exactly," Al said, "it's just a sample of the way they figure things. Brush for fuel is scarce. Burning every third pole leaves one standing on each side of the ones that they burn. Ten poles that will have to be replaced, but thirty poles will have to be climbed and strung with new line."

Reece looked at Al, amazed at the way his friend's mind worked. Peering intently at the burning poles, Reece could see movement as figures circled into the flaring light from the shadows while clouds of shooting sparks spiraled upwards.

"I'm going to get my binoculars," Rodriguez said, hurrying to his tent.

"Hah! Now I see them -- nothing but naked savages dancing around one of our poles -- I'll give them something to dance about!" Neilson rushed over to his table and unrolled one of the maps.

"What's he doing?" Reece asked Al.

"Calculating the distance with his scale. Now the fool's running to get his rifle."

"You mean he's gonna try and shoot 'em from here?"

"The man's a fool -- always has to win. Well, he won't win this one. He doesn't understand Yaquis. They're a good half-mile away, but if he kills one we can forget about finishing this line," Al said, a serious frown clouding his boyish features.

Reece knew immediately that Al was right.

The impulsive Swede could ruin all of his plans, with just one bullet. He had to be stopped. Reece's legs shook with anxiety when the Swede came hurrying over, pushing cartridges into the rifle's breech as he ran.

Rodriguez stepped out of his tent, hesitating, his mouth open wide as if he was going to speak.

For just a moment Reece saw himself as a boy, once again playing Blackman. Without stopping to think he lowered his head and charged straight at the Swede.

CHAPTER 10

THE SWEDE'S SURPRISE

Reece drove his shoulder into the side of the unsuspecting Swede's left knee, complete surprise giving Reece the advantage. The Swede's legs buckled, tumbling him into the dirt. Instinctively, he cradled the rifle against his chest when he fell, protecting it at the expense of his body. Up in an instant and shouting curses, he kicked Reece in his ribs and stomach. Reece rolled to the side as the crazed man lunged forward, raising the rifle butt above Reece's head for a smashing blow.

The raised weapon stopped in mid-air. "Hold it right there!" Rodriguez ordered, gripping the rifle's barrel behind the Swede's back.

Reece couldn't believe it. The Swede slowly released his hold on the wooden stock and stood panting above him, a baffled look on his face. The captain's quick action had saved Reece from serious injury or even death. He lay on his back in the dirt, looking up at the Swede, wondering if in the last few seconds his actions had doomed any chance for escape. Had he, too, become like Thompson, foolishly believing he could defy all odds?

"The Sergeant will deal with you later -- I'll see to that, you dumb bastard." Rodriguez snarled down at Reece.

Rodriguez took the Swede's arm and led him aside, talking quietly as they walked. Seeing Reece struggling to get to his feet, Al hurried over. Holding onto Al's arm, Reece steadied himself. Taking shallow breaths he eased the pain in his chest.

After a short interval, Rodriguez walked back over, an incredulous look on his face.

"I thought he was gonna' shoot me," Reece lied, hoping Rodriguez might believe him since he had seen the Swede shoot the jar out of his hand.

The captain looked at Reece. A trace of amusement crossed his face. "You two get back to work."

As he turned and left Al grinned and whispered, "You've done it again my friend. I don't know what's gotten into you."

"I lost my head an' now I just know I'm gonna be sent back." Reece shook his head and looked at the ground in despair.

"I'm not so sure about that. Besides, you said yourself what a great cook you are."

"Maybe I'm not as good as I said." Reece answered, holding his side, gently pressing his fingers against his ribs where the Swede's boot struck.

"You may not believe this but I think the captain was both surprised and tickled when he saw you knock the Swede on his ass. He had a smirk on his face until the Swede leaped up and started kicking you."

"You really think so?"

"Yeah. They don't really like each other that much -- but they need each other. I heard that the captain and the warden are to get a bonus if the line's completed on time."

"I hope you're right. I can't stand the thought of being locked up again. But that Swede's gonna' really hate me now."

"Maybe not as much as you think. After all, he was the one standing at the end of the fight -- you were the one in the dirt. He knows he hurt you pretty bad. Any time he wins at anything he won't be too unhappy. I have to tell you though, I was really surprised you jumped him. That took a lot of nerve."

"I don't know." Reece shook his head and stared at the ground. He'd never acted like this before. He knew he didn't even dare tell Al he was obsessed with ideas for escape, especially now since he'd gotten the letter from Eula Mae.

"The best way to handle this is to pretend it never happened. Just do your job. Believe me, when the Swede has time to think about it he's going to be glad you stopped him from killing any of the Yaquis."

"I'm gonna' do my best."

"Good. Now lets take a look at your side."

The Swede and the captain spent the following day discussing their problem with the Yaquis. There was no point, they finally agreed, to invest more money or time until they'd resolved the problem. Limesand had convinced them it would be foolish to ignore the Yaquis' interest as the railroad directors had done for a stretch of 11 years. Shutting down the railroad had been easy. Each time the rail crews rebuilt the wooden trestle spanning a river in Copper Canyon, the Yaquis burned it.

After the decision by Rodriguez and the Swede, Limesand confided to Reece his belief of the one thing that convinced the Swede. "It was the orange flames of every third pole lighting the sky. That told the Swede a lot more than words."

Rodriguez and the Swede took Harper and Limesand on a mission to locate the Yaquis' leaders. Three more days were spent in negotiating an annual payment for use of the Yaquis' lands. "The Indians," Limesand said, grinning, upon his return, "are learning the ways of the white man." His face showed concern. "Say, did Sanchez do anything to you while I was gone?"

"No. I can't understand it. He walked right past me a couple of times but never said a word. Both times he looked at me kinda' funny."

"I'll bet him and the captain had a real good laugh about your little run-in with the Swede." Al chuckled, his look of concern disappearing. Glancing toward Rodriguez, he said, "We better get busy."

"I hope they just forget me. I don't even look at 'em if I don't have to."

A small crew was sent back to replace the blackened poles and string new copper lines. The following three weeks were filled with back-breaking labor before the line was completed to the crest of the Sierra Madre. The way was often blocked. The Swede spent long days surveying the best route for the line's location. The maps he had made didn't always have sufficient detail for terrain and soil conditions. Sheer cliffs and overhanging granite ledges made treacherous footing for both men and mules climbing the western slopes above the Rio Papigochic. Reece had hoped the young wrangler with the crippled hand would fail and loose control of the unbroken animals. It hadn't happened. The slowed progress of installing poles in rocky ground gave the wrangler time to train the mules to carry full cans of water.

The thin blankets each prisoner had been issued were scant protection from the cold night air on the divide's timbered crest. The nights, however, were a welcome relief from the scorching heat of the desert.

On the morning they were moving the camp, they broke out of the timber and walked to the edge of a long shelf. "Here's the place I told you about, John," Al said, looking in the direction of the rising sun, still low above the horizon. They stood looking down on a vast sweeping plateau. The eastern slopes were cut with steep sided canyons and valleys. "Juarez is there, off to the north, but you can't see it from here."

"I never saw nothin' like this where I come from." Reece replied in a hushed tone, feeling awed at the remote expanse.

"You can see smoke at the head of that canyon." Al pointed to a thin gray ribbon rising from a chasm between two canyon walls. "It's probably the home of an Indian family or maybe two or three. If there's a good spring and some little slivers of land that's not too steep, they'll plant some squash and a few hills of beans and as many rows of corn as they have room for."

"Shore would be easy to get lost out there." Reece answered before he thought. Most everything reminded him of his plans to escape and try to find his way north when the time was right. Al was caught up in explaining the wilderness that stretched as far as Reece could see, and continued talking.

"The Tarahumara build the walls of their houses with rock slabs and adobe bricks they make and dry in the sun -- usually one small room covered with scraps of sheet iron, when they can find it. We'll see some before long when we get near the Babicora."

"What's the Babicora?"

"It's a million-acre ranch. Used to be owned by a United States Senator, named George Hearst. Ever hear of him?"

"Can't say I did." Reece was embarrassed that he knew so little about the many things Al had seen and read about.

"Before the Mexican government sold it to Hearst for 30 cents an acre it was the ancestral home of the Tarahumara for thousands of years or so it is believed. Nobody really knows how long they'd lived there."

"How could anybody sell somethin' that didn't rightly belong to 'em?"

"Hey, old man, I thought you said you were from Oklahoma and you're asking me how it happened? Didn't you read about the Indian Territory in your history books when you went to school or were you too busy trying to look up some girl's dress?" Al laughed and punched Reece on the shoulder.

Reece was embarrassed, hesitating to respond when Al changed the subject.

"There's a couple of Indians now carrying something on their backs."

Reece turned, just in time to see two figures disappear down through the trees, both were hidden under bulky loads jutting high above their heads.

During the following week the Tarahumara were seen more often, some with their families moving their flocks of sheep and goats, others racing along the divide's timbered crest as Al predicted,

Reece's ribs were almost healed but he was now discouraged. His plans couldn't work unless he had access to the remoteness of the line's location. He had to hide water. If he was allowed to run with the mules he could develop stamina and hide jars of water.

They turned south, stringing the lines along the eastern slopes, paralleling the Sierra's crest. Another week passed before a guard came staggering into camp. There had been an accident he reported in broken English. The wrangler was badly hurt.

The Swede ran over from his table, asking the exhausted guard a barrage of questions.

"Give him a chance to get his breath," Rodriguez admonished the Swede.

Reece's spirits soared when he heard enough to know there'd been trouble with the wrangler's horse and the mules.

"Where's Limesand?" the Swede asked sharply, turning toward Reece then glancing around the campsite. "He's had medical training -- go find him hobo. Now!" the Swede demanded when he didn't see Limesand in camp.

Reece hurried toward the grove of scrub oak thickets where Al was searching for firewood, calling for him as he ran.

"Over here, John. What's all the yelling about?"

"Come on. There's been a bad accident. That wrangler Puente's been hurt and the Swede wants you -- said something about your medical training." As they hurried down to the camp Reece realized he was pleased about another man's misfortune. He hated himself for the way he felt but he couldn't stop being glad that it happened. This could be his chance. After all, he'd lately heard the Swede refer to him by a couple of new names: hillbilly and plowboy. It could be the break he'd hoped for.

It was almost midnight when four men came into camp, carrying Puente on a stretcher. Al walked alongside, holding Puente's wrist and checking his pulse. Reece got a glimpse of Puente's head. One side was covered with blood where the cheek and eye socket were crushed. Reece walked into the darkness and vomited; his selfish prayers had been answered. Could it be only the devil who'd been listening?

Limesand stayed by the man's side until morning, bathing his battered head, washing it with atropine and warm water while Reece tended to the lanterns and fire. Even though there was no sign of life, Limesand talked to Puente throughout the night, with quiet reassurance.

The sun was breaking the horizon when Limesand stood and bowed his head. Puente was dead.

Breakfast was served late. The guards and prisoners were somber, talking only in subdued voices. Puente had been well-liked, respected by both the other guards and prisoners. He never abused his authority.

When most of the men were finished eating, the captain got to his feet. He commented briefly on Puente's loyal service, then explained the details of the accident.

"Puente got a late start and tried to take a short-cut, riding down into a steep arroyo. His horse stumbled and started sliding in loose shale 'til it dropped its rump and slid into a pine tree. Puente didn't let go of the lead rope, so the mules followed him down. The first one slid by his horse on the left and the second one went by on the right and then the others piled into them -- all that weight, they couldn't stop." Rodriguez stopped, shook his head and lowered his voice. "The lead rope between the first two mules caught Puente high across his back and crushed him against the tree... A little later he slid off his horse and fell..."

Reece knew that the kind of accident that killed Puente wasn't that unusual. He'd worked with packmules in Colorado when he cooked for hunting camps. Lashing the bloody carcasses of elk and deer onto the backs of young skittish mules and packing them off mountains so steep the mules could barely stand had been a dangerous and risky business.

Rodriguez cleared his throat. "Puente was kicked in the head and never regained consciousness. Limesand stayed with him all night -- did everything he could. Now we've got a new problem. I've got to pick someone to take Puente's place -- unless we have a volunteer."

The group became strangely quiet. Where the captain had their rapt attention now there was only silence. The men either looked away or down at their plates.

Reece was so excited his legs trembled. If a guard didn't volunteer would they consider a prisoner? He desperately wanted the job but didn't want to call attention to himself. He couldn't appear anxious.

Rodriguez looked from table to table, studying the guards and then the prisoners. As usual, when making a decision, he rubbed his chin and smoothed his mustache while he pondered the problem.

Reece glanced over to his left. The Swede was staring in his direction. His hopes soared. A plowboy would know about mules, the goddam Swede would know that. Rodriguez walked between the tables, eyeing the men closely.

"Some of you must've worked on farms. I know you did. I've seen the files on all of you, I just can't remember which ones. Raise your hand if you ever worked with mules."

A small man at a rear table raised his hand and hesitantly asked. "Do a burro count?"

"Hell no, a burro is nothing like a mule, even though a mule's father is a jackass -- of course lots of fathers are jackasses." Rodriguez answered. A wave of laughter eased the nervous tension of the moment.

The Swede showed no indication he'd heard Rodriguez's attempt at humor. "I think you're overlooking someone," the Swede offered seriously. "I've heard the hobo over there telling Limesand about his days when he worked as a field hand and plowed with mules." Neilson nodded in Reece's direction.

Rodriguez looked at Reece while tapping his fingers on the table top, pondering the Swede's suggestion. "No. I don't think so. I'd prefer one of the guards since they have to be out along the line -- working alone a lot of the time."

The Swede stood and looked over the men who kept averting their eyes and trying to avoid being noticed. "We do need someone with experience -- someone who can handle mules that need a firm hand -- young mules that can be dangerous and hard to handle."

Reece felt an emptiness in the pit of his stomach. He'd come close to getting his chance to work out his plans for an attempt to escape.

One of the guards seated at the rear table said something to Rodriguez. The captain turned and looked directly at Reece. "Reece, I'm told you've been seen feeding that honey-colored mule -- the mean one -- probably the one that killed Puente -- said the mule was eating out of your hand. Is that true?"

"*Sí, Señor* Rodriguez."

"Did you ever work with mules?"

"*Sí, Capitán.*"

"Then I'd suggest we give Reece a shot at it," the Swede said, nodding his head with enthusiasm.

Reece could hardly believe what he'd just heard. Now that they needed an experienced hand, the uppity bastard had decided to show him a little respect. While the two men talked among themselves and with the guard that had reported seeing Reece feed the honey-colored mule, Reece whispered to Limesand. "You hear that? The son-of-a-bitch has heard that I got a name, just like everybody else."

"Didn't I tell you? Knocking him on his ass really got his attention," Limesand whispered out of the side of his mouth.

"Then it's settled. We'll work out the details later. Someone will have to be assigned to help with the cooking, Reece, you'll still help with the evening meal." Rodriguez turned to the Swede. "One more thing. Reece won't be using the horse that Puente rode. No prisoner is allowed to even get on a horse. He'll have to lead the mules at a fast trot."

"I don't know about that, he's at least twice Puente's age. He may not be able to last if he can't ride a horse -- but that's your call, Captain. The fact that Reece is experienced with mules means the most to me."

Reece tried to hide his feelings. He knew his new job would take long hours of punishing effort. But he was determined to show them one thing -- his age wasn't going to matter. Just thinking about the letters from Eula Mae would keep him going. He crossed his fingers under the table and waited.

Rodriguez turned back and gave Reece a hard look. "Reece, you better watch your step. You may be out of sight of the guards a lot of the time but I'll have someone checking on you when you least expect it. Is that clear?"

"*Sí, Señor* Rodriguez. Me an' the mules'll be there with the water any time the men get thirsty. I promise."

CHAPTER 11

CHICKEN BONES

By the fourth day of running with the mules, Reece knew he'd been given an almost impossible task. Overweight and in his late forties, his best years were only a memory. He was convinced, however, that any other man in the crew would find the ordeal exhausting. At night, weariness from the days running gave him a few hours sleep and escape from the throbbing pain in the tendons alongside his shin bones. It was on a night when the throbbing seemed the worst that Reece dreamed he was running down the long rows in a cotton field in Kansas while Glen Cunningham raced on ahead of him, finally disappearing into a distant haze.

They were on rocky slopes, east of the Sierra's crest. Line crews slowed their pace when the diggers hit miles of shale. The Swede studied his maps. Within three weeks, he calculated, they would come to a long plateau of open sage and sand. He insisted the crews must cover twice the distance. They'd lost time when the Yaquis stole their stock. Reece worried that the additional miles could far exceed his limits of endurance. But for now the slowed pace would give him a chance to get in better condition.

Stopping the mules, he dipped water from one of the ten-gallon cans carried in the panniers strapped on the sides of Jake, the lead mule. He poured the cooling water over his head and down the front of his shirt, the closest thing to a bath with clean water since the bus accident. After taking a long drink, he trotted up the trail the mule's hooves had cut on his earlier run that morning. Reece listened to the creaking of the split willow strands, woven into the framework of the swaying panniers, while the mules loped along behind him, water in the cans sloshing in rhythm with their strides. He'd wrapped and tied dishtowels around his jars of water carried in the bottom of the cans to keep them quiet when they gently bumped against the metal sides.

The young mules were strong, carrying the 200 pound loads with little sign of stress. Within less than half an hour Reece's legs began to weaken. He struggled on as best he could but he was late with the water delivery. The guard warned him, "If you're this late again, Reece, I'll report you to the *capitán*."

Reece's days were long, one almost running over into the next. Limesand's earlier suggestion to just do the best he could each day was encouragement enough for Reece to keep on trying. He had so little time now to work with his friend, one of the few men he'd ever trusted. Still, he didn't dare hint that he was working on a plan to escape. If Limesand was ever questioned by Sanchez or beaten, he might blurt out what he knew of Reece's plans. With his sentence ending in less than a year, it would be foolish for Limesand to consider any attempt to escape. Reece realized his friend had an easy life and for him the rigors of fleeing through the mountains and desert would be a chance doomed to fail.

Near the end of a long stretch where the trail climbed into the timber near the mountain's crest, Reece stopped the panting mules. He watched as Indian runners came into view, gliding through the trees with little apparent effort. Their arms and legs moved in a gentle rhythm, while their thong-covered feet found the best footing.

Reece changed his own style of running on his toes and the balls of his feet to the more flat-footed manner the Indians used. Within days the nagging pain in his lower legs subsided. Each grueling day hardened his body for the escape, he prayed, would one day come. Taking one day at a time helped him keep his fervent hopes alive. On the days when the longer distances made him weary and near complete exhaustion, he'd picture Eula Mae as a little girl in pigtails, wearing a pretty, flowered dress. On some days he'd picture her sitting in the front row of her college classes, getting A's in all of her subjects. The surge of emotion he felt would push his body to higher limits.

Almost daily now, Reece saw small children picking their way through thickets of thorn bush and spiny ocotillo, helping their families drive goats and sheep to distant waterholes. Reece knew the searing drought had hit the high desert even harder than the dust bowl and the withered plain states back home. Browse was scarce. Lack of moisture in the rocky ground kept new growth from sprouting on the shrubs and grasses, leaving flocks little more than skin and bones. The goats fared best. They could stand on their hind legs and reach higher than the sheep, their nimble muzzles adapted for plucking tender shoots, sprouting between the thorns.

The children were shy with round pretty faces, haunting dark eyes and black hair contrasting sharply with their sun-bleached muslin shirts. If they passed near the line camp at meal time, they would stop and peek through the mesquite at the guards and prisoners eating their food.

When the captain saw them lurking near camp he'd yell and curse them and then chuckle as they fled through the mesquite.

The Swede reviewed his maps and calculated they'd now come at least 100 miles from Nacozari. He stated it was time for a feast. He promised that when they reached the 200-mile point, almost due west of Chihuahua, musicians and dancers would be trucked to the campsite and another feast would be prepared like most had never seen before. It had now been over 20 days since they'd left Nacozari.

On the following morning Reece and Limesand were up early. A Mexican wearing a large sombrero was waiting out by the corrals with a string of burros. Crates of chickens and fresh fruits and vegetables were strapped onto the backs of the sleepy pack animals. It was just another long day for Reece and Limesand, cooking and serving the large crew and the guards.

By first light on the day after the feast, Reece finished feeding the mules and began adjusting the breeching harness on Jake's rump. Jake raised his head and his ears pointed toward the back of the corral. He'd either heard or smelled something or caught a glimpse of movement.

Reece stood still and listened. He heard cracking sounds coming from back of the corral where Limesand had dumped the chicken bones. "Them damn coyotes are still following us," he muttered to himself, tightening the leather straps that held the panniers in place. Since he now spent most of his days alone, he noticed he often talked to himself. He listened again. The sounds persisted. He picked up a rock, crawled through the pole rails of the corral and sneaked through the brush. Something black moved not fifty feet ahead. It wasn't the tawny color of a coyote. Another one moved, but in the early morning light Reece couldn't be sure what they were. The whites of two round, dark eyes now showed on the nearest one, holding still and staring back at Reece. After a moment his stomach churned when he realized that he was watching two children who'd been cracking chicken bones and eating the marrow.

Reece eased back then noticed another movement farther over in the mesquite. It looked like a woman hunched under a dark blanket, fringed with tassel. Long dark hair streaked with gray hung down her back.

Reece slipped away and went to find Limesand.

"If you got any food left over, save it for me." Reece looked around and whispered, "There's two kids an' an old woman hidin' out behind the corrals. The kids are eatin' the chicken bones you throwed out last night."

"I'm not surprised. Lots of them starve every year. The marrow in the chicken bones is a real treat for them and very nourishing, too." Limesand's face showed a kind of sadness Reece had seldom seen before. "Most of their corn and squash plants have withered in the drought these last three years. Beans do a little better. They don't take as much water -- but you're from the farm, I don't suppose I need to tell you that."

"Just save me anything you can. I'll get it to 'em somehow but you be careful. Don't take any chances if anyone's around. You ain't got that much time left on your sentence to risk gettin' caught."

"You're the one who should be careful. They need you to run the line but they'll nail your ass if you get careless -- you know it's strictly against the captain's rules."

"I know. But I'm gonna' see that them kids get something to eat. I been hungry myself and it ain't no fun." Reece wondered if Eula Mae always had plenty of food when she was a child. He wheeled and walked away, well aware that Rodriguez had been more hostile toward all Indians since the Yaquis stole their stock and burned the ten telegraph poles.

After filling the water cans, Reece made sure no one else was around. He pulled from the bushes two half-gallon glass fruit jars he'd washed and hidden earlier. He filled them with water and sealed them with zinc lids, wrapped them with the dish towels and sunk them to the bottom of the water cans ready to be loaded on Jake. The ten-gallon containers, originally made to hold milk dairymen sent to creameries, were the perfect hiding place for his secret water supply. When he found an isolated place near a telegraph pole, out of anyone's sight, he'd stop and remove them and bury them in the ground. He'd count off the poles from the nearest prominent point and mark it in the notebook he'd stolen from the Swede's writing table.

Seeing a pole ahead, partly screened by creosote bushes, Reece led Jake up close and took the jars from the water cans. He unfastened the top buttons on his pants before he started digging. If anyone ever surprised him he'd claim he'd only stopped to relieve himself. After covering the jars with dirt and rocks, Reece pulled the notebook from a pocket he'd sewn on the inside of his shirt and checked the count. During the last few weeks he'd hidden 42 jars. The numbers of the poles were coded with references to the most prominent point around. The number of poles from the prominent point and the direction were referenced by the number of birds he claimed he'd seen -- he'd noted the number and the direction they were supposedly flying. Reece figured he'd need almost two gallons of water each day if he escaped and reached the remote eastern slopes and bluffs along the Sierra's crest.

They reached the long open stretch of sage the Swede's maps had shown. The crews averaged eight miles a day where the soil was easy to dig. Two trips out along the line and back now required Reece to trot over 30 miles. Helping with the cooking and clean-up in the late afternoon and evenings meant he never finished his chores until way after dark.

It took less than a week to install the poles and lines across the high plateau. Reece prayed each night for his tiring legs to hold out until they reached the higher mountains he could see on the horizon to the south. In another 30 miles he hoped the towering rock outcroppings would slow the line crews. A sprinkling of snow showed on the north side of the mountain's highest peaks.

They'd now reached a remote section of steep-sided arroyos where the earth's crust had been folded into high, narrow ridges, like wrinkles in a blanket. Vegetation was sparse and stunted.

The captain made an announcement at the first breakfast in the new camp. "For about the next 80 miles we'll be crossing some steep, desolate country. In some places we can drive trucks up backroads that lead off the highway running south from Casas Grandes -- some of the overgrown roadways lead to old abandoned silver mines. From the end of these roads all food and water'll have to be trucked in to a point where they can be met by pack mules. We'll get our water from lakes that haven't been ruined by alkali."

Rodriguez leaned over and said something to the Swede. They each pointed to some lines on one of the Swede's maps and continued their conversation.

The mention of more work for the pack mules, Reece reckoned, meant more work for him. But it didn't seem possible. His days now were 18 hours long with little chance for a rest.

The Swede filled his pipe, lit it, and took one more look at his map and got to his feet. He cleared his throat and waited until there was complete silence before he began speaking.

"You're probably wondering where we'll get the telegraph poles when we reach the back-country." He pointed to the granite walls towering in the distance, "There's timber on the slopes near Madera. Some other stands grow on the western slopes of the divide southwest of Madera and there's some growing above J. Matta Ortiz.

"We've put out the word that we'll pay fifty cents apiece for poles that are at least 26 feet long. Most of the trees we'll need are growing within 20 miles of where we'll be building the line when we need them."

"Can you believe that tight-fisted son-of-a-bitch?" Limesand asked, shaking his head negatively.

"Shh" Reece cautioned, "he'll hear you."

Rodriguez raised his head and glared in the general direction of Limesand and Reece, apparently unable to determine who'd been talking.

The Swede continued. "Some of the Indians who live on the slopes above the Babicora agreed to cut and carry the poles to where we'll need them. We gave out pieces of cord that measure twenty six feet. It's up to them to cut the poles we need and carry them to us." The Swede rolled up his maps and returned to his writing table.

Limesand sat with his lips pursed, his brow wrinkled into a deep frown. "All that timber is claimed by corporations in the states. They got it for almost nothing from that bloody dictator, Diaz." Reece noticed Limesand's jaws clench as he watched the Swede, sitting at his table, strike a match and try to re-light his pipe. "It all belonged to the Indians before that goddam Diaz sold them out."

Reece had never before heard Limesand take the Lord's name in vain.

Continuing to denounce the long-dead dictator, Limesand added, "The timbered areas are patrolled by guards on horseback, carrying semi-automatic rifles. Any trees cut for the line will have to be taken from the highest and most dangerous slopes that the lazy guards can't ride up to on horseback. They have standing orders to shoot on sight any Indians caught cutting trees."

The crews reached a saddle where the windswept land, lying between massive bluffs, was barren except for scattered greasewood and tumbleweeds. Harper stood on the leeward side of his horse, looking south, trying to hold a partly unrolled map against the horse's flank. Gusting winds whipped sheets of sand across the high desert, blowing it through the pass and into the upper reaches of Copper Canyon. Diggers kept their backs to the howling winds.

Reece waited for the blowing sands to subside before he took the lids from the water cans and started moving along the line of thirsty workers. Looking up he saw two hulking forms emerge from behind the limestone bluff toward the south. Silhouetted against the skyline for a moment, they then moved down toward them. As the strange forms loomed closer Reece saw they were two Indians, dwarfed under long dark poles carried over their hunched shoulders. Both men came on with a fast shuffling gait across the uneven footing.

Harper turned his head and watched their final approach. Now Reece could see where the logs were cushioned against the top of the men's shoulders with pieces of folded sheepskin. Harper stood with his mouth ajar. Like Reece he'd probably never seen such a feat of strength and endurance. The logs appeared to be at least twice the weight of the men carrying them.

"Over there. Drop them over there," Harper said, pointing to a stake driven in the ground. A red flag tied to the top fluttered in the windy pass.

Harper took a tape and checked the logs for length. He nodded and opened a metal box. Reece watched as Harper counted out some coins. He then took out a pencil and made a note in a small tablet he carried in the box.

Without saying a word, the men, who looked like brothers, turned and trotted up the slope they'd just come down, the muscles in their legs rippling under dark skin.

Harper turned to face Reece and shook his head. "The closest trees this size are growing at least twenty miles from here. I've heard of these Tarahumara runners before but never expected anything like this."

For the next two weeks there was a steady stream of men bringing logs from early morning until after dark.

Reece now spent little time helping with the cooking. Packing water from the trucks parked at the ends of abandoned mining roads took all of the daylight hours. On many days Reece knew he'd covered more than 40 miles.

The day had been especially hot. Reece stopped in the shade of a stand of dwarf Pinon trees to give the sweating mules a short rest.

It was the last run of the day. Reece took the final swallow from the gourd dipper then hung it from a strap on Jake's pannier. Turning he saw a burro tied below the trail. Its body was almost hidden under bundles of thorn-covered branches, leaves and what appeared to be greenish white flowers. Across the top of the load a mass of cream-colored tangled roots, many at least six feet in length, were lashed in place. What appeared to be a goatskin water bag hung from a piece of hemp tied near the burro's shoulder.

The barely visible burro stood motionless except for an occasional flick of its tail. With its head hanging low, it appeared to be asleep. The load on its back was unlike any other Reece had seen on burros Indians sometimes led through the mountains. He took Jake's lead rope and started to move on. After a few steps he stopped and looked again at the tethered animal: a nagging thought telling him that he'd noticed something familiar.

Something hanging below the burro's flanks caught Reece's eye. A fringe of six-inch long, dark-brown tassels were attached to the edge of a blanket that protected the animal's back and flanks from the load of thorns. He then saw what caused his nagging thoughts, compelling a second look. The blanket's edge showed the same dark and white design pattern he'd seen the old woman wearing the morning he'd watched the children cracking chicken bones. Could it be a coincidence?

What could they possibly be doing wandering around these mountains, he wondered? He thought perhaps he had a clue. The cream-colored roots could be the answer. They looked to be the same as those from the spikenard plant Limesand had dug and made into a poultice for the festering cuts on Reece's face. Could the burro's owner be some kind of medicine woman?

It seemed likely that the blanket was the one he'd seen before. If it was the old woman's, where was she now and was she still traveling with the two children? Another question crossed his mind that puzzled him even more. How could she possibly find enough water to sustain three people and a burro in the desolate creosote and chaparral-covered wasteland? She'd have to know more about the remote desert and possible sources of water than the people who'd made the Swede's maps.

A grave concern suddenly gripped Reece. Had the old woman been watching him and stealing his jars of buried water?

CHAPTER 12

DESERT BIGHORN

"I can fry you a little slice of ham, John, and slip it in with your lunch. The Swede'll never miss it," Limesand said in a low voice. "He and the captain are still busy talking out by the corral." Limesand slid two skillets to the back of the grate. "Something's going on, I guess. Rodriguez got up real early this morning."

Reece watched, trance-like as the flames licked at a piece of wood.

"Well, what's the matter, Mr. Reece? Since when did you ever turn down ham or have you lost your hearing? I know, you're probably thinking about Eula Mae."

"Oh yes -- that's it," Reece answered. "Yeah, some ham. That would be good." He didn't want Limesand to know of his concern for his jars of buried water that might have been stolen. The problem he faced had no answer. There was no way for him to go back now along the line to see if they were missing. Without them in place he had no plan.

"You feeling all right, old friend?" Limesand asked, glancing out towards the pole corral.

"I was just thinking about some sheep I saw crossing a rock slide above the line a couple of days ago." Changing the subject should keep Limesand's attention for awhile.

"I'm talking about sneaking you a piece of fried ham and you're thinking about sheep." Limesand laughed. "Maybe I should fry you a nice big piece of greasy mutton."

Reece was too worried to listen to Limesand's idle chatter. After a few moments of silence, Limesand raised his voice and impatiently declared, "I don't get it, John. What's eating you, anyway?"

Harper looked over from the Swede's table, where he was sorting a stack of papers. His look of suspicion got Reece's attention.

"Keep your voice down. I think Harper's trying to hear what we're sayin'." Reece looked around to see if anyone else was still in camp. He now suspected everyone except Limesand. "The sheep I saw wasn't just any sheep -- they was bighorn -- desert bighorn. They ain't that many of them left, you know."

"I've been working in Sonora and Chihuahua for over ten years and I've never even seen one. It seems like I did hear something about them -- that they're protected -- no one's allowed to hunt them."

"No one's been allowed to hunt them for over twenty years. They stay as far from people as they can, up high, mostly in the rocks. You ain't gonna see any desert bighorn when you're drivin' along some road."

"Too late now, here they come, but I'll fix you a piece of ham in the morning if no one's around, while you're loading the mules."

Both Rodriguez and the Swede walked over and joined Harper. Pushing Harper's stacks of papers aside, the Swede unrolled his largest map.

"Reece, any of that coffee left?" the Swede asked, raising his cup. "If there is, bring it over."

"Half a pot," Reece answered, stepping over and filling the Swede's cup, careful to avoid splattering coffee on the map. "Any for you, Captain?" he asked, first holding the pot out toward Rodriguez, then Harper. Both men shook their heads.

Reece took little notice of the Swede's apparent change in attitude. Just because he didn't rap his cup for service any more didn't mean a thing. Anxious to be on his way, Reece looked over to where the mules were tied, loaded and ready to be led up the trail. He had thought of a way that might keep his water cache safe.

The Swede added his blend of sugar and cinnamon to his coffee and turned to Harper. "Jess, bring me up to date on how things are going."

"Sure Mr. Neilson, I got it all down right here. It's going real good, I'm pleased to report. We're getting plenty of poles every day. It's hard to believe what those Indians will do for fifty cents, cutting and carrying…"

"Tell me if you see any problems ahead that we should be thinking about."

"Yes sir. We'll need more rolls of wire in another couple of weeks and another thousand insulators." Reece stayed busy wiping the tops of nearby tables while Harper turned the pages in a sheaf of papers. "It's all right here in my memorandum on page seven."

"I'll remember that."

"Best I can figure, right now, we're about fifteen miles from the nearest timber. It takes most of the Indians a day and a half to make a round trip and bring a log. Beats me how one man can carry that much weight, that far and…"

"Forget about them. They got nothing better to do." The Swede turned to Rodriguez. "One of the guards said he saw large bear tracks that crossed a sandy wash and went into a manzanita thicket -- could have been a grizzly. There's supposed to be a few of them left in these mountains."

"I heard about someone seeing some big tracks," Rodriguez said. It was obvious to Reece the two men were getting bored again. They'd probably take one of the trucks and head for the closest town or maybe go back to Casas Grandes or down to Chihuahua for the line supplies.

"I'd sure like to get a crack at one of them old boars. If it wasn't so far, I'd like to take a little side trip east of here over to Sierra del Nido. A few grizzlies killed there have weighed up to 700 pounds." The Swede looked closely at his map and pursed his lips as if relishing the thought of hunting one of the coveted trophies.

"Without dogs, wouldn't it be hard to find one in the brush?" Rodriguez asked.

"Maybe we could ask the Indians if they've seen any sign of bears or know where they den up."

Rodriguez laughed. "You'd never find one that way. They stay as far away from grizzlies as they can -- and there's a damn good reason -- none of them own a rifle that I've ever heard of."

"If I might add, they do travel through some wild country on their way to cut the logs." Harper said softly, apparently concerned his remarks might seem to contradict the captain.

"It wouldn't hurt to ask," the Swede nodded in agreement.

"I did see one family camped not far from here," Harper said. "There's two brothers that bring a log each day -- they're the only ones that do. They eat with their family and get a short nap and then they're off again. They must have found a spring that's got enough water for the five of them and their burro."

"Five of them and a burro?" Reece blurted before he thought, alarmed at how much water that many people and a burro would drink.

"Yeah." Harper looked at Reece with a quizzical expression. "You seen them too?"

"Say, what do you think of Reece seeing some sheep, some desert bighorn?" Limesand asked.

Reece was relieved Limesand had quickly taken the attention away from his sudden question that had both Rodriguez and the Swede eyeing him suspiciously.

The Swede had raised his hand to make a point and opened his mouth as if to speak. From the corner of his eye, Reece could see the man's hand remained fixed, his mouth open, yet strangely silent. Something had been said or done, Reece realized, causing Neilson's odd reaction. Reece waited for some clue that might let him know the cause of the man's behavior.

The Swede lowered his hand slowly to the top of the table and turned squarely to face Reece. After a long pause he asked in a superior manner, "And just when, Reece, did you ever see a desert bighorn before?"

"I never did."

"Did you ever see a picture of one?"

Reece hesitated to answer, confused about the Swede's questions. He had no idea what he'd done or said to offend the man.

"In case you've forgotten the question, I asked if you'd ever seen a picture of a desert bighorn?"

"Uh no, can't say that I have."

"Can you describe for us just what it is that made you think you'd seen desert bighorn?" Smirking, the Swede turned to Rodriguez and winked.

"Well I saw a band of maybe fifteen in all crossin' a rock slide -- up high above the line. There was five or six ewes, some lambs, and a couple of yearlings. Following along behind was a three-quarter curl ram."

The Swede stood, his mouth agape. After a long pause he asked, "Did you say a three-quarter curl ram? Where did you ever hear anyone use that term?"

Reece again hesitated to answer, completely baffled by the Swede abruptly getting to his feet, staring hard at him, and asking another question.

"I'm waiting for your answer."

"I was a cook for a huntin' camp near Black Sage pass in Colorado a couple of times. Two hunters killed bighorn sheep one year an' the next year another hunter got one. That one was killed on a narrow ledge of a cliff. The guide paid me two dollars to climb up an' carry it down."

"Rocky Mountain Bighorn?"

"Yeah."

The Swede continued staring at Reece, almost like he'd forgotten there was anyone else around. His superior manner changed and he asked in a civil way. "Did any of the sheep hunters ever mention the term 'Grand Slam'?"

"About all they ever talked about."

Now the Swede was the one who spent long moments before responding. "Do you think you could find the place again where you saw them?" Neilson's voice was almost casual with a poorly disguised attempt to be pleasant.

79

Reece saw what the strange line of questioning was leading to. Even though the Swede had no legal right to hunt the rare desert bighorn, that was exactly what he was planning to do.

"I might. They're up yonder." Reece nodded toward the mountain's highest peaks.

The Swede whispered something to Rodriguez. After an exchange of comments Rodriguez nodded. The Swede's face broke into a big grin, his eyes wide and shinning. Rodriguez looked over and said, "Wait here, Reece."

The captain got to his feet and motioned to the Swede. Both men walked out to a shelf that overlooked a narrow canyon where smoke was rising from a small village at the bottom.

Reece was disgusted with himself. His idle comment to Limesand was apt to start an intensive hunt for the sheep that could take several days. His own plan to eliminate the problem with his water supply would have to wait -- just when he'd thought of a way to stop the old woman from wandering through the mountains.

If he could catch the old flop-eared burro alone he could kill it, slash its neck and flanks and drag a bush behind him to wipe out his tracks, making it look like a bear attacked it. Without the burro the woman would surely leave. He couldn't risk losing his chance to escape for the life of one near-worthless animal.

It was mostly Limesand's fault. If he hadn't kept talking about cooking some ham and then blurting out that Reece had seen bighorn sheep he would have already been on his way with the mules, following Sanchez and his crew up the line.

Rodriguez and the Swede came walking back toward their table. "There's been a change in plans, Jess," the Swede said, beaming with enthusiasm. "Captain Rodriguez has an idea that should work out just fine. You'll ride your horse and lead the mules for the next few days."

"Yes sir, Mister Neilson. I see Reece has them loaded and ready to go."

"Sergeant Sanchez will be in complete charge of the project and you'll be his assistant."

"Yes sir."

"We're going to take Reece and that big mule he calls Jake, and one other mule, on a little side-trip up to those higher bluffs." The Swede pointed toward the limestone cliffs that glistened in the morning sun. "Oh yes, and we're going to need your backpack."

"Yes sir, Mister Neilson."

Reece felt an immediate sense of desperation. The freedom he'd had to run the line was gone. He could feel his legs trembling with anxiety. There was a manzanita thicket no more than 100 yards away. While the men's back was turned Reece knew he could sprint behind the captain's tent in seconds and be out of sight before either man could grab a gun. Surely some of his water jars would still be where he'd buried them. He glanced at Limesand. The salesman was watching him closely with a look of deep concern. He looked at Reece and frowned and shook his head. How could he possibly know what he was thinking. Had he seen him washing and filling empty jars?

His crazy impulse passed when he realized the timing wasn't right. Too many Indians were working along the line. They'd be paid a generous reward to run him down and they'd likely welcome the challenge to chase an escaped *gringo*.

It took until almost noon for Limesand to select and prepare the food the Swede listed. While the guns and hunting equipment were being sorted and made ready for packing, Reece saddled the two horses Rodriguez selected for the trip. Jake and the black mare mule brayed when Harper started up the trail with the other pack mules.

Reece lashed blankets and a small tent across the top of Jake's load. Removing one of the water cans, Reece packed the wicker pannier with the food supplies then dipped some water from the can on the opposite side to balance the black mule's load.

While Reece was strapping the rifle scabbards onto both saddles, Limesand came over carrying their lunches.

"I'm worried about you, John. You've been acting troubled all morning. Since you found out you have a daughter you've been like a different person. Something's going on in your head that wasn't there before." He put his hand on Reece's arm and added, "What ever you do, don't do anything foolish."

Reece idly drew a line in the dust with the toe of his badly worn shoe, avoiding Limesand's stern expression.

"Hey my friend, cheer up. Things will get better, you'll see." Al playfully punched Reece on his shoulder. "Tell me. Just what is this 'Grand Slam' the Swede was talking about, anyway?"

Reece hesitated to speak. He knew Al only wanted the best for him. He thought of Al's earlier advice and knew he had better follow it and try to make the best of each day. So this was the day that counted. He looked over to where Rodriguez and Neilson were sorting items on their table. The Swede was whistling, his foot tapping in time with the tune. He began loading Harper's back pack with cameras and film and boxes of ammunition and what appeared to be other personal items, including a shaving kit.

"All right, I'll tell you about a 'Grand Slam.'" Reece said lowering his voice. "Most men, I spec, spend most of the time thinkin' about women or gettin' their hands on a lot of money -- but sheep hunters, they seem different, somehow. First, they generally try to kill a Rocky Mountain bighorn. Then, if they get one, they're hooked. Next, they want to go up to Alaska or some place called British...I can't remember the name of the rest of it..."

"Columbia?"

"Yeah, that's it. That's where they try to kill a stone or a dall sheep. Then, if they get one of them, they get a little crazy. But if they get all three, then they go plumb *loco*." Reece nodded over towards the Swede and winked at Al.

"Only a very few ever get all three an' then hardly any of them get a chance to hunt a desert bighorn. The seasons been closed in most of the western states for a long time. Sometimes a few desert sheep permits are allowed in a drawing."

"But then, what you're saying is if somehow they get a desert bighorn, then have all four, it's called "the 'Grand Slam' which makes them a member of a very special group?"

"That's right. It's a rich man's club, but money alone can't get you in. It takes the kind of man that's plumb out of his mind, one that'll climb mountains in all kinds of weather, a man that don't know fear, one that'll risk his life on high, ice-covered ledges to get the trophy of his dreams. A little over a hundred in the whole world have done it, or so I've been told."

"And just what is a three-quarter curl?"

"The horns on a real old ram will flare out and grow into a complete circle. A plumb purty sight they are. But only a few live that long. But when the horns have growed three fourths of the way around they can be killed as a legal trophy."

"Say Reece, do you know what this is?" The Swede held up a knife with a carved bone handle and a short glistening curved blade that came to a sharp point.

"Yeah, I know what it is."

The excited Swede waited for Reece to say more. When he didn't add anything to his brief answer Neilson asked, "Then what the hell is it?"

"It's a skinning knife."

"Ever used one?"

"Yeah." Reece kept his answers brief. It was beginning to visibly annoy the Swede. Al's back was toward Rodriguez and the Swede as he busied himself at the cooking table. He looked at Reece and grinned and made a sad face, mocking the Swede. Reece's body tingled. Al knew just how to pump up his spirits when he was feeling discouraged. He hoped someday when Eula Mae finished her college classes she'd be just like Al.

The Swede stared at Reece. It was obvious the man was frustrated with his short answers, but pleased he knew how to use a skinning knife. He also had to know that the plowboy was baiting him in a little game of wits.

While Rodriguez watched the two men, with an obvious look of amusement, Reece tried to show no trace of emotion or any reaction to the Swede's line of questioning.

The Swede looked at Reece and asked politely, "You ever caped out a trophy animal like a bighorn?"

"Yeah."

"Then let's get going, Captain. I can hardly wait. If this trip works out as we've planned I'll certainly make it well worth your while." Neilson did a little figure-eight dance, his feet tapping in the dust like a giddy child.

Rodriguez grinned and mounted his horse and turned to Reece saying, "Get that pack on your back and move it. We got a long ways to go before dark."

Reece grabbed Jake's lead rope and led off at a fast trot when he heard the captain whack his horse sharply with his riding crop.

He'd lead them on a trip they'd never forget.

CHAPTER 13

THE SHEEP HUNT

Reece held a steady trot. If the Indians could do it for a whole day he could do it for at least ten miles. He'd done it before, with the mules, to see if he had the stamina. There had been a difference then. On that day he wasn't carrying a backpack.

By the end of the first hour they overtook Sanchez where he was directing the crew stringing wire on the overhead crossarms. Without slowing their pace, Rodriguez called to Sanchez, as they passed, "You're in charge Sergeant until we get back. I'm taking the Swede on a little trip up the mountain. We may be gone for a couple of days."

"Good hunting, *Capitán*."

Rodriguez waved and urged his horse forward. When they reached the rockslide where he'd seen the sheep, Reece slowed his pace, circling southward below the slide on the mountain's shoulder. Near the end of the slide the sage-covered slopes steepened into a long incline leading to a bench, overgrown with clumps of mesquite.

Reece angled upward on a curving course, following a faint trail showing no recent footprints. If the trail continued in its present direction Reece figured, it could take them to the back side of the bluffs overlooking Copper Canyon.

"Hold up, Reece!" The captain called out.

"Whoa Jake," Reece said, stepping off the trail and looking back at the two mounted horsemen trailing over a hundred yards behind. The sides of the mules were heaving, their wet hair glistening in the mid-afternoon sun.

The lathered horses plodded up the trail, their breathing labored, as neither mounts nor riders were accustomed to such a test of endurance. Both men dismounted and steadied themselves, bracing their hands against the saddle skirting until their cramped leg muscles relaxed. They each began checking their cinch straps rather than let Reece see they'd suffered more from riding than he had on foot.

Jake relieved himself, the foaming liquid puddling at first, then running back against his rear hooves. At the familiar sound the other mule and both horses, in near-perfect unison, relaxed and streamed their urine into puddles where hooves had gouged the dirt.

Neilson led his horse up alongside Jake and looked across the expanse of broken rock on the mountain's shoulder. Then he swept his gaze across the long sweeping curve to the north. His ruddy face was flushed from the heat and the excitement at a chance to kill a bighorn.

"Just where did you see the sheep?"

"Back yonder," Reece said, pointing to the spot he'd last seen the sheep, "'bout where the rock slide curves out of sight."

"Which way were they headed?"

"Up to our left, toward the south."

Neilson raised his binoculars, slowly sweeping them across the jumble of sharp edged scree that had broken from the face of the limestone bluffs looming against the skyline.

"Were they feeding or just walking along?"

"Just working their way across the rocks -- nuthin' much up there for them to eat." Reece saw the Swede cut his eyes in his direction for a moment.

"You sure you saw sheep up there?" The Swede eyed Reece suspiciously, "We better not find out we're being taken on some wild-goose chase."

Reece pointed again to the spot where he'd seen them walking in single file. He shook his head, "No, they was right there." The sheep would be hard to spot, he knew, for he'd seen them headed north, in the opposite direction from where he'd said. They could be fifteen miles away by now from the south-facing bluffs of the mountain where Reece was headed. There was no way for his reported direction to be proven a lie. The sheep left no tracks where they'd crossed the rock.

"It's no goose chase -- carryin' this pack on my back like a mule ain't no fun for me."

The Swede smirked, the two gold fillings in his front teeth flashing in the sunlight. He looked back at Rodriguez. "Captain, that saddle up there between the two bluffs would be a good place to make camp. We can glass for miles -- got a good chance to see them if they're still on this side of the mountain. From there, we might work around and check the upper slopes on the back side above the canyons."

"You're the hunter. You'd be the best judge of that."

While the Swede studied the higher slopes with his binoculars he said to Reece, "Get me a dipper of water." When he'd finished drinking it, he said, "Fill it again." Reece handed him another dipper of water and watched in disbelief as the man poured it over his back and shoulders and splashed some on his face and throat. At this rate the water wouldn't last more than two days. Without water, the horses and mules would become weak and exhausted.

Within two hours they reached the eastern end of the high valley, notched between two eroded gray cliffs, rays of the fast dropping sun streaming through the narrow pass.

"Put the tent there where it'll be out of the wind," said the Swede pointing to the sheltered side of a boulder the size of a house. The mass of fallen rock blocked most of the entrance into the pass, leaving an opening of no more than 20 feet.

The heated air currents, rising from the barrancas on the western side of the imposing crest of the Sierra, whistled through the high mountain gap.

While the Swede glassed the upper rock ledges, streaked with bands of fading light and shadows, the captain began sorting his belongings.

Reece erected the tent where the Swede had pointed and took the ropes from the panniers he'd stacked by the tent. He drove the stock to the middle of the pass where the winds had withered and bent the sparse grasses clinging to the shallow soil.

Looping and tying the ropes around each animal's forelegs at the knees, Reece fashioned hobbles that would keep them from wandering away in search of water.

After Reece had cooked their supper and served the two men sitting inside the canvas shelter, he was warned to stay away from the water cans sitting against the wall of the tent.

As shadows settled onto the valley floor, Reece rolled into his blanket and looked up at the purple-dark walls lofting into the darkness. The Swede's earlier excitement had waned when the last rays of light showed no trace of animals on the mountain's rock ledges. At least for now, the ram was safe. Tomorrow would have its own problems and cause for worry. With no water for the stock and little chance for the Swede to see a bighorn, vain hopes would soon be dashed and tempers short. Reece tucked his blanket around his head and tried to sleep. It was of little use. One blanket gave scant shelter from the rocky ground and the cold. The winds, howling through the pass, increased.

A sliver of moon, sliding behind thin clouds, slowly moved along the opening between the hazy tops of the narrow canyon walls. Reece listened to the wind and the snoring of the two men sleeping comfortably on soft bedding inside the tent.

As Reece dozed in fitful moments of blurred consciousness he fantasized with thoughts of escape.

It would be easy to slip away.. He could wrap and tie Jake's feet with the towels folded neatly in the backpack he was using for a pillow, quietly lead him past the tent and ride him back down the trail. If he was lucky, Jake might not even buck. The load he'd been carrying was at least 40 pounds more than Reece now weighed.

The big, strong mule was like an overgrown pup, nuzzling Reece each morning until he'd been slipped a lump of sugar. The two of them could make a run for it. But the timing wasn't right, as yet. Too many people were working along the Sierra's crest. Within hours, the captain could have 100 Indian runners after him with no more than the promise of a $10 reward.

Reece knew he'd have to pick a time when the line was nearly finished. By then, he figured, they'd be another 200 miles below the border. This would give him some advantages. Telegraph poles would again be trucked to the line. There'd be no timber close enough for even the Indians to cut and carry to the line -- just cactus and mesquite dotting the desert.

If his plan worked, no one would know in which direction he'd gone. The farther Rodriguez had to spread his search party the easier it would be to slip between them. If he was really lucky, and the captain feared there'd be publicity about a prisoner escaping, he'd hesitate to bring in outside help to chase down one lone man. He might be too proud to bring in the natives who knew the mountains and desert.

Reece sat upright, his heart pounding wildly, now wide awake. The one Indian he feared the most was not some famed runner or tracker but an old gray-haired woman he'd seen huddled under a blanket. If all of the Indians were thieves, as he'd heard so often, she alone may have thwarted all his plans. She could continue for weeks gathering plants for use in some pagan ceremony or crude attempt at pretending to be a doctor if she had a ready supply of water.

It would be at least two more days before they'd return to camp and he'd have a chance to slip out after dark and see if she'd stolen his buried jars. Maybe he could find her tethered burro, and kill it, forcing a change in her routine of collecting roots and leaves from plants growing along the mountain's crest. Reece lay in the darkness for what seemed like hours, waiting for the trials of the coming day. During the last few hours he could hear the snoring of only one man. He was sure the Swede was the quiet one in the tent, unable to sleep, obsessed with visions of rams, their heads weighted under massive horns.

Reece propped his head up on the backpack and sat watching for the first trace of light to appear on the eastern skyline. He was troubled about his earlier decision. Deliberately leading the construction camp's two prominent leaders away from the band of skittish sheep could be a disaster. Both men would take pleasure in exacting revenge on anyone even suspected of being so foolish. But even more important, the longer it took for the Swede to find the desert sheep, the longer Reece would have to wait before he could check on his hidden jars.

The long night finally ended when a pink glow backlit the wisp of clouds streaked low on the distant horizon.

The Swede rose earlier than usual, before the sun broke above the dark line where the earth met the sky. Reece was already up, checking on the stock, when he remembered he'd forgotten to sneak a lump of sugar from the Swede's supply. When Reece removed the hobbles, Jake followed him back to the campsite, restless with the change in routine and the lack of feed and water.

The Swede met Reece and said quietly, "The captains sleeping for awhile this morning but you got work to do. Get a fire going and make some coffee and then hurry and fix me some breakfast. I want to be glassing for sheep at first light when they're apt to be out feeding -- and you'd better hope I see a ram today," he added, fixing Reece with a hard stare. Playing the Swede for a fool, Reece realized, may have been a serious mistake.

Neilson continued watching Reece as he scurried about, looking for dead branches and leaves to start a fire. Reece took a hatchet and chopped down a dead mesquite tree on the bench near camp, worried that the noise might wake the captain. When the sharpened blade easily split the hardened wood Reece wished instead he could be splitting the head of the man whose eyes seemed riveted on his every movement.

The Swede walked over and said, "I think you're a liar, Reece. I haven't been able to find a single track where even one sheep has been."

Reece could feel his hands trembling as he placed smaller sticks on the fire. He hesitated to answer for fear his voice would reveal that the Swede's suspicions were right.

"Hurry up, Reece. Don't take all day, and don't give the stock any of the water. If the desert bighorn can go for seven days without water, they ought to be able to go for three or four. Oxen did it when my grandpa drove a team across the desert of the Great Salt Lake. As for you, you ask me when you want a drink and I'll let you know if I think you've earned it." He laughed and then added, "That'll give you a good incentive to get busy and find that ram."

"Yes sir, Mister Neilson, I promise I'll do my best to help you find the sheep," Reece answered, realizing he'd gotten himself and the stock into a bad situation by leading the Swede so far away from the sheep. He remembered the hunters in Colorado talking about how the desert sheep split off in small groups. With waterholes scarce and springs trickling only a few gallons a day, at most, only groups of no more than ten or twenty could survive in any area. It was too late to explain that he'd deliberately lied as the Swede suspected. Even if Reece tried, there would be almost no chance that he could now find the animals he'd seen three days before, headed north in single file.

It was late afternoon and the Swede continued to scour every ledge on the mountain's western face for any sign of sheep. His binoculars were seldom taken from his eyes for more than a minute. In mid-morning, as he'd led his horse through the pass, he'd found faint outlines of cloven hoofprints. The Swede had been elated, no longer questioning Reece's claim of seeing sheep, even allowing him a dipper of water.

They'd hurried back and loaded the water cans and camp supplies onto the mules and moved on through the pass before noon, then started north along the steep slopes above the barrancas. The captain was obviously bored, but willing to let the Swede take plenty of time to find the trophy of his dreams. The captain idly glassed the slopes from time to time with little apparent belief he'd spot a bighorn. However, the promise of a generous bonus if the Swede had a successful hunt kept the captain's interest whetted.

They continued on northward along the narrow ledges on the Sierra's flanks. The view down into Copper Canyon was awesome. Thousands of feet below them they could see the thin, curving line of the Rio Papigochic. As the Swede had insisted, Reece walked ahead, leading Jake slowly where loose shale made the footing treacherous.

"What's that up there?" the Swede asked, his voice little more than a hoarse whisper. "Looks like mountain mahogany. At this elevation, it's the bighorn's favorite browse."

Reece saw clumps of small trees with dark, reddish-brown bark and oval-shaped leaves. The tops would reach the height of a man riding through on horseback. He stopped and waited for the Swede to come up alongside.

"Stay here," said the Swede, moving cautiously across a narrow ledge until he reached a point where the footing widened. He stooped low over an opening in the shrubs where a thin layer of grit covered the broken granite slabs. The Swede moved in a small circle, studying the ground and picking up bits of leaves and stems. He examined the leaves growing on the lower limbs where some had been cropped short. Picking up small round sheep droppings, he pressed them between his fingertips to check for moisture and firmness. Reece had seen elk hunters near the Black Sage pass hunting camp in Colorado do the same thing.

The Swede half-stood, sniffing the air and moving his head from side to side in an attempt to peer through the heavy foliage and see farther along the ledge, past the growth of shrubs. When he looked back and waved to Rodriguez, Reece could see the man's eyes shining with excitement.

"They've been here sometime within the last twenty-four hours," he whispered.

A glance to the side told Reece the captain was already counting his bonus, a wide grin on his face radiating pleasure.

The Swede bent low, crept back and joined the captain. "We'll have a good chance of seeing sheep within the next few miles. Bits of remaining leaves that have been bitten off or stripped from stems are fresh. They don't show any discoloration at the edges," he said holding out fragments of leaves with sharply-notched margins.

Rodriguez looked at the pale, green pieces and nodded in apparent agreement. "I see what you mean. Let's go find them."

If the Swede found cause for such excitement, this obviously pleased the captain.

The Swede eyed the sheer bluffs ahead where they rose from the narrow ledges the men had been traversing. He peered cautiously into the gaping chasm of Copper Canyon. "We'll have to figure the best way to go after them. It'll be quieter if we sneak along without the stock clomping along behind us. We can tie them up or Reece can stay here with them. For the next mile it's going to be slow going, but you can see where the bluffs recede and curve around into a basin," the Swede extended his arm and swept his hand across and then upward, pointing out the area he'd described. "That's where I think we'll find them. I can see clumps of mahogany from here that are growing on most of the benches -- clear to the skyline."

"Want me to fill the canteens?" Reece asked. There was no longer any use trying to lead the Swede away from the sheep. Reece had tried by leading the avid hunter around the south side of the mountain. The fresh tracks they'd found indicated the sheep had circled the imposing gray cliffs on the north and returned to their feeding grounds on the western slopes.

The Swede shook his canteen. "I got plenty. How about you, Captain?"

"I filled mine a little bit ago. I'm all right for now."

"Remember Reece, you get all the water you can drink when I get that ram."

Reece nodded. He'd never gone so long before with so little water. The physical pounding his body had taken during the past weeks had developed his strength and stamina. At least the Swede's harsh demands were helping him weigh his chances for surviving in the desert. He glanced up at the sun, trying to calculate the amount of remaining daylight. They had another hour at the most, he reckoned.

The Swede looked at his watch and studied the shadows being cast by some of the lower bluffs to the west across Copper Canyon. "Let's tie the stock here and all get moving. Reece, be careful with that backpack. I've got a camera and flashlight in there and I think we could be taking some pictures before dark."

Reece was tired and thirsty and he knew the animals were starting to suffer. Jake was listless as Reece tied him to a mahogany bush where he could get some nourishment and a little moisture from the leaves. Jake had stumbled a couple of times earlier when the shale slipped from beneath his feet.

The Swede led off, sneaking forward in a half-crouch while watching ahead for any sign of animals feeding on the higher slopes.

Reece had seen before the Swede's shooting ability. Watching him move now Reece could see a demonstration of the man's years of experience at hunting big game animals -- his feet slipping quietly from one step to the next while his eyes appeared to stay fixed on the higher slopes. Within a half hour he stopped suddenly and turned, motioning for the captain and Reece to get down. He held his hand to his mouth to signal for silence, then pointed toward an area halfway up the slope.

Reece saw the movement of several gray-brown animals, their white rumps little more than shifting dots as they fed through clumps of mahogany.

The Swede and the captain studied them through their binoculars with keen anticipation. Reece saw a rusty-red form emerge from behind a boulder, just above the main group. The late evening sun glistened on its dark sides. It looked like the ram with the three-quarter curl horns he'd seen earlier. He hesitated to speak when the Swede turned his head and whispered something to the captain.

"Wait a second," the captain interrupted. "I think I've spotted what we came for." Rodriguez pointed toward the ram.

The Swede quickly swung his binoculars in line with where the captain was pointing. Reece saw the tension harden on the man's face. He appeared to be holding his breath. There was no doubt he was now watching the rare and majestic trophy. Finally, he let out a sigh and turned back to the captain.

"Hey, *Señor* Rodriguez," he whispered, "that's the one we've been trying to find -- he's a real beauty," the Swede said solemnly. After a moment of silence, while he studied the ram, he reached over and lightly slapped Rodriguez on the back and added. *"Gracias, Señor, gracias."*

Reece knew this would be the moment of truth for the Swede. He knew killing the animal would be a clear violation of Mexican laws. The Swede whispered to Rodriguez and glanced back at Reece. The sheep were feeding, completely unaware of the menacing presence below. Reece's nervousness increased when Rodriguez and the Swede continued exchanging nods and brief bits of conversation that he couldn't overhear. Clearly, their repeated looks in his direction showed a deep level of concern that a potential witness was present.

A decision had been reached, Reece realized, when Rodriguez reached back toward him and said, "Hand me the backpack." He took it and passed it to the Swede. Placing it on a flat rock in front of him, the Swede lay prone and nestled the magnum rifle carefully across it.

Reece knew both men had decided that, for some reason, he wouldn't be a serious risk in their future plans. Reece took a deep breath, then held it, waiting to see the unsuspecting bighorn collapse when the marksman pulled the trigger. The ram was no farther away than he was the day the half-drunk Swede shot the jar out of his hand, at a distance of 300 yards. Even though the light was fading, the Swede took his time. He wouldn't hurry the shot of a lifetime.

When the powder in the cartridge exploded Reece blinked then quickly re-focused on the still-standing ram. Seconds passed before it slowly crumpled to the ground and rolled onto its back, only its legs and feet remaining visible. After several seconds passed it gave a couple of feeble kicks and then remained motionless. Rodriguez and the Swede let out whoops and shook hands, both men grinning from ear to ear. They'd each gotten what they wanted. The Swede fumbled with the backpack, then dug out his camera and a roll of film.

Reece didn't comment or look at either man. He felt sick at his stomach. This was all his fault. He'd been raised to keep his mouth shut, but his idle remark to Al had resulted in the animal's death. He watched as the other sheep moved quickly up through the mahogany, distancing themselves from the danger below. Off to the right, another dark form caught Reece's attention when he saw it limping, trying to join the others. Even at the increased distance, Reece saw it was a large animal with dark shoulders and flanks, possibly hampered by age and near the end of its lifespan. As it slowed and angled upward across a ledge, it became silhouetted against the skyline. Reece gasped when he saw the massive full curve of its magnificent horns, widely flared and bluntly broomed off at the ends. Its slim neck and small head looked out of proportion to the massive horns.

"Remember this, Reece?"

Turning his head, Reece looked directly at the Swede.

He had pulled the skinning knife from the leather scabbard on his belt and was holding it up, twisting the shiny blade back and forth.

"Why are you looking so startled, Reece? I'm sure if you really worked in hunting camps you've seen animals killed before," the captain said, a questioning look on his face.

"I- I never shot an animal -- guess I'm not so used to it as you think." Reece kept his gaze straight ahead, hoping they'd believe him. In minutes it would be too dark to see the ram on the skyline. He'd be out of sight when he crossed the ridgetop where the other sheep had disappeared, one by one. He realized now that the older ram, staying off by himself, had probably been defeated by the younger ram in a battle to breed with the ewes. Not thinking, Reece stole another glance at the ram he was sure would rank near the top in the record books.

Without saying a word, the Swede grabbed his binoculars and began sweeping them across the upper basin. He'd never trusted Reece since the day he'd been bowled over backward by the hobo's sneak attack.

"Holy Christ! Holy mother of Christ! I don't believe it! Captain, look, up on the skyline," the Swede exclaimed, chambering another cartridge into the rifle's breech.

Rodriguez took long seconds to spot the ram and when he did, he turned to the Swede and shook his head, saying, "You shot the wrong one didn't you, I..."

"What'll we do now?" The Swede interrupted shaking his head, his face changing from an expression of elation to one of disgust.

The captain crawled over by Neilson and whispered a few words before the Swede interrupted him again, "Look, I'll triple what I offered you before if..." he said, his pleading voice rising in frustration and urgency. He brought up the binoculars again and clenched his jaws as he watched the silhouetted ram. It stopped and stood motionless, while the shadows kept creeping up to the skyline. There was another hurried but indistinct conversation with a couple of glances back at Reece. He did hear part of a comment, "…the warden's a good friend of the governor…" There was another question by Rodriguez, but Reece couldn't hear it.

"Hard to say, maybe just a little over 600 yards," the Swede answered. "I'll hold the cross-hairs the depth of his brisket above the top of his shoulders.

"All right, I guess it can't make that much difference whether it's one or two…." Rodriguez said in a matter-of-fact voice. The promise of a tripled bonus was too good to turn down.

With the light fading fast and the ram only a few steps away from following the other sheep over the crest and out of sight, the Swede had a difficult choice. A hurried shot at such a long distance could easily be a miss. However, the normally methodical Swede had to know that a hurried shot at such an unbelievable trophy was better than none at all -- this one would definitely be a once-in-a-lifetime chance.

Lying prone, with the sling wrapped tightly around his forearm, the Swede squinted through the scope. After only a few moment's hesitation, he pulled the trigger.

Reece felt the acrid smoke of the burnt powder enter his nostrils while he closely watched the distant target, his ears again ringing from the force of the blast.

When the bullet struck, the ram staggered. His front legs collapsed, leaving his rump sticking awkwardly in the air, his hind legs refusing to buckle. With his hind legs driving hard, he drove forward, his head skidding like a plow. The ram stopped and staggered to his feet then lurched out of sight, his left shoulder broken and his foreleg dragging on the ground.

CHAPTER 14

BLOOD TRAIL

As Reece watched the ram lurch out of sight, he heard the Swede curse.

"Goddammit! I can't find him in the scope!" The Swede grabbed his binoculars, giving him a wider field of vision, and scanned the skyline. The force of exploding powder had jolted the rifle's barrel and moved the alignment of the telescopic sight off the target. In the seconds he'd taken trying to realign the scope, the ram had disappeared.

''That was one unbelievable shot, Swede!" Rodriguez said, shaking his head and grinning. "I knew you were good, but I didn't know you were that good."

"Where the hell did he go? I still can't spot him --"

"You hit him in the shoulder -- looked like you broke it. He went down in front, then got up and wobbled after the others -- dragging his left front leg." Rodriguez raised his binoculars. "He won't go far."

"For Christ's sake!" the Swede muttered. He looked up to his left where the first ram had fallen. The lighter shades of hair on the ram's belly and two of its legs showed where it lay on its side among the rocks. The curl on one horn showed where the end was hooked against a rock. The quickly changing shadows would soon darken the hillside. "Now what the hell do we do?" he asked.

Rodriguez studied the fading skyline where the bighorn sheep had stood, outlined briefly before the Swede fired the crippling shot. Reece watched as the captain began nervously rubbing his palms together. If the aged ram got away, Rodriguez would lose his triple bonus and the Swede would lose a trophy that should easily make the record books.

Neilson turned and looked at Reece. The two shots that had echoed off of the basin's sloping sides had set in motion a new level of complexity. He knew that for the next several hours he'd be kept busy. He hoped that he'd be allowed to return to the mules and get the water he'd been promised when the Swede found sheep tracks. Never before had Reece gone as long with so little water. He was sure the suffering of the horses and mules was worse.

"We could make camp right here and go after the ram at daybreak," Rodriguez said, looking back in the direction of the skyline. "Or Reece could gut and skin the one you killed and let the meat cool out tonight. Then we could load it on the mules and head on back at daybreak. It's up to you, but we're getting low on water. The last time I filled my canteen the water in the can was well past half-way down. One more day and we may find ourselves on foot. It's hard to tell."

When Rodriguez mentioned the shortage of water and the possibility that mounts and pack animals might collapse from dehydration, the Swede's expression changed from a look of irritation to one of anguish.

All of his observations of the Swede convinced Reece that the Swede would forget the smaller ram he'd killed and go after the bigger ram. He'd ignore the limited water supply. He wasn't a man who'd settle for anything except the best. Neilson sat staring toward the vanishing skyline, apparently weighing the choices the captain had mentioned. The experienced hunter knew there could be no certainty in pursuing the animal that had made it over the crest. He took out his pipe, cleaned the bowl and filled it with fresh tobacco, never taking his gaze from the last place he'd seen the ram. Tamping the tobacco with his forefinger and lighting it, he took a long draw, inhaling the smoke from the curved stem. After a long pause he looked back to where the sloping face of the basin ended at a steep incline above the canyons.

In the last of the light, Reece could see the way to the north along the canyon was passable only to the sure-footed sheep. There would be no way to take the horses and mules any farther. The high narrow ledges on the limestone bluff gave the sheep refuge from predators, except those carrying a rifle. Time had long ago adapted the rough-textured pads on the bottoms of their cloven hooves for clinging to the rock's slippery surfaces.

Neilson turned back and faced the captain, cradling the bowl of the pipe in his palm. "I can't pass up a chance like this." He paused and shook his head, then rubbed his fingers up along his jaw, feeling the stubble of his whiskers while staring fixedly at the mountain's crest. "The horns on that ram are massive -- almost unbelievable -- with a spread at the tips of at least twenty-four, maybe twenty-five inches. From the base of the curls to the tip of the horns will easily measure over forty inches -- could go even forty-three or maybe even forty-five. He's gotta be fourteen -- maybe fifteen years old. Only a very few ever reach that age -- could very well be one of the top five in the record book."

"His silhouette when he topped the ridge and stood like a statute, looking back one last time, sure made one unforgettable picture," the captain added.

Neilson sat in silence, still staring at the skyline that was now but a faint blur, his brow wrinkling at times with apparent concern. He had to know that such a record ram would raise a thousand questions if it were ever mounted and put on display for public admiration.

"Reece can go cut the tenderloins from the one over there," the Swede nodded toward his left, "and then go get our bedding and food and water. We can camp right here and have broiled tenderloin for supper -- but being on top of the ridge at first light is all that's important to me."

"Yeah, we can camp right here -- shouldn't be any problem. But we'll have to go after that ram on foot. The horses would never make it up that rock face leading to the second ledge. It's too steep. And there's no use in bringing all the animals, that jagged bluff where the basin ends above the canyon means we'll have to circle back the way we came in when we go to leave. Sheep can cross it but the horses can't."

"I'd noticed that," the Swede nodded in agreement. "We can use my flashlights and climb to the ridge top before daylight. It's not that steep once we get above the lower benches."

"There's another thing you might want to think about," Rodriguez suggested. "If the crippled one gets away the one here will be ruined by the time we get back. The meat will spoil when the morning sun hits it. It'll bloat within a few hours."

"You're right, and buzzards and coyotes could ruin the head and cape." The Swede's brow furrowed again and his heavy jaws clenched. The captain's analysis clearly disturbed him. The exuberance of a few minutes before had been replaced with indecision and the possibility that instead of having two rare and magnificent trophies he'd have none. "I don't even want to think about losing the one on the ridge top, but... it could happen," he commented and turned to Reece. "All right Reece, take this knife and cape that one out and bring back the tenderloin, then go get one of the mules and the camping equipment."

"Someone's gonna have to hold me a light. Skinnin' aroun' the eyelids an' mouth ain't even easy in daytime, an' I gotta cut away the skin where it joins the base of the horns. To do it right could take a couple of hours, an' then I'll need to find some wood to cook the loin."

Both men stared at Reece, their faces showing impatience. They were probably as tired and hungry as he was but they'd had all of the water they wanted to drink. Now that it was getting dark, it was obvious they really didn't want to hear him mention any complications they'd overlooked.

"There's somethin' else," he added hesitantly when neither man spoke. "The saddles an' panniers should be taken off the horses an' the mule we left tied up back yonder. If I skin out the ram first, the mule's gonna be hard to load with my arms an' hands all covered with blood. The smell's gonna spook him somethin' bad. One of you will need to go back with me an' hold him. An' leadin' him along the top of that narrow trail above the drop-off in the dark's gonna be real tricky -- for me an' the mule, too." If he could convince them to let him go get the mule and equipment first, he could get a much-needed drink. Neither man would want to go with him and help him load Jake. That he could be sure of. Returning for Jake and bringing back the camping supplies, setting up the tent, skinning the ram and then finding wood and cooking the bastard's supper would take Reece until at least midnight. And they'd want him up again a couple of hours before daylight to fix their breakfast and load his backpack with food and water to continue the hunt on top of the mesa.

"Goddammit Reece, there's something about you that really gets under my skin." The Swede muttered, frowning, without taking the stem of his pipe from his mouth, puffs of smoke escaping from around the stem he held between his clenched teeth as he spoke. It was another one of the Neilson's mannerisms that Reece despised.

"I'm sorry, Mr. Neilson, I'm just tryin' to do the best I know how." Reece replied softly and lowered his head in an attempt to convey submissive respect. It was something he had to be careful about, realizing how much he'd changed since he'd been working on his plan to escape and he'd gotten the letter from Eula Mae. Inside, he was now inspired, a much different person from the one he'd been on the day they started building the line.

His physical strength and endurance had improved, far beyond his hopes. Only time would tell, however, if he was really prepared for the ultimate test in the desert.

He wondered if the Kansas boy who'd been told he'd never walk again had felt such inspiration as the tendons in his burned legs slowly healed and he was able to take his first steps.

Though he tried to appear respectful to both Neilson and the captain, he felt sure that the Swede suspected he couldn't be trusted.

He'd need to reassure them he was only a humble prisoner marking off each day of his ten year sentence. But someday he was going to see his daughter. If he had to kiss their asses every day, he'd do it. He could hardly wait to hear if Eula Mae had gotten the letter Al helped him write.

After both men discussed the situation, Rodriguez made a decision. "Reece, you go get the mule and load him with everything we'll need to camp here tonight -- and don't even think about giving any of the water to the animals. You understand me?"

"*Sí, Capitán*. I'm ready to leave right now."

Reece hurried to reach the place they'd left the stock, anxious to take advantage of the dwindling twilight. When he saw the bluffs rising abruptly before him, he moved cautiously as he entered the darkened shadows and started across the narrow ledge. He remembered that the loose shale sloped steeply downward toward the gaping dark canyon that was no longer visible. Unable to see anything but the shadowy outline of the limestone bluff looming into the darkness, he lost track of how far he'd come. Fear gripped him when a flake of shale suddenly gave way under his foot and slid noisily over the canyon's brink, shattering on impact when he heard it strike a protruding ledge far below. The echoes down in the canyon were a gripping reminder of unseen dangers, while his overpowering thirst conflicted with his fear of making one fateful misstep in the darkness. When he felt along the wall's surface for guidance, he realized his fingers were trembling each time they touched the wall of limestone. He stopped for a moment to steady himself, anxiety and exertion making him dizzy when combined with the altitude and his dehydration. He moved with more caution until his outstretched hand finally touched leaves at shoulder height. He'd reached the point where the ledge widened and the mountain mahogany grew in clumps. For the next 200 yards the footing was solid, Reece remembered, as he hurried toward the place they'd tied the stock. A low nicker told him that the slight breeze had carried his scent to one of the horses. As he moved away from the darkened wall, more light reached the ledge where the canyon widened. Water was just ahead. Within minutes he'd have all that he could drink.

Suddenly he stumbled, and heard a slight groan. He'd fallen over one of the horses that was lying down. The saddle horn jabbed him painfully in his side, but the horse made no attempt to rise. Reece knew immediately that it was the bay mare, the Swede's mount, when his forearm brushed across the stiff bristles of her shorn mane.

Jake's outline showed where he stood head down and motionless, tied another twenty feet ahead. When Reece's hand touched his shoulder, he raised his head briefly and turned toward him. Reece grabbed the dipper hanging on the front of the panniers. When he shoved it down into the water can he was startled when the dipper struck a hard object that slowly gave way, and then moved aside like a piece of floating ice.

His heart raced when he realized the dipper had struck one of the jars of water he'd sunk to the bottom of the can, before first light, two days before. With a trembling hand, Reece filled the dipper. As he pulled it out of the can it rattled against the metal sides until it cleared the opening and he brought it to his parched lips. The cool water bathed his swollen tongue with the sweetest water he'd ever tasted.

If either Rodriguez or the Swede hadn't been so hurried when they'd last filled their canteens, all of his plans would now be nothing but a painful memory and he'd be on his way back to the prison. No lie could have covered for his scheme of carrying jars of water in the bottom of the metal cans. That he'd completely forgotten about them shook his earlier confidence that he had a well-thought-out escape plan.

He ran his hands over an area of solid rock until he found a slight depression, took one of the jars and poured the water into the shallow rocky bowl. Reece led Jake over and stopped him by the water. The listless mule lowered his head then slurped loudly at the much needed but meager drink. Reece heaved the empty jar over the canyon's edge and listened, finally hearing it strike far below.

Taking the jar from the other can, he took off the lid and gave the water to Jake, then threw the jar over the edge. Within seconds it struck a projection, shattering with a booming sound that echoed off the canyon walls.

The black mule and the captain's mount were both standing, neither appearing to be as weak as the bay. The sounds of Jake loudly slurping the water riveted their attention, the silhouette of their ears pointed in his direction. Reece felt badly that they both needed water as they anxiously waited their turn at the makeshift trough. The 30 gallons they'd started with was down to no more than six or seven. Unsure of what he should do, he hesitated, and then decided against sharing any more with the stock.

Reece removed the panniers from the mule and the saddle from the captain's sorrel gelding. It was the least he could do for them.

It took all of his strength to roll the Swede's mare off of the leather strap that held the cinch tight on her saddle. When he got the latigo loosened and slid the saddle off her back she made an attempt to rise, stretching both front hooves out in front of her. Reece reached under the back of her shoulder, giving her encouragement but only minimal support in his efforts to lift her. Her legs straining to rise and shaking with exertion, her front quarters slowly cleared the ground, then stopped in place for a moment before she fell back with a deep sigh. It was no use. Her muscles were not as conditioned as the mule's had become on their daily runs with the water cans. Reece stroked her neck, sadly realizing the dehydrated mare's chances for recovery were slim at best. He took one of the aluminum cooking pans and gave her a little water.

Pouring all of the remaining water in one can and loading the other pannier with the food, tent and bedding, he started back toward the basin where the Swede and the captain waited. Jake followed close behind, accustomed to being led by Reece and trusting him for direction. When they reached the ledge where the trail narrowed, Reece stopped and gripped the lead rope close against Jake's halter. They'd move with extra caution since the mule's weight would put more pressure on any loose pieces of shale. If Jake panicked when the dangerous footing slipped beneath his hooves, they could both slide over the precipice in seconds. Reece had one advantage. Darkness and the black depths of the canyon would conceal the real danger from the trusting mule. Reece listened as Jake carefully planted each foot, the metal shoes scraping the rock's surfaces, the mule instinctively seeking then testing the support with each slow step as he shifted his weight. The sides of the metal water can scraped noisily against the bluff where the cylinder extended above the pannier.

Reece could hardly believe it when they safely reached firm footing on the other side without any serious incident. He then realized he'd never seen a single horse he would have led across the ledge in total darkness. Hopefully, the sheep-hunt would soon be over and he would no longer be required to scramble across narrow ledges in total darkness. Two days more at the most and they should be back to the base camp: a day to go after the ram and then most of another day to make the return trip. Traveling on foot could mean more problems before they'd ever reach camp.

Light showed ahead. The two men waiting for Reece and Jake had found enough dry sage to build a fire. As Reece approached the light, the captain demanded, "Hurry up, Reece. You've been gone for over an hour. Did you bring everything I told you to?" The yellow light from the blazing sage bathed the impatient faces of Rodriguez and the Swede.

"*Sí, Capitán.* I got it all right here."

"How many gallons of water did you bring?" the Swede asked.

"Bout four or five, I ain't got nothin' to measure it with, but I brung all there was."

"No more than five? You liar, who do you think you're fooling?" You must have drunk it and given it to the stock," Rodriguez snapped.

"No *Señor*, I only drunk a little bit an' didn't give them a single drop."

"What was that loud noise -- sounded like a big piece of glass shattering?" asked the Swede.

"It was just a piece of shale fell down in the canyon -- I didn't hear nothin' else."

"I better not catch you lying to me," Rodriguez threatened, his heavy dark eyebrows outlining the reflected brightness of the firelight from his flashing eyes.

" I would never lie to you, *Señor* Rodriguez," Reece replied, trying to sound both meek and humble.

"Maybe I should mention, one of the horses is down -- tried to get up but couldn't..."

"Which one?" the Swede asked.

"The one you ride, the bay."

"Holy mother of Christ. What else can go wrong?" The Swede got up from where he'd been hunkering near the fire and stood with his hands on his hips, looking back toward the place where the animals were tied. Nothing else was said for several minutes as both men seemed to be weighing the risk of prolonging the hunt. The flickering light from the last of the burning stems of the sage reflected off the Swede's troubled features. Finally he spoke. "It doesn't really matter now. We're going after that ram, right, Captain?"

"We've come this far, we may as well give it one more day. If all of the stock dies Reece can run back and get some more for us to ride out of here."

It was past midnight when Reece lay down for what he knew would be a short night's sleep. It would have been even later if Rodriguez and the Swede hadn't decided against even bothering with skinning the cape from the smaller ram. They wanted to save the batteries in their flashlights, they'd said.

When Reece was sent to cut the loin strips from the ram's back he hated ever having seen the sheep. Slicing the skin on its back, he removed the loins and felt the warmth of its flesh. He left the rest for the scavengers. It was the most nauseating thing he'd ever done. Taking no more than two pounds of meat from the 300-pound animal was a shameful and wanton deed.

He was thankful for at least one condition: darkness made him unable to see the magnificent head with its lifeless glazed eyes staring blankly and unfocused.

From the top of the mountain, the vastness of the lands to the east was a stunning spectacle. The sun was just below the horizon, spreading the dawn light across the tops of the higher land forms, the valleys still shrouded in the night's shadows.

Pain radiated from Reece's collar bones where the straps on the heavy pack hung from narrow straps across his shoulders. Both Rodriguez and the Swede were sitting on a low rock ledge, still breathing hard and exhausted from the climb. Neither seemed interested in conversation or enjoying the endless sweep of mountains and desert spreading to the endless horizons. By the time the captain and the Swede were able to continue it would be light enough to search the ground for blood spots. The hoof on the broken leg would also leave drag marks if the ram crossed patches of shallow soil.

Reece could see the small white tent he'd erected at the bottom of the basin's slope. A ribbon of smoke was rising from the campfire where he'd cooked breakfast for the two men sitting quietly on the ledge. Jake's honey-colored back was partly hidden by the mahogany tree where he was tied.

As soon as the Swede could breathe normally, he'd be anxious to be up and searching for the trophy ram.

Sorting out the trail of the wounded sheep from the ones it had tried to follow could take some time. But once the blood trail was found, the wounded animal's tracks could be quickly isolated and followed. Reece knew the Swede would become driven with impatience when there was no longer any question of the direction the quarry had fled. The Swede was seldom given to any form of moderation. His enthusiasm would send him in relentless pursuit until he'd found the trophy or become completely exhausted. Reece wiped his brow across his sleeve and waited for a signal or word to begin the search. His clothes were damp with sweat. Climbing the long slope with the heavy load in the backpack had been another test of his endurance.

When the Swede got to his feet he looked at Reece, then nodded in the general direction where the frightened sheep had run, leaving fresh tracks across the mesa's top. Scattered mahogany shrubs grew in sparse clumps toward the southern end of the flat-topped mesa, another two miles ahead of them. Low-spreading sagebrush dotted the mesa's top where the broad sweep of limestone had collected a layer of grit and sand.

On the western side of the mesa wind and rain had eroded the shallow soil, leaving barren stretches of exposed shale and large slabs of gray limestone. Boulders and rock outcroppings jutted above the surrounding mesa's level expanse. Pockets of stunted mahogany could be seen growing among the boulders.

The sharp hooves of the sheep showed a definite trail where they'd fled toward the south. Tracking was slow for the first two hours, with only an occasional spot of dried blood until Reece found a place where the ram had lain near a clump of sage. A dark red stain showed on the coarse gravel where the blood had pooled. Raking across the blood with his fingertips, Reece felt moisture in the middle where most of the coagulated blood had collected. It had been several hours since the ram had lain there.

The tracks leaving the place where the ram had rested showed it had turned abruptly westward toward the more inaccessible and rocky ridges. The other sheep had kept going south where the mesa top was more open and the terrain easier for flight. Predators could be seen at a greater distance. The crippled ram had given up following the ewes and lambs across the mesa top and instinctively chosen the more inaccessible terrain. The eroded rock ledges and huge boulders would have places to hide. Tracks, if any, would be few and far between. Dried drops of blood would be harder to spot along the ram's flight path on the gravelly surface.

After the Swede climbed the most prominent outcroppings he glassed the top of the entire mesa toward the south, then announced, "No sign of any of them out there -- the ram's gotta be up here somewhere in the rocks. With a broken leg and losing blood he can't go far," he added, a wide grin spreading across his broad face.

For hours they searched through the crevices and boulders, repeatedly backtracking to find the last place where blood had dripped onto the rocks, then scouring ahead, searching all possible hiding places. A couple of times when Reece had seen where the sheep had left a few drops of blood he'd said nothing. He'd simply moved on and circled back as if diligently looking for the place where the ram had made his final bed. By mid-afternoon Reece realized his actions were foolish. The Swede would stay until dark, unwilling to give up the chase. This could only increase the agony of the horses and mules and nothing could be gained by their added suffering.

Going back to the last place he'd seen the blood sign, Reece bent low and searched for any trace where the sheep had fled. Within less than an hour he found a slight depression between two large boulders, holding a trace of soil that the wind and rain had left undisturbed. A groove crossed it where the sheep had dragged its hoof. Cloven tracks of the other hooves pointed to an area ahead where mahogany trees clung to the shallow soil.

It was late afternoon when the white rump of the ram showed just ahead where it lay on its side. Reece approached quietly. He could see where it had tried to push through a narrow opening where the bushes grew close together, covering the entrance into a shallow cave where a slab of granite projected over the edge of one lying beneath it. One of the ram's massive horns had hooked around the slender trunk of a mahogany where it had fallen, then tried to back out and free itself. Reece felt a rush of nausea when he looked at the furrows in the gravel showing where the ram had lain and futilely raked its hooves in its death throes.

The magnificent animal had finally escaped the relentless pursuit of its predators.

CHAPTER 15

FRIED HAM

The setting sun hung low, just above the horizon, the fiery ball casting a pink glow across the basin's limestone ledges.

Reece slowed his descent, shading his eyes with his hand as he looked down toward the tent at the bottom of the slope. There was no sign of the honey-colored mule.

"Get going, Reece. It's a long way to base camp. And you and Sanchez better be back here with water and fresh horses by noon tomorrow."

"*Sí. Señor*. I'll do my best..."

Reece quickened his pace, watching his footing on the weathered rock's crumbling surfaces as he hurried down the steep grade. Now that the hunt was over, Rodriguez and the Swede were tired and impatient to return to the main camp. The earlier excitement of the chase had masked their fatigue since the first ram was spotted. Neither of the men nor their mounts had been in condition for the events of the past three days. Reece knew there was little chance now either of the saddle horses would survive. Even if they lived, they'd be too weak to carry a rider.

When Reece had overheard the captain's earlier comments to the Swede, he'd known they would send him back for fresh mounts and water as soon as they reached the tent. Finding his way in the darkness for the near twenty-mile return would sap his waning energy.

The bloody ram's skin and head were strapped onto the backpack; the massive horn jutted above his head and shoulders. Reece held to the faster pace, moving downward in a zigzag line, balancing the shifting weight on his back with his upraised arms when he changed directions. When he reached a ledge and moved horizontally, shadows of the flared horns cast a looming, grotesque outline against the layered wall of rock.

Each curled horn had measured a fraction over forty-three inches in length. The Swede had repeatedly stretched a cloth tape around the outside curves and then remeasured the circumferences, marveling at both their length and girth while excitedly discussing the kill with Rodriguez. Getting the illegally killed animal listed into the record books, they'd both agreed, could require a generous bribe for the proper officials.

While the two men had taken two rolls of film, often exchanging places and holding the dead sheep's head in lifelike poses, Reece had sneaked a long drink of water from the pack. Afterward, he'd poured the last of the water, filling the two men's canteens barely halfway.

Reece squinted into the sun's blinding rays as he kept the lead and continued his brisk descent. He, too, was anxious to return to the base camp and resume his regular duties. At least now the chase was over. Two more days and he'd be back, working with Al and running with the mules.

First, he'd check on the jars of water he'd most recently buried. He hoped the old woman hadn't found them all.

But of special interest to Reece, Rodriguez and the Swede had talked of going into Chihuahua. They wanted to take the prized trophy to a man who worked with fine leathers and had made the captain's dress boots. The bootmaker would know the most discreet taxidermist in Chihuahua.

It would also take a few days to see if the warden could get a special hunting permit from the governor. If not, Rodriguez had said, sneaking the trophy across the border would be quite simple.

He'd attended the military academy in Mexico City with the officer in charge of the border crossing at El Paso. Both men had talked of spending their time in the city's best cantinas with some lady friends of the captain. While none of this was important to Reece, it did mean they'd have the mail brought up from the prison while they caroused in Chihuahua. There might even be a letter from his daughter. Hearing that Eula Mae had received the reply Al helped him write would be the biggest thrill he'd ever had. Distracted by his thoughts of a possible letter, Reece cut back too quickly, losing his balance on the loose gravel when he changed direction at the end of a ledge. The Swede cursed when Reece slipped and fell. He'd instinctively spread his forearms, catching the impact on his palms, driving the sharp-edged grit into the fleshy part on the heels of his hands. The quick reaction had prevented the horn's tips from striking the rocks, which Reece knew was the Swede's only concern. He was up in an instant, moving on down the slope, wiping the grit and blood on his dirty pants.

After skinning the entire sheep, as the Swede instructed, Reece had cut away all of the fat deposits from the hide. He'd rubbed the flesh side of the skin with the salt the confident Swede had put in the pack the morning they'd left on the hunt.

They reached the tent while it was still light enough to see.

"Put the hide in the burlap bag and hang it on the shady side of the tallest mahogany," Neilson ordered.

Both men sat down and removed their boots and socks and began rubbing their blistered feet. While Reece rolled the hide with the fleshy side out and placed it in the loosely woven sack, he kept looking for some sign of Jake. As he approached the clump of trees, Jake struggled to his feet. The weary mule was still alive. With a little luck, he might last another day, resting in the shade of the mahogany.

Rodriguez took a drink from his canteen and replaced the cap, then sat looking across the dark-hued expanse of Copper Canyon. The Swede lay back and closed his eyes, resting his head on a folded blanket. Reece sneaked over and scratched Jake behind his ears and patted him on his shoulder, wishing he'd never gotten the patient animal into such a grave situation.

"Goddammit, Reece! Get away from that mule and get your ass out of here! You got a long way to go to get to camp. You tell Sanchez I want him to saddle the fastest horses and hurry. And bring a mule with two cans of water -- and tell Sanchez to have the cook fix us a lunch. Another thing, Reece, you better remember what I already told you. You don't ever say one word about this trip to anyone, not even your *gringo* friend, Limesand."

"*Sí, Capitán.* I'll not say a word and I'm on my way right now. I'll run as fast as I can." Reece threw the captain a brief salute and left in a long-striding trot.

It was past midnight when Reece reached the point where he could see the overhead crossarms of the telegraph line where they'd last seen Sanchez and his crew stringing wire between the poles. Even though his legs and feet ached from three days and nights with little rest or sleep he felt relieved to be within five or six miles of camp.

When the trail crossed a deep arroyo Reece began counting off telegraph poles. Near the base of the fourth pole he found two half-gallon jars of water he'd buried a couple of days before he'd led the hunters out of camp. As he rested his weary legs and drank the water from one of the jars he felt an unusual sense of calm. For some strange reason the old Tarahumara woman hadn't found all of his hidden jars.

After a period of fitful sleep Reece was awakened by the cry of a bird he'd often heard at night when he was little more than a toddler. The strange cry of the nocturnal whippoorwill that had frightened him then still carried its eerie effect, its mournful calls an almost identical repeating of its name. His stern mother had scared him by saying some boy named Will had been naughty and now his mother would have to whip him.

Light showed ahead as Reece neared the campsite. As he got closer he saw a form hovered over the table preparing food for the guards. It could be Al. A steaming pot sat on the grate covering the fire. Reece felt a lump in his throat when he was sure that the darkened figure at the table was Al's. It seemed so long since he'd seen his friend and then the dismal thought of Al finishing his sentence within less than a year and returning to his family in San Diego made Reece's chest tighten. His short-lived joy was replaced with a sense of fear and sadness. It was hard for Reece to be happy for Al knowing he still had over nine years to serve on his own sentence if his hopes for escape failed. Al's family had some money and the judge had been lenient. He'd given Al a light sentence when he was caught buying illegal drugs to take across the border.

Reece waited in the shadows, trying to sort out his feelings. It was another case of families with money being treated better than those that were poor. After he thought about the difference in the way he and Al had been treated, Reece decided it was the system that was to blame -- not his best friend. Watching Al preparing food while everyone else seemed to be sleeping made Reece feel guilty. Al would never ask for special favors for himself.

Moving past a small table covered with sprinklings of flour and white mounds of bread dough ready for baking, Reece cleared his throat. He didn't want to startle the busy cook.

"Hello Al, I see you're up early. What's for breakfast?"

Al spun around, dropping the potato he was peeling, quickly stepping forward and grabbing Reece by his shoulders then hugging him. "Where you been, John? I've been worried about you!"

Reece hesitated, then gave a Al a brief hug. He'd never before had another man put his arms around him except the time a hobo, just outside the train switching yards in Tulsa, tried to throw him off the top of a moving boxcar.

"You didn't kill them, did you?" Al's face showed concern when he looked around the area and didn't see Rodriguez or the Swede. "What are you doing coming in here at this time of the morning by yourself -- you're not in trouble, are you?"

"Just plumb worn out is all -- no real trouble more'n usual."

"I thought you'd be back in a couple of days at the most. You didn't take enough water for more than that."

"I know that now. Believe me, I know."

"Did you find the bunch of sheep with the ram?"

Reece looked around. A moving lantern out at the corrals meant someone was strapping the panniers onto the mules. The shadowy form of two men moved in and out of the lantern's yellow light.

"I'm not supposed to say nuthin' about what happened since we left -- nuthin' a'tall. Rodriguez warned me twice. Wait a few days and I think the whole camp will be talkin' about what happened. You'll hear 'em."

"It's good to see you," Al said, patting Reece on his shoulder. "Sit down and I'll fix you some breakfast."

"Some of that coffee would sure taste good -- 'specially if you slip in some of that brown sugar."

Al raised his eyebrows and made a silly face. "Well now," he said, turning completely around, peering into the darkness with an exaggerated and inquiring look of surveillance. "Since I don't see your good friend Mr. Neilson anywhere about I'll assume that would be just fine with him."

Al and Reece both laughed. Reece then felt a wave of sadness as he watched Al get a cup and fill it with the steaming liquid from the pot. It would all be so different when his friend finished his sentence and caught the train to California. There'd be no one to laugh with then -- not a soul he could trust.

"I saved you some half-gallon pickle jars -- washed them too." Al paused then added with a mischievous grin, " I know how you like to collect them. You told me once how you used to catch fireflies in them when you were a kid and made yourself a lantern -- no, I believe you said you called them lightning bugs."

Reece sipped his coffee and stared at the fire. It was best, he knew, for Al's sake, that he never discuss anything about his plans for escape. If he got away in the next few months they wouldn't hesitate to beat Al into telling them anything he'd heard of Reece's escape plans. Sanchez would enjoy the job of making Al talk.

"Yeah, we called them lightin' bugs. Chasin' them was a lotta fun as soon as it got dark, if you didn't step on a copperhead snake or a rusty nail. We never wore shoes in the summertime." Reece looked up at Al and raised his cup. "Thanks for the coffee. It tastes real good." He turned back to the fire and grinned and quietly added, "Thanks for the pickle jars, too, they're just the right size. They'll come in handy if I ever see any of them lightin' bugs flyin' around out here."

Al looked out toward the corral as he reached for the coffee pot. "I'll fry you some ham but don't let anyone see you eating it. Here, let me fill your cup again."

"A piece of fried ham -- I can't even remember the last time I had any."

Al opened the door to the wooden cabinet where the Swede kept his personal supplies and took out the ham, wrapped in heavy white paper stamped with the words "Swift's Premium," then reached for a knife.

"Now I've got to do something I've been dreadin'," Reece said, biting at a piece of sun-chapped skin that was peeling on his lower lip.

"What's that?"

"I got to go wake up Sanchez. He'll start cussin' an' throw a boot or somethin' at me."

"You better have a good reason to wake him up this early. He can be meaner than a snake."

The thick slice of ham began to sizzle the instant Al laid it on the grate by the coffee pot. Reece closed his eyes and took a deep breath, savoring the aroma that he remembered from his childhood. When times were good, his father would sometimes save a ham from one of the hogs he killed to sell and they'd have a piece of it for their Christmas dinner. Reece remembered how he'd bow his head -- when his father cleared his throat to signal the beginning of the mealtime prayer -- then he'd peek at the special treat, wishing his father would hurry up and get to the part that went '...in Jesus's name, Amen.'

"You're not going to doze off, are you John, while I'm fixing your breakfast?"

"Sorry. No. I was just restin' my eyes for a minute. Ain't had much sleep lately. Rodriguez sent me for Sanchez. Him an' the Swede's back yonder in the mountains 'bout fifteen, maybe twenty miles, footsore an' plumb worn out. They're out of water an' their horses are down -- can't hardly raise their heads off the ground they're so weak..."

"How can anyone be so cruel to..."

"Not their fault. It's all mine. I'm the one that led them on a wild-goose chase 'til we was damn near out of water -- all my fault, not theirs -- thought I could save the ram..."

"Then they got one?"

"I didn't say whether they did or not -- I gotta go wake up Sanchez."

"Aw, let him sleep a little longer, might improve his disposition."

"I doubt it. I don't think anything'll ever improve that bastard. Most likely he was just born mean."

Al took a fork and turned the ham then laid a piece of bread on the edge of the grate to warm. "We haven't had a chance to talk for…"

"Say, you haven't seen that old woman an' the two kids have you?" Reece was hoping they'd left the area and gone back down out of the mountains and taken their sorry looking burro with them. The little beast would drink as much water as the three of them.

"Funny you'd ask. Harper was talking about them the other day. He was setting here at the table going through his daily ledger, figuring out how many poles the Indians had brought in to build the line. He said that two brothers have brought in over twice as many poles as the next two men combined. He said they are the sons of the old grandma who's still gathering plants and grinding them into powders for medicine."

"Medicine, huh? Well, what about the kids?"

"Day before yesterday they were out behind the corral digging up roots of some kind with sharp-pointed sticks. I sneaked out and left a jar of peanut butter setting near the little one and motioned for him to come get it. I came back and hid and watched him and the girl taste it. I heard something behind me and turned as Harper walked past. I know he saw me but he looked the other way. He walked off whistling as he went."

Reece hesitated to ask Al the question that he desperately needed an answer to, then decided he'd have to find out sooner or later. "What do you think they do for water?"

"I wondered about that too. One of the Indians bringing logs told Harper who she was when he inquired about her and asked what she was doing up here. Her family was driven off the Babicora when it was sold to that United States Senator, George Hearst, the one I told you about."

"I remember you telling me about it, I 'specially remember the part of him gettin' all that good land for thirty cents an acre. What about the water…?"

"I'm coming to that. Later, when she had a family and her two sons were still quite small that's when she became a midwife -- knows these mountains better than any one -- knows the location of every spring and water hole for two hundred miles along this mountain range. When any of her people are sick or hurt or a woman's going to have a baby, she's the one they send a runner for. She's the only doctor these mountain people have -- sometimes it takes days for her and her burro to reach them when the mountain passes are covered with snow. The old woman, it seems, is somewhat of a legend in these mountains to all of the Tarahumara people."

"I never would've figured it."

Al reached over and picked up the smoking bread and juggled it in his cupped hands while it cooled then took a fork and placed the slab of ham on the bread. "Here, this'll help you get your strength back. You're going to need it. Looks like you got another forty miles to cover today -- time you go out and bring them back."

"I don't even want to think about it right now. I just want to sit here an' enjoy this, it smells so good." Reece slid the meat over to where his first bite would be equal with both meat and bread and took a bite, then closed his eyes while he chewed it. He swallowed and added, "*Gracias, gracias*, my friend. I never had a piece of ham that tasted so good -- not even when I was a kid." While Reece alternated with large bites and gulps of coffee, Al began sliding the mounds of bread dough into the cast-iron oven.

"Another thing about the medicine woman I heard that's kind of strange. She's worked for white foremen on farms for years but she refuses to speak a word of English. They say her family worked for a Mormon farmer near Casas Grandes so you know she has to understand the language. One of the guards, I think it was Morales, said no one ever remembers seeing her smile. She's always got such a stern expression as if saying, get out of my way -- I'm coming through. She just tells those grandkids something once and they do it."

"My own ma was a lot like that. Gonna' do things that didn't seem possible to most folks. So, this old Indian woman knows the locations of all the springs. Knows these mountains better than anyone?" Reece was greatly relieved at hearing that the old grandma might not be a thief. She had to have been finding water for years without any help from him.

"Morales says he's heard she really despises all white men."

"I can understand that. Don't like a lot of 'em myself. An' you can include most of these Mexican guards in that bunch too." Reece felt guilty that he'd called the woman a thief if only when talking to himself. Knowing there was now a good chance that his water jars were still in place made him feel much better. Within a week or two he might get a letter from Eula Mae. His spirits were higher than they'd been for over a month -- it felt like his heart had swelled up inside of him, pounding hard with new hope and expectations.

Al sat down on a bench directly across from Reece, his face taking on a somber expression that wasn't typical for Al.

"John, we need to have a talk. I'm not sure just what you're up to and maybe it's best you don't tell me. I just hate to think about maybe getting out of here and leaving you behind. As much as I want to go home and be with family the thought of leaving you here is a worry to me..."

"Awful nice of you to feel that way -- it's more'n anyone could rightly hope for." The light from the fire showed the depth of Al's feelings. His eyes reflected the yellow flames of the glowing embers.

"I can't believe how much you've changed since that day I got you into so much trouble. When Sanchez headed right for us and grabbed you around the neck instead of me and started choking you and dragging you -- I-I wanted to tell them it was me that was talking but I was so scared I could hardly breathe." Al sniffled and wiped his nose on his sleeve. He grinned and added, "Being the cook, I should have better manners."

"I don't hold nuthin' against you for that, been that scared myself lots of times. Besides, you done apologized before."

"John, you don't even look like the same person you did on that day. You must have lost forty or fifty pounds and your skin and hair have both changed color spending so much time out in the sun. Your clothes hang on you like loose rags. You've been worked so hard, but you don't ever really complain about it. You drive yourself like something's after you and you're trying to outrun it…"

"Never felt better in my whole life…Now ain't that a whopper of a lie? I'm so tired right now I can hardly stand up." Reece chuckled, then stretched out the front of his loose baggy shirt. "Room for two of me in here now."

Al's face changed again, registering a serious expression. "I have no way of knowing where I might move to when I finish my sentence but I want you to know how to reach me if you ever need me for anything."

"I'd like that. You being the best friend I ever had."

"Or if you ever need a place to hide out for a while, I got a place in mind. It's just across the border about eighty miles east of Nogales -- more or less, that is, I'm not real sure about the distance but you'll know it if you ever get there. It's a real pretty place with lots of trees and water."

"I just might need something like that for a spell, a fellow never really knows nuthin' for sure."

"My uncle's the foreman there. It's the biggest cattle ranch anywhere around. It's called Kino Springs. My uncle's name is Clarence. Clarence Bigelow. He's my mother's brother."

"How would he know for sure we been friends?"

"Tell him Bo Bo sent you. It was the name he called me when I was just a kid and he knows how much I hated it. He'd know I wouldn't tell just anyone that name. My uncle took me on his horse one time way up in the hills to an old sheep-herders cabin where…"

"Oh hell! I forgot to wake up Sanchez. You'll have to tell me later," Reece called over his shoulder as he hurried toward the Sergeant's tent.

Reece led the three horses he'd saddled and the two mules that would carry the water over by the table where Al was frying potatoes.

"I forgot to tell you Rodriguez wants you to fix a lunch for him an' the Swede. Has Sanchez showed up yet?"

"No, but I heard him yelling at you when you woke him. He'll be by in a little while, I'm sure. He'd be the last one in this camp that would ever miss a meal. I'll fry him some eggs and salt pork to go with the potatoes while I'm fixing something for the captain and Neilson."

"While you're doing that I'll go fill up the water cans," Reece said as he led the mules away. While he was filling the cans from the barrels on one of the trucks he heard Sanchez yelling curses at Al.

"I know somebody's been eatin' ham and you're giving me salt pork! I can smell it, Limesand, and let me tell you nobody makes a fool of Sergeant Sanchez and gets away with it. You understand me, you lying bastard?"

"It mu-must have been a little piece stuck on the edge of the gra-grate from when the captain and the Swede had breakfast just before they left to go hunting. I-I'm sure that must be it. Here let me put the lunches in the saddle bags. I even put you in a couple of candy bars and an extra apple."

"Four days and that little piece is still sizzling on the grate? You really better watch yourself, you goddam smart-aleck *gringo.*"

Reece led the mules over and mounted the black gelding that Harper had told him to take. Sanchez's tirade made him nervous. The sergeant had caught Al in an obvious lie and Reece knew he'd take out his anger on anyone near.

"Get the hell off that horse, Reece. Just who do you think you are? You know the *capitán* never lets any prisoner ride a horse," Sanchez said, untying the long whip coiled just below his saddle horn, as Reece dismounted.

"I'm gonna see just how fast you can run, you lazy bastard," Sanchez yelled, spurring his horse and lashing Reece across his back with his bullwhip.

CHAPTER 16

SANCHEZ'S WHIP

When the second lash struck Reece's back, he stumbled from the shock of the shooting pain. Gritting his teeth to keep from crying out, he regained his balance and sprinted straight ahead.

The tearing sound he'd heard was the impact of the knot on the end of the plaited rawhide whip when it ripped his shirt. Enjoying the fried ham less than an hour before he had no inkling of the price he'd soon pay.

Sanchez had ordered him to run. Now he had to run like he'd never run before or the beating would continue. Al's lies about the ham had infuriated the suspicious sergeant.

The first few miles would be the hardest. After that, the weight of the burly guard and the heat would soon tire his mount.

The strong-armed sergeant, John had seen on many occasions, was a skilled craftsman when it came to meting out punishment. Grabbing and choking any nearby prisoner until he collapsed was his favorite. Beating them with his whip was a close second. Reece had now experienced both.

Sanchez often bragged that blowflies would light on the end of his whip where a prisoner's blood had soaked into the leather.

Glancing back at Sanchez, when he heard the man grunt with exertion, Reece flinched and ducked his head when he saw the sergeant's raised arm, whipping the lash back to deliver another blow. In the same motion the guard's boots drove forward in the stirrups, then kicked back hard, driving his spurs into his horse's flanks. Reece bent low and drove his legs with all of his strength, straining to stay out of the whip's long reach.

Hearing curses, Reece stole another glance behind him. The sergeant, off-balance and half-turned in the saddle, jerked on the lead rope of the first horse in the pack train strung out behind him. It appeared the flailing whip, looping back over Sanchez's horse's rump, had struck the frightened roan's head, tied first in line behind the sergeant's horse. The roan reared and flung its neck and head from side to side in an attempt to break away and escape the whip's backlash.

Seeing Sanchez drop his bullwhip in the confusion, Reece took advantage of the sergeant's delay and kept sprinting until his lungs ached from exertion. Never before had he run as fast for such a distance. After running hard for what he knew would be over a mile, his legs weakened. He could no longer maintain the pace. When he'd seen the Indians running for hours, they'd been moving much slower.

Looking back again, he could see that he now had a lead of at least 300 yards. The sergeant's attention was kept distracted by the packstring holding their heads high, pulling back on their halter ropes and being dragged along by the Sergeant's tiring mount.

The whip's curling backlash had saved Reece from a vicious beating, at least for now. The temperamental sergeant's mood swings could subside quickly once he'd struck a painful blow or been satisfied with a look of terror on his victim's face. Al had said the man enjoyed seeing the immediate results of his actions; a cowering prisoner was reassurance the sergeant was still in control.

Wielding a whip when he had both feet planted on the ground was easy. However, Sanchez had found the act of whipping a man on the run from the back of a horse much more difficult.

Reece's tracks showed in the dirt where he'd come down the trail in the middle of the night on his way to camp. A couple of miles behind him he'd passed the point where he'd found his jars of water and taken a short nap.

During the first hour, Reece kept his lead. As the sergeant fell farther behind, Reece gradually slowed his pace. The new trail along the line was well defined. The tracks of men and animals had beaten a path through the stunted sage and grasses as they built the line. Where the trail forked, the one leading off to the right toward the crest had been little more than a trace until the hooves of the hunting party's horses and mules had passed. The distinct tracks, now four days old, began angling upward, gradually leading away from the line of recently set telegraph poles that continued on in a southeasterly direction toward the distant town of Durango.

Reece reckoned they'd come at least eight miles when the high limestone mesa came into view on the western skyline. When he reached the beginning of the rock slide where he'd first spotted the sheep they were within less than a mile of the sheer eastern face of the mesa. Dark objects in the sky moved across a white thunder cloud, drifting high above Copper Canyon and the Rio Papigochic. Reece felt an immediate sense of shame. More than a dozen buzzards slowly circled above the mesa's top. He knew at a glance they had likely spotted the carcasses of either one or both rams.

The sight of the gathering buzzards and exhaustion from the hard running in the heat left him weary. He stopped and reached out to steady himself against a boulder lying above the trail. Looking back, he watched as Sanchez came into view again, riding through a stand of creosote bushes less than a quarter mile down the slope. Reece closed his eyes and swallowed hard. It was no use. Vomit suddenly erupted from his throat and sprayed across the top of the boulder. His legs began to shake. He sat down and waited until the sergeant caught up and reined his horse to a stop.

"Get up, you lazy bastard," Sanchez ordered, dismounting and walking forward with his whip coiled in his hand, his arm half-raised in a threatening position. He grinned and added, "Looks like I've got a job to finish."

Reece struggled to his feet and stared up at the buzzards circling the mesa. Other vultures were still arriving from the south. It was impossible to count them.

He pointed to the circling vultures. "That's a bad sign. I-I think I'm gonna die," he said, without looking at the sergeant. "You'll have to go on without me," Reece added, his voice barely above a whisper.

"What -- what did you say?"

"You'll have to go on without me ... I..." Reece's voice trailed off without finishing his answer.

"What are you talkin' about?"

Reece feebly brushed away the large black flies attracted by the vomit. Fear gripped him when he noticed the pink flecks of ham spread among the contents of his stomach that had gushed across the rock. If Sanchez came closer and examined the stinking mass he would know for sure Al had lied to him.

When Reece didn't answer the sergeant's question there was a short period of silence, broken only by the rapid breathing of the winded horses.

"You can't die now," Sanchez snarled, "and you better not be lyin' to me," he added after a pause, his voice sounding puzzled by the real meaning of Reece's comments.

When Reece didn't respond, Sanchez's temper showed when he blurted. "You and that other cook are both liars. You don't fool no one."

Reece stood quietly, his eyes fixed on the ground. He desperately hoped the Sergeant wouldn't notice the damning evidence the flies had swarmed to in even greater numbers.

"You got to go with me because I don't know where to even start looking for the *capitán*." Sanchez's voice had an edge of concern. "You said they were out of water and they'd be waitin' for us."

Reece sat back down and put his head between his knees and said in a subdued voice, "I think I puked my guts out." Without looking up he waved in the general direction of the sheer wall of the mesa. "They're up yonder. Just keep going up this trail." Reece took several deep breaths and pressed the palm of his hand on his heart and muttered, "You ought to find them on the back side of the mountains, somewhere."

Sanchez moved back by his horse and laid his whip across the saddle. Reece watched him out of the corner of his eye. Sanchez took his canteen's strap off the saddle horn and brought it to Reece saying, "Here. Maybe a drink will make you feel better." He stepped back away from Reece, saying, "You stink," when he smelled the vomit.

Reece raised his head and wiped his mouth on his sleeve. "You may as well just shoot me and put me out of my misery. I can't run no more," his voice hoarse and barely above a whisper. He paused, then shook his head and again looked at the ground. Large red ants were crawling across the trail. He forced himself to slowly remove the canteen cap and continued watching the ants without bringing the canteen to his dried lips. "My pa had a bad heart -- died when I was nine," Reece lied, rubbing his fingers across the left side of his chest.

Sanchez looked up at the vastness of the Sierra Madre. The jagged tops of the mountain range to the south stretched for another twenty miles. "Rest for awhile, it might make you feel better." Sanchez's comment for the first time ever in Reece's presence indicated a concern for the welfare of a prisoner. If the sergeant failed to bring the captain fresh mounts, food and water, he would be in real trouble. Sanchez had to be thinking of the berating he would get. He had to know he could be reduced in rank with loss of pay. But Reece felt sure the sergeant feared most a verbal tirade by the captain in the presence of others. Al had said Rodriguez's previous military schooling prepared him well for an understanding of men's basic weaknesses, especially men of inferior rank.

"I think maybe you better ride one of the horses," the sergeant offered in a voice sounding worried and unsure of what to do.

With the roan in the lead, Reece took his time, riding slumped in the saddle. He could see that the horse's right eye was badly swollen, the closed lid showing only a narrow slit of the eyeball. Flies crawled below the edge where clear mucous with flecks of blood oozed through the lower line of eyelashes. A glance back at the sergeant showed a definite look of concern on his scowling features, the man's eyes squinting against the bright sun. He nervously looked back and forth across the dull expanse of high desert that lay below the bluffs.

The scant soil covering ended. They were now crossing a stretch of the upper slopes where layers of sharp-edged shale left no tracks. The roan slowed, picking his way carefully across the unsure footing.

If Reece was unable to travel, the sergeant was clearly worried he'd never find his way to where Rodriguez was waiting.

He'd have no idea there was a narrow pass through the mountains where the hunters had camped the first night of the hunt. The house-sized boulder that had blocked the wind from the hunter's tent hid the narrow valley from the view of anyone approaching until they were within less than 200 feet of the opening.

The roan's ears pointed straight ahead. He'd either smelled or heard something that lay in the general direction of the cleft where the opening was still hidden from view.

At the entrance to the pass the roan slowed and began taking shorter, more tentative steps. His instincts seemed to be telling him to flee from this dark-sided chasm where the walls rose a thousand feet above his line of sight. Somehow he seemed to know that the ones that didn't run would have become victims of predators hiding in places such as this. At Reece's urgings the roan continued, eyeing every shadow as they entered. His vision, now limited to one eye, seemed to make him much more nervous than usual.

A ring of blackened stones held the remains of charred sticks where John had cooked supper for Rodriguez and the Swede.

"This where you camped?"

"*Sí, Señor.*"

Reece half-turned in the saddle and studied the nearby rock formations. He could see that Sanchez was awed by the height of the walls that dwarfed them. He had to be thinking of the near impossible task of finding his way alone through the vastness of the Sierra's range.

The sun's rays slanted down onto the sparse grass that had been cropped short. Here and there a single blade or two the grazing animals had missed, waved gently in the slight breeze. It appeared to Reece it was nature's way of trying to save a few scattered seed-plants for the coming year.

It would soon be noon.

Piles of dried manure lay just inside the entrance where the horses and pack mules had spent the first night without water.

A shot rang out. The walls of the pass seemed to amplify the sounds. The roan stopped and jerked up his head, ready to bolt in an instant. He stood with both ears pointing toward the far end of the pass where it ended high above the Copper Canyon gorge. John could feel the horse's body quivering against the inside of his thighs and lower legs.

After a long pause, the blast of another shot bounced off the hard rock walls. After a long silence Sanchez asked, "What do you think that was?" His voice was timid, not like a man who enjoyed his reputation of being tough and unforgiving.

The towering walls and the sharp reverberating blast of a big-bore rifle intimidated the sergeant.

"It's hard to say the way rifle sounds bounce around in the mountains. Could be they've moved back to where we tied the horses an' one of the mules. Maybe they just put the two horses out of their misery, they were almost dead when I left. Course it could be they was tryin' to signal us…to hurry up an' bring the water. Can't really say -- it's just a guess."

"Think it could be bandits? Maybe Yaquis? We can't be far from Sonora."

Reece wished Al could be with him now just so he could enjoy hearing the concern in the sergeant's voice. "Don't think so. Pretty sure it was the Swede's heavy-caliber magnum. Most likely no one else in all of Mexico has a custom-made rifle like the two he brung with him." Reece could never forget the blistering afternoon when the half-drunk Swede shot the glass jar out of his hand. The thought still rankled him. "A Yaqui wouldn't make enough money in a lifetime to buy the gun that made that sound, even if he lived to be a hundred."

"How much further 'til we get to the end of this place, where you said the *capitán* might be waiting?"

"'Bout a mile and a half. Can't say for sure."

"We better hurry. It could be they're trying to get our attention and signaling for water. You seem to be feeling better. When we get almost there you'll have to get off and walk. The *capitán* won't like it if he sees you riding a horse."

Sanchez had changed from being a vicious guard, anxious to whip a near-helpless prisoner into a bloody pulp, into a man visibly shaken with uncertainty. The thought of being alone in desolate, remote mountains, and bewildered as to which way to go, was bothering Sanchez. The added anxiety of knowing Captain Rodriguez was out of water and awaiting his arrival had badly rattled his nerves.

"I think I can walk for a ways," Reece said, his voice sounding stronger. He didn't want to overdo his little scheme.

The sun was straight overhead when Reece stopped the bald-faced roan, and said. "We're less than half a mile from where we tied the horses."

When they reached the end of the pass where the opening ended high above Copper Canyon, the sergeant stopped and dismounted. "Here, hold my horse," he said, leading it up alongside Reece where he'd dismounted. Sanchez looked around and asked, "Is this where you left them?" He took a few steps then leaned forward, peering into the deep chasm cut by the Rio Papigochic, a thin ribbon of glistening water winding along the canyon floor more than two thousand feet below them.

"It's about another 300 yards on up yonder." Reece pointed toward the north along the narrow shelf lying below the western wall of the flat-topped mesa. "The small trees you see are mahogany. The place where they're growin' widens out for a ways before it drops straight down into the canyon. That's where the Swede found sign that the sheep were here. They'd been eatin' on the mahogany leaves."

Within a short distance the roan stopped and snorted, the one good eye fixed on the spot where Reece had pointed. Rodriguez stepped out from behind a growth of mountain mahogany and shielded his eyes with his hand. "That had better be you, Sanchez."

"*Sí, Capitán,* it's me. We got plenty of water and something for you to eat. Got three good horses too."

The Swede got to his feet and hobbled after Rodriguez as the two groups walked toward each other. Reece noticed the captain was limping, favoring his right foot.

"I thought you'd never get here," the captain grumbled when he came near Reece and Sanchez. "What took you so long?"

"You know the *gringo*, he's kinda lazy. I had to use my whip to get him moving." As the captain reached them Sanchez added, "Turn around *gringo* and show the *capitán* your back. A pair of scissors couldn't have cut it any straighter." Sanchez laughed as he reached for Rodriguez's canteen. "Here, let me fill it for you,*Capitán.*"

Reece was sure the torn gaping shirt left no question as to where the lash had struck.

"That no doubt got his attention," Rodriguez chuckled and reached for his canteen.

The Swede caught up and handed his canteen to Reece, saying, "Hurry up and fill mine, too. You should have been here hours ago."

"*Señor* Reece got a little bit sick. Tried to puke his guts out. He felt better real fast when he saw me untie my whip again." Sanchez made no mention of how upset he was when he thought he might have to go on alone or that he'd told Reece to mount one of the horses.

"You brought two mules with water cans. I only told Reece to bring one." Rodriguez said when he noticed the Swede pouring water from the dipper on his head and down his back, then splashing it onto his face and throat.

'I'm sorry, I didn't know how many mules you'd told Reece to bring, *Capitán*. Him and Harper had them ready when it was time to leave," Sanchez said, and shrugged his shoulders.

"*Señor* Rodriguez, I thought if we had some extra water we might save the two pack mules even if the horses are down --"

"I took care of the horses," the Swede interrupted. "They're no problem -- shot them both in the head and put them out of their misery just awhile ago. You must have been close enough to hear the shots."

"I heard them when we were just entering the pass, sounded like lightning struck the mountain," Sanchez said, grinning and nodding his head.

When the Swede noticed Reece's look of anguish he smirked and said, "Buzzards gotta eat too."

"Fill it up again," Rodriguez said, handing his canteen to Reece and turning to Sanchez. "Swede killed the grand-daddy of all rams. We carried the head and hide on back to where we tied the stock. We wrapped it in a blanket to keep the flies and bugs off it but it's gotta be taken care of real soon."

"I'm anxious to get it into Chihuahua and have it put in cold-storage until the taxidermist can work on it," the Swede said. "We need to leave right now. If we hurry we can have it there by noon tomorrow." Reece could see the normally ruddy face of the Swede had become sunburned during the past four days. The skin on his nose had peeled into pale round scales like the ones growing on the sides of a hand-sized perch. Reece was pleased to hear they'd be leaving right away and going to Chihuahua. That was the place they'd pick up the mail.

"What about the saddles and equipment and the two mules -- are we gonna take them?" Sanchez asked.

"Let's just leave everything," the Swede urged. "We can report that the Yaquis stole them, too. That way if we leave right now and ride hard we can make it back to camp before dark."

"I like the idea. I want to get into Chihuahua and get a bath and some clean clothes and spend a night with a beautiful woman," Rodriguez said, a wide grin spreading across his face, his perfect set of teeth showing under his dark mustache. "In fact, I got a couple in mind right now that I know will be glad to see me."

"If you're gonna push the horses hard I can get a pan an' give them a good drink 'fore you leave," Reece offered.

"What'll we do with Reece if he can't keep up?" Sanchez asked. "He really was sick this morning."

"I could keep one of the mules with me an' any water that's left an' try to save Jake an' Bell an' pack out the tent an' saddles an' the two panniers even if we leave the water can. We'll need all of the stock an' equipment to finish."

"Are we going to listen to this hobo talk all day when we could be on our way out of here?" The Swede's impatience with a prisoner's opinion was making his sunburned face even redder.

"Think we can trust Reece to not run away and go on back to camp by himself?" Rodriguez asked Sanchez.

The Swede scoffed, "Run away? First of all, he'd either get lost or die from thirst and starvation. For ten dollars I could hire a dozen Indian runners to go after him and bring him back," the Swede turned to Reece, looking him up and down, and laughed. "If the buzzards left anything besides his old worn-out shoes."

After Reece watered the horses, the three men left leading one mule with the Swede's prized trophy tied on top of its packframe. Reece watched them spur their mounts into a fast trot.

Reece watched as the riders and the pack mule rounded a slight bend in the pass and disappeared from view with the captain still in the lead. None of them had bothered to look back.

So far, Reece's plan was working. The three men's goal was to get down out of the high country as fast as possible while Reece's goal was to save the mules. He hurried to where Bell lay in the shade of a mahogany. Just past the mule the two nearby horses lay where the Swede had shot them. It was a sickening sight. The mouths of the horses were partly open, their tongues hanging limp from their jaws. Flies crawled up out of sight into their open mouths and nostrils.

Reece turned his head away to keep from vomiting again. He took a round aluminum pan and filled it with water. The mare mule raised her head and began sipping the water from the shallow pan. After she'd drunk at least a gallon, Reece took the pan away. He didn't want the mule to drink too much at one time, fearing it could make her sick.

The backpack the Swede had used to carry his trophy down from where Reece had left Rodriguez and the Swede at the tent was leaning against a knee-high bush. Reece grabbed it and strapped on the can containing the remains of the water. Reece dreaded going back across the dangerous shale but couldn't bring himself to leave Jake to die.

At least three gallons of the water remained that he could share with Jake. Hurrying toward the basin Reece was careful of his footing. He was at the narrow ledge in a matter of minutes. He slowed and as he made his way across he looked down. As he reached the beginning of the basin he saw buzzards fighting, beating each other with their wings and beaks. Was he too late? It was then he realized it was the carcass of the first killed ram, the smaller one, that the vultures were fighting over.

Reece found Jake lying in the shade. He raised his head as Reece approached, then lowered his muzzle back to the ground. Reece spent the better part of an hour letting the mule sip small amounts of water. He rubbed Jake's head and took a leafy branch and brushed the flies away from his head and neck.

As Jake's strength slowly returned he raised his head and looked around. Another hour passed and the weary mule struggled to his feet. Reece's hopes soared. Jake was going to live.

Reece walked him in circles, noting his wobbly gait as he moved. It was midafternoon when Reece made his decision to leave the tent and camping equipment. He hoped it would be the last hunting trip he'd ever go on.

With the water can strapped onto his backpack Reece led Jake back towards the place where Bell was waiting. When they reached the dangerous stretch of loose shale, Reece stopped and thought for a moment. Before, they'd crossed it in total darkness. The listless mule didn't hesitate when Reece decided to go on across.

Moving a half-step at a time they'd passed the midpoint when the loose shale shifted from under Jake's front feet, dropping him to his knees. The trusting mule seemed to sense that he shouldn't struggle. When bits of gravel and small slivers began slipping from under his knees, he pawed hard at the moving surface to regain his footing. His pawing sent another trickle of slivers with more and larger pieces of shale sliding toward the edge of the precipice.

Reece felt the limestone he was standing on shift when the coarse grit under it became a thin moving stream flowing after the sliding shale.

Tons of rock and shale suddenly broke loose, cascading toward the precipice under a cloud of dust, carrying Jake over the edge and out of sight.

With his fingers hooked like claws over the edge of a rock at the base of the wall, Reece kept himself from being swept along with the mule and cascading rock into the chasm of Copper Canyon.

With his heart pounding wildly, minutes passed as he clung to the rock without making any attempt to move a foot or hand, taking shallow breaths and trying to stop his legs from trembling.

When all sounds of sliding shale had ceased and the dust settled Reece still waited before making any attempt to crawl to safety. Inside his head, events of his life flashed by as if carried along by a lightning bolt.

Inching his fingers along the rock's edge he clung to, Reece finally reached solid ground. He tried to stand, then sunk to his knees, tears running down his cheeks.

The honey-colored mule was dead.

CHAPTER 17

THE COBBLER

It was twilight on the sixth morning since Rodriguez and the Swede had left for Chihuahua. During their absence Reece had gotten some much needed rest. He rolled over and pushed himself into a sitting position. He had been unable to sleep since midnight when he'd heard the whine of a truck's motor climbing the last steep grade to camp. The slurred voices of Rodriguez and the Swede had awakened the entire camp. It could only mean one thing: they'd sleep until noon or the heat of the midmorning sun drove them from their tents.

If they'd brought mail it wouldn't be given out until evening, after the day's work was finished. Al was snoring on the blanket he'd spread over a layer of pine needles where he'd finally gone back to sleep.

Reece was convinced he was the most excited of all the line crew. Waiting to see if he'd gotten a letter from Eula Mae would make this one of his longest days since he'd become a prisoner.

Keeping busy every minute would help a little; he'd begin his chores earlier than usual by feeding and watering the pack mules. He'd keep his mind busy reviewing every detail in his plans for escape.

Nearby treetops, now only blurred silhouettes, would soon be distinct. A mourning dove began its melancholy calls to its mate, setting on a crudely built nest in a cedar near the corral. Reece had noticed the nest a few days earlier when he'd been getting water from one of the trucks. Looking up he'd seen the two white eggs she'd laid, showing through the loosely woven sticks in the bottom of the flimsy structure.

"You already awake, John?" Al asked, setting up and rubbing his eyes.

"Been awake ever since them two noisy drunks come back from Chihuahua in the middle of the night. Never could go back to sleep."

"They sure made a lot of noise," Al agreed. There was a period of silence before Al added, "I hope you don't get too disappointed if they brought the mail. For the last few days you've been on edge and I know how you've been counting on a letter. I'm sure you'll get one soon, if not today." Al's concern showed his usual way of trying to see the good in everything, trying to keep John's spirits up and yet prepare him for the possibility of a crushing disappointment.

"I heard a chicken squawk awhile ago -- must have brought back some young roosters for fryin'." Reece tried changing the subject. He was afraid that talking about a letter that might not even yet be written could put a jinx on ever receiving it. His mother had been superstitious. She'd warned Reece many times about wanting something real bad -- said it could put a hex on things and you just might never get them. And even if you did get them, you might not feel the pleasure you'd hoped for.

"Maybe we're goin' to have some kind of party. The Swede promised us one some time ago -- said we'd have one when we finished the first 200 miles of line," Al got to his feet and stretched.

"Feels more like we already done five hundred miles to me."

"Sure it would for you, running out to the end of the line and back two and sometimes three times a day could be closer to a thousand -- maybe even two thousand. Say, do you smell something familiar?" Al asked, raising his nose and sniffing the air.

"Yeah, I can smell a pile of mule turds -- fact is I can smell a whole bunch of--"

"No," Al interrupted. "I smell something sweet like fresh peaches. Can't you smell them?"

"I've heard horse turds called road apples before but never heard anybody call 'em peaches -- hey, I believe you're right. I can smell 'em now." Reece lowered his voice and looked around and whispered, "You stay here an' I'll sneak over an' see if I can find out what all they brung back."

Reece peered over the sideboards on the truck bed. Burlap sacks were stacked along one side. He could feel the distinctive shapes of unshucked corn through the coarse fabric. He pulled an ear out of a sack and quickly shucked it. Biting into the sweet juicy kernels he felt the cool strands of moist corn silk growing on the end of the cob tickle his nose and stir his memory. When he'd been a hobo he'd once snatched ears from stalks in a field while being chased by a farmer and his dogs.

He stuffed three more ears into his pockets while starting around to the other side of the truck. Some of the chickens in the crates lashed to the tailgate began making low quavering twitters, warning the others they'd seen or heard nearby movements in the dim light. It was a sound Reece remembered. More than a few times he'd stolen chickens and roasted them on a stick in a hobo jungle when he couldn't find work.

Waiting for the chickens to calm down and go back to sleep, Reece watched to see if the night guard had been alerted by their cautioning noises. When all was quiet he slipped around the front of the truck and back along the other side. Baskets of fresh peaches sat within easy reach. Reece felt the sticky juice run through his fingers when he squeezed a soft peach lying at the top of a basket. Shoving the ripened flesh into his mouth he pulled away the pit, tossed it out of sight in the brush same as he'd done with the corn shucks. Then he grabbed another peach. After eating it he pulled up his shirttail and gently placed a few more in the makeshift bag and sneaked back to where Al was waiting.

"Here Al, I brung you somethin' for breakfast -- fresh corn an' juicy ripe peaches. I bet we are gonna have a feast tonight like you said but this way we can get an early start."

"You took a big chance, John, but thanks just the same."

"No different than when you sliced off a piece of the Swede's special ham for me," Reece answered. "The two of us will probably spend most of the afternoon draggin' in wood an' heatin' water to boil the corn an' scald the chickens."

"What about the peaches? You know they may want us to cook them too," Al said.

"We got plenty of flour an' bakin' powder an' cinnamon, an' if they brung butter an' brown sugar I can make some dandy cobblers. With all them dutch ovens we got we can make enough where everybody can have a helpin'." Reece figured taking water to the crews and helping with the extra cooking would be more than enough to keep his mind busy. Still, if he got a chance later, he'd try to peek into the captain's tent and see if they had really brought the mail sack.

It was when Reece returned at midday for another load of water that Al motioned him over to where he was chopping wood.

"They brought the mail. Lopez told me. He was the guard that drove them into Chihuahua." Al grinned and shook his head saying, "Remember, don't go getting your hopes too high." Before Reece could say anything, Al added, "Lopez said that the Swede planned to move the camp within the next three days. The new camp will be almost thirty miles south of here where it's not so steep. We will be far from any trees but trucks can haul in all the poles and equipment we'll need --"

"Then we won't be seeing much more of the Indians?"

"No. We'll be out of the mountains then and,it'll be mostly just high desert. But don't worry, we'll see plenty of rattlesnakes and scorpions. That's where the line will start bearing more to the southeast. Within the next month we're scheduled to cross the Rio Conchos about sixty miles west of Camargo."

"I hate them damn rattlers, never could figure what the Lord Almighty put them here for anyhow. Them an' flies too."

"The Almighty, as you call him, has got a purpose even if we don't understand it. But if you watch where you're stepping you can usually avoid the rattlers," Al said, jumping aside and yelling, "There's one behind you -- look out!" He rolled his eyes in mock terror then doubled over laughing as Reece scrambled forward before realizing it was just another of Al's little pranks.

As soon as Reece recovered from his momentary fright he said, "You beat all I ever saw, scaring people half to death an' always playin' the fool like you do." Reece laughed at how easily Al had tricked him. Still, he couldn't resist glancing back again to make sure it really was just another of Al's jokes.

"Can you give a hand with splitting some wood? You can handle an axe a lot better than I can. I need to get the water in the pots boiling right away."

"Be glad to, but I gotta get movin' soon with one more run of water. The crew's really humpin' it -- tryin' to finish early -- can't hardly wait to get their mail." The comment about mail brought a questioning glance from Al. Reece grabbed the wooden handle of the axe and began splitting the sawed logs. Al was right, he'd always been good at striking the sharp blade at the precise point where he intended. When he'd split all of the wood he carried it over and laid it near the cooking table while thinking about Al's earlier remarks. Once they were far from the Sierra's crest and the Indians were no longer needed to bring in poles for the line, the higher mountains would be mostly deserted again.

One man sneaking along below the limestone bluffs would be hard to find, especially if he had a good lead and no one knew which way he'd headed. The very thought made Reece's skin tingle with anticipation. He swallowed when his mouth became wet with saliva. Another thought crossed his mind that troubled him, dampening the hopes of the first. It was a vision his mind couldn't shake, a picture of mounted guards with tracking dogs to run him down.

When Reece returned for another armload of wood and started back toward the cooking table he stopped in mid-stride, turned around and inquired. "Then Camargo must be about three hundred miles below the border?"

Al hesitated and looked off into the distance before he responded. "Let's see now, I'm not too familiar with the area we're headed into but I'd say it could be a little more or a little less than 300 miles -- I'm really not sure. You could ask the Swede. He can tell from his maps."

"I wouldn't ask that bastard what month it is. He never could stand me 'til he found out I'd worked a lot with mules an' he needed me -- 'fore that he never called me nuthin' but hobo."

"You really shouldn't keep dwelling on that and carrying a grudge against him like you do. Just forget it, John."

"You don't know what it's like, havin' people look down on you for things you can't help none. You never been in my shoes."

"Forget about what he might think -- it's not that important. What he thinks doesn't change who he is or who you are either. I'd much rather have you for a friend."

"Oh, I--I better get busy an'..." Reece stammered, embarrassed but pleased by Al's unexpected compliment. He walked over and grabbed the trunk of a palo verde that had fallen long ago and dragged it to the chopping block. "I gotta take another load to the crew," said Reece, picking up Bell's lead rope and leading her and the other mules over to the water barrels.

By early afternoon the crews' shirts were drenched with sweat. They'd almost reached the point Harper had assigned for the day. After the line crew drained every drop of water from the cans, Reece hurried back down the trail toward camp. Al would need more help to get everything ready before the evening light dimmed.

He stopped abruptly and studied the ground. Fresh tracks showed crossing the trail the mules had cut within the last hour when he'd led them on the last water run for the day. The old mid-wife had driven her burro down from a high ridge that was covered with a stand of condalia. The tracks showed where they'd all walked along in single file. The girl's tracks showed last where she'd often stepped on her brother's footprints.

While Reece knelt and examined the ground, he could see that the burro's right rearhoof print turned outward more than the one on the left. He remembered that its right ear also drooped more than the left one did. He'd always noticed things about stock he'd worked around. A few blue-black fleshy berries and some seed had been dropped in one of the burro's tracks. Probably by the boy, Reece assumed, trying to eat some of the condalia berries as he trudged along.

Al had said the tasty fruit picked from the vast condalia thickets was a favorite of many Indian tribes that lived in high desert regions. Seeds could easily be squeezed from the fruit and the remaining pulp dried for ease of storage and future use. Al had also said that Indians on the move favored the sun-dried lightweight berries and it made good feed for their stock.

The burro was old. Possibly over twenty years in age. It didn't matter, he knew. He'd likely never see any of them again but the girl's tracks made him think of his own daughter.

He guessed that the Indian girl was maybe thirteen. It was hard to tell. He couldn't help wonder what Eula Mae had been like when she was about that age and growing up. A wave of guilt swept over him when he thought again of how he'd never even done one thing to help her -- never even known that she existed.

Reece looked in the direction the tracks had taken. There was no sign of the little party that had crossed his trail. He broke into a fast trot, leading the mules back to camp where he could give Al a hand with the cooking. The mules crowded close behind him, their loads light, the metal cans in the panniers emptied of all their water. They needed no urging. They knew they'd made the last run of the day and now it would be their turn for feed and water and a much needed rest. First, however, they'd find a soft dusty area in the corral and roll, massaging their hot sweat-streaked skin for relief where the panniers and cinch straps had trapped their body heat since early morning.

Even though he was tired, Reece kept the fast pace. He'd make peach cobblers like none of the prisoners or guards had ever tasted before. When he'd made cobblers for the hunting camps in Colorado, the hunters had all given him a good tip at the end of the hunts. All had agreed they'd never tasted any cobbler as good as the ones he'd made.

The mules were breathing hard when Reece led them into camp and stopped them in the shade of a grove of scrub pine. They'd never been led down the trail at such a pace. He'd stopped them only once for less than a minute when an empty water can bounced out of a pannier and rolled down a slope.

"Look at the dust you made coming down the trail so fast," Al said, walking over and pointing to where a pall of dust still hung above the trail. "Something chasing you?"

"Naw, just showin' off I guess." Reece answered, panting hard and trying to catch his breath. He couldn't tell Al that he'd really pretended he was being chased for the last hour and he just wanted to see if he could run fast for the entire distance.

Someday, he knew, it could be for real.

"Guess what I saw back up yonder about a mile from where the line crew's just finishing up for the day?" Reece asked.

"Oh, I don't know, maybe a mountain lion?" Al replied.

"No. Nuthin' like that. I saw where the old midwife an' the kids had crossed the tracks I made on my way up to the crew. They'd been pickin' berries off some condalia bushes growin' on a rocky knob above the trail. Some of the berries had been dropped in one of the burro's tracks."

"Not much else for them to eat this time of the year, especially up this high. It's so hot and dry even the varmints move down to lower elevations," Al said.

"Hard to believe how tough some folks have it havin' to live off so little. It shore ain't easy makin' it in these parts."

"When we move the camp most of the men carrying in logs for the line will go back to their families. They'll take the little bit of money they made and try to make it last until they find some other kind of work," Al said.

Sweat ran down Reece's face and dripped off his nose as he squatted near the fire. With a small metal shovel, he heaped coals around the dutch ovens and placed a thin layer of hot ash and embers over the cast-iron lids. Al and some of the prisoners usually assigned to cook for the prison crew, tended to the cooking of the corn and fryers. Burst of laughter and singing by both prisoners and guards filled the air as small groups huddled around the tables and waited for the special feast. Reece listened to the comments about the mail they hoped to get. He was sure none was more anxious than he was.

Both the captain and the Swede seemed to be in high spirits. They had also been drinking tequila for the last hour. Neilson smiled and nodded when men mentioned the trophy rams they'd heard about. Word had quickly gotten out about the bighorn and the normally aloof Swede seemed to revel in the attention he was getting. Answers to questions about the women they'd met in Chihuahua were listened to with keen attention before loud guffaws drowned out many of the replies.

Reece's earlier excitement ended abruptly. Hearing any discussion of the hunt was too painful. Losing Jake still left an empty feeling in his stomach. The young trusting mule deserved a better fate than the one Reece's actions had brought him.

A loud cheer erupted when Rodriguez went into his tent, brought out the sack of mail and asked, "Anyone want their mail?"

There was an agonizing wait for Reece until Rodriguez called out the name Kilgore, the last prisoner's name before Limesand.

Kilgore was a tall man whose dark hair stood up like the bristles on a brush. His blue eyes and easy smile gave no clue to the man's quick temper. He was serving seven years for stabbing a Mexican pimp in Tijuana in a fight over a payment to a whore. Kilgore had rammed the point of a cow's horn he'd bought as a souvenir into the pimp's side.

Reece heard Al's name called as he was spreading another layer of embers over an oven lid. He watched as Al stepped forward, a wide grin spread across his face as the captain handed him two letters. One addressed with large red letters written in crayon was on top. Al dabbed at his eyes and moved back out of Reece's sight. After what seemed like an eternity, the captain called out the name Reece was waiting for.

"Ramirez!" His was the last name before Reece. Reece held his breath while the captain stopped and took another drink of tequila and said something to a man standing near, then looked down at the bundle of mail in his hand.

"Reece!" Dropping the shovel he was using to spread the ashes, Reece banged it against the cast-iron lid of the oven. Rodiguez stood holding the letter out toward Reece, a questioning look on his face. Hurrying forward Reece tripped over a piece of firewood and lurched against the nearest table.

"Clumsy fool," the Swede muttered.

With a shaking hand, Reece reached and took the letter, his eyes lowered away from the direct gaze of the captain.

"*Gracias, gracias,*" he whispered and backed away, glancing at the name in the upper left hand corner. As he turned back to his chores he found it difficult to take a deep breath. The name Eula Mae Reece was neatly typed on the top line. Changing the spelling of her last name meant his daughter had gotten his letter. It was all he could have hoped for. He looked over to where he'd last seen Al.

His smiling friend waved and nodded his head, pleased that Reece had gotten mail too. Being a slow reader it took Reece several minutes to read the three-page letter as he tried to keep an eye on the ovens. A slight breeze had come up and he had to be ready to brush off any excess embers on the lids. The oxygen in the air currents moving over the lids could fan the embers into overheating and quickly burn the top layers of the cobblers.

Reece reread two sentences near the end of the second page three times. The statement made him tense with an added anxiety: "I've been taking extra classes and I'm going to graduate second in my class on June 15th. All of the other girls will have family here to see them graduate. How I wish you could be here too." The date was barely three months away.

Reece looked at the ground and dug the toe of his shoe into the dirt. When troubled or unsure of what he should do it was a habit he'd resorted to as a child whenever his mother would scold him or demand an answer as to why he'd failed to please her. This letter could change his plans and he couldn't tell a soul.

Rodriguez finished handing out the mail and declared it was time to eat. The hungry men devoured the food. Their comments made it clear they'd never expected such a feast. Within minutes after the men began eating their food, the drone of a truck motor could be heard in the distance.

The Swede stood and all noise ceased, except the whine of the laboring motor. "I promised you a feast and a party when we reached this point. The truck you hear coming up the mountain will be bringing musicians and dancing girls but…"

The Swede's voice was drowned out with a loud cheer. He grinned and added, "But, they are not to be touched or be subjected to any crude remarks. This is a family of professional entertainers."

A low, polite groan of disappointment came from the prisoners and guards at all the tables.

When Al got a minute from his duties of serving the guards he came over and nudged John with his elbow, saying, "Didn't I tell you to just be patient?"

"My daughter gonna' be a college graduate real soon, just like you, Al. What do you think of that?" Reece blurted, his chest swelling with pride. "Remember I told you she's the first in my family to ever go past the eighth grade?" Nothing he'd ever done had given him a real feeling of accomplishment. And now, someone he'd never heard of until a couple of months before had given him an almost overwhelming feeling of fulfillment.

"Put plenty of food aside for our guests," the captain ordered.

"There'll be eight to ten of them -- and bring me another bowl of that cobbler."

"Get me one too while you're at it," the Swede said.

Al moved quickly to do as the captain ordered, setting food aside on the back of the grate to keep it warm. Reece filled clean bowls of cobbler for both men and then realized that he and Al and the others assigned to serve the meal would only get any leftovers.

It was after the pretty dancing girls arrived and the musicians began tuning their guitars that Reece noticed a movement out in the bushes. In the fading light he saw the movement again. It was the girl and her little brother. A shadow farther back was indistinct but he was sure it was the old grandma. It had to be. The music undoubtedly fascinated the children. Or, he thought it just might be the smell of the delicious cobblers he'd made.

"If anyone asks, that was the last of the cobbler," Reece said, winking as

Al hurried over.

"Sanchez and the captain have both asked for another bowl. What will I tell them?" Al asked, a worried look on his face.

"Tell them there ain't no more. Tell them we didn't know another ten people were comin' to supper."

Taking a rag from a bench, Reece glanced around. Everyone's attention was riveted on the entertainers while Al served them their food.

No one knew exactly how many ovens Reece had used to make the cobblers. Even he had lost count. But one still remained, covered with a layer of gray ash. In the dim light no one else would even notice it if they were standing within arm's length. When he was sure no one was looking he wrapped the rag around the hot metal wire handle and sneaked over through the brush. In his other hand Reece carried two pieces of wood he'd split earlier in the afternoon. While the children watched, he scooped cobbler onto each clean flake of wood and left it within fifty feet of where they squatted. He backed away motioning for them to come get it.

Reece could hear the musicians as they began playing Mexican songs that he was only vaguely familiar with. The voices of the singers blended with the guitars into a beautiful melody even though Reece didn't understand many of the words. It was the end of a perfect evening, he thought, as he watched the children enjoying their surprise treat.

While Reece stood holding the handle of the oven at his side he saw the old woman suddenly step forward out of the shadows and hold up both arms, her fingers spread with palms forward, as if she was trying to tell him something. Almost immediately he had a sudden sensation of flying -- spots flashed before his eyes and his ears rang with a sound of clanging cymbals. A sensation of stabbing pain awakened him to the fact his face was pressed into a layer of fine dust and the side of his head throbbed.

Something slid down over his cheekbone and ran into his mouth.

The taste of blood told him he'd been struck a vicious blow from a massive force he hadn't seen.

CHAPTER 18

NO SECOND CHANCE

A man's gruff voice penetrated Reece's dreamlike state. Without opening his eyes, he could picture the dirt floor he was sleeping on in an empty barn. But something wasn't right. It wasn't the sound of his cousin's slow stuttering voice, and the dirt was much too warm. Other voices and the sound of a man's laughter nearby became distinct, then faded into silence. The sounds of guitar music and a woman singing became clear, and then, it too, faded away.

He woke to the taste of blood running into the corner of his mouth, oozing over his tongue. He choked and gasped for air, then opened his eyes. A man's large boot was inches from his face.

"He's not dead, *Capitán*. Want me go ahead an' kill him?" Sanchez's voice was unmistakable.

"Uh, no, wait." Reece had never before heard such hesitation in the captain's voice. "Let me think about it for a minute. We don't really know this family that's watching us. If someone reports we killed a *gringo* and it gets into the newspapers, it could cause trouble." After a pause the captain spoke forcefully. "Tell them to start the music again."

Sanchez called something in Spanish to one of the other guards and the strumming of guitars started again.

Rodriguez lowered his voice. "Now we'll have time to figure out what to do with this lying bastard," his words laced with contempt.

Reece knew he'd made two bad mistakes. He'd disobeyed orders, feeding children hanging around the camp and he'd lied about the remaining cobbler. Without question, Sanchez would now carry out any form of punishment Rodriguez wanted. It would just be a matter of time.

The Swede chuckled, "You've got a special way of getting a man's attention, sergeant. This one went down like you'd hit him alongside the head with a pick handle."

"I could step on his neck and crush his windpipe," Sanchez offered, sliding the toe of his boot over and pressing it against Reece's throat. Reece knew his life meant nothing to the three men standing over him. And having been a witness to the poaching of a record desert bighorn would also count against him.

All he could do was pray he might live to someday see his daughter. Time for Reece stood still while his fate was being decided.

Past Sanchez's boot, Reece could see the dutch oven where it had landed against a bush. The thickened peach juices and pieces of crust were seeping over the side, then spreading across the dirt. The still-steaming liquid meant he'd been unconscious for no more than a few minutes.

Sanchez lifted Reece's chin with the toe of his boot.

"I think we ought to wait, we can take care of all of this later," the Swede objected. "We still need him to handle the stock until we find another man to replace him. On this last section of the line the crews will be spread from eight to ten miles most days and we'll be moving fast. That's a lot of ground to cover to deliver water and it'll be hotter than hell. Besides, he's our best muleskinner. He's in good shape now and he can cover a lot of ground."

"How many more miles until we reach the Conchos?" Rodriguez asked.

"The map shows about a hundred and sixty. Right after we cross the river we're going to meet the United States congressmen. Since they'll be coming down from Washington to inspect the line, we don't want any trouble to spoil it," the Swede said. "Hell, they're still hollering about having to send Pershing and 10,000 troops down here twenty years ago to chase after Pancho Villa."

"They should remember that Pershing never caught up with Villa but his own people shot him down." Rodriguez said in a matter-of-fact voice, giving no hint of how he felt about the matter.

"The calvary learned a lesson. You can't ride horses across the desert without a source of water but they killed a lot of them trying. It was the last time they tried to fight a war on horseback."

"That's all behind us. Then we'll meet the congressmen, west of Camargo and on the south side of the Rio Conchos?"

"Yeah. They'll probably be down here for at least a week or maybe longer. They picked that spot so they'd be in easy driving distance to Chihuahua, where they can get all of the comforts of home," the Swede paused and laughed. He then said slowly, emphasizing each word, "And some they probably can't even get at home."

Reece heard both the captain and Sanchez chuckle. It was an encouraging sign. The Swede had a quick way of sizing up all the advantages and disadvantages in a business situation. Reece knew the captain respected

Neilson for that. After all, that was what an educated man like the Swede had been trained for. Except for the evening he'd tried to shoot naked Yaquis dancing around burning telegraph poles, the Swede had pretty much controlled his temper. He had avoided any hasty action that could jeopardize the large cash bonuses both he and Rodriguez hoped to share. And, they'd all had their fun seeing Reece half-killed and sent sprawling into the dirt.

"You're right. I hadn't thought of it that way. Reece can be taken care of later when the time is right," Rodriguez agreed.

"Timing's important in any action." The Swede emphasized the word 'timing' as if it were the captain's original thought. "I'm sure the visiting congressmen will be happy to meet some of your lady friends, Sir *Capitán*, especially any friends of that beautiful Carmen you introduced me to. They could be a big help in getting the new contracts signed."

"I'm pleased to help any way I can. You really like that Carmen, don't you?" Even though Reece didn't dare to look up at any of the men, Rodriguez's voice sounded as if his anger had subsided.

"Wish we weren't moving so far south of Chihuahua. I'd like to see a lot more of that woman, but that's where the job is," the Swede said.

"Oh. There's something she didn't let you see?" The captain's voice had a ring of mock surprise.

The Swede laughed and said, "We were talking about the contracts. Once they're signed we can build the rest of the line on down to Durango -- should get it approved in no more than two weeks at the most." The Swede paused, then added, "But if the men from Washington found out that an American citizen had been killed, it could make them nervous, and could cause an investigation, if they were afraid the word might leak out -- this being a joint venture between our two countries."

"I do not understand your government, *Señor*. He is nothing but a drifter and a prisoner."

"Yes, I know, but it's different in our country. Even the stupid and lazy ones have rights. It's something I don't personally agree with, but a representative has to at least pretend he cares about them, too. We can't afford to put any of the congressmen in an embarrassing position, especially at this time."

While the Swede had talked, Reece realized a case was being made for his survival, at least for now. They still needed him.

"What about them, *Capitán* ? They're sneaking off through the trees." From the position of Sanchez's boots Reece could tell the sergeant was now facing the area where the Indian woman had been standing when she raised her hands.

"¡*Vamos*! ¡*Vamos*!" Rodriguez yelled, then began cursing in Spanish at the old woman.

A strange thought crossed Reece's mind. Was it possible that when the woman had suddenly raised her hands she had been trying to signal him he was in danger?

"Come on, Swede, let's go on back as if nothing had happened and enjoy the show."

When the captain and the Swede turned and walked away, Sanchez waited until their voices faded.

A hard blow struck Reece in the side, suddenly forcing the wind from his lungs like a blown tire.

"Remember the day when your lying friend cooked ham for you and fried salt pork for me?" Sanchez snarled. "You got off easy but I'm gonna make your friend sorry he ever had a mother."

The sounds of Sanchez's boots scuffing across the hard-packed ground died away. Reece waited until the evening shadows had darkened into night. He raised his throbbing head slightly to look around. He knew Sanchez's boot had either broken or badly bruised the ribs along his right side, where the force of his kick struck. Each breath wracked his upper body with paralyzing pain.

From the increasing tempo of the singing and guitar playing at the camp, Reece was sure the party would last for hours. If he was lucky, the captain would get drunk and completely forget about him. The sergeant, however, was the man Reece feared the most. The brooding guard who had set up Thompson for a futile escape attempt into the desert would take any prisoner's slightest offense personally. Now Al would feel the wrath of a man who would enjoy the chance to beat and humiliate him. Reece was convinced that the longer the man brooded, the more severe Al's punishment would be.

The faint sound of footsteps were coming up from somewhere behind him. Reece desperately wanted to look around but he was afraid to move. It might be better, he thought, if he appeared to be dead.

"It's me, John. You're going to be all right." Al whispered, kneeling beside him, gently sliding a warm wet towel across the side of Reece's face. "I saw the three of them sneak out and follow you, but there was nothing I could do."

"Wait. Don't let Sanchez see…see you near me." Reece paused to take another breath. "He knows you lied to him about the ham. He's the one who hit me."

"Sanchez is over listening to the music, but I'll keep an eye out for him."

Al touched the side of Reece's face. "You got a nasty cut across your ear and a lump on the side of your head, but I can sew your ear up later. Where do you hurt the most?"

"It's my right side, I-I can't hardly breathe, it hurts so bad. It's where Sanchez kicked me."

Al lightly moved his fingers over Reece's ribcage. "They could be broken. I can't tell for sure but I don't think they are. Maybe they're just bruised, but I'll have to wrap you tight to keep them from moving in case they're broken. They'll heal quicker that way. I'll be right back. I know where there's a piece of canvas from a torn tent flap and some tape."

"Don't let Sanchez see what you're doing. No tellin' what he might do to you if he does."

On the day after Sanchez's surprise assault, Reece passed out twice when he tried to lift the cans of water up and into the panniers. On the second day he got up earlier than usual and put the empty cans into the panniers. Dipping a small pail into the water barrels, he slowly filled the water cans.

The days following were long and painful but the nights were even worse. Sleeping in a sitting position to relieve the pressure on his ribcage gave him brief periods of fitful rest. While his bruised ribs slowly healed he found himself avoiding all contact with the three men who'd caused him so much misery. Even at a distance Reece avoided any eye contact. As he trotted along each day, leading the water caravan, he often thought of the Cunningham boy and the years of painful healing he must have endured.

Reece fantasized during most of his waking hours with thoughts of escape, the best revenge he could ever hope for.

The crews were spread out over ten miles on some days where wide expanses of sand made the digging easier and faster. The extra distances he had to cover left him exhausted, long before his day's work was finished.

There was little time now for him to work with Al, and he missed the friendly chatter of the salesman. Reece had never worked around another man he'd enjoyed so many laughs with. Al still tried to make the best of every situation. The one thing that bothered him the most, which he still tried to hide, was that he desperately missed his children. Many nights after they'd gone to bed, Reece would hear Al sniffling.

There was one advantage for Reece. His busy schedule made it easier to avoid contact with the three men who'd stood over him on the day he'd expected Sanchez to stomp out his life.

Several times each day, he thought about the evening he was almost killed and the discussion that immediately followed. The one remark he dwelled on was the one the Swede made to Rodriguez: "Timing's important in any action."

The days passed slowly. He'd counted them ever since he got the second letter from Eula Mae. He made notes in a small notebook where he kept a record of his buried water jars. Each day he made sure the crews had plenty of water. He wanted to see them reach the river as soon as possible. At the end of two weeks, his ribs were feeling much better.

They were all scheduled to be returned to the prison until the new contracts were signed and new equipment for building the new section of the line arrived. Because of the heat, he'd heard one of the guards say, "We'll travel in trucks at night."

Leaping from a truck when it was climbing a sandy hummock should be much easier than jumping from a rolling freight car. Within seconds he believed he could sprint out of the glare of the headlights of any truck following close behind.

Even though his ribcage was still tender, the rest of his body was in top condition. He was sure few men his age had ever worked as hard to develop their stamina. He was ready to make his move, convinced the time was right, realizing it would be the most important decision he'd ever make.

Many of the other prisoners had whispered about the idea of escaping until Thompson's withered remains had been brought in from the desert. Reece believed he had three advantages: buried water and some jars of hidden food, but most important, the will to make any sacrifice to see his daughter.

From the top of a long rise he could now see the Conchos. One more day and they'd be across and ready for the return trip to the prison. The Swede had been astonished at the speed with which the last 160 miles of line had been built. The crew had averaged over 11 miles a day.

The evening the line was finished and the men were still eating their supper, the Swede stood on top of a table and bragged, "No crew in the states ever had such a record of building a telegraph line. And this line has been built by you men over impossible terrain. You're to be commended for such an outstanding feat." Reece had never seen a construction superintendent who knew more about the power of recognition. The man willingly gave credit where it was due.

Most of the prisoners and guards had stood and cheered, but Reece was not one of them.

"Now I would like for your captain to step up here and join me. He deserves a lot of credit for selecting the best men to do the job." The Swede reached out and shook Rodriguez's hand, then turned and motioned to someone sitting at the next table.

Reece seethed with anger when he saw the beautiful custom-made rifle handed up. It was the one with the ivory inlays of an elk's head contrasting against the dark walnut stock -- the one the half-drunk Swede had used to shoot the glass jar from Reece's hand.

There was a rousing cheer as the captain smiled and took the gift. "*Gracias, gracias*," he said to the Swede, nodding his appreciation, then holding the gleaming weapon above his head, turning completely around for all to see the expensive present. Al had said the Swede was convinced they'd get the new contract but Reece knew it wouldn't mean a thing to him. He'd never be used to work on the line running down to Durango.

Within two days, all the crew would be returned to the prison east of Matamoros. Reece had to make his move before he was again locked behind the stone walls. If he didn't, he might never get another chance to leave the prison alive. He knew the Swede was right. The timing of Reece's leap into the darkness would determine his best chances of escape.

The last campsite was bustling with activity. Trucks were loaded with equipment and supplies. The stock would be driven along the Rio Parral to a small farm, where they'd be pastured until the matter of the contract was decided.

Al was packing the cooking utensils and supplies into wooden boxes when Reece sidled over. "We'll be on our way in a couple of hours, Al, but in case we don't get put in the same truck there's somethin' I want to tell you."

"What's wrong, John? You look so serious."

Reece licked his lips and rubbed his hands together and looked around to see if anyone was watching them. "I want to say good-bye. Just in case we don't see each other again for awhile I'm…"

"What are you talking about, where're you planning to go?" Al's asked, his face tensing without any trace of his usual friendly expression.

"It's likely best if you don't really know. I'm planning a little trip an' I might leave sudden-like tonight when we're…"

"It's the letter, I know it. You been thinking about this trip for a long time but the letter from your daughter's made you a little crazy, John. Are you sure it's the right time to…?"

"I'm goin', but I didn't want to leave without telling you how much I 'preciate you being my friend an' all." Reece noticed that Al had referred to the 'timing' and its importance, but Reece had made up his mind. "If I make it, someday I'm gonna' come see you out in California. I'm remembering you telling me about your uncle at Kino Springs, just across the border in Arizona. I'll get in touch with him to find out where you might be."

"You better come, and be sure and bring Eula Mae. I want to meet her and tell her what a fine daddy she's got. She don't really know you like I do. And I'll explain to her how I taught you how to cook." Al grinned, and then he frowned, and his face took on a worried look like Reece had never seen before and said, "Really, my friend, I'm asking you to not do this foolish thing you've planned so long. You know they'll come after you with everything they've got."

"No! I'm goin' I tell you. It's the only chance I've got. You'll be out in less than a year," Reece said emphatically. "You got family who can help you..."

"You two lyin' lazy bastards get busy! We're pulling out of here as soon as this stuff is loaded," Sanchez snapped impatiently, then added, "Reece, you'll be ridin' in the first truck, sittin' beside a guard and he'll tell you some of the things I'm gonna do to you when I get you back where you belong."

"Sí, Señor Sanchez," Reece barely whispered. His knees felt suddenly weak. He kneeled to the ground, shuffling items around him to appear busy, unable to focus, his head spinning with Sanchez's startling announcement.

Reece stole a glance up at the towering guard, who was looking at Al and grinning. At a glance Reece could see his friend was nervous.

"Limesand, your day's comin' too and you can't believe how much I'm gonna enjoy it." Sanchez turned and walked down along the line of trucks and went out of sight behind one near the end of the line.

Al's face lost its color. He knew the sergeant would keep his word. He tried to ignore it by saying, "John, I think you're making a big mistake -- remember what happened to Thompson. I don't ever want to see them bringing you in like that."

Reece barely heard Al's remarks as his mouth lost its saliva and the muscles in his throat tightened into a hard knot. He made no attempt to stand, convinced his legs would buckle if he tried. He stared at the ground and slowly shook his head in disbelief. The months of carefully made plans had been wasted. Once he was behind the prison walls again they'd keep him there until the day he died. There would be no second chance. Sneaking food to the Indian children had been an act Rodriguez could never forgive. He'd seen it as an act of complete defiance and disrespect.

The trucks were strung out for almost a mile as they labored over the dunes of wind-blown sand. The headlights of the trailing trucks were often obscured by spiraling sheets of fine grit the truck's spinning tires whipped into the hot night air.

Reece sat with his back to the cab of the truck with a guard alongside and at least another thirty men packed in around him. It would have been a perfect time to leap from the truck and sprint into the darkness if he were still just another prisoner.

Neither the heat nor the crowded conditions now mattered.

During his lifetime he'd suffered many setbacks but none such as this. He stared straight ahead at the silhouette of the man sitting in front of him, his mind and body now numbed by the misery and sadness sweeping over him. He'd lost track of Al. There was no way to even tell which truck he was riding in.

It was sometime after midnight when the truck he was riding in rolled through the open prison gates.

The stench and darkness were more depressing now than the first morning he'd climbed from a truck and looked around at his new home. He glanced up when a movement caught his eye.

The silhouetted upper body of a guard walking on the west wall of the compound was backlit by the half-moon dropping toward the horizon. The polished barrel of his rifle had caught the moon's rays when he turned and walked back toward the gun tower.

CHAPTER 19

TRAPPED ANTS

Six long days passed and Reece had seen Al only once, across the prisoner's dining hall. They'd exchanged a brief wave and both hurried on their way. They now ate in different shifts and slept in different wings of the prison.

Unable to concentrate on even the simplest duties for the first three days, Reece was now glad he'd been assigned to paint the walls and scrub the floor in the guards' dining room. As long as he kept busy he was left alone. The enthusiasm he'd felt after getting the letter from Eula Mae about her upcoming graduation had vanished without a trace. His spirits had soared beyond any previous experience until the fateful evening when he had to sit alongside one of the guards.

He had no appetite but forced himself to eat the meager rations. His mind dwelled on the ride through the sand dunes. The near-perfect conditions that had existed for an escape into the night now haunted him with an overwhelming gloom. Unable to sleep for more than brief periods of time, he felt weak and dejected.

While down on his hands and knees, Reece scrubbed and waxed the floor in the guard's dining room. The simple lonely job was a blessing. He needed to be alone to sort out his thoughts and fears. All of the elation and freedom he'd felt working on the line had turned to despair. He'd never get a second chance at freedom now.

At least ten days passed before Reece finished the cleaning and painting. He'd lost count. The routine passing of days no longer mattered. His new assignment by the guard, Flores, was to clean the storage area behind the kitchen. Crates with rotting vegetables and garbage had to be sorted and stacked for hauling to a nearby desert canyon.

Reece crawled along the back wall of the compound, using a small broom to thoroughly clean every bit of debris from the seam where the base of the stone wall joined the rough concrete floor. Foraging cockroaches and ants searching through the decaying litter darted aside. He would soon have the area ready for inspection.

Reece felt a sudden stinging pain just above the tongue of his shoe. Jerking up his pant leg, he slapped an ant that had sunk its pincers into the skin above his ankle. Within minutes, a large red welt covered the spot where the disturbed ant had bitten him.

When he reached the heavy timbered gate at the rear of the storage yard, he noticed a column of red ants carrying bits of discarded food through a narrow slit under the door sill. He envied them their freedom as he watched the ants scurrying back and forth in a ragged line, much like he'd done when taking water to the crews, their jaws locked onto the provisions they'd scavenged from the refuse.

Reece idly moved the broom back and forth as he watched the busy ants. He was almost finished for the day and he'd soon be taken back to his cellblock. Even though he'd lost all hope of having another chance to escape, he began thinking of a new possibility -- one more chance -- a desperate chance at best -- one that could only mean freedom or certain death. There could be no other outcome.

His mind began to race as never before as a plan took shape for one more high-risk attempt at freedom.

Leaping to his feet, he frantically began searching through the garbage for something he'd seen earlier but had forgotten which box he'd put it in. There would be little time to sort through the dozens of boxes stacked as high as he could reach along the wall.

A surge of new energy gave him almost unbelievable strength as he pawed through one box after another, dumping the contents on the clean concrete floor and scattering them for easier viewing. Sweat running into his eyes made it difficult to quickly scan the strewn debris. The once clean floor and neatly stacked boxes soon looked the same as when he'd started the cleaning project.

After what seemed like hours he spotted the item he was searching for, partly hidden under the moldy leaves of a head of lettuce. Reece grabbed the drinking glass with a crack spiraling up one side.

"Reece, what the hell have you been doing?" Flores boomed coming through the screen door that led out of the kitchen. "This place is a bigger mess than when you started this morning."

"I'm very sorry, *Señor* Flores, I got real sick but I'm feeling much better now. If you can just give me another hour I'll get it all cleaned up, I promise," Reece pleaded.

"You'll miss your supper but that's your problem," Flores snapped.

"Within one hour I'll be back and you'd better have this place spotless," Flores added, striding back into the kitchen.

It was sometime near midnight. Reece lay wide awake on his mattress, his clothes still damp from hurrying to refill and stack the boxes in the storage area. When he was sure all around were sleeping soundly, he brought out his jar of red ants and carefully removed the rag he'd tied over the top of the glass. Pressing the open mouth of the glass against his cheek, he kept the ants from escaping. Within seconds, Reece could feel the agitated ants crawling over his cheekbone looking for any avenue of escape. He slightly raised the edge of the glass, relieving the pressing ring on one side. He shuddered when he felt the pincers of several ants biting at the skin on his cheek, desperate in their attempt to gnaw their way to freedom.

He gritted his teeth as the painful minutes passed, while sliding the mouth of the jar up over his forehead and down the other side of his face then under his chin and across his throat. The diligent ants never gave up in their attempt to escape the glass enclosure, attacking his skin along the rim of the glass as soon as he gave them the slightest opening.

It was long past midnight when one man sat up on his mattress, then got up to relieve himself at the bucket in the corner. He stumbled over Reece's legs and muttered, "What the hell you doing sleeping on the floor, Reece?"

Reece groaned and turned over without answering. He'd already released the frantic ants and hidden the glass in his mattress. He was sure when daylight came his strange appearance would quickly result in a guard being summoned. Although exhausted, he felt a new surge of hope. Unable to sleep, he listened for the first waking sounds of the pigeons that nested under the eaves of the prison roof.

"Guard! Guard! There's something wrong with Reece. He's gasping for air and his face is red and swollen!"

As he heard the approaching steps of the guard, Reece flailed his head from side to side and pulled his knees up to his chest. He groaned and gasped for air.

After a brief look at Reece, the guard exclaimed, "I'd better get the *capitán*!" His footsteps faded as he ran down the hall. Reece hoped Rodriguez would become so alarmed when he saw his face that he would send him to the small hospital near Matamoros. Prison guards had often joked about the *capitán* being interested in a nurse named Maria who worked at the hospital.

There was a good chance the captain would personally drive Reece to the hospital.

"This had better be something unusual," Reece heard the captain's agitated voice when he entered the cell block and the sounds of his boot heels striking the concrete floor came closer. "Waking me up at daylight to show me a sick prisoner may cost you a month's pay."

When they reached the cell, Rodriguez asked, "What's this man's name?"

"Reece. John Reece."

"Reece?" Rodriguez muttered sarcastically.

Reece lay with his face toward the wall. Seeing all the welts at once would give Rodriguez a bigger shock.

"Turn him over. Let me see what you're talking about," Rodriguez said impatiently.

"*Madre mía.*" Rodriguez's voice was slow and deliberate, indicating the depth of his concerns. He backed up a couple of steps, "This could be something serious." There was another pause while he collected his thoughts and decided on what should be done next. "Get Flores in here and have him take a look at this man and then tell him to check the roster in my office for the names of all the men who worked on the line crew!"

"*Sí, Capitán.*"

"I need to know if any other men on the crew have developed these symptoms and get Gonzsales to start checking on all the other prisoners, too. We need to get on this right away! Tell him to report to me in my quarters as soon as possible."

"I'll run and wake Flores, *Capitán*, then I'll be right back."

"Don't forget Gonzsales!" Rodriguez yelled as the guard's running steps faded.

Within minutes Flores came hurrying down the hall, asking rapidfire questions of the guard on duty. Flores stopped when he reached the cell where Reece lay with his knees pulled up to his chest.

"My God, what's happened to his face? It looks like hell!" Flores said aloud. "You say this man is Reece? If it is he sure didn't look like this when I brought him in about dark. But he did say he'd been sick earlier in the day."

"It's John Reece, *Señor* Flores. I'm sure about that. He's one of the cooks they brought back from working on the line. He lost so much weight while he was gone, I hardly recognized him."

"I'll be back as soon as I check the rest of the men who were with him. They could have picked up something in the desert. If they did we could have an epidemic on our hands! Let me know if you hear anything from Gonzales."

Within minutes after the guards left Reece struggled to his feet, went to the bucket and relieved himself. He lay back down on his mattress and continued breathing hard, rolling his head from side to side at times while spit drooled from the corners of his mouth.

He knew there was little concern for the well-being of any one prisoner, especially him. However, there was a chance his plan might work. Someone would probably take him in to see the doctor. From the reaction by the guards, he could tell his face must present a disgusting sight. He knew his eyes were almost swollen shut. The guards' fears of some deadly disease spreading throughout the entire prison population and all who worked there was all he could have hoped for.

While waiting for the guard's return he thought again of his plan of racing into the darkness. If he could have leaped from the truck near where the Rio San Juan ran into the Conchos, he would have had a good chance of making it to the mountains. By now, with a little luck, he could have been almost to the border.

The vast desolation of the Sierra chain of peaks that extended the Rocky Mountains into Mexico could swallow up an entire army sent to run him down.

"Here comes the *capitán* and he's got Flores and Gonzales with him." It sounded like Kilgore's voice from somewhere down the cell-block.

"So far Reece is the only one." Reece heard the unmistakable high-pitched voice of Flores giving a report to Rodriguez. "By tomorrow who knows how many there could be."

"We better get him in to the hospital and have Doctor Alvarez see if he can tell what's wrong with him." Rodriguez's voice had an urgency to it. "We don't want this thing to spread. Reece could have picked up something from those damn dirty Indians hanging around our camp. Sometimes they get sick and die off like flies."

Reece knew there was a good chance Rodriguez would be the one to drive him to the hospital. If the rumors were true that Rodriguez was bothered by the nurse Maria's lack of interest in his attempts to court her he wouldn't pass up another opportunity to try again. Most women would no doubt be pleased to be seen with the tall muscular captain. For some reason, the captain couldn't accept the fact that the hospital nurse showed so little interest toward him. Her reserved manner was a challenge to his ego.

This time he'd have an excuse to show off the expensive custom-made rifle the Swede had given him as a present. Most anyone, Reece knew, would have to be impressed with the beautiful ivory inlays contrasting against the dark grain of the rifle's walnut stock.

"I'm going to go shave and shower and change my clothes. While I'm gone, Flores, I want you to get my handcuffs from the wall in my office and put them on Reece. Cuff him in front. If he has to take a leak he can do it without me having to get near him to remove the cuffs," Rodriguez ordered.

"*Sí. Capitán.*"

"Another thing, go ahead and put him in the back of my truck and watch him until I get there."

"Get on your feet, Reece. You're going for a ride," Flores said sharply.

Reece slowly struggled to his feet and stood on wobbly legs as Rodriguez took out his watch and checked the time.

"Five minutes after ten. That'll work just fine," Rodriguez smiled and pivoted with the precision of his military school training and started down the corridor.

Reece noticed the broad shoulders of the captain and his agile movements when he was in a hurry. The former champion boxer would be a dreadful opponent for any man half Reece's age.

CHAPTER 20

DOCTOR'S OFFICE

The recently installed telephone on the wall at the nurses' station began to ring. Assuming the call would likely be for him, Dr. Alvarez listened, waiting for the nurse to answer it. He took another long deep drag on the Camel cigarette he'd lit when he sat down at his desk. It was almost noon and this was the first break he had been able to take. He hadn't counted them but he knew he must have seen over twenty patients since 7:00 a. m. He felt the soothing rich taste of the tobacco relax him. Leaning back, he blew the smoke at the ceiling in his office, adding slightly to the 14 years' worth of tobacco residue that formed a greenish-brown patina in a large circle above his desk.

"I'm sorry doctor, but there's another call for you," the nurse said, poking her head into his office doorway and frowning. "It's from the prison."

Alvarez stepped into the hall and picked up the telephone. "Hello, this is Dr…"

"This is Captain Rodriguez. I'll be in the clinic with a prisoner in one half-hour," Rodriguez interrupted Alvarez, making no attempt at a cordial greeting.

Alvarez felt the blood rush to his face and neck. He took a short breath and held it. The sound of the captain's voice evoked a bitter memory. Alvarez was well aware of Rodriguez's attraction to his favorite nurse, Maria. He had had a serious altercation with the captain in Maria's presence at the warden's daughter's wedding the previous summer. Alvarez seethed every time Rodriguez found an excuse to visit the hospital.

"I see." Alvarez's hand trembled as he held the receiver but he tried to keep his voice calm. Alvarez glanced at the clock. "Can't this wait until after lunch? We've been swamped all morning and…"

"No! This is an emergency," the captain interrupted again. "This man's got ugly red spots on his face. It could be something contagious, even the beginning of some kind of plague!" Even though Rodriguez's voice on the new telephone was scratchy, it came through loud and insistent.

Alvarez was determined to keep his composure. The captain's habit of timing his arrival at the prison to coincide with the midday meal was irritating to him. When a prisoner wasn't considered dangerous, it gave Rodriguez a chance to sit in the patio with his favorite nurse Maria while Alvarez was busy with the patient. The quiet attractive nurse who seldom showed much emotion had never been married as far as Dr. Alvarez knew. She was the one Alvarez relied on when he was performing a difficult surgery.

Alvarez paused, considering his options. "This doesn't sound like an emergency, really nothing that serious. If you could just wait until…"

Rodriguez interrupted again, saying in a slow and sarcastic tone, "I told you I'm coming in now and I expect you to take care of this man. We must know what he's got! Or would you prefer I tell the warden that you are now refusing to handle prison emergencies?"

"All right, bring the prisoner in," said the doctor wearily. Alvarez's slow response had only made Rodriguez more demanding.

Alvarez walked down the hall to check on a teen-aged boy who had lost a lot of blood from a nosebleed earlier in the morning. The bleeding had stopped after Alvarez had gently pushed a caustic stick up the boy's bleeding nostril, searing the exposed vein. Alvarez saw that the boy was sleeping peacefully and that his pulse was strong.

Returning to his office, Alvarez stopped when he reached the door with the divided panes that led out to the patio. He could see Maria bending over, brushing the top of one of the benches at the table under one of the olive trees. The slight swaying of her hips with each stroke of her moving hand excited Alvarez. He glanced around to see if anyone had noticed him watching her. The staff had either gone to lunch or were busy with patients.

It was no secret that he was very fond of the pretty, shapely nurse. He'd overheard comments on more than one occasion. Even his wife, the mother of his six children, had sharply questioned him about his rumored interest. Of course, he had denied it. Still, he would have been flattered if he thought Maria had ever given him a second thought in any kind of romantic way. His reflection in the glass panes confirmed what he had known for many years. He was short and overweight. His hair was thinning. The long strands he tried to comb across the balding area on the top of his head would usually slip back down toward his ears before noon. Sweating from exertion in the summer heat often made him look unkept and slovenly. He knew there was little he could do about it.

Alvarez turned away from his reflection and returned to his office. Through the windows on the east wall of his office he could now see a column of dust trailing a vehicle coming fast along the dirt road that led to the prison.

He estimated the distance to the rising dust trail at no more than four or five miles. If it was the truck Rodriguez usually drove, it had come about halfway from the prison and they would arrive within minutes.

Dr. Alvarez waited for the arrival of the vehicle and tried to read a brief article on the recommended treatment for typhoid fever. While trying to concentrate on the article, Alvarez nervously tapped a yellow wooden pencil against the head of a brass armadillo with green glassy eyes. He used the gift from his father-in-law as a paperweight.

Alvarez's mind, however, was still on the nurse now sitting on a bench in the shade. By gripping the arms on his chair and pushing himself up a few inches, he could see Maria through his office window. The grove of olive trees was less than forty yards from the west wall of his office. The flat-roofed addition to the hospital had been built as an office and storage room for Alvarez. The three exterior walls gave him privacy and a view to the east, south and west.

Alvarez was disgusted with the very thought of Rodriguez arriving and joining Maria at the table.

After reading to the bottom of the first page, the doctor realized he couldn't remember anything that he had just read. He would need to reread the entire article later. Alvarez closed his eyes but the recollection of the wedding day at the warden's estate wouldn't go away. Rodriguez, in a drunken state, had shoved the new bride's husband against a table. The young groom had confronted the captain for fondling his new wife while on the dance floor. When Alvarez tried to intercede, Rodriguez became enraged and the confrontation quickly escalated into a mismatched challenge.

The sound of a vehicle bouncing over the ruts in the graveled parking and delivery area jerked Alvarez's thoughts out of the past. Rodriguez was driving, while a man in prison clothes sat in the back against the tailgate. White bed sheets, hanging on a cotton clothesline, waved gently in the breeze, partially blocking Alvarez's view of the men as they got out of the truck and started for the back door of the hospital.

Partially hidden behind the window curtain, Dr. Alvarez watched the captain follow several steps behind the prisoner. The man's ruddy complexion and sun-bleached hair gave him the appearance of an *americano*. Walking unsteadily up to the rear entry, the man showed obvious difficulty climbing the four steps to the landing, losing his balance and almost falling when he reached the third stone step. On his second try, with his handcuffed wrists extended forward for balance and his fingers trembling noticeably, he made it onto the landing with slow, careful steps.

Alvarez sat down at his desk. He was holding a medical journal, as if in deep concentration, when the head nurse ushered Rodriguez and his prisoner into the room.

"This is the man I was telling you about. You can see I was right," Rodriguez blurted.

"Here is the file on this man doctor. It doesn't have much about him except that his height is 5' 10" and he weighed 207 pounds when he first arrived at the prison," said the duty nurse, handing the folder to the doctor. She smiled and added, "It does look like we will need to weigh him again, however. About 160 pounds at the most, I'd say."

Nurse Gomez was standing slightly to the rear of the captain. She caught the doctor's eye and pointed toward Rodriguez's waistline. Shrugging her shoulders, she grinned. It was obvious to both that the captain had gained several pounds around his midsection.

"His name is Reece. *Señor* John Reece. He is an *americano* and he is forty-seven years old," the nurse continued.

"Thank you, Miss Gomez." Alvarez detected a strong whiff of perfume that he assumed the young nurse was wearing that he hadn't noticed earlier.

Dr. Alvarez now had the captain on his ground. He waited for a few moments as he moved closer to the prisoner, noting spittle drooling down Reece's chin and his unblinking half-closed eyes staring downward. Alvarez casually took his stethoscope from a shelf while he glanced at the swollen markings on Reece's face and forehead. He then acknowledged Rodriguez's opening comment.

"Your concerns are understandable in light of this man's appearance." After unbuttoning Reece's shirt, Alvarez pushed it down off his shoulders to below his elbows, just above his cuffed wrists. In the small mirror on the wall Alvarez could see the tense look on Rodriguez's face. The captain was clearly concerned about Reece's condition. Alvarez saw no reason to hurry his diagnosis. It was a pleasure to see Rodriguez looking so worried. He had to be thinking how quickly a serious disease could spread throughout a confined area like a prison.

"*Señor* Reece," Alvarez said, placing the stethoscope on Reece's upper shoulders, "I need you to take a few deep breaths."

At first, Reece gave no indication he'd heard the doctor, then, without any outward change in appearance, he breathed deeply. Almost immediately, Reece leaned forward in a fit of coughing. When Reece reached out to a small table to steady himself, Rodriguez backed up by the door, his eyes widening. Alvarez frowned and peered over the top of his glasses at Reece, knowing his reaction would worry Rodriguez.

Moving the stethoscope across Reece's back, Alvarez listened for any signs of obstruction or wheezing. The lungs were clear with no indication of congestion. Alvarez made no comment on his findings, but at a glance he saw that Rodriguez had shifted his position to where he could also glance out the window at Maria.

After taking Reece's blood pressure, Alvarez was puzzled but not too surprised. "Miss Gomez, please note that *Señor* Reece's systolic pressure is 110. The diastolic pressure is 60 and his heart rate is 46 beats per minute. His lungs are clear." Alvarez doubted Rodriguez would understand the significance of the numbers. "Did you get those figures recorded, Miss Gomez?" Alvarez could now see the flirtatious nurse's profile in the mirror on the wall.

"*Sí,* Doctor," Miss Gomez said, looking up at Rodriguez and smiling as she moistened the pencil eraser with her tongue and slid it across her lower lip. When Rodriguez didn't seem to notice her, the attractive nurse turned and straightened some papers on the doctor's desk. With her lips in a pout she seemed peeved, well aware that Rodriguez's attention, like Alvarez's, was divided between the prisoner and Maria.

Alvarez rubbed his hand over the muscles on Reece's upper shoulders and arms. They were lean and hard. Except for the spittle drooling down Reece's chin and the fit of coughing, he appeared to be in excellent condition for a man half his age. The marks on his face were a different matter.

"The man's lost a lot of weight in the last few months. Has he been ill?"

"No, he's been working on the telegraph line we're building down across the high desert from Nacozari -- had an easy job taking water to the crews -- sometimes he helped with the cooking."

"I see. What about this nasty scar across his ear? Looks like he's taken an awful wallop to the head not long ago. Any chance he got kicked by a mule?"

"Stop wasting my time. What do you make of the spots on his face? Are they contagious or not?"

"What's this?" thought Alvarez, "The captain is going to allow a doctor to have a medical opinion?"

"Frankly, I'm puzzled but it doesn't appear to be too serious," Alvarez said, shaking his head, even though he doubted Reece was seriously ill or even ill at all. Alvarez knew of Rodriguez's concerns about germs and any kind of a disease. The man was obsessed with his own personal cleanliness, wearing a clean, pressed uniform each day, his boots polished to a high sheen. Alvarez felt envious that Rodriguez had a job that provided leisure and plenty of time for meticulous grooming. Since Alvarez's mid-teens his studies had taken long hours each day. Sometimes he'd heard roosters crow, announcing the dawn, before he realized he'd studied all night.

In the mirror Alvarez could see that Rodriguez was now beginning to relax, repeatedly glancing toward the patio and smoothing his mustache. Seeing that the doctor did not fear to rub his hands over Reece's back had lessened the captain's concerns, Alvarez assumed.

Reece still hadn't made a sound except for the coughing or even looked around the room. If he had any feelings at the moment he was keeping them to himself.

The spots on Reece's face appeared to be individual lacerations or possible bite marks by a horde of insects. Surely, anyone subjected to such an attack would be well aware of it at the time of occurrence. They didn't indicate any kind of plague Alvarez had studied about in medical school.

"This may take some time to diagnose," Alvarez said, shrugging his shoulders and laying the stethoscope back on a shelf. "I'll need to read some reference material. It certainly is unusual, something I've never seen before." Alvarez wanted to talk to the man in private.

"Fine, I'll wait outside, Doctor."

Alvarez could hardly believe it. Rodriguez for the first time had referred to him as a doctor. Alvarez turned to the nurse, "You may go ahead and go to lunch, too, Miss Gomez. I don't think I'm going to need any assistance in this matter."

Rodriguez opened the door for Miss Gomez. "You won't have to worry about this one -- he won't give you any trouble, you can count on it." The captain started to follow the nurse out the door. He stopped and grinned and nodding his head for emphasis, added, "*Señor* Reece will behave himself -- he has a real good memory."

Reece glanced briefly to his left as Rodriguez followed Miss Gomez through the open door, then lowered his eyes to the floor again.

"You can check back in about 20 minutes or so, *Capitán*. I should know something by then," Alvarez said.

As the door closed behind Rodriguez, the doctor turned to take a magnifying glass from a shelf. He idly polished off the dust on the glass with the tail of his stained smock.

As Alvarez continued to polish the glass he heard the squeaking of the captain's boots when he left the chair outside the door. Alvarez wondered if Reece knew the routine when prisoners were brought into the hospital. He seemed to be aware that the captain was leaving the assigned station, glancing briefly in the direction of the squeaking sounds.

Alvarez watched while partially screened by the curtain on the office window that overlooked the patio. Rodriguez didn't emerge from the side door. Alvarez turned when he heard the sound of a door closing. Rodriguez was on the steps on the opposite side of his office where Reece had almost fallen as they entered from the parking lot. He was going toward his truck. From the cab of the vehicle Rodriguez took a long leather case and walked around the rear wall of Alvarez's office toward the patio. It looked like a saddle scabbard for a rifle. But why, Alvarez wondered, would Rodriguez be carrying a rifle over to the table where Maria was sitting?

Maria smiled and said something to Rodriguez as he approached. Alvarez immediately felt contempt and hatred boiling up inside him. He had been mildly annoyed when Miss Gomez had tried to subtly flirt with Rodriguez. Seeing the smile on Maria's beautiful round face and the flash of her white teeth when she greeted the handsome captain, however, was a totally different matter. The picturesque setting with the two people engaged in conversation was maddening to Alvarez. He continued to watch for several minutes, straining to hear their conversation, but they were too far away to hear, except for an occasional word. He wished that he was standing in the captain's place and that Rodriguez had the responsibility of examining the unsightly sores on his prisoner's face.

Alvarez looked down when he realized he was still vigorously rubbing the round magnifying lens and gritting his teeth.

After laying the case on the end of the table, Rodriguez put the toe of his right boot on the bench, inches from Maria's shapely thigh. The noonday sun glistened off the highly polished boot. Alvarez looked down at his own shabby, unpolished shoes and realized he should spend some of his salary on himself. He immediately thought of his spendthrift wife and the fashionable way she dressed herself and the children.

Remembering he had a patient, Alvarez glanced at Reece but was unable to pull himself away from the window. The man with splotches on his face could wait. This wasn't an emergency. He turned back to the couple whose features were accentuated by the filtered shadows of the olive leaves gently waving in the breeze.

When Rodriguez drew a rifle with a dark, glinting stock from the scabbard and held it up for Maria to see, Alvarez felt a knot twist inside his stomach. "I hope the bastard rots in hell!" he muttered under his breath.

With another quick glimpse at Reece, Alvarez noticed the man lower his eyes. For a moment it appeared he, too, might have been checking on the whereabouts of Rodriguez but then Reece reached out to the back of Alvarez's chair to steady himself, feebly coughing like an old man.

Alvarez moved close to Reece and began to study the sores on the side of his face with the magnifying glass. "These look like some kind of bite…"

"Don't make a sound or I'll slit your goddam throat!"

Something sharp was pressing lightly against the doctor's jugular vein. He then remembered he had earlier left a small scalpel lying on a table when he lanced a patient's boil. With one hand Reece had a tight grip on Alvarez's collar and the other hand held the scalpel. Alvarez knew immediately that even though Reece was handcuffed, one quick thrust with the sharp, short-bladed knife could easily sever his jugular. Terrified, he jerked his head backward. The sting of the blade slicing along under his jawbone was immediate.

"Please, *Señor* Reece -- I mean you no harm."

Reece moved closer, his face inches from the doctor's, forcing Alvarez back against the door to the storage and supply room. Alvarez could feel blood running down from where the blade had slashed from just below his ear to a point under his chin.

"Then you better not make a sound an' do exactly as I say. I'll kill you 'fore I go back to that stinkin' prison!"

"Yes! Yes! I -- I'll do anything you say. What do you want me to do?" Alvarez glanced out to the patio. Rodriguez was facing away from the hospital, gesturing with his left hand in his discussion with Maria. The lazy captain of the guards had left Alvarez alone with a vicious killer.

"Show me where you keep your hot water bottles, rolls of tape an' ether." Reece's eyes swept the room. "And I'll keep the knife."

The man who less than a minute before appeared ready to collapse now moved with a calm self-control. At a glance, Reece took in the situation with Rodriguez in the patio. "I'll take the magnifying glass and I'll need a screwdriver."

"May -- may I ask what you want the ether for? You're not going to use it on me -- are you?" Alvarez asked the man whose face was a mask of quiet determination, a man who must have spent months calculating the odds on such a high-risk attempt at freedom. But it was the demand for the anesthetic that frightened Alvarez. The careless use of ether by an untrained person could easily cripple or kill an individual. Even highly skilled doctors often made mistakes.

"No, the ether ain't for you. I really don't want to hurt you none, doctor, 'less you cross me. It's just that you are my only way to escape. You gotta move fast 'cause I jest got minutes to get out of here 'fore Rodriguez comes back."

"But -- but how could you ever hope to get away with your hands all...?"

"A set of extra keys is tied to the springs under the truck seat."

"But what about the swollen lumps on your face, aren't you worried about them? Don't you want me to..."

"Nothin' but ant bites."

"Ant bites?" Alvarez could scarcely believe what he'd heard.

He knew this bold cunning prisoner would kill him in an instant if he had to. Anyone who let ants crawl over his face and bite him had to have a disposition of unbelievable resolve.

"They were trapped in a glass. Now get the things I need!" Reece tightened his grip on Alvarez's collar, their legs bumping together as Reece crowded against him, backing him through the narrow doorway into the supply room.

"Put 'em all right there," said Reece, nodding toward a small table by Alvarez's desk.

Alvarez felt a sense of relief. Reece wasn't acting on a sudden impulse. As long as he received complete cooperation there would be no reason for Reece to kill him. Alvarez knew he hadn't been hurt too badly yet. The bleeding from the cut on his throat was barely dripping onto his smock,

"I may die in a Mexican desert but I ain't gonna' die in a Mexican prison," the lean determined prisoner stated quietly.

Hearing the sound of raised voices from the direction of the olive trees, both Alvarez and Reece looked out the window.

Rodriguez had a frown on his face as he stood with the leather scabbard in one hand and the rifle in the other. Could it be that Maria didn't think it appropriate for the captain to display such a weapon at the hospital?

"May I ask what you want the hot water bottles for?" Alvarez couldn't imagine Reece's intended use.

"Canteens." Reece glanced again out the window on the west wall. "Get that can of ether, too." Reece nodded toward one of the shelves in the closet. "Hurry! I gotta' get out of here," Reece ordered curtly.

Dumping the contents from the field pack he used on his bird-watching walks, Alvarez stuffed the items Reece had demanded into the canvas container. Of course, Alvarez realized, the rubber bottles would make perfect canteens if Reece knew of some magic way to squeeze water from the hot desert sands. Still, this man had spent a lot of time in the desert between the prison and Nacozari, below the border town of Nogales. Canteens for carrying water would be the most vital equipment for crossing the desert. Alvarez realized Reece could become famous if he beat all odds, making good his escape.

There would be reporters asking questions. Best of all, Alvarez thought -- this could be big trouble for the smug Rodriguez who had left a dangerous prisoner alone with the doctor.

"I put in some salt tablets. You'll need them too, long before you reach the states -- and here is a pouch of dried fruit. You should take it too."

"I need a towel an' open that can of ether!"

Alvarez's hands began to shake, "You said you were going to take it with you -- that you didn't mean to hurt…"

"I don't. Now open it!"

"But it'll evaporate almost immediately," explained Alvarez.

"I may need it right away if I don't get outta' here quick!" Reece said, cutting his eyes toward the olive trees. "Hurry an' don't ask so many questions. I'll keep my thumb over the opening an' you can wrap the towel around my hands…"

"I can be sent to prison if I help you!" Alvarez pleaded, realizing the ether might be used in some way in an attack on Rodriguez.

"Not now with that cut on your throat -- strip me off a piece of that widest tape an' unroll ten feet of that gauze an' cut it off."

"Now put your hands behind your back so I can wrap 'em an' hold still while I put the tape across your mouth. I can open the ether if I need it."

As Reece started to put the tape over Alvarez's mouth the doctor said, "One moment please. I just want you to know I don't hold any of this against you. I've seen desperate men try to escape before, but I believe you just might be the first to make it. I certainly hope so. You can rest assured you'll be in my prayers."

"Thank you doctor -- but let me tell you -- if you're lying to me an' you call out a warnin' I'll slit your throat from ear to ear like you was a fattenin' hog!" The expression on Reece's face hardened. Rodriguez appeared ready to leave the patio and return to his truck with the rifle. His back was toward Maria as he jammed the rifle back into the scabbard.

After taping Alvarez's mouth, Reece clumsily worked the gauze around Alvarez's wrists and back between his forearms. Alvarez realized it was a part of Reece's plan that he hadn't been able to practice. The handcuffs made it difficult for Reece to wrap the gauze and tie a tight knot.

"Leavin' you taped up like this, nobody'll blame you 'cause I got away. You can get it loose in a while."

Reece moved to the open window overlooking the parking area. He sliced away the screens, rolled them up and crammed them into the canvas bag while keeping an eye on Rodriguez.

Alvarez wondered why the prisoner would want the screens.

Reece seemed to note the confusion on Alvarez's face. "Rattlers an' thorns." Reece pointed to his lower legs.

Alvarez could see that when the metal mesh was wrapped in layers and fastened around Reece's lower thighs and down to his ankles, the lightweight screen would make perfect leggings. Alvarez nodded enthusiastically.

Reece reached out the open window where he'd cut the screens away and lowered the bag to the ground then turned quickly back to Alvarez. "Sit down here on the floor by the table." Reece picked up a corner of the table and put the leg back down between Alvarez's forearms, just above where his hands were tied. He looked around the room then glanced out toward the parking area. Reece looked troubled as his eyes swept the room again. He squatted, peering back under the overhanging shelves on Alvarez's rolltop desk. Alvarez nervously watched as Reece slid the hospital's prized microscope toward him and picked it up. He then sat it on the corner of the table above the leg standing between Alvarez's bound wrists. Alvarez would now be unable to simply tilt the table and free himself. It would take time to untie the knotted gauze bindings. The precarious position of the expensive microscope would ensure Reece the extra minutes he needed. Alvarez was amazed. It was obvious Reece had little formal education but in a game of wits his moves were astonishing.

Reece grabbed the can of ether, sat it on the table, jabbed the point of the screwdriver into the metal top then covered the hole with his thumb. Pulling a white towel off a shelf with his teeth, Reece shook out the folds and draped it over his hands, slipped out the door and quietly closed it.

The strong odor of ether immediately filled the room.

Alvarez listened intently. He then realized Reece was sitting in the chair just outside of his office door when the chair back scraped against the wall.

Alvarez slid his wrists up the table leg until he could kneel and peek over the window sill. He watched Rodriguez walking briskly up to the steps of the rear entrance. The captain was scowling. Alvarez was pleased. It seemed obvious something had gone wrong with Rodriguez's visit with Maria.

When Rodriguez disappeared into the door leading into the hall that ran past the laundry room, Alvarez listened and strained to hear any conversation when the captain reached the area where Reece was waiting.

"What are you doing sitting out here?" Rodriguez asked in an irritated sounding voice.

"A man got hurt," Alvarez heard Reece cough before he added slowly, "an he's bleedin' real bad...the nurse tole me to wait for you out here." Reece's voice sounded weak and wheezy.

"What's the towel for?"

"Got medicine on it..." There was another pause then Alvarez heard Reece add, "Doctor said if I ain't well in two days -- bring me back." Alvarez realized that even though his mouth was taped his face muscles were straining to pull his lips into a grin. He listened with pleasure as Reece began another fit of coughing. Alvarez marveled that Reece could sit there with such patience and control, setting his trap for the unsuspecting captain.

"It sure does stink. Just what kind of rotten disease did the doctor say you have?" Rodriguez asked, a sarcastic tone in his voice.

"Jest some big words, I didn't know none of 'em -- but said what I got ain't ketchin'."

"Come on, let's get out of here!" Rodriguez ordered sharply.

Alvarez listened as the sounds of the men's footsteps moved down the hall toward the door that led out to the captain's parked truck. The doctor's knees were shaking as he watched Reece hesitate before attempting the four steps to the ground. Slowly, Reece descended the stairs then wobbled unsteadily toward the truck, still keeping up his act to fool Rodriguez.

As both men reached the truck, Alvarez realized he was holding his breath. If Reece was going to make his move it would have to be now before Rodriguez climbed into the truck's cab. Was it possible the handcuffed prisoner would lose his nerve? Alvarez didn't think so.

Rodriguez took out his keys and pointed toward the open truck bed. When he turned and opened the door the towel was just a white blur as Reece leaped onto Rodriguez's back, hooking the short links on his cuffed wrists over Rodriguez's head and up under his chin. Rodriguez whirled and fought desperately to escape from the suffocating, ether-laced towel held tightly against his nose and mouth. He slammed Reece from side to side and then banged him back over the truck's fender. Alvarez watched the two men struggle through the open window. Alvarez was gripping his fist tightly when it became apparent Reece couldn't let go even if he tried.

Blood began to spurt from Reece's scarred ear when Rodriguez lunged backward, knocking Reece's head against the edge of the open door frame. Reece, however, was still able to keep the towel clutched over Rodriguez's face. Finally, the powerful legs of the captain wobbled as he staggered around in a small circle. He stopped, gave a muffled cry and went down hard, his face driving into the parking lot's dirt and graveled surface.

Alvarez watched in disbelief. Reece grabbed the key ring from where Rodriguez dropped it, switched the handcuffs onto the captain and dragged his limp form back into the building.

Within seconds Reece ran out of the rear door carrying Rodriguez's boots. He raced to where the dried sheets were hanging on the cotton clothesline, stripped away the bedding and slashed the lines from between the dark weathered post. Alvarez ducked out of sight when he saw Reece wheel and dart toward the window. He heard Reece's pounding feet as he came on full speed for the bag he'd lowered. Less than five feet from the window, Alvarez heard him slide to a stop, grunt, suck in a deep breath and start back for the parking area. Alvarez peeked over the window sill and saw Reece in an all-out sprint to the truck.

Dr. Alvarez watched as the escaping prisoner gunned the motor, flooding the engine. The motor sputtered and died. In haste Reece had given it too much gas. Long minutes passed before Reece was able to start the motor again. When it finally caught, Reece let out the clutch, sending a spray of gravel and dirt over the clean sheets lying scattered where Reece had dropped them. Reece cut the wheels sharply down a lane that would lead to the long alkali valley to the west. A column of rising dust soon obscured the speeding truck from view.

The lone nurse on duty during the siesta suddenly stepped out onto the landing at the top of the stairs. She glanced in the direction of the trail of dust. Putting her hands on her hips with her feet spread she stood looking at the sheets spotted with dirt and pebbles. She shook her head in bewilderment and went back inside.

Beads of sweat were running down Alvarez's face when he realized he was still kneeling and looking down the long valley where the last of the dust was settling. When his hands finally pulled free of the gauze bindings, Alvarez stood on cramped legs and looked into the mirror below the clock. The tape across his mouth only partly hid his strained expression. Alvarez raised his chin and looked with disappointment at the cut under his jaw where the blood had begun to coagulate. It would heal in a few days with no chance of leaving any scar. If there were to be interviews and pictures appearing later in newspapers, such a shallow wound could be an embarrassment. Jokes could be made about anything so trivial.

If, however, he was found where things in his office had been broken and knocked about, it would all make for a much more interesting story. It could all be done quietly, now. A few glass vials could be broken under water in his basin, dried and left scattered on the floor.

Since the nurses would be returning soon, he'd have to hurry with his other idea. Standing in front of the mirror, Dr. Alvarez tilted his head again and lightly touched the skin where the blade had left a clean shallow cut. If the cut was deepened and made more obvious, that would definitely make his story more compelling.

A piece of broken glass would do the job nicely, after an application of a topical dressing to deaden the pain. Most important, Maria might even be impressed. After all, he had been attacked by a desperate prisoner and survived. Alvarez could honestly say Reece had slashed his throat with a knife. The thought of Rodriguez being punished even more if the gash was more life-threatening pleased Alvarez.

With blood on his smock and the floor, who would ever question him? Afterwards, Alvarez could push his hands back inside the gauze Reece had clumsily wrapped around his wrists. When he heard the steps of approaching nurses, he could lie down and kick at the closed door.

Dr. Alvarez reached for a bottle of novocaine and removed the cap. He took a sponge and rubbed the liquid along the thin red line running under his jawbone. He looked at himself in the mirror again, pushing a strand of hair across the bald area on top of his head where a shock of thick auburn hair had once grown. His heart was racing wildly. He'd seldom felt such exhilaration.

The sounds of rapid footsteps came from somewhere in the building. There was no time to let the Novocaine take effect. Holding his head at an angle, Dr. Alvarez with a shaking hand raked the point of the glass forward.

Blood gushed from the jagged cut. Alvarez realized that in his haste he had made the cut too deep. Feeling faint, he tried to wrap the gauze he'd taken from his wrists around his face and under his jaw where the blood was flowing freely.

CHAPTER 21

FLIGHT

It was like a strange dream -- an ominous floating sensation, with muffled sounds nearby. When the sounds became more distinct, Captain Rodriguez realized he was hearing the laughter of young women. He tried to turn his head to see where they were. Some type of cloth lay on the side of his face and as he tried to move, the dreamy euphoria abruptly faded. His face was pressed against a grit-covered floor. He knew he was no longer dreaming when he tasted blood on his lips and a revolting odor surged into his nostrils. It was then he realized the cloth lying over his cheek reeked of stale urine. He swallowed hard to keep from vomiting while fear and panic gripped him.

Stabbing pain encircled his wrists when he struggled to get to his feet. It was then he knew his hands were manacled behind his back. The metal clamps cutting into his wrists numbed his hands and fingers.

Lashing out with both feet, the terrified captain rolled over and thrust himself up into a kneeling position. Soiled bed sheets and dirty garments slid off his head and shoulders, bunching around his thighs. The sudden realization that he had been lying under a pile of dirty laundry sent a chill across his back and lifted the hair on the nape of his neck. The warm, bitter taste of bile suddenly flooded his throat then gushed from his mouth, spraying across the sheets and clothing. He was overwhelmed with disgust and confusion.

He strained until the muscles and tendons in his neck and shoulders popped, but his hands stayed locked behind him. He had never known such a feeling of helplessness. Hundreds of times he'd placed men in handcuffs and never given it a second thought. It was different now.

Rodriguez struggled up and stood weaving until his head began to clear. He looked down at his stocking-covered feet. His custom-made boots were nowhere in sight. The ring of keys he kept snapped on a belt loop was also missing. Suddenly he realized that his prisoner must be missing too and he could only guess at what other events might have occurred. He vaguely remembered falling, his face driving into the gravel. The captain tasted the blood in his mouth again and his tongue probed the deep cut inside his lower lip.

"*Capitán* Rodriguez, why are you sleeping in the laundry room -- have you been drinking?"

Rodriguez turned and saw two young women standing in the doorway of the dimly lit room. One of them nervously giggled.

The captain's thinking was now more lucid. It was his prisoner John Reece who'd jumped him, holding something stinking over his face and around his neck and almost choking him to death. It must have been Reece who'd handcuffed and hid him under that pile of filth!

But where was his prisoner now? One thing the captain was absolutely sure of -- when he found Reece, he would curse the day he was born.

One of the women cleared her throat, bringing the captain's attention back to his immediate problem.

He must appear calm while he thought of a way to keep others from learning of his shameful predicament. "You must hurry and do exactly as I say. Go out in back and look under the seat in the green prison truck. You'll find a keyring tied to the springs. Bring it to me and if anyone asks you what you are doing, don't tell them anything! Don't tell them anything at all. Now go!"

Both women turned and hurried out the door. Rodriguez looked around the room. As his eyes adjusted to the dim light, he saw pale yellow bars of lye soap stacked on a shelf behind a wooden bench where three galvanized tubs sat in a row. Washboards with rows of ribbed metal ridges used for rubbing the dirt and stains from clothing and bedding were hanging on nails on the opposite wall. There were galvanized pails that he knew were for carrying in heated water from the three-legged black cast-iron pots that sat out past the clothes lines in back of the building. The very thought of women picking up the hospital's soiled garments and sheets with their bare hands, dipping them down into hot soapy water and then rubbing them on the washboards until they were clean, filled him with revulsion.

Long-suppressed memories of his childhood flooded his thoughts. As a small boy he'd stood and watched his mother bending over the side of a hot steaming tub of water, her hands moving with a ceaseless rhythm for what seemed like most all of the daylight hours.

It was one way she made a living: washing and ironing clothes for the more successful people in a mining village that they had moved to when he was just a toddler. It was just one of several indignities he knew she suffered due to their poverty. The image of seeing his mother's hair clinging to the sides of her sweating face and working until her hands were red and shriveled still haunted him. He hated it then and he still hated the thought of the drudgery she endured.

There were days when his mother cleaned the home of the owner of the mine whose wife was an invalid. Some nights his mother didn't come home until the roosters began crowing at dawn. Those were the times he hated the most. Staying in the darkened shack alone was frightening. The many strange sounds he heard would keep him awake until exhaustion finally brought merciful sleep.

He remembered that in the days following the nights he spent alone his mother would be strangely quiet, often holding him close and stroking his hair with tears in her eyes. Those were often the best days, too. There would be milk and sometimes an egg for his breakfast. He remembered the special times when his mother would even buy a little butter and on occasions she would bring home a small piece of meat. Once, she even brought him an orange. It was the first orange he had ever tasted. She laughed when he bit into it and suddenly spat on the floor and wiped his mouth on his sleeve. She then showed him how to take off the peel to find the fruit inside.

Things changed by the time he was eight, when he became more aware of the little world around him. The chasing and taunting by the other boys at that time was especially humiliating. Some older boys told him his mother was a whore.

It was then he made the painful connection between the nights he spent alone and the extra money his mother had for food.

Rodriguez had an excellent memory for the faces and names of those who had once abused him. Two of those who taunted him then, however, were aware that their past ridiculing of him carried a high price. They were now inmates, each sentenced to a twenty-year term.

While he waited for the women's return, he felt a sense of apprehension. He hoped that word of this shocking encounter with the prisoner John Reece would not spread.

At least, Rodriguez realized, no other workers at the hospital were apt to wander into the smelly, humid room and see that the prison captain was now a temporary victim. But revenge would soon be his. Any minute now, he knew the women would return with the keys and he would be freed, ready to strike out after the prisoner who had, without a doubt, fled the hospital.

Minutes passed and the waiting became intolerable but Rodriguez realized his present options were few. The one he counted on the most were the hidden keys and the fact that the young women knew his name. That meant they knew his reputation. Fear was a powerful weapon. No one used it to a greater advantage than he did. Fear could paralyze a man or an entire village without a single physical restraint -- a far more powerful weapon than any destructive device ever made by man.

The women would keep their mouths shut. He would see to that as soon as they returned. The prisoner's escape was only a temporary problem. John Reece would soon be either found dead, like Thompson, or run down and captured. And that would be a day to enjoy.

One thought troubled him even more than his hands being shackled behind his back. Rodriguez was chagrined that he'd allowed an uneducated field hand, a peon, possibly feigning an illness, to escape.

It shouldn't have taken so long to retrieve the keys. Rodriguez grew concerned that the young women may have become so frightened that they, too, may have fled the hospital grounds. If they didn't return soon he was unsure of his next move.

The stale air in the room stank. There was only one small window on the wall that Rodriguez calculated must be just above the steps where Reece had appeared about to fall. Rodriguez moved over near the side of the window. He would peek out and see if he could see the returning laundry workers without letting anyone get even a glimpse of him through the small window panes.

Strangely, white bed sheets that had been hanging on the clothes lines were lying scattered on the ground. When he raised his head a little higher a shadowy movement across the walkway at the window on the opposite wall caught his eye. Rodriguez jerked his head back. It had been at the window of Alvarez's office.

Rodriguez felt his body begin to shake with rage and a new surge of frustration. The doctor had been in on the scheme to help the prisoner get away. There could be no other explanation. Dr. Alvarez had fooled him, too. Alvarez must have been brooding since the time Rodriguez slapped him and challenged him to fight on the day of the warden's daughter's wedding. Now he was hiding in his office and laughing at the captain's plight. Where were the two stupid laundry workers?

This was a day that had started out so promising. He'd showered and put on a freshly cleaned uniform and then laced his expensive boots. He'd polished the walnut stock on the gift from Neilson before sliding it back into the leather scabbard.

When he was talking to Maria under the gently waving branches of the olive tree, he'd been intrigued by the moving shadows contrasted against the flawless creamy skin on her face. Her soft laughter and smile had made him feel like a king.

Within moments his good fortune changed abruptly when he slid the gleaming rifle from the scabbard. Maria's brow wrinkled and her full lips became taut. Her one simple statement still rang in his ears: "A hospital is no place for showing off such an instrument for killing. Please take it away immediately!"

The door squeaked as it swung open slowly and the two women tiptoed into the room. Both had troubled looks on their faces.

"Did you find the keys?"

"I'm very sorry *Capitán,* but there isn't any truck out back, " said the one who had asked him the questions. She kept her eyes averted and her head down. "We -- we went all around the building and there isn't any green prison truck anywhere."

Rodriguez was speechless. The prisoner had somehow stolen his truck. His mind wildly raced in circles. His earlier humiliation was now unbelievably compounded. The perplexing struggle with the prisoner behind the hospital could have been covered up and a plausible story concocted as to how he'd temporarily gotten away. His official report for the files could have been written in such a way that it would have enhanced the captain's reputation. The two laundry workers could have easily been frightened into complete silence. All would have been readily accomplished if the nurses had brought him his keys.

Now Captain Rodriguez must get word of his plight to his most trusted guard, Sanchez. He could bring a key, and just as important, he would keep his mouth shut.

Rodriguez glared at both women until they shifted nervously and he was sure they were both totally frightened at the many ways he could cause their families harm. Then he spoke to them calmly.

"I want both of you to run out to the prison. Tell the guard at the gate that you are whores and that *Señor* Sanchez sent for you."

"Oh please, *Capitán* Rodriguez, as soon as we finish washing the clothes and cleaning the laundry room, I must go right home. My husband and children will be waiting for me. He'll beat me if I don't come home quickly and fix his supper," said the heavier woman who hadn't spoken before.

"What's your husband's name?"

"Manuel Ybarra, *Señor* Rodriguez, but -- but please do not cause him any harm, he is a good man even though he sometimes beats me when I need it and…"

170

"Who does he work for?" Rodriguez snarled. Scaring this poor peasant woman half out of her senses would guarantee her obedience.

The woman opened her mouth as if to speak and then began to sob quietly. It was easy to see that she was beginning to understand her family's plight. She really didn't have any other choice but to do exactly as he commanded.

"I'll do anything you wish, *Capitán*," she finally stammered. "I--I love my husband and my babies -- please don't --" The woman began to sob again and the other laundry worker spoke up.

"Yes, *Capitán*, I'll go too. But it will take us awhile to reach the prison, at least two or three hours."

"No. I'm not going to stay here for two hours, like this," he growled. "I want you to leave right now and run like you've never run before! If anyone tries to ask you any questions tell them that *capitán* Rodriguez sent you on an errand. That'll shut them up. Remember, don't talk to anyone except *Señor* Sanchez. Now get out of here and run as fast as you can. I'll be counting every minute until *Señor* Sanchez arrives."

The air in the hot, humid room became even more unbearable. Time passed slowly as Rodriguez huddled in a darkened corner behind the wash tubs. Salty sweat from his forehead ran down his face, stinging his eyes. His shirt clung to his shoulders and sides, making the skin on his back itch. He twisted around and rubbed his shoulder blades against the corner of the bench holding the tubs.

He became increasingly more restless and anxious for Sanchez's return until he heard a commotion somewhere outside the closed door to the hallway. He watched the door intently, afraid it would burst open at any minute and others would discover his humbling situation.

There were excited voices of women, all trying to talk at once. The name "Dr Alvarez" was repeated often until the captain finally determined that the doctor had been hurt. That a prisoner tried to kill him. One shrill voice could be heard clearly above the others.

"And where was *Capitán* Rodriguez? He knows the rules when he brings a prisoner to the hospital and...".

Another woman's voice interrupted, "*¡Capitán Rodriguez es un imbécil,* an incompetent fool! He left the prisoner unattended while he was showing off a big gun and bothering Maria when she was trying to eat her lunch."

The assertion that he was both incompetent and making unwelcome advances to Maria was especially demeaning. It became difficult to refrain from rushing out into the hallway to confront his accusers.

There only seemed to be complete agreement on one matter: the nurses now considered the cowardly doctor a hero.

CHAPTER 22

THE CHASE

Rodriguez paced back and forth in his office. The clock on the shelf above his desk showed that it was now 3:20 a.m. There would be no sleep for him this night.

There was a light knock on the door and Sergeant Sanchez quietly entered the room carrying a kerosene lamp. He sat it on Rodriguez's desk.

"Thanks, Sergeant." Rodriguez bit the ends on his mustache and shook his head. "I don't know what I would have done without you these last few hours. You know I won't forget it."

"I hope I can always be there when you need me, *Capitán*, an' if I ever get my hands on that *gringo* I'll wring his neck just like a chicken's." Sanchez placed one of his meaty fists on top of the other, wrenching them in opposite directions. His dark, scowling face was accentuated by the reflections of the lamp's yellow light.

"I've been going over these old maps of the area I think Reece could be headed for. But until we find the truck we won't really know where to look for him. He can't get far, though, there wasn't much gas in the truck -- no more than a gallon or maybe two -- I didn't take time to fill it before leaving for the hospital."

"That should help us find him sooner," Sanchez said.

"It could be the one thing that's gone right," Rodriguez agreed. "I hope we can catch him right away before word of his escape gets out. *Ojalá que sí.* Like I told you, I want to keep this matter as quiet as possible. When you talk to Flores take him aside and tell him that Reece sneaked out of the hospital and stole the truck. He'll keep his mouth shut. We can count on that." Rodriguez, for the first time in over twelve hours, felt like his luck might be changing for the better.

"What about the rifle? I saw it in the truck when you left for the hospital. I remember you saying it'll shoot three or four times as far as our Mausers and if the conditions were just right, you said the Swede could kill a man with it at

173

up to a mile or maybe even farther. Won't that be a problem?"

Rodriguez hesitated before responding. Sanchez had brought up a matter he'd hardly had time to think about. He couldn't believe how many things had gone wrong in such a short time. He was still so mortified that he could barely bring himself to even think about Reece having his prized gift from the Swede. But he didn't want Sanchez to even suspect his doubts of making an easy capture of Reece. The recent actions by the quiet man who had seldom talked to any prisoner besides the other cook, Limesand, had been such a shocking surprise. Rodriguez didn't want Sanchez to know that he was already conceding they wouldn't find Reece's body like they'd found Thompson's. First, they'd have to find the truck and then look for Reece's tracks. Concerns with the rifle would have to be dealt with later.

"The rifle may be a problem that we'll just have to deal with. We'll keep our distance 'til we figure out where he is and work out a plan to jump him when he doesn't expect it," Rodriguez explained, growing increasingly more irritated with the chain of events triggered by his own mistakes at the hospital.

Rodriguez was still hesitant to admit to Sanchez that all of Reece's actions were now appearing to be part of an elaborate scheme. The man's deceptiveness and timing were too precise to be the random acts of a desperate prisoner. "This man Reece is sneaky and hard to predict and I want us to be behind the hospital where he stole the truck as soon as it's light enough to see tire marks."

"*Sí, Capitán,* we'll be ready to leave anytime," said Sanchez, picking up the lamp that showed just a trace of fluid remaining in the bowl, then opening the door into the hallway. "I'll check back with you later," he added, then closed the door quietly behind him.

Rodriguez took the refilled lamp from his desk. He rolled the small brass wheel with its serrated edges between his thumb and forefinger, raising the tip of the wick and exposing more of the oil-soaked woven cotton's surface to the eager flame. The increased light flooded across the map on the wall.

For the last four hours the captain had studied the dim lines and the hand-printed names of locations on the map. There was a good possibility they could locate the truck's tire marks and at least determine the direction Reece had fled. Reece must have had some definite route in mind that he'd follow if he ever managed to escape. There was only one logical choice that Rodriguez could think of -- Reece would try to stay out of sight until he reached the rough terrain that led into the mountains. He would probably drive the truck into the nearest foothills and abandon it.

Recalling again the nurses' accusations, Rodriguez had difficulty concentrating. He held the light close to the map and once more reviewed its prominent features. He began to realize the truck could have been driven up any of a dozen old abandoned mining roads that didn't even show on the map.

There was a light tapping on the door as Sanchez slowly opened it. "Excuse me, *Capitán*, Flores wants to know if you want him to bring any dogs."

Rodriguez hadn't considered the possible need for taking dogs with them. He thought for a moment then said, "Until we find Reece's trail, dogs would probably just get in the way. If we catch sight of him out in the open he'd shoot any dog we sent after him. If he's already reached the arroyos along the foothills we'll need horses to keep the dogs in sight, otherwise he'll kill them too. And I know none of us are in condition to run him down on foot."

"*Sí, Capitán*, I'll tell Flores what you said."

"Tell him and then come on back and I'll show you on the map where I think Reece might have headed."

"*Sí, Capitán*, I'll be right back."

Most of the roads, Rodriguez remembered, ran up from a long alkali valley into the high desert on the eastern slopes of the Sierra Madre that lay southwest of Chihuahua. That could take Reece into the general direction of where they'd built the telegraph line. It would be the area of the remote Mexican mountains and desert that Reece would be most familiar with. Rodriguez felt a measure of hope. It was the most positive thought he'd had since he'd awakened on the laundry room floor. At least for now, only four other people knew of Reece's escape. Sanchez and Flores were his most trusted guards. Neither would tell a soul and he was sure the two laundry workers would be afraid to even discuss the matter between themselves as to how the prison captain had been found. Then he remembered the shadowy figure at the window in the doctor's office. If the doctor was found alone in his office with his throat cut, then who had been peering out the window? And there was something else that didn't add up. Why would Reece want to kill the only man trying to help him?

The idea that Reece had been able to escape without any help from Alvarez made the entire episode even more embarrassing.

There would be an investigation, especially now that the doctor had been injured. Still, the very thought that the pudgy doctor had survived a ferocious fight in his office and a slashing by the man who'd then overpowered the prison captain was impossible for Rodriguez to accept. He shook his head in disbelief as he sat the lamp back on his desk.

A full moon was sinking in the west, sending angled rays of soft light through the divided window panes above his desk. Reece was out there somewhere, possibly wide awake too and looking up at the very same moon.

When Sanchez returned, Rodriguez nodded toward the map and said, "Hold the light for me and I'll show you where I think we're going to find Reece's trail." Rodriguez pointed to an area on the map and added. "This area is about five miles from the hospital. These lines here show where the arroyos that drain into the valley cut up into the foothills. Of course, he could've headed down this valley showing here and driven the truck until it ran out of gas. He could have made a run for the mountains, but I really believe he'll take the shortest route into the closest and most rugged foothills he sees."

"And just abandon the truck?"

"*Sí.*"

"What do you think he'll do for water? There can't be many springs and he wouldn't have any way of knowing the location of the few that might still exist. It hasn't rained for months."

Rodriguez felt the muscles around his chest tighten as he pursed his lips. He hesitated to answer Sanchez's question. He was faced with another embarrassing thought. Besides his canteen he'd kept a jug of water in the truck for the past three weeks due to a slow leak in the radiator. Rodriguez decided to keep the matter to himself. He'd suffered enough from revealing his mistakes without adding another oversight to the ones Sanchez already knew about.

"Reece will soon learn that playing a game of chance in the desert is one based on impossible odds. Thompson found that out, but he found it out too late. I'm sure all the trump cards are in our hands. We'll just have to play each one at the right time."

"Thompson thought he was so smart and that all Mexicans are so dumb. But you showed him, *Capitán.*" Sanchez said, then laughed. "We'll catch this one too an' have some fun with him."

"This one may not be as easy, but we'll get him." Rodriguez said with as much confidence in his voice as he could muster. At the same time, however, he was, feeling a strange sense of uneasiness -- something he couldn't fathom kept nagging at his confidence. "Maybe we should take both of the dogs -- give them a little experience and some exercise."

"*Sí, Capitán.* Flores will like that. He's real proud of the dogs and he's done a good job training them."

"Go tell him while I finish getting ready. I'll be along shortly."

Rodriguez wanted to leave a short note on his desk in case the warden heard of Reece's escape and came by his office for a report.

The report would be brief and lacking in specifics. Rodriguez hoped the matter would be resolved before the warden even learned of any escape.

"Sí, Capitán, we'll wait with the dogs out at the gate."

Rodriguez nodded as Sanchez left the room, then sat down at his desk and took out a sheet of paper. He looked around the room, trying to collect his thoughts. He gazed at a slightly out-of-focus, faded picture of himself and his mother, taken when he was about five years old. They were sitting on the wooden steps of the unpainted shack where they'd lived in a remote mining town. It was the only picture that was ever made of the two of them together that he had seen. In the lamplight it was hard to tell what he was wearing but he still remembered the starched, white shirt his mother put on him just before the picture was taken. He remembered the lines in her face as she stooped to comb his hair and button the shirt and reminded him to sit up straight.

Looking out the window, Rodriguez could see the early light of dawn creeping into the shadows. He decided he'd write the report later.

The dogs whined as he approached the truck and climbed into the crowded cab.

"Good morning, *Capitán.* I hear you've been up most of the night," Flores said in greeting.

"All of it," Rodriguez snapped. "Let's go."

As the truck bounced along the rutted road to the hospital, jackrabbits scurried back and forth, confused in the glow of the truck's headlights. The tension in all three men became apparent. They seldom spoke and when they did it was in quiet, muffled voices.

Rodriguez could see that the other two guards were getting excited about the impending chase. Tracking down another human being with dogs and guns was a rare event. This time Rodriguez felt the tension more than he'd ever felt it before. He was worried about the prisoner's one unusual advantage -- the deadly gift from the Swede.

When they were within the last hundred yards of the rear of the hospital, Flores said, "*Capitán,* if we stop here we won't drive over any tire marks where the truck was parked. I can slip in on foot and look around and no one will even know what I'm doing."

"That's a good idea. Stop the truck over there behind that clump of creosote, Sergeant," Rodriguez said, pointing to the side of the roadway where a stand of slender dust-covered bushes grew almost as high as the cab of the truck. "We'll be mostly hidden from anyone passing by. Turn off the headlights."

Rodriguez and Sanchez sat in the truck, watching Flores take his flashlight and approach the place where the truck had been parked. In the early morning light they saw him moving slowly, his head bent low, looking for any sign showing where the prison truck had been driven away from the hospital. Flores slowly circled the area twice, carefully placing his feet to avoid obscuring any tracks. He stopped and raised his hand and motioned for them to follow in the truck as he trotted along a faint road where weeds had overgrown the old ruts. Recent tread marks could now be seen where tires rolling over the sand and dust had flattened two narrow strips of weeds. After circling back, Flores jumped on the running board and gave directions to Sanchez as he increased the truck's speed.

Rodriguez checked again to make sure his pistol was loaded. With nervous anticipation he slid his fingers up and down the wooden stock of the Mauser rifle standing upright between his legs. Considering its limited effective range gave him an uneasy feeling when he thought again of the rifle Reece had in his possession.

They'd come about five miles from the hospital when Rodriguez pointed to the mountain range off to the right where they could see the lower foothills rising to meet the distant flanks of the Sierra Madre and said, "That's the area I think he'll be headed for. I think we'll soon see where he turned and went in that direction."

Red shale stretched for miles both to the right and left of the path they were following. Boulders the size of the truck had been scattered at random across the gently sloping plain to the right that ended at the foothills. Indian rice grass and desert needle grass grew in profusion where the soil deposits were deep enough to retain a little moisture.

Within a couple of miles the terrain changed abruptly, leveling off with a monotonous sameness to its features.

The long flat valley was dry and desolate, mostly an unbroken expanse of salt flats with patches of stunted sage stretching for thirty or forty miles. Decades earlier miners looking for silver had combed the arroyos running along its northern slopes that led into the vast Sierra range. Traces of bleached bones had been found where they'd slowly turned to dust and been carried away on the howling winds, showing the fate of many lonely prospectors and their pack animals.

The old roadway faded away and forked into even less traveled lanes. A lone coyote stood on a slight mound and watched them pass. Finally, the narrow lane disappeared altogether where earlier drivers had chosen their own directions through the valley. The distinct tread marks of the stolen truck continued to show plainly again where the vehicle had continued, following a westerly direction. They rode on in silence.

Over an hour passed and Rodriguez became even more concerned. Reece's actions were puzzling. The truck should be out of gas by now. They were now some 20 miles or more from the hospital. The valley had widened and the foothills to the north were now at least 10 to 15 miles away. Without a single tree or outcropping on the valley floor, it made it difficult to judge the distance. Shallow arroyos showed where the occasional rains of previous years and the wind had carried away the loose soil.

A dark object appeared ahead. It looked to be no more than a foot or two tall. It was hard to tell, viewing it through the shimmering heat waves that lay across the valley, giving the appearance of glistening distant lakes. The image ahead slowly took form. It was a dark triangle, now less than a mile ahead.

"Slow down, I don't like the looks of whatever that is." Rodriguez was concerned that it could be one of Reece's tricks.

Sanchez shifted from second gear, the gear they had been traveling in for most of the way. With the gears in low the truck crept forward until they were within no more than a half mile from the strange-looking object.

"Stop here," Rodriguez said, stepping out of the truck after it rolled to a stop. He adjusted the center focus wheel on the field glasses then sucked in his breath, explaining, "That's the truck down in a ditch with just a piece of the tailgate showing. That son-of-a-bitch has had a wreck! Goddammit, we got him now!"

While Rodriguez continued to study the situation Flores timidly asked, "If he wasn't hurt too bad don't you think he might have run into the hills, *Capitán?*"

Rodriguez swung his binoculars toward the distant slopes without responding and methodically searched for any sign of Reece. After a long period of silence he lowered the binoculars, leaving them hanging from the leather strap around his neck. He took out his handkerchief, removed his hat and wiped the sweat from the inside of the hat band. He wanted to think carefully. He turned to Flores and saw a troubling frown, his face grim.

"What's bothering you, Flores? You look worried."

"I-I was just wondering. Reece could be hurt but still be watching us. He could have heard the truck's motor and be trying to figure the distance to where we are and lining one of us up in the rifle's telescope. We're no more than half a mi..."

"Get in the truck and let's get out of here!" Rodriguez yelled.

The tires spun, whipping up alkali dust as Sanchez turned the truck in a tight circle and drove at top speed until they were well over a mile from the wreck.

CHAPTER 23

WRECKED TRUCK

After moving back to a safer distance, the perplexed captain stood silently, pondering the situation. First gazing at the massive mountain range to the northwest, Rodriguez then looked at the desolate salt flats where the valley curved to the southwest and disappeared into a distant blur.

Sanchez took the jug of water from the truck and poured each of them a drink. The panting dogs whined and sniffed at the open jug while their lolling tongues dripped saliva onto the wooden floor of the truck bed. For almost a month the oppressive heat had exceeded 100 degrees each day, sometimes reaching 110 degrees by midday.

After a period of time Rodriguez made his decision. "We'll drive in a big circle," he said with a sweep of his arm, "completely around the wreck, staying out at least a mile and a half. If we find Reece's tracks we'll know which way he went and from his tracks probably be able to tell whether or not he's hurt."

"*Sí, Capitán.* That's a good idea," Sanchez said, climbing into the truck and starting the motor.

As the truck rolled forward and gained momentum, Rodriguez felt good about his decision. Flores stood on the running board watching for any sign of Reece's tracks.

"Circle to the northwest first. We might find his trail right away and save time but I'm hoping we don't find a single track. That would mean we got him for sure. We don't want to lose any more time. If we find tracks we know he's got almost a twenty-hour head start and that could cause us trouble."

Now they had a chance to determine Reece's plan of escape or learn if the chase was already over. With just a little luck, Rodriguez hoped to write a brief report for the warden and the files by late afternoon.

They'd completed the first half of the circle and hadn't seen a single track. Rodriguez was elated. "Looks like he didn't head into the mountains, but I can't believe he would have started out into such a barren wasteland," Rodriguez said, looking down the long alkali valley. "Let's hurry and complete the circle."

If we don't see any tracks it'll mean Reece is either already dead or we'll have him in our custody within hours."

As they reached the point where the tire marks showed they'd started the circle, all three men let out a whoop. Captain Rodriguez reached and shook hands with the two guards and said, "I can't wait to get my hands on that son-of-a-bitch."

All three men turned and looked toward the section of dark green tailgate that was barely visible through the heat waves.

"Let's have another drink of water and give some to the dogs, too. We've done our job and done it well." Rodriguez was ecstatic.

After they'd each had a drink, Sanchez asked, "Are we gonna go on in and drag him out, or just wait here and hope he crawls out in the open? It's got to be like an oven in that truck."

"We better wait while we think about it some more. Let's be absolutely sure we're right. I want to make one more circle around about two miles out from the truck. What do you think, Flores?"

"I think it's a wise decision. Indians sometimes drag a bush behind them, wiping out their tracks for miles. Reece could have done that or walked where the patches of sage grew the thickest, stepping under or on as many plants as possible for some distance. If he did it would be hard to spot his tracks. I tried to watch for that when we circled the truck but I could have missed it," Flores said.

"That all makes sense to me," Rodriguez agreed. "He's from that state, Oklahoma where they put all the Indian tribes. Who knows, he's sneaky enough to be part Indian. If he wasn't hurt, I'd bet he'd only be careful for a mile or so before he made a run for the hills." Rodriguez glassed the foothills again with the binoculars without seeing any sign of movement. "All right, let's make another loop and take it a little slower."

Sanchez put the truck in low gear and drove slowly while looking down at the ground from the driver's side. They stopped once when Flores spotted a depression under a sagebush the size of a man's boot print. He stepped down from the running board and looked under the bush and said, "Just a place where a jackrabbit scratched out some dirt, looking for a little shade. They don't seem to like this heat any more than we do. Here's fresh tracks where it must have heard us coming and hopped off through the sage."

"Good work, Flores. Looks like our luck is still holding and Reece is still in there." By the time the larger circle had been completed, the sun had reached a point almost directly overhead. Rodriguez said, "He's in there all right, but it looks like we'll have to wait him out." After looking at his watch he asked, "How much water do we have?"

Sanchez picked up the metal can, wrapped in burlap and said, "Maybe a gallon and a half."

Within fifteen minutes Rodriguez said, "This heat's unbearable. We can't sit here forever waiting for that goddam *gringo* to show himself. We need to figure out some way to check on him without getting anyone killed."

"I think I can do it, *Capitán*," Flores offered.

"What do you mean?"

"While we were circling, I looked over once and couldn't see any part of the truck. That means there's a little mound of dirt maybe two or three feet high not far from where it's lying in the ditch. It we make one more circle I'm sure I can spot it. I can get out of the truck at that point and take Lobo with me and sneak within maybe no more than two hundred yards or less and then send in Lobo. If Reece is in there and able to move at all he'll come out screaming -- or the dog will kill him. Next to Blue he's the best dog we've got."

"Either that or Reece will kill Lobo," Rodriguez warned.

"I don't think so, *Capitán*, not much chance Reece can react that fast."

Rodriguez looked at the panting dogs. "All right, give him some more water and go ahead. But be careful. We may have to sacrifice a dog, but don't get yourself killed in the meantime."

After driving for no more than half a mile Flores said, "There it is. I can sneak in from here. If you keep driving around in circles it'll keep Reece's attention in case he's watching. We'll move into position and wait for you to reach a point straight across from where we are now. Once I show El Lobo the target of attack he can cover the last hundred yards in less than seven seconds. If we're lucky, Reece will be watching the circling truck and never see the dog coming."

"Good thinking, Flores, but be careful. Oh, and another thing, take off your shirt and wave it when you want us to come on in."

Flores grinned and nodded.

Rodriguez stood on the running board as Sanchez continued to slowly circle the wreck. He marveled at the tenacity and spirit of his youngest guard as he watched him start across the burning salt flats, crouched low and moving fast with the dog following close behind him. He couldn't help thinking of the contrast between the two guards that he'd brought with him. Unlike Sanchez, Flores had infinite patience and the ability to cope in any kind of emergency. Where Sanchez was large and clumsy, Flores was small and agile, quick thinking and decisive. As a former wrestler, he was known for being able to take down men almost twice his size.

As the truck rolled on, circling the wreck at a safe distance, Rodriguez soon lost sight of the diminutive guard and the dog.

"Pick up the speed a little until we get around to where I can see Flores again," Rodriguez said. "I want to keep an eye on him in case he needs us."

As they neared the point opposite from where Flores had started his stalking of Reece, Rodriguez said, "Slow down. I'm going to step off and watch Flores on his final approach, but just keep on driving," Rodriguez said, squatting low and bringing his binoculars up to his eyes.

Flores was kneeling alongside the dog and pointing toward the wreck when Rodriguez finished adjusting the focus wheel on the binoculars. The ears on the gray wolf-like animal were erect, his head pointed toward the hiding place of his intended victim, his tail sticking straight out behind him.

Like a gray streak, the dog suddenly bolted toward the wrecked truck that showed no sign of life or sound that Rodriguez could see or hear. Rodriguez held his breath as Lobo streaked over and through the sage, rapidly closing the distance to the wreck, his pounding feet raking clusters of white alkali dust into the air behind him. Rodriguez had time for one fleeting regret: there was little chance now they could take Reece alive. It would all be over in an instant.

When Lobo dived out of sight Rodriguez stood and cheered. Reece had not even seen the dog sent in to kill him.

Within seconds the dog was back out, running in tight circles around the wreck, his nose inches from the ground. He stopped suddenly and looked in Flores' direction, his ears and head erect as if waiting for another signal from his trainer.

Rodriguez had a sinking feeling. Was it possible Reece was dead and the dog simply ignored him, or had he somehow sneaked away and the intense heat had vaporized any remaining scent?

CHAPTER 24

THE PUZZLE

Rodriguez watched, dumbfounded and puzzled. Flores sprinted toward the wreck. He dropped out of sight momentarily, like the dog, then came out and waved his shirt as a signal to come on in. Sanchez wheeled the truck in Rodriguez's direction, hurrying to pick up the captain and drive in to learn the prisoner's fate.

As the truck closed the distance, Rodriguez could see Flores walking in circles around the wreck, the dog loping in larger circles out into the sage, searching for Reece's trail.

"This makes no sense at all! What the hell could have happened? Flores and the dog act like there's no sign of Reece." The elation and renewed confidence of the last hours had vanished, replaced with worry and thoughts of his pending trouble with the hospital and Reece's attack on Alvarez.

He had to admit to himself that his attraction for the woman Maria had been his weakness. The thought that at that very moment she might be feeding or even bathing Dr. Alvarez was enough to drive him half crazy.

Now this. As the truck slid to a stop Rodriguez knew from the troubled look on the young guard's face he wouldn't like what he was about to see or hear.

"No sign of Reece?" Rodriguez could no longer disguise the anguish he felt.

"Take a look, *Capitán*. No body and not even a single track. And Lobo can't pick up even a trace of scent. I can't explain it."

"*¡No lo Creo!*" Rodriguez was overwhelmed. "It just can't be!"

There was no plausible explanation for what they found. There was no body inside of the truck lying on its side, nose down in the boulder-strewn wash. All three men peered inside and studied the situation.

"Look at this," said Flores finally. "The steering wheel was tied in place with a white rope running down to the clutch pedal. The rope must have broken when the wheels hit the bank. And look here on the dash -- the throttle cable is set to keep it going probably at about ten miles an hour. See this, it's in second gear. It may have gone for an hour or more with no one in it. I tell you, I don't believe we've ever had a prisoner like this one before."

Rodriguez was speechless. Flores didn't really know anything about Reece at all but now he'd discovered in minutes what the man the captain was trying to capture was really like. It didn't seem possible that the *gringo* had given him the slip again and was now well into his second day on the run without leaving a clue in which direction.

"Hand me a piece of the rope," Rodriguez said bitterly.

"Here's the part that was tied to the steering wheel to keep the truck going in a straight line. You can see where it's been cut with a sharp knife within the last few days," Flores said, handing the cotton rope to the captain.

Rodriguez examined the rope briefly, then remembered the sheets lying on the ground at the back of the hospital. It was another one of Reece's stunts. Captain Rodriguez felt a quick stab of fear that he might never find out how Reece had vanished.

"Where's my new rifle? It's gone too. *¡Es impossible!* I just don't understand it." The captain looked back up the valley toward the hospital, now almost 30 miles away. He didn't want Sanchez and Flores to know that this discovery was almost more than he could bear. Going two days and a night without any sleep was taking a heavy toll on both his nerves and stamina. This shocking finding in the scorching heat left him with the feeling he might collapse at any moment.

The captain took a long slow drink of water, then poured a stream of the water over his head and neck, then down over the front of his shirt. The concern for his own state of health was at least for now taking precedence over the immediate whereabouts of the escaped prisoner, Reece. The extra weight the rich foods had added to his waistline while they'd built the telegraph line was adding to his weariness.

The captain stood quietly without any comment. His men mustn't know that their captain possessed as many weaknesses as any other man. In time, he desperately hoped Reece would show some faults. Surely, the man would make some mistakes. If he did, that's when they would get him.

As Rodriguez gazed at the unbroken stretch of sand and sage he again wondered just what took place in the doctor's office. The more he thought about it, the more he was convinced the pampered doctor was lying or in some way helping the hated *gringo*. Why would Reece cut the doctor's throat, then tie him up and gag him? If it was a deep cut the doctor would have surely bled to death. Why didn't Reece just kill him? And why didn't the doctor yell for help? Now the doctor was a hero. That was the especially galling part to Rodriguez. He would have to think about all of it later when he wasn't so exhausted.

But then what about his own encounter? The *gringo* could have easily killed him too. The captain began to tire of the puzzle that made no sense at all. The immediate problem of finding the spot where Reece jumped from the truck, leaving it in gear with the throttle set and the steering wheel tied to the clutch pedal, needed an urgent answer. If Reece had leaped onto a rocky surface or one covered with grass at some point along the way his boots would have left no imprints. Or as Flores said, he could have taken a piece of sage and dragged it behind him, easily wiping out his tracks as he went.

Rodriguez drove slowly back along the route they took from the hospital. Sanchez and Flores walking along at some distance out to each side. Eventually, he was sure they would find where Reece ran for the mountain range to the northwest. The captain knew from his years of experience that it was human nature for a man, when frightened or pursued, to seek familiar territory. And to the northwest was where the prison crew built the telegraph line.

It was almost dark when Rodriguez heard a shout. Sanchez was waving his shirt and yelling excitedly. The captain let out a long sigh of relief, sure they finally were getting a break.

Only the tracks of Reece could cause such wild enthusiasm.

Lights from the prison showed ahead, less than ten miles away. All three men were bone tired. They badly needed food and rest. Rodriguez knew he needed sleep more than anything else but he was wide awake with a feeling of intense exhilaration. Finding the trail of John Reece was the first thing that he could feel good about in the last two days.

For the last hour his thoughts had been dominated about their best chances for going after Reece. They would need trucks and horses and barrels of water and plenty of food. And also feed for the horses and mules and dogs. The captain was now convinced that Reece was already somewhere in the mountains. He would have taken enough water with him to at least reach the higher slopes. How Reece planned to survive after that was still the biggest puzzle. The latest trick by the *gringo* convinced the captain he was dealing with a desperate man -- but one who was unbelievably sly, calculating and ingenious in so many different ways -- a man Rodriguez only thought he knew. One who didn't make many mistakes -- but one who would be eventually run down.

The white stone wall of the prison showed directly ahead in the truck's lights as the full moon broke the eastern horizon.

"Here's the plan. By tomorrow the trail we found could be too old for a dog to follow. We'll prepare for a couple of hard days of riding horses once we cut his trail again. I want you to get everything we'll need loaded by early morning -- don't forget anything we can possibly use. I'm holding you both responsible, and if either of you make any mistakes it's going to be your ass. After you get it all ready, come wake me and we'll check it over together. At dawn tomorrow we'll truck the horses and equipment as far up as we can drive. Be sure and load at least enough water to last four or five days. Any questions?"

"We'll get ready, *Capitán*, and then come and get you," said Sanchez enthusiastically.

"I'll go tell Raul as soon as we stop the truck, *Capitán*," said Flores.

"Good, I'll expect to see you both before daylight. And don't forget to bring Blue, she's the only dog that has a chance to pick up a scent in this heat, especially if it's been made a day or two --"

"But we can't take her," interrupted Flores. "She just had a litter of pups and…"

"Goddammit, Flores, I said we're taking her. To hell with them goddam pups."

"Yes sir, *Capitán*, I know how important it is to all of us but…"

"Wait a minute, you could be right. In fact, I'm sure you are but not in the way you think. Blue will be so worried about her pups and her tits will get all swelled up an' sore an' she just might try to sneak back here to nurse them if she ever gets out of our sight."

"That's another good reason, *Capitán*, that we shouldn't take her, her pups could grow up to be good tracking dogs just --"

"I said we're taking her. Now get that straight in your head, Flores!" yelled Rodriguez. "We're not going to let that bastard get away just because of your worrying about a litter of pups. Take all them pups out in front of Blue's pen and kill them where she can see you do it."

"Please. Please, *Capitán*, I can't do that, Blue would never trust me again, she's so shy an' --" Flores stopped in mid-sentence, unable to continue. Rodriguez could see the eyes of his young guard glistening in the moonlight. He waited a bit before he responded to his dog trainer's plea.

"Grow up, Flores, and don't act like an old woman. Blue's our best chance to track down Reece. You know that as well as I do," Rodriguez said. "We've got to have her. Tell Raul to kill the pups just like I told you to do and tell him to do it now before he starts getting the horses and mules ready. *¡Ahora mismo!*"

"Tell him to bloody them real good and throw them back in the pen with Blue. That way she'll know they're dead long before we leave and her milk will start to dry up sooner -- then when we find Reece's trail we can put her on it and she'll stay with it 'til she drops or finds him. I want that bastard brought in alive more than you'll ever know."

The truck slowed as the guard on the gate swung the iron framework wide for them to enter. Rodriguez heard Flores swallow hard a couple of times. The young guard was just going to have to grow up and become a real man. He was just too much of a woman. The captain then added one last demand.

"Tell Raul to take one of the pups and flatten its head good and wire its body up tight to Blue's collar. By morning she'll know her pups are dead. *Todos muertos.*"

CHAPTER 25

COUNT DOWN

It was late afternoon on the day John Reece escaped from the hospital. He'd moved at a steady trot for the last three hours, anxious to increase the distance from the point where he'd jumped from the slow-moving truck.

When the foothills steepened into a long sweeping curve, dotted with scattered mesquite and yucca, Reece stopped and looked back at the alkali valley, now at least twenty miles away. He pulled the telescope he'd removed from the captain's rifle from his backpack. The screwdriver from Alvarez's office had been all he needed to loosen the screws on the mounting bracket and leave the heavy weapon under a pile of rocks.

Raising the metal tube holding the magnifying lenses, he studied the hazy expanse where he'd sent the truck on its way.

There was no sign of movement or telltale column of dust, but any delayed pursuit, he knew, would only be temporary.

Was it possible, he wondered, that the captain was still lying hidden in the laundry room? Had the smothering action with the ether-soaked towel been too much for Captain Rodriguez?

There had been a moment of hesitation before he'd leaped onto the back of the unsuspecting captain. It was a life or death decision with nothing in between, taking every bit of courage Reece could muster. When the struggling captain's legs finally buckled and his head struck the ground Reece felt a strange sense of power like he'd never felt before. He was awed that the most dangerous act of his entire life had, for the moment, left him strangely calm and without a trace of fear.

The sequence of the actions at the hospital had happened so quickly, Reece found it hard to believe his escape plan had worked so well. He was free, at least for now. The distraction of both men by the pretty nurse had been even more than he had hoped for. Unwittingly, at critical moments, she'd been the focus of both men's attention.

Reece looked down at the wire mesh window screens he'd wrapped in layers around his lower legs. The lightweight leggings rested easily on the top of his insteps, sliding up and down an inch or two with each stride. Moving at a fast pace through mesquite and boulders, he'd had little cause to worry about any hidden rattlers or scorpions that might strike out, knowing the tightly woven metal would protect his lower legs.

The once highly polished boots Reece had stripped from Rodriguez's feet were now scuffed from striking against the rough edges of rocks.

Feeling a fleeting sense of relief, Reece took out one of the salt tablets Alvarez had given him and removed the stopper from a hot-water bottle. He filled his mouth with the water he'd taken from the can in Rodriguez's truck and tasted the salt on his tongue as the flat pellet slowly dissolved. Raising his chin, he let the water trickle down his throat. He slowly chewed two pieces of the dried fruit Alvarez had given him.

Reece shook his head in wonder when he thought of the moment the impulsive idea of capturing ants in a glass had struck him. The simple act had made it possible to set the entire series of events in motion. After a few moments he began to relax. Believing he'd taken the weapon with him would give his pursuers something to worry about.

Reece hurried on, climbing a steeper, barren slope on the vast Sierra range. Scattered acacia trees began appearing on benches where they clung to the shallow arid soil. Bent by the prevailing winds from the west, the small trees leaned downslope, toward the alkali valley that was now only a blur.

Stunted blue-green sage stretched to the west as far as he could see across the high desert. When the sun dropped toward the horizon, the silhouetted mass of granite that formed the crest of the Sierra slowly took shape.

A flat slab of granite no more than a foot high was to Reece's right. He eased himself down, immediately becoming aware of the pain in the tendons of his tiring legs. It would soon be dark. He reckoned he'd covered almost forty miles since abandoning the truck. The border could be another 500 miles away. He had no way of knowing for sure.

As long shadows crept across the land, Reece felt a sense of fear. Being alone in such a towering mountain range was unnerving, but even the sighting of another human being at a distance could put his chances of reaching the border at risk.

In addition to all who would come after him there would be a constant threat ahead: a chance encounter with any roving Indians that might spot him or cut his trail. His boot tracks would reveal at a glance that the one who'd passed wasn't wearing thin strips of hide on his feet.

Being constantly aware of his surroundings and ready to flee into the most remote and desolate areas would be his best chance to avoid capture. His risk would increase as he went farther north, along the eastern slopes of the Sierra range where roving Indians herded their flocks.

Nearer to the border he would have to cross the lower-lying lands that were developed into ranches and farms. The report of any chance sighting could result in a desperate act by the captain -- the posting of a price on John Reece's head.

As the darkness closed in around him, Reece found himself glancing into the deepening shadows.

At midday the alkali valley had been like an oven. The evening air on the higher slopes was already turning cold. It was hard to keep his teeth from chattering. With little water and food left and no blankets he knew sleep would not come easy.

He pulled a well-worn envelope from inside his shirt and removed a letter he'd read hundreds of times. In the fading light he could still see where the lines started and stopped. The darkness didn't matter, he knew the words in each line from memory. In another twenty-seven days Eula Mae would graduate from nursing college.

CHAPTER 26

WRANGLER'S NIGHT OFF

Crossing the compound, Flores unlocked the gate that connected a long corridor to the guards' quarters. It was 8:40 p.m. and nearing the end of a day that had started two hours before sunup. He still had to see that the trucks, horses and supplies were loaded and ready to leave before daylight.

Tired and depressed, Flores dreaded the worst assignment he'd ever been given: seeing to the killing of Blue's pups, even though he knew the captain might be right. The minute she was loose she'd be trying to find her way back home if she didn't know her pups were dead. The best tracking dog Flores ever saw would yield to her mothering instincts and no amount of training could change that. But successfully following a days-old trail in the dry desert air would require Blue's total attention.

As he neared the double-door entry to the officer's dining room the sounds of loud laughter and excited voices came from the nearby kitchen. One voice, rising above the others, excitedly predicted, "Captain Rodriguez is going to find out what it's like to have his own ass in trouble and I can't wait to see it!" A quick burst of laughter and hooting drowned out the speaker's voice.

Flores stopped in mid-stride and listened intently as another speaker, who sounded like Limesand, laugh and say, "Don't forget Sanchez! Maybe the warden's just mad enough to put them both in the same cell!"

"Yes! Yes! I'd love it! I'd love it!" The voice was a little bit timid but the message was clear and unmistakable. The speaker no doubt hated Sanchez even more than he hated Rodriguez.

"I never saw the warden so mad before. Did you see the look on his face when he came in here the second time with the hospital director and we had to tell them we still hadn't seen or heard a thing from anybody?"

"He looked like his eyeballs were gonna pop right out of his head!" someone added, chortling loudly at his own retelling of the warden's agitated state.

The first speaker, who Flores now recognized as Kilgore, now argued in a more serious tone, "The warden's mad at both of them, but it was Rodriguez who left Reece alone with the doctor -- that's what started the whole damn thing. But who would have thought that old man would cut the doctor's throat within a hair on a gnat's ass of his jugular vein and then escape into the desert in the captain's truck?"

"Go Reece go!" someone urged with enthusiasm.

"I guess nobody's figured out yet just how Reece did it or where the captain was when Reece got his keys. But a lot of people are laying bets." Limesand paused then added, "Someone said a guard at the gate saw the captain and Sanchez and a smaller guard leave before daylight this morning. He figured it must've been Flores because they had dogs with them."

"They're gonna crack down on all of us now," someone else whined in a worried voice.

The levity and bravado stopped and the voices became serious, suddenly worried that a successful escape could cause a sudden punitive action against all other prisoners.

"I seen the lumps myself the morning they took Reece out of his cell block," Kilgore's voice was unmistakable. "They looked bad and he could barely walk -- didn't seem to know where he was."

"Leaving Reece alone with the doctor was bad enough but failing to make a report to the warden about the doctor's injuries and a prisoner's escape is going to cause the captain nothing but trouble." Flores couldn't recognize the speaker's voice.

"Making the warden look like a fool is gonna have a price. And just where Sanchez fits into all of this and where they've been all day is anybody's guess. One thing for sure, most of us sure had Reece figured wrong," Kilgore added.

"You're right there," Limesand agreed, his voice sounding sympathetic.

"Reece always hid his feelings," Kilgore continued. "I could see it when the Swede tried to rile him -- called him names and make fun of the way he talked -- lots of times Reece was boiling mad inside but he didn't let it show. Just kept doing his job -- not lettin' on all the time he was working on a plan."

"That could be," Limesand said.

Flores listened intently, dumbfounded that he was learning more about Reece's escape from overhearing the trustees working in the kitchen than he'd learned from spending 16 hours with the two men who had the daily responsibility of running the prison. Flores had known better than to ask either of them any questions but news of Reece's escape had obviously spread, exciting all the inmates.

Even if they captured Reece right away, Flores knew the entire incident would still cause a major embarrassment for the warden and Captain Rodriguez. A worsening of the doctor's condition could add to both men's troubles.

Flores turned and sneaked quietly back to his quarters. He was thinking he'd come back later and get something to eat when he remembered that Raul had a day off and would have to be located so he could help with the stock and…killing the pups. Flores felt depressed -- it would be such a cruel thing to do and maybe unnecessary. Flores had a feeling that even with Blue searching far and wide from daylight until dark across the vast Sierra Madre, John Reece was going to be a hard man to run down.

Flores was puzzled. How had such a chain of events been possible? Was the man's escape the result of dumb luck or a well thought out scheme, crafted by the hobo?

One thing Flores had learned soon after he came to work at the prison: it was impossible to look at any inmate and tell what crime he'd been convicted of. Kilgore, himself, was a good example. His pleasant unlined face and easy smile gave no indication he'd be the kind of person who would've stabbed a man with a cow's horn in a fight over a whore in Tijuana.

Flores sat down at a small table to make a list of things Sanchez had told him to do -- things that had to be done before they could start the chase at first light. He couldn't remember when he'd been so tired and he was convinced the ordeal of going after Reece was just beginning.

A noise in the hall and the sound of a door closing meant Sanchez had come in from the compound and gone into his room.

It was then that Flores thought of a comment by a guard who'd been on the gate the evening Reece escaped. It could be another piece of the puzzle. The guard mentioned he'd sent for Sanchez at the insistence of two women standing at the gate, tearfully begging to speak to the sergeant. Within minutes after a brief conversation with the women, Sanchez had sped from the compound, returning at sundown with the captain. The guard had noticed that Rodriguez's uniform appeared soiled and wrinkled as Sanchez barely slowed at the gate.

The incident could be related to the escape. It was hard to tell. Flores was only sure of one thing: he'd never mention hearing anything about it to the captain's loyal sergeant.

Flores could hear the sounds of agitated voices coming closer. It sounded like two men in a heated discussion.

Someone knocked loudly on Sanchez's door. "You in there, Sanchez?" Flores recognized that it was the strained and hoarse voice of the warden.

"*Sí, Señor.* What can I do for…"

"I'll tell what you had better do! You had better tell your *capitán* to report to me as soon as you can find him. Is that clear?"

"*Sí, Señor,* please come in and wait here while I go find him."

Flores heard the door close and the sound of rapid footsteps hurrying down the hall. He opened his door a crack and saw Sanchez disappear through a doorway.

There was much to be done and no time to sit and think about what might have happened. The captain would have to resolve his own problems with the agitated warden.

Hurrying out to where the prison trucks were parked, Flores knew he had to find Raul and tell him the urgency of the situation and give him Rodriguez's specific instructions.

The small two-room house where Raul's girlfriend Cecelia lived was no more than three miles away. As the truck sped down the road Flores could see scattered lights ahead. Kerosene lamps and lanterns dimly showed through the stunted mesquite trees growing along the winding dirt lane that led to the quarry village. For a brief moment, the glowing reflections from a cat's eyes showed from under a clump of weeds before the cat turned and slunk back out of sight.

Off to his left, Flores could see the bright electric lights of the large irrigated farm that was owned by a rich family who lived in southern California. He had seen the huge generators that supplied the power to the farm buildings and the pumps that ran day and night, sucking water from deep wells. The rock quarry buildings were off to his right.

He reached a stretch where a row of dusty cottonwood trees stood along each side of the road. As he began passing the small modest cottages he could smell the unmistakable odor of the pigpens where the more fortunate families lived. They would later have meat to put on their tables.

The women who lived in the houses often found work during the year in the fields of the American farmer while most of the men cut and chiseled stones in the quarry.

He passed the now abandoned shack where his cousin had lived almost twenty years before. The door was hanging open at an angle, still attached to one hinge at the top. The two windows that had been on the front of the house were now dark gaping holes.

Shadows from trees in the yard moved across the rear walls of the two front rooms from the truck's headlights as it passed. Flores had visited there as a small boy on many occasions with his family. He slowed the truck as he drove past the village well. It had been a great source of pride among the people who depended on it for their daily water. It had been dug over 100 years before. Large stones lined its walls to a depth of over 150 feet. All the roughness on the stones surfaces that faced inward had been worn smooth. Countless thousands of buckets of water had banged against the stones as they were drawn slowly upward from the darkened depths below.

When no adults were around, Flores and his cousin would climb up on the wooden box that covered the opening and supported the posts and beam for the overhead pulley. They would carefully lay back the door hinged with strips of weather-blackened leather and holler down into the darkness before running away to look for some other source of amusement.

The truck's headlights now flashed across a shed where the road curved to the right. Flores could see a dim circle where the browse had been eaten down short by a goat tied to a wooden stake in the middle. A newly born kid, its still-wet coat glistening in the truck's lights, stood on wobbly legs and tried to nurse. The nanny goat was licking her newest offspring and Flores could see the wet afterbirth clinging to the underside of her tail.

A garden just past the staked goat showed rows of slender gray weathered sticks where pole-bean vines twisted and climbed their way to the top, their lush dark leaves evidence that many trips had been made to the deep well for buckets of water.

When Flores saw a wire-enclosed chicken house off to his right and a garden with rows of squash and corn, he knew that Cecelia and her mother lived in the next house.

Flores stopped the truck in front of the small, unpainted adobe dwelling. As he walked up the path he could see through the sagging and torn screen door that both Cecelia and Raul were sitting close on the small sofa. It looked as if the young woman's blouse was partly unbuttoned. The lamp on the small table was turned down low, the tip of the flame barely showing. Shadows cast by the two empty tequila bottles sitting nearby made dark splotches across the faces and upper bodies of both Cecelia and Raul. A sliver of light showed along the side of the curtained doorway that led to the other small room. It appeared Cecelia's mother had discreetly retired for the evening.

Flores knew his task was going to be more difficult when he reached to knock and then saw that one of Raul's hands was up under Cecelia's skirt. Completely unaware of his presence on the lean-to porch, they were kissing passionately. Flores saw he had arrived at a bad time but then he realized if he had arrived five minutes later it could have been even worse. Forgetting his mission, Flores stared, feeling his face redden from embarrassment. He had never been with a woman, himself. He stepped back, unsure of his next move. Flores thought for a moment and then quietly returned to the truck and slowly opened the door -- then he slammed it hard and started clomping up the path taking small steps and calling out -- "Hey, Raul, you in there? The *capitán* wants to see you."

A dark shadow stepped up to the screen door and responded, "Who the hell wants to know? If that's you, Flores, you can just get your ass out of here -- it's my night off, the first one I've had in nearly two weeks." Cecelia was getting up, buttoning her blouse and straightening her skirt.

"Hello, Cecelia, I'm very sorry to have to come out here like this but the *capitán* --"

"Goddammit, I knew this was going to happen when I heard last night the count showed someone was missing," said Raul bitterly. "It just ain't my lucky day."

"I'm sorry, Raul. The *capitán* wants you right away. Reece is the prisoner who got --"

"Reece? The *gringo* ? I don't believe it. Where the hell would he go?"

"It's a long story -- look's like he fooled the *capitán* into thinking he was sick -- did something to make his face swell up and got away from the hospital and took the *capitán*'s truck. There's a lot I don't know, but I do know the *capitán* wants you there right away. Everything's got to be ready to go before daylight," Flores said, hoping to convince Raul to come along without a fight.

"Reece won't get far. Thompson didn't and he was a hell of a lot younger and one tough son-of-a-bitch," Raul said. "You go on back now and I'll come in later. I can get everything ready in no more than three hours. Just leave me a list of what the *capitán* wants done and how many of us are going," Raul said, emphatically, his voice rising with increased irritation.

Flores could see that Cecelia was holding one arm tightly around Raul's waist and pressing her breast against the back of his shoulder. The light coming through the narrow gap between the curtain and the edge of the door opening increased slightly. Cecelia's mother was not asleep. She appeared to be listening to the guard's discussion.

It wasn't going to be easy convincing a young man off-duty and in a high state of sexual arousal that he should leave his girlfriend and go load some feed and water for a bunch of horses and mules. He would have to be told about the dogs.

"Raul, the *capitán* insists we take Blue since she's the best one at tracking -- but you may not know she just had pups --"

"Goddammit, Flores, I don't care about some bitch an' her pups. That's your problem. I told you I'll take care of my business and you take care of yours. Now just get out of here and leave us alone."

Flores swallowed and took a deep breath. Valuable time was being wasted. He wished he wasn't the kind of person who was so easily disturbed by the plight of helpless creatures. Raul was right. The dogs were his responsibility. Still, he simply couldn't kill the pups himself.

Raul turned to go back inside and started to close the door, muttering curses as he put his arm around Cecelia.

"The *capitán* wants you to kill Blue's pups!" implored Flores before Raul could close the door. He was embarrassed when his voice cracked, sure that the two women would know that he probably didn't have the nerve to be a prison guard.

The tall slim wrangler stepped outside and stooped down, his face now inches from Flores. "You're lying, Flores. You know damn well the *capitán* didn't tell you that. He knows what my job is and so do you. Get off the porch and get the hell out of here or I'm gonna' knock you on your ass!"

Flores knew in the guard's half-drunk state, he could flip him into the middle of the small front yard. It would solve nothing and only make matters worse.

Backing up a couple of steps, Flores calmly said. "I'll tell the *capitán* you refused to follow his orders. I've been with him and Sanchez since before daylight looking for Reece and the truck. I tell you the man's half-crazy at times. Something happened at the hospital but I don't know for sure what it was. I do know he wants you to kill the pups and leave them in the pen with Blue and tie the little one's body to her collar so by morning she'll know they're all dead. He's afraid that if we don't do it she'll keep trying to sneak back to her pups. He knows I -- I can't --"

Flores paused and swallowed hard and waited hopefully for a response from the highly agitated wrangler.

There was an embarrassing period of time when Raul didn't make any comment but just stared at Flores. Flores finally added, "I simply can't do it myself. I raised her from a pup on a bottle. That's why Rodriguez wants you to do it."

Raul still made no response. He just glared at Flores, taking deep breaths, his nostrils flaring wide with each breath.

Flores continued in little more than a hoarse whisper. "You had better be sure you're doing the right thing. The *capitán* is going to be furious if you refuse his order. I'm telling you as a friend, Raul, he's in no mood --"

"All right goddamn', just shut up, I'm coming with you, but --"

"Wait a minute, Raul, come on back in. I want to talk to you before you go," said Cecelia. Her mother had stepped into the room and she was whispering in her daughter's ear but Flores could hear nothing of the conversation.

Raul went back inside and stood close to Cecelia. She seemed to be telling him something in an emphatic manner.

"Wait for me in the truck, I'll be with you soon," said Raul, his voice less hostile now.

Flores sat in the truck, relieved that Raul had finally listened to reason. After a few minutes he saw the light of a lantern swinging alongside the legs of someone walking in the side-yard, toward the back of the house. He heard the bleat of a goat and the squawk of chickens that had been disturbed on their roost. Within minutes Raul joined him saying, "Let's go."

They drove the first mile in silence until Raul started talking without a hint of hard feelings. "I'm sorry, Flores. I know you're just doing your job but you caught me at a bad time. So Reece is the one who got away? That's a surprise."

"I think we're in for more surprises. We just don't know much about him -- he kept mostly to himself. But the other cook, Limesand, now he might know something."

"By the time we get moving in the morning he's going to have a two-day lead on us," Raul said, then asked, "Got any idea where we should start lookin'?"

"Yeah, but it took us all day just to figure it out. He drove the truck down that long alkali valley that starts about seven miles from the hospital. We found the truck where it ran into an arroyo about 30 miles from where he stole it. But there wasn't a track anywhere around it in the dust. He'd tied the steering wheel down to the clutch pedal, put it in second gear and set the throttle about ten miles an hour and jumped out when he first drove into the valley. He'd jumped where a stretch of shale and sage brush ran toward the hills for several miles and he left no tracks there either --"

"I'm beginning to see why the *capitán* is so mad. But we'll get him. That trick sending an empty truck on its way while he ran off in a different direction,"

Raul laughed, then added, "sounds pretty smart to me."

"I don't know how he got away from the hospital but I overheard one of the cooks say he'd seen him when the *capitán* took him from the cell-block. He said Reece's face was all swollen with lumps on it and he looked like he was so weak he was about to fall down."

"Could be another stunt like the one with the truck, since he was able to run off into the mountains. Can't be too sick if he did that," Raul said, then asked, "Think the lumps were all part of it too?"

"I'm beginning to think so. There's even a rumor he cut Dr. Alvarez's throat --"

"*Dios mío,*" Raul interrupted. "Sounds like we got a wild man on the loose. But he just never seemed like the kind that would do anything like what you're telling me."

"You'd already been sent back to work at the prison when Reece got in trouble with the *capitán*," Flores said.

"I never heard anything about that. What happened?" Raul asked.

"We were a little over halfway when the Swede put on a feast and brought in entertainers," Flores said as he slowed the truck when two dogs showed in the truck's headlights, running across the road. "They caught Reece slipping one of the desserts he'd made to some of the Indian kids that kept following us. He had saved one back and when the *capitán* and the Swede wanted another helping Reece lied and said there wasn't anymore. I heard he'd sneaked them scraps of food before when they were hanging around --"

"What did they do to Reece?" Raul asked.

"I didn't see it myself, hardly anyone did, most of us were watching the dancers. One of the guards said Sanchez sneaked up behind Reece and hit him hard across the side of his head...damn near killed him while the *capitán* and the Swede watched."

"He's a hard one to figure," answered Raul. "Does something dumb like that and then pulls off the slickest escape I've ever heard of."

"Some prisoners are like wild animals -- you pen them up and they never stop trying to find a way out," Flores said.

Flores slowed on the last curve where the road had a deep rut from past seasonal rains that had washed across the road. The prison was no more than a few hundred yards away. "Well, it don't make any difference how smart this man is. Where he's headed there's no water. He can't be carrying enough to last more than two or three days," Flores said. "We'll get him in less than a week."

"I don't know," Raul said. "Seems to me we may be chasing a running fool."

Flores drove the truck past the stables and on to the kennels. The truck's headlights swept across the pens as he turned in to park. He felt the muscles in his throat tighten when he saw Blue lying on her side. The sleeping pups didn't move when she raised her head and shoulders and watched the guards get out of the truck.

Then she lay back down.

CHAPTER 27

THE LONG CLIMB

A pink glow tinted the undersides of clouds layered in bands above the eastern horizon. The skyline on the mountains to the west was slowly taking shape.

The trucks and trailers sat, loaded with barrels of water and hay and grain. Flores hung the pack saddles and panniers on a rack and then watched as Raul opened the gate to old Tom's stall. The blind gray-muzzled mule sniffed Raul's hands. After he felt the tug on his lead rope he walked up the ramp into the stock trailer. The steady mule wouldn't shy if they tied a dead man's body across his back.

The two dogs and the food for the guards would be loaded last.

Flores returned to the kitchen where a trustee was preparing breakfast for Rodriguez.

Sanchez marched three sleepy-eyed prisoners through the doorway. The boxes of food for the guards sat on tables in the dining room. The trustees, who cooked and served the guards, had been up all night preparing food and packing supplies for the search party going after Reece.

"Get a move on and get this stuff loaded, fast," ordered Sanchez in a tone that left no doubt what he meant. Shaking off the drowsiness, the men hurriedly began loading the boxes, stealthy glances showing their fear of the moody sergeant.

Sanchez, his face scowling in the lamp light, asked Flores, "You and Raul got everything ready to go?"

"*Sí*, Sergeant. We're all set and ready to pull out when you and the *capitán* say the word."

"You sure you didn't forget anything?" Sanchez's equal spacing and inflection of each word indicated he had a specific thought in mind.

"No, I don't think so." Flores shook his head slowly, then swallowed in a nervous reaction to Sanchez's pointed questioning, trying to think of something he might have forgotten. He'd carefully gone over the list of things he'd been told to do and, after he and Raul had finished, checked it again.

"You got that bitch you call Blue?"

"*Sí,* Sergeant. She's tied out by the truck."

"Raul take care of her pups like the *capitán* said?"

Flores hesitated and swallowed again. He looked at the floor, and, after clearing his throat, answered softly, "Flies are already crawling over the bloody hair on her throat."

"And you brought an old shirt or something of Reece's so she'll get the scent and know who we're looking for?"

"Uh, no -- no I--I forgot..."

"I guess you were going to write Reece's name in the sand or maybe draw his picture with a stick and show it to her?" Sanchez's words were slow and flat, with no more emotion than if he were reading aloud the label on a can of tomato sauce. Whenever Sanchez spoke in this manner Flores knew the man's nasty disposition was rising to the surface, apt to erupt at any moment.

"I'm -- sorry, Sergeant Sanchez. I guess I forgot..."

"When we found the wrecked truck, you make a big show of going in after Reece."

"I was just trying to do my job, *Señor* Sanchez. I didn't mean..."

"You thought you were clever when you showed the *capitán* how the steering wheel had been tied to the clutch pedal and the throttle set at slow speed, with the truck in gear -- like anyone could see."

"I'm not sure what I did wrong about that, I..."

"You're supposed to be the great tracker -- one who keeps his eyes open instead of his mouth."

"Did I miss something that would have helped us look for Reece?" Flores was disappointed that the sergeant seemed to dislike him.

"You didn't notice a pair of old shoes in the truck?"

"Seems like I might have seen them -- I can't be sure. I guess if I did, I thought they were the *capitán*'s." Flores remembered how Rodriguez seemed pleased with his plan for taking Lobo and going in to flush Reece from the overturned truck. Was it possible Sanchez was jealous of the brief comments of praise Rodriguez had extended to Flores for doing his job? Flores realized now that he shouldn't have spoken up so quickly. Sanchez should have had first chance to explain Reece's stunt with the truck.

"Did you ever see the *capitán* wear old worn-out shoes?"

"No, *Señor* Sanchez. I never did see...but I'll go right now and look for some of Reece's clothes. Maybe I can find..."

"Forget that. I've got Reece's old shoes in a sack. But I'm warning you, Flores, you don't address the *capitán* in my presence unless he speaks directly to you."

"I'll remember that and do my very best, *Señor* Sanchez," Flores assured the sergeant. He hesitated for a moment and then asked, "Did Reece run off into the mountains without his shoes?"

Sanchez looked flustered for a moment, caught off-guard by Flores' question. Sanchez turned around when he heard the unmistakable sounds of *Capitán* Rodriguez striding down the hall to the dining room, the hard heels of his boots striking the concrete floors, echoing in the corridor.

"You don't say anything about this to anyone," Sanchez cautioned quietly. "You understand me, Flores?"

"*Sí, Señor* Sanchez. I won't say a word." Flores wondered if Sanchez's irritation meant that Reece had stripped the *capitán*'s expensive boots off his feet before he fled.

"I'll give the shoes to you later, when no one's around. Remember, don't mention this to anyone," Sanchez warned again, giving Flores a hard stare.

"*Sí, Señor* Sanchez." Perhaps Sanchez was trying to save Rodriguez further embarrassment about the theft of his boots. Flores was puzzled. Details of Reece's escape might never be revealed. It seemed unlikely, but somehow Reece must have overpowered the captain.

Off to the left the door opened and the captain came into the room. Flores noticed that Rodriguez hadn't shaved for a couple of days. It wasn't like the man to neglect his personal appearance. His hair was tousled and his bloodshot eyes were little more than narrow slits, squinting against the glare of the lamplight.

Both Flores and Raul greeted the captain. When he nodded toward the seats across the table from where he sat down, they quickly joined him.

The cook that was still on duty hurried over with the food he'd just finished preparing for Rodriguez.

"Here you are, *Capitán*, just the way you like your breakfast. We missed you --"

Rodriguez waved the cook away without comment and then unrolled a map and laid it alongside the steaming dishes of food. He took a couple of bites of egg and then picked up the cup of coffee.

Flores noted the captain looked tired as his eyes moved slowly across the scope of the map, from the Arizona and New Mexico border at the top, to the sweep of the Rio Grande to the east, and then west to where the land ended at the Sea of Cortez. A prominent, meandering line down near the middle of the map showed the border between the states of Sonora on the west and Chihuahua on the east.

Squinting, Rodriguez leaned to the side, pouring over details where the map was smudged. Without taking his eyes from the map, Rodriguez took a sip from the porcelain mug.

After setting the mug back on the table, Rodriguez shook his head and pursed his lips. Flores had never seen the captain with such a look of determination. His jaw muscles clinched spasmodically. He took a couple of deep breaths and said, "We've got to get after this bastard -- he's got a big head start so we've got to make every move count. First, I want to know if everything's been prepared and loaded as I instructed."

"*Sí, Capitán,* it has," Sanchez assured Rodriguez.

Rodriguez nodded his approval. "Now here's the plan. We'll drive up this old mining road for about 30 miles," Rodriguez said, pointing to a wide yellow line on the map, shaded in with a crayon, that started at the hospital and followed straight for about ten miles into the lower foothills. At that point the yellow line on the map began to curve back and forth as it wound up into the higher elevations.

"This map was made by a survey crew the Swede sent down here over a year ago. He used it every day -- that's why it's so wrinkled." While still looking at the map, Rodriguez took his fork, poked at his plate until he felt the tines stick into a slice of fried potato. Holding the fork just below his mouth, he paused and added, "It could help us figure out where Reece is headed." While he slowly chewed the mouthful of food his heavy brow wrinkled again. "I'm beginning to worry that his escape wasn't some crazy impulse. The man must have spent a lot of time working on a plan, but he never seemed like the type who…" Rodriguez shook his head without finishing the sentence, his mouth set in a grim expression. Flores could see that even discussing Reece exasperated the captain. "I can't believe it's taken so long just to finally start. That stunt of his with the truck wasted a hell of a lot of our time -- cost us a whole day." said the captain disgustedly.

Rodriguez sat rubbing the stubble on his jaws, staring at the map in an almost trancelike state. After a long pause, he picked up his coffee cup, raised it halfway to his lips, hesitated, then set it down again. Spreading both hands, he ran them across the map in an attempt to smooth the outer edges where the map was starting to roll toward the middle. Storage in a leather cylinder had formed a curling set in the paper's fibers.

Sliding his cup over on one corner, Rodriguez said, "Here, Flores, hold your hand on that edge so I can read the map."

"*Sí, Capitán.*"

"The telegraph line runs southeast from here, just east of Nacozari, to about here." The captain then pointed to a line marked with x's, running at a southeasterly slant from near the top of the map. "Here's the village of La Junta. We crossed the road about ten miles east of the village at this point. The road runs on to Cuauntemoc before it swings in a big loop and heads northeast to Chihuahua."

Rodriguez stopped and rubbed his eyes before he continued. "From this point here, near La Junta, the line bears in a more southerly route to where we stopped west of Parral. These little inverted 'v' marks, running along here west of the x's," Rodriguez ran his finger along the meandering line of inverted marks, "they show the location of the Sierra's Crest." Rodriguez shook his head again and then looked first at Sanchez and then Flores. "There's almost no chance Reece could ever make it to the crest, but, if he does we're in trouble. There are a few springs here where the headwaters of the Rio Conchos start. We can't let this bastard get away. We've got to get as far as we can with the trucks and then ride hard to cut him off from reaching the higher mountains where he'll have too many places to hide."

"Thompson was a lot younger and he didn't last more than twenty miles. My guess is we'll find Reece along here where the slopes start getting steep," Sanchez said, pointing to an area of the map not far above the end of the winding yellow line.

"No. I don't think so." Rodriguez looked up from the map and began hurriedly eating his breakfast. He stopped abruptly and picked up the crayon.

"This is about where the telegraph line ended. If we can get within fifteen miles with the trucks and trailers we can unload and set up a base camp about here." Rodriguez drew a small yellow circle on the map. "We can ride out and try to pick up Reece's trail. He should be somewhere in this general area. We'll take our binoculars and watch for any circling buzzards. Maybe we'll get lucky and get him by evening. I'm not looking forward to having to ride one of them damn horses for more than a day or two at the most," he growled.

Flores nodded and noticed that the captain now seemed in better spirits than when he'd come in late the evening before, exhausted and dejected. The action of finally preparing for the chase had buoyed the captain's spirits. But the thought of riding horseback for long hours in the scorching heat wasn't anything that Flores felt good about either. It was the only way, however, to cover any amount of territory in steep, rough terrain, and the captain knew it.

"A friend and I were up in that area a few months ago, near one of the old silver mines, hunting for quail and rabbits," said Flores. "We didn't see anything but a couple of bobcats. The road's not so good up there but…" Flores stopped in mid-sentence when he remembered Sanchez's warning about offering his opinion unless Rodriguez specifically addressed him. A glance to the side confirmed Sanchez's glare of disapproval.

"You were saying?" Rodriguez asked.

"Yes, uh…" Flores hesitated, knowing he'd offended Sanchez again. He licked his lips and continued, "The old roads across the arroyos are washed out in places. We'll need to go slow when we cross them. The water barrels and stock are heavy."

Rodriguez's brow wrinkled again upon Flores' comment about the roads. He slid the plate of eggs and potatoes closer, took a couple of bites of egg and then picked up the cup of coffee and took a quick swallow. Pushing back from the table he rolled up the map, stood, and said curtly, "Let's go!"

Sanchez drove the truck out that would be first in line. Captain Rodriguez was riding with Sergeant Sanchez. Rodriguez made it clear that he wasn't about to follow in someone else's dust. The bales of hay and sacks of grain were in the smaller lead truck. Raul drove the larger truck with the barrels of water, towing the trailer with the horses and mules.

Dust from the vehicle in front usually obscured it from the view of those following. Raul drove some fifty yards behind. Flores was glad that he could barely see Blue, standing on top of the highest hay bale.

He'd busied himself with other duties and avoided Raul when he brought the bitch around and loaded her last. They rode on in silence for almost an hour.

The first few miles were flat and the procession moved at a moderate speed of up to fifteen miles an hour. After that, when the winding road wound into the lower hills, the trucks slowed and ground on upward in their lowest gears. There was more rock and gravel on the road now and there wasn't so much dust.

Raul was also following closer at the lower speed and Flores could now see the dark bloodstain under Blue's lower jaw. He started to ask Raul to follow back away from the lead truck but then realized that might start the old arguments and hostilities again. He thought of how he'd put Raul in a difficult position by asking him to kill the pups and decided not to say anything.

Spiny ocotillo shrubs began appearing on both sides of the road. On ahead, at the higher elevations, they could be seen growing in greater profusion, flaring upward, shaped like a cone of dead sticks growing from a common root.

Raul commented about the beauty of the spiny, scarlet-flowered shrubs but Flores made no response other than a terse, "I guess so."

When the old road steepened, both trucks were stopped to allow their boiling radiators to cool. It was no more than two hours after daylight but the sun was quickly warming the clear and cloudless desert air.

The captain stood alongside the lead truck, glassing the steep rocky ridges above. He then turned and adjusted the binoculars to the valley where the wrecked truck had been found.

Lobo was sleeping in the shade of the stacked crates of food and supplies. Blue stayed on the top bale of hay, her eyes seldom leaving the white outline of the prison that could barely be seen in the distance. Flies gathered on the matted lumps of blood that had dried and stained the bitch's white throat and the lightly-shaded hair on her chest and front legs.

Flores looked away. He simply couldn't stand to watch Blue's solemn vigil for her pups.

When the radiators cooled they added more water from one of the barrels and then the procession climbed on up to the higher elevations.

The truck Flores was riding in suddenly jerked to a stop. Raul swore and blew the horn so the men up ahead would know that there was a problem.

The axle on the heavily loaded truck seemed to have caught on something underneath. The wheels were spinning but the truck would no longer move either forward or backward.

Raul jumped out and dropped to his knees trying to see back under the truck bed. He lifted his head with a grim expression showing his disgust and said. "The *capitán* is goin' to be really mad at me now."

Flores knelt by Raul and immediately saw that the top of a rock was jammed up against the bed of the truck. It was lodged between the rear end housing and the leaf springs by the right rear wheel. They would have to take the trailer loose and drag it back before the truck could be jacked up and moved off the boulder. Raul swore quietly when they heard gravel crunching under the approaching boots steps of Rodriguez and Sanchez.

"The *capitán* will blame me for this, you just wait and see."

Flores was surprised at Raul's comment about the Captain.

"Not so loud, Raul. He'll hear you." whispered Flores.

"Goddammit Raul, now what's wrong?" yelled Rodriguez.

"I'm sorry, *Capitán*. We're caught on a big rock but---"

"Now how the hell did you do that?"

"I'm not sure *Capitán*, but the barrels of water are so heavy ---we can unload the stock trailer and drag it back by tying ropes to old Tom's packsaddle. He's strong and he can pull it, since it's downhill."

"And how do we unload the barrels of water on the truck? I hope you can see what a mess you have gotten us into. I told you to be careful, didn't I? You damn well know we don't need any more delays," snapped Rodriguez.

"I'm sorry, *Capitán*, I should have been more careful. But I'm sure we can get it loose once we---"

"We're not going to waste any more time because of your carelessness. We'll make camp right here. It's several miles from where I wanted to stop but this way we won't waste so much time. You better learn how to listen, Raul, when I tell you something. I don't want any more dumb mistakes."

"*Sí, Capitán*. I'll be more careful," answered Raul. He turned his face away to hide his embarrassment and began opening the gate on the trailer to unload the horses and mules.

Flores wondered if the captain realized just how unreasonable he was being. There was no way Raul or anyone else could have gotten the heavily loaded trailer across the rocks without them dragging on the axle. But it wasn't like the captain to ever consider that he could be wrong about anything. If something went wrong he could always find someone else to blame. He always did.

Flores knew that Raul would not soon forget the totally unjustified criticism and accusations made by Rodriguez. A small force working in the inhospitable mountains was dangerous enough without adding uncalled-for insults.

Rodriguez and Sanchez got out both sets of binoculars and began scouring the mountainside for any sign of circling buzzards. Flores and Raul saddled the horses and loaded enough supplies of water and food on one of the young mules to last them throughout the rest of the day.

The other mules were then tethered near the arroyo where the trailer was caught on the rock.

"We'll head off to that point up there," said the captain. "From there we can see for miles in any direction." They rode for over two hours, stopping only once for a few minutes to let the sweating horses rest.

The horses labored on through broken, rocky terrain. Thornbush, that clawed at the rider's leather chaps, cruelly raked the flanks of their mounts.

After riding and glassing the high-desert slopes for miles in every direction the guards moved on higher into the mountains.

Flores rode off to the side of the other guards. He kept glancing at the ground for any signs of tracks while the dogs plodded along through the dust and the heat of the midday sun.

It was late afternoon when the tracks of a man clearly showed where he'd crossed the dry, sandy bottom of an arroyo. It was obvious to Flores that the man had been making no attempt to conceal his trail as he headed on deeper into the mountains. The length of the stride and the almost direct line of the tracks gave no indication of a man wandering aimlessly in the desert or in any danger of collapsing from the heat or exhaustion.

The other guards rode over and joined Flores when he called.

Rodriguez got down from his horse and took a long drink from his canteen, handed it to Raul and then grinned and said. "Fill it up again. I think we are finally in luck." He then studied the tracks and took the map from his saddle bag. He studied both the direction where the tracks were headed and noted the location of two distant mountain peaks then declared, "We should be about here," he said, pointing to a spot on the map. He looked again to check his bearings.

"We are at least 50 miles from the prison. Where in the hell could that *gringo* be headed, but more important than that, what is he doing for water? There can't be any within 20 miles of here. Get that bitch over here and get her going on his trail. Maybe we can jump him within a couple of hours. He can't be far ahead."

Flores took one of Reece's worn-out shoes from his saddlebag and when Rodriguez wasn't looking, knelt by Blue and let her smell it and quietly gave her the command to follow. He could see where insects had left tiny tracks in the bottom of each footprint. Mice trails wandered in and out of three depressions. The edges of the footprints had crumbled before the ants and other insects crawled across the slumping sands.

Blue sniffed along the ground in a half circle before moving slowly in the general direction of where the footprints led.

"We should try to follow them by sight where we can. They appear to have been made on the day the prisoner got away or perhaps the morning after. Blue's got his scent now but there's little left and the breeze has drifted it in different directions. No dog could…"

"Lazy bitch! Raul, you should have killed her when you killed her worthless pups. The tracks can't be that old. I don't think that Reece could have gotten this far on the day after he---"

The excitement of a few moments before quickly vanished. For some reason the captain didn't seem to want to even speak of what happened on the day that Reece vanished into the desert. Flores was convinced now that some totally humiliating experience occurred at the hospital. He wondered if he'd ever learn the details of Reece's escape.

When no orders were given, Flores began following the tracks, leading his horse behind him as the others followed in single file. Since the man who made the tracks had been making no attempt to hide his trail, Flores only needed to slow up when they climbed to higher rocky ground and the man's boots made no prints, for sometimes long stretches. There they slowed and followed Blue. After several miles, Reece's tracks showed where he'd abruptly changed directions. Flores was puzzled by Reece's reason for changing course where the terrain remained the same.

Within a couple of miles a startled flock of white-winged doves suddenly took flight. They'd flown from a seep where a clear basin of water pooled, dripping from a fissure in the rocky ledge above.

A dried rattler skin hung over a limb on a small, mesquite tree. Blackened rocks and ash remained in a small circle where Reece sat and ate. He had likely seen a flash of light from the doves or other birds' feathers, banking their wings in flight as they descended to the water. In the distance, patches of snow clung to shaded crevices on the Sierra's limestone peaks.

There was no longer any question in Flores' mind that the *gringo* passed this way two days before or early in the morning of the second day. He could afford to be a little careless. The scope on the rifle would reveal any trail of dust in the distance that could be made by men coming after him. Flores had no doubts that the escaped prisoner would be much more careful in the days ahead, if his pursuers were gaining in the chase.

The dejection on the captain's face showed his final recognition that the ordeal was just beginning. The fact that the tracks had gone for at least two miles in an almost straight line to the spring was all the proof needed.

Captain Rodriguez stared at the spot where the water pooled in a shallow rock basin. He then placed his hand on the fissure in the slab above where the water seeped through the crack then idly tasted the moisture on his fingers. He looked up towards the high mountain range to the northwest where the trail appeared to be leading, almost as if he were in a trance.

"How could he possibly have known about the location of this tiny spring in all of this?" the captain asked quietly as if only talking to himself and not expecting any reply. He continued gazing back and forth across the high desert mountain slopes that stretched both north and south as far as the eye could see. Flores opened his mouth to explain his thoughts on the matter and then decided to keep quiet. He had not been asked his opinion.

It was almost two hours after dark when they neared the location where they had left the trucks and trailer. "I think it's somewhere off down below, about another mile or so," said Flores.

The sudden and unmistakable braying of a mule broke the silence of the warm desert air. The young mule Raul was leading gave an immediate and raucous response to its stablemate. Flores felt goose bumps race across his back as the eerie sounds echoed up and down the mountainsides in the stillness on the darkened slopes. One of the mules at camp had likely heard or smelled the returning men and animals.

After the horses and mules were fed and watered, Flores built a small fire to heat some food for their supper. Sanchez and the captain were busy clearing away rocks and rolling out their thin cotton mattresses.

Flores looked up as Raul came into the range of the light from the fire.

"I didn't get a chance to finish apologizing for what I did last night. I had no right to--"

"Yeah, you got me in trouble with both Cecelia and her mother. Now you owe me one. But her mother really don't like me much anyhow. A couple of times she's told me she don't want to see my ugly face aroun' there any more. But as long as I bring the food for the table and buy Cecelia some clothes, well..."

Flores could see Raul grinning in the firelight.

"I couldn't have come at a worse time. That I'm sure of and it seemed like Cecelia and her mother were disgusted with both of us standing and arguing like we were on the porch. But I guess you and Cecelia worked it out when you went out in the back yard. I heard you when you disturbed the goat and the..."

"That wasn't me out there. That was Cecelia's mother. That reminds me. You'd better tie Blue up or she won't be here in the morning."

"I know her tits are all swollen and sore. It's even hard for her to walk when she hasn't been nursed all day. It'll take a few more days for her milk to cake and then it'll start to dry up." said Flores, looking over at Blue where she was lying near his bedroll. "It's hard to see her in such misery. She didn't even seem very hungry when I fed her. *Es muy triste.* She's grieving for her pups."

"After Rodriguez goes to sleep you'd better milk her."

"Goddam you, Raul. You cruel bastard. Don't mess with me like this. Why should I milk…"

"Well aren't you something! I never heard you cuss before. And after the special favors you asked for."

"I saw the dried bl…, the blo…" stammered Flores. "Where you tied the little one to her collar."

Raul looked over to where the sergeant and Rodriguez were finishing spreading out their bedrolls then turned back to Raul.

"Aw grow up and quit carrying on so, you snivling little shit." Raul reached over and put his arm around Flores shoulders.

"That is nothing but chicken blood."

CHAPTER 28

KEEPER OF THE FLOCK

It was the third day of the mounted chase. The horses were ridden hard in the searing heat with no water and little rest. Flores, riding in the lead position, kept glancing at the ground for any sign of bootprints, while the dejected captain rode last in line. Lobo and Blue had trouble keeping pace with the long-legged horses, pushing their way over and through scattered clumps of chaparral that often brushed against the rider's stirrups. Raul urged his tiring mount alongside Flores, then pointed off to the right and quietly said, "I saw something moving right over there."

Flores reined his horse around and watched the spot where Raul was pointing. Then he saw it. A dark object moved a few feet, stopped briefly, and then moved again. When his eyes adjusted to the distance, other movements caught his eye. A flock of sheep and goats were feeding through a field of tall mesquite, with no herder anywhere in sight. Flores continued to watch, then spotted a small boy following the flock, crouching low and glancing in the rider's direction, trying to sneak through the spiny shrubs without being seen.

A glance behind him showed Flores that Rodriguez and Sanchez were studying the area through their binoculars.

"Come on, let's get him!" Rodriguez yelled, spurring his horse into a gallop. "He might have seen something!"

After the guards ran the boy down and cut him off with their horses, he froze in a half-crouch, his eyes wide with fright of the looming, uniformed men on horseback who had him surrounded.

"Flores, see if you can find out if he's seen anyone," Rodriguez ordered.

Flores dismounted, slowly, knelt in front of the boy in the dirt, and spoke to him kindly, first in Spanish, then, adding in his limited knowledge of the Tarahumara language, he tried to calm the boy and assure him they meant him no harm. They only wanted to ask him if he had seen a *gringo*.

Minutes passed before the boy stopped shaking enough to tell Flores he had seen a man trotting along below the telegraph lines the previous day. When asked which way, the boy pointed in a northwesterly direction. After additional questioning, Flores turned to the captain. "The best I can tell from what he's saying, when the man saw he was being watched, he turned and ran into the higher mountains."

"Tell him he's got to go with us and show us where he last saw the man!" Rodriguez voice was coarse and insistent.

After Flores told the boy what the captain wanted, the boy began to tremble again, shook his head, and pointed toward his flock, moving out of his sight into the thickets.

Rodriguez cursed when the boy shook his head. "Then ask him if the man was carrying a rifle."

When the boy kept shaking his head and couldn't understand Flores' question about a rifle, Rodriguez, in exasperation, yelled, "*¡Estúpido!* Look here, you little dummy!" and drew the Mauser from his saddle scabbard in an attempt to show him what Flores was talking about. When the barrel of the long repeating rifle cleared the scabbard, the boy panicked, ducked under Rodriguez's horse's belly, then dashed out of sight into the thickest growth of mesquite.

In was mid afternoon on the following day when they gave up trying to follow Reece. They had found his tracks near the telegraph line where the boy had seen him. The tracks disappeared into a steep rockslide where there was no chance horses could keep their footing on the treacherous shale. The riders were too exhausted to dismount and pursue the runner on foot, even if they'd known the direction he'd fled.

Flores wondered what Rodriguez's thoughts were as the captain sat silent on his horse, looking at the spot where the last boot track ended at the edge of the shale.

Darkness was creeping across the slopes as Raul started the truck's motor and pulled out into the dust kicked up by the truck Sanchez was driving.

"It'll be good to get back and get a hot shower," Raul said. "I don't think I've ever been as dirty or more tired than I am right now."

"It's been a rotten trip," Flores said. "I feel really bad we chased down a little kid and scared him half-to-death."

"Ducking under the *capitán*'s horse was a pretty neat trick to get away," Raul chuckled. "Then running like a scared rabbit right into the thorns. I tell you, these Indian kids have to grow up tough or they don't make it."

"Seeing him run into the thorns made the skin on my back crawl," Flores said.

"What do you think the *capitán* will do now?" Raul asked.

"Don't have any idea."

"Think he'll call in the *federales* ?"

"Not much chance he will."

"I don't think we've been within forty miles of Reece in the last three days. This country's just too big," Raul said, reaching for the switch and turning on the truck's headlights.

"You're right," Flores agreed. "Remember when we were kids, all the stories about Geronimo and his little band of Apaches? Over 5000 *gringo* soldiers couldn't catch them. They just kept slipping back and forth across the border and hid in the Chiricahuas."

"Yeah, and how about that Pancho Villa? More than ten thousand *americanos* couldn't find him when he hid out here in the Sierra Madre," Raul said. "But they did kill a lot of his men."

"One's thing's different in this case. The *capitán* knows where Reece is headed."

"If we can't run him down on horseback there is one way to get him, that's figuring if he finds water and food, somehow. Nail up a bunch of reward posters and you'll have these people looking for him behind every bush. Reece is smart enough to know that if he's not caught soon, a price will be put on his head and..."

"If that happens," Flores interrupted, "Reece's days will be numbered. Search parties will swarm through these Madres. They'll run him down like a pack of dogs and fight over who gets the reward."

CHAPTER 29

HORSE THIEF

Reece had moved on at first light when the air was cool. From a slight rise at the edge of the desolate plain, Reece looked back toward the south across the sand and sage. It was the ninth day since he'd fled the hospital and he was facing a new problem he'd thought about many times. When they'd built the line across the open stretch of high desert they had moved at a fast clip. Digging holes and hauling in telegraph poles had been easy. Reece knew there was at least 40 miles of the open country he had to cross where there were few places to hide. If he was spotted in the open, he'd have little chance to run to cover before Lobo or a guard mounted on either of the two fast Arab horses chased him down.

Earlier, he'd hoped to start across this area at night, knowing moonlight on the light-colored sands would make it possible to find his way along the telegraph lines. Now, he was too pressed for time to hide and wait for nightfall.

Reece rested and massaged the tendons along his shinbones. Taking the rifle-scope from his backpack he scanned the country to the south. Within a short time he spotted four riders, miles away, emerge from behind a low hill, moving in single file. His heart rate quickened and blood pounded through the arteries in his neck. He still hadn't been able to lose them.

Meandering across rock and shale, they appeared to be waiting for the dogs to find his trail. They hadn't reached the open sands where his tracks would clearly show.

To the north, he could see the one place where the flat plain was broken by the looming walls of chalk-colored mesas and buttes, rising 1000 feet or more. He remembered the gentle slopes around the mesas' lower flanks where scrub mesquite grew. Below the slopes, shallow basins trapped the meager rainfall, shed by the mesas' rocky surfaces.

On one of his return trips from delivering water, Reece had led the mules over and let them graze on the needlegrass and Indian ricegrass growing in the basins. The dried grasses that provided the mules a well-needed bulk in their diet. Thinking of the grasses, a plan began to take shape. Perhaps he could use those same grasses to help him steal one of the guards' horses.

He had to make a tough decision. The men on horseback were less than fifteen miles away. Within a few hours, if they continued in the same direction, they would cut his trail.

His only other choice was to flee back to the southeast where he'd skirted a mountain range the day before. It was an even riskier choice. He had used up all of the hidden water along his backtrail.

Reece made his decision. Up and running in a crouch, he headed for the mesa. He could hear the water sloshing in the water bottles. It was the only thing he felt good about. He had to gain a little time to set his plan in motion. Halfway to the mesa Reece began to tire. The deep sands were straining the muscles in his legs. He stopped for a quick glance through the scope. Now moving in his general direction, the riders appeared to be still waiting for the dogs to find his trail. Reece felt in the backpack. The magnifying glass he'd taken from Alvarez's office was still there. He moved on at a fast trot and reached the scattered clumps of sage that ringed the edge of the shallow basin where the dried grasses grew across the expanse of silt. Across the basin, on the mesa's lower slopes, mesquite grew among the sparse grasses and rocks that had rolled down from the mesa's flanks.

Reece selected a few rocks and carried them back to the other side where the sage and grasses grew together. He grabbed some of the dried grasses and placed them in a pile. Taking the magnifying lens he held it less than a foot above the grasses, adjusting the height until the sun's rays focused into a small white dot. Within seconds the grass began to smoke, then a tiny flame appeared. He snuffed the flame and grabbed the rocks. He stacked them so the lens's handle placed between the rocks would hold the glass flat. It would be held at the same elevation above the grasses that he'd just ignited. He slid the stack of rocks over into the shade under the edge of a sage bush. Grabbing several handfulls of grass he placed them under the lens. Reece calculated that within a little over an hour the sun would reach the lens. When the heated grasses burst into flames and spread across the basin, smoke would surely bring the armed riders hurrying to the fire. By then they would likely have found his tracks.

Reece planned to climb up a broad boulder-strewn ravine cut into the western wall of the mesa. Once on the top he'd run in a large circle around the mesa's outer rim. The dogs would have no trouble in following his scent along his trail. Near the completion of the circle there was a steep eroded crevice on the mesa's flanks near where the fire should have completed its burn. He'd estimated the crevice to be no more than 400 yards from where the fire should start. When they neared the mesa the dogs would find his scent. The guards would, without a doubt, come scrambling up after him, assuming he'd accidentally started the fire and fled to the mesa's top. Everything should work as planned if all of them left their horses tied below, leaving no guard to watch them. If they left no guard he should be able to sneak back down and steal the young gray gelding and run the other horses off. If his plan did work he'd leave the guards stranded in the desert and gain a lead of at least a couple of days, maybe even more.

From the mesa's rim Reece looked down on the trap he'd set.

Everything was in place and the grasses were beginning to smoke. The horses and riders, now less than five miles away, were moving in a direct line toward the mesa. They were, no doubt, following his tracks in the sand. Moving at a trot, the horses were bunched behind the two dogs, running at a lope out in front, easily following his scent.

Within moments flames flared upward mixed with swirling smoke, then began spreading across the basin, moving toward the mesquite. The fire would soon burn out where the soil changed to rock.

Watching the group coming after him, Reece saw the horses break into a gallop and come racing across the plain. Reece left the rim and began a fast trot in a circle around the mesa's top. Within no more than thirty minutes he'd completed most of the circle and reached the rim by the steep sloping ravine where mesquite clung to fissures in the rocks. He could hear Lobo barking, in hot pursuit on Reece's trail, when the dog reached the top of the mesa.

Looking down he could see how well his plan was working. No riders waited below. The horses had been hastily tied to low mesquite shrubs. Two of them were all ready loose and dragging their reins, grazing where needlegrass grew in small clumps among the rocks and mesquite, above the edge of the burn. The fire had quickly blackened several acres of grasses. Smoking twigs and mesquite stumps showed the fire had ignited them, too, where the scattered shrubs had sprouted along the edge of the grasses.

As he started to descend the steep crevice he heard Lobo barking excitedly, sounding if he was now coming in Reece's direction. The slight breeze on top of the mesa, Reece quickly realized, had carried his scent across the top. Either Lobo or Blue had scented him. They were cutting directly across instead of following his scent around the perimeter of the mesa's top as he had planned.

Reece scrambled down the slick rocky surface in the steep ravine. Grabbing at anything he could find and ripping out small bushes growing out of the rock's tiny crevices, he tried to slow his rapid and dangerous descent. Tumbling and sliding from one cluster of shrubs to another he barely kept control -- hoping and praying he wouldn't break any bones in his headlong flight to keep ahead of Lobo.

When he neared the bottom of the crevice he glanced up. He got a glimpse of the dog bouncing from side to side where the crevice's steep sides joined at the bottom, his four clawed feet giving him better control in his race down after Reece.

Sliding down the last twenty feet of the crevice, Reece bounced up and sprinted toward the horses. With his legs driving hard and gulping for air he rapidly covered the distance. He saw the horses throw up their heads, puzzled at the strange form racing toward them. He knew guards had reached the rim when he heard shots and then bullets striking rocks behind him. The barking of a dog trying to catch him added to the noisy bedlam. Reece was within fifty yards of the gray when the two grazing horses panicked. They broke into a gallop and raced around the edge of the burn. When they reached the scattered sage they slowed, stopped and snorted and nervously watched and waited for the other two horses to join them.

Reece was within thirty feet of the gray when it fought to break away from its lead rope, tied to a sturdy mesquite. The nearby bay suddenly broke loose and bolted to join the others. Reece reached the gray just as it jerked the mesquite bush up by the roots. It whirled as he reached out to the saddle skirting and tried to grasp the cantle. With the gray's head pulled to the side by the bouncing bush, Reece reached again for the saddle as his legs began to wobble. He could hear Lobo closing fast, no more than a few yards behind him.

The lead rope broke, freeing the Arab to run at top speed straight across the blackened grass toward the other horses now fleeing across the plain.

Exhausted and weary, his legs near collapsing and his lungs aching, Reece staggered as he slowed. Running on instinct and blinded by smoke, he lost track of the direction he'd been headed. He could hear the panting of the dog right behind him. The race was over. He'd never catch a horse or outrun Lobo.

The excited barking of the dog changed. Frenzied and painful sounding yelps replaced the barking. Reece looked around. Through the smoke he could make out the form of the dog trying to find his way back out of the burn. The smoldering twigs and stumps had saved Reece from the dog's intended attack. Blue, running at a distance behind Lobo, stopped when she saw the frightened dog running back toward her in an attempt to escape from the hot coals and ashes. Reece could feel the heat of the ashes through his boots.

Reece headed north, straining to keep out of the limited range of the Mausers. His plan hadn't worked as he'd intended but now, at least, they were all on foot and the horses would soon be miles away. After he'd run for a few hundred yards he glanced back. He wasn't surprised that none had tried to chase him. The four men and their dog with the burned footpads had other concerns to deal with.

CHAPTER 30

RAUL'S MISTAKE

It was the thirteenth day since the prisoner had escaped into the desert. Flores watched the late afternoon sun drop to just above the snow-dusted bluffs on the western skyline.

The captain had been enraged when Reece's stunt with the fire left them stranded. It had taken the rest of the day and half of the night to reach the trucks and trailers. With little water and food with them the ordeal had been exhausting. It had taken another day to find the horses and return to Chihuahua where Lobo was left in the care of a veterinarian. That evening Rodriguez had gotten roaring drunk.

Now the horses and the pack mule at the back of the line plodded along in single file, their hooves kicking up puffs of dust while Blue lagged behind.

Riding at the head of the line, Captain Rodriguez reined his horse around and waited for the other guards to catch up. Taking off his hat, he wiped the sweat from his forehead onto the sleeve of his wrinkled shirt.

As he stopped his own mount in front of Rodriguez, Flores noticed the layer of fine dust coating the captain's clothes and saddle bags. While Rodriguez sat quietly, slumped in his saddle, he gazed out across the sparse clumps of needle grass that covered the high plateau. For the first time, Flores noticed the deep lines in Rodriguez's face and the gray hairs showing in the discouraged captain's whiskers. It was hard to believe that anyone could appear to have aged so much in barely two weeks. Flores knew, however, that the hard riding and lack of sleep hadn't left the other three of them looking any better. The week's stubble on his own face and his grit-stung eyes were proof of that. The drooping heads and listless eyes of the horses showed the weariness from their ordeal.

Rodriguez turned back and glanced briefly at Flores while idly wiping the sweatband in his hat.

"How far do you think it is back to camp?" he asked, his voice revealing his discouragement.

"Maybe fifteen miles, it's hard to say. We've ridden in a wide circle for maybe twenty or twenty-five miles."

"Let's turn back. It'll be dark before we get to the trucks, even if we start now. I'm convinced that somehow Reece has moved on north and could be another fifteen or twenty miles ahead of us," Rodriguez said, shaking his head, his bewilderment showing. He put his hat back on, adjusted the chin strap and then, after a long pause continued, "All the tracks we've seen today indicate he's kept the lead he got on us. We haven't gained a bit. It's hard to figure. We keep looking where he's been at least one or two days before."

Rodriguez shifted his hips in the saddle, rested his left hand on the cantle and looked back up at the distant mountains, clearly frustrated that the search had proven to be in the wrong area again. His face took on a hard look. "But he could be anywhere up there, watching us right now through the scope on my rifle."

When Rodriguez voiced his own startling concerns, Flores looked up at the bluffs and felt a chill race over his shoulders. He remembered the Swede bragging that in competition he'd hit targets no bigger than a rabbit at almost half a mile. Still, Flores doubted Reece would risk shooting at the guards. But, there was no doubt in Flores' mind, the man had some reason for taking the heavy weapon from the wrecked truck. Flores was sure of one thing. He knew it must be nearly impossible for Rodriguez to even talk about the theft of his highly-prized rifle.

Both Sanchez and Raul sat quietly on their horses, looking off into the distance.

Rodriguez sat staring up at the mountain range without comment for several more minutes before he turned back toward Flores and continued, "That Reece is a strange one. I still don't understand why he makes wide detours around the head of the canyons where there might be a chance of a small spring, except for that first day where we found his camp by the seep and that rattler's skin hanging on a bush. He just keeps moving on north."

Flores nodded in agreement, but he was puzzled, too. He thought about what the captain had said many times, that Reece was such a strange one. His tracks would go in an almost straight line for miles then veer off in a different direction. Usually they would cross back somewhere along where the telegraph line was built -- but, like the captain had observed, Reece avoided canyons where there was any chance of water. How could anyone travel without water across the hot sands where the heat waves kept dancing ahead of them? It was a puzzle that seemed to have no answer.

"I think you're right, *Capitán*," Flores said. "Maybe we should go on back to the prison and get more water and supplies, then we could try again farther north after we study the maps of that area. But if we don't find him soon -- how about offering a reward?"

"Damn you, Flores, you still don't understand, do you?" Rodriguez said, frowning. "It's our job to find any prisoner who gets away. Someday, before long, I expect to be named warden -- and this man's escape is embarrassing enough without letting the whole damn country know about it."

Flores hesitated before he responded to the captain's heated remarks, still wondering how a man as old as Reece and in handcuffs could have fled from the hospital in the prison truck. In such a situation any guard would be embarrassed -- but especially the captain of the guards. "I'm sorry, *Capitán*, it's just that--"

"If the word gets out that we are looking for someone we can't catch, we'll be seen as a bunch of fools," the captain said irritably, his face reddening with anger."

"*Lo siento mucho, Capitán,* I never thought of it that way." Flores realized that once again he'd provoked the captain -- even though he was only trying to be helpful. It was hard to foresee the kinds of simple remarks that could so easily offend Rodriguez. He hoped the subject of Reece running off the horses and leaving them on foot wouldn't be brought up for discussion again.

They were all tired and discouraged. The last two days of riding had been hard, with little sleep, and they still hadn't even caught sight of Reece again. One thing was clear, however, this prisoner who ran into the desert wasn't like any of the others. Reece seemed to have a definite plan -- though they were at a loss to figure out just what it was.

"We're just about out of water and..."

"Don't you think I know that, Flores?" snapped Rodriguez.

Rodriguez sat looking northward for several minutes. The only sounds were the labored breathing of the horses and the panting of the dogs, standing in the shade cast by the horses and riders.

Looking over at Sanchez, Rodriguez shook his head and said, "I'm convinced we'll never catch Reece from behind. I guess all of that running with the mules put him in good condition. And he knows the area well. Chasing wildly after someone is a waste of time."

"I think you're right, *Capitán*," Sanchez agreed. "If we could get ahead of him and set up an ambush..."

"Yes. I've been thinking of that. We've got to move fast and try to set up some kind of a base camp -- some place where we can make a quicker strike when we find fresh tracks or catch sight of that bastard -- and then get the dogs after him right away when we do."

The captain's idea about setting up an ambush made sense to Flores. There seemed to be so little chance to run Reece down since they seldom even knew which way he'd fled. After thinking about the possibility of moving on north and spreading a line of hidden guards or soldiers across a wide expanse of high desert, Flores became worried. If Reece tried to come through an area assigned to him he knew he'd never be able to shoot an unarmed man from ambush, and that could cost him his job.

Pondering his dilemma, Flores dismounted and picked up the near forefoot of the bay mare he was riding. A stretch of rocks they'd crossed earlier had left her limping. With his knife, he pried out a sharp stone that was tightly wedged between the frog of the mare's hoof and the inside curved lip of the metal horseshoe.

"*Señor* Rodriguez, this hauling in barrels of water and feed and supplies for ourselves is a hard thing to do," said Raul. The wrangler's statement surprised Flores, since Raul seldom offered any suggestions of his own, especially when the captain was in a bad mood. And Flores couldn't think of any previous time when the captain had been so frustrated, except the day they found the wrecked truck.

Rodriguez glared at Raul in apparent disbelief. "You think I can't see that for myself? You think I'm so dumb that I need that kind of advice from you?" Rodriguez asked, obviously annoyed.

"I mean no disrespect, *Capitán*." Raul said, biting his lower lip and quietly looked away from his captain's stern, haughty stare.

"Then why do you tell me these things that I can see for myself? Is there some point in what you are trying to say?"

"Ye -- yes, *Capitán*. I believe you were right when you said that the *gringo* is maybe still twenty miles ahead of us -- that he is no longer in this area at all," offered Raul in a subdued voice.

"So, just what is your point, besides that you agree we are wasting our time?" Rodriguez asked, sarcastically.

Flores was convinced that his long-time friend had some specific idea that might be worth considering. But it was clear the wrangler was so intimidated by the captain's anger that it was hard for Raul to express himself.

"You might remember that I was born in a little village near Chihuahua and…"

"I don't give a goddam where you were born. I told you, get to the point or shut up your babbling," said Rodriguez. He took out his watch, glanced at it briefly and then shoved it back into his pocket.

"*Sí, Capitán.*" Raul's voice was barely audible. He turned and looked back toward the lower slopes where the trucks and the other mules would be waiting. Raul then pursed his lips as if to speak, hesitated, then shook his head and said, "I'm sorry, *Capitán.*"

Although Flores was bothered by Raul's decision to forego any more attempts to explain his earlier comments, he felt sure that Raul had observed something of significance. Flores knew the man too well. Raul could be forceful when dealing with anyone other than those whose rank was higher than his. With those who ranked above him, he readily acquiesced.

Flores wanted to speak up on behalf of his friend, but then thought better of it. The overbearing captain made others reluctant to incur his scorn. He seldom spoke to Raul without a tone of ridicule.

Flores stepped back alongside of the packmule and filled his canteen. He then held it up toward the others and asked, "Anyone else?"

"Yeah. Fill mine too," said Rodriguez. When Sanchez and Raul held out their canteens and nodded, Flores filled them and as he handed them back he noticed Blue was still standing in the shade cast by the belly of his mare, panting and watching him closely. She was obviously tiring, badly. Her teats were swollen and oozing drops of milk. Small lacerations showed on her flanks where thorns had scraped against the sides and stomach of the mongrel bitch. Taking a shallow wooden bowl from his saddlebags, Flores filled it with water and placed it down in front of Blue. She wagged her short tail, then lapped hungrily at the water, quickly emptying the bowl and licking away the drops clinging to the inside rim. Flores filled the bowl again.

Flores took a long drink from his canteen. He was pleased that the captain wanted to return to the prison. Later, when the shadows lengthened, he would ask Raul to ride on ahead with Rodriguez and Sanchez. Since the bay mare had been noticeably limping, Flores would have an excuse to lag behind where he could carry Blue on the saddle behind him without the captain knowing. When they got back to the prison, he would sneak her out to Cecelia's and let her spend the night with her pups. He could hardly wait to see the excitement when Blue first spotted her litter.

Replacing the cap on his canteen, Rodriguez, stared off into the distance, making no move to leave the mountain. He finally spoke, his voice now calm. "I don't want any of you to try to kill Reece if you see him. Shoot him only in the legs. Is that clear?"

"*Sí, Capitán,*" they all spoke at once.

"I want that bastard alive! I want to drag him behind my horse, running at top speed, right in through the main prison gate!"

After another long pause, Rodriguez spoke in a more normal tone. "We've got to have a plan. First we'll set up the ambush. I've already got a place in mind for that. We know where Reece is headed. He seldom strays more than a few miles from the Sierra's crest or the telegraph line." Rodriguez paused, with a strangely amused look on his face, then added, "The Swede's begged me for a chance to help us get him. When he heard of Reece's escape he came to the prison and left me a note. He's still negotiating for the rest of the line's completion."

"The *americano* who built the line?" Flores asked, puzzled that a prominent man like the contractor would want to be involved in such a scheme.

"I'm going to tell you something and if any one of you ever repeats it, I'll see that you regret it every day for the rest of your life. Is that clear?"

"*Sí, Capitán,*" they again answered in unison.

"The Swede got drunk in a bar in Chihuahua and got into a fight over a week ago. A taxidermist in the city had been bragging and showing friends the bighorn ram the Swede killed. Someone found out he'd killed it without any kind of permit in an area closed to hunting for over twenty years. Only two other desert bighorn rams in the record books that have been killed are bigger." Rodriguez took another drink from his canteen, wiped his mouth on his sleeve, took off his hat and wiped his forehead on his other sleeve. "The Swede's paid a lot of money to the right people so he can take the trophy home and have it entered in the record books."

"I see what you mean, *capitán*." Sanchez said.

"That's not the part that really worries me. A newspaper reporter from Mexico City has been around asking questions about how and where the ram was killed. He's also been talking to everyone who works at the hospital, trying to find out who we're chasing and how...." Rodriguez looked away, and picked at the peeling skin on his lower lip.

Flores was puzzled. "But how could anyone as far away as Mexico City have found out about...?"

"That damn Juarez! That's how. It had to be him who called the newspaper reporter."

Flores knew the captain was probably right. The bitter rivalry between Lieutenant Juarez and Rodriguez had increased in recent months. Since marrying the warden's niece the lieutenant had been even more arrogant than before.

Sanchez shook his head. "I don't know *nada, Capitán.*"

"That's the answer you'd all better remember. None of you know anything!" Rodriguez paused and looked at each man, his words of warning leaving no doubt as to just what he meant. "Don't let me see or hear of any of you even standing near a newspaper reporter. Besides me and the Swede, only one other man knows what happened." Rodriguez nodded toward the north. "When we get Reece back to the prison I got a special treat for him and when I'm through, he won't even be able to remember his own name."

Again there was a long pause. Flores had never seen the captain in such an agitated state. Looking at nothing Flores could see, the captain's eyes flashed excitedly. Straightening his legs and pressing the toes on his boots against the bottom of his stirrups, Rodriguez pushed himself up, sitting straight and tall. Flores wondered if Rodriguez was picturing a victorious return to the prison, dragging Reece in on a rope in front of all the prisoners.

After several minutes when nothing more was said, Rodriguez broke the silence, saying, "We need a base camp high in the mountains where we can strike in different directions -- north or south or even higher up if we spot him up along the rimrock or bottom of the cliffs."

"Hauling water for the stock is goin' to slow us down every time," said Sanchez, who, as Flores had noticed many times, usually just listened when the captain was expressing an idea.

"There -- there's a place that's got some water," stammered Raul in a barely audible voice.

The captain, ignoring Raul as usual, turned to Sanchez and said, "Yes, we need to take full advantage of the location of any springs that are within a few miles of the telegraph lines." Rodriguez jutted out his chin and nodded his head, obviously pleased that even the others were now showing a new eagerness to continue the pursuit of the man who had again vanished into the wastelands.

Flores tried to picture the quiet, docile Reece running high across the rocks and diving into thorn thickets and chaparral when he saw armed men on horseback coming after him. The rifle scope and the man's hardened physical condition had so far kept the odds in Reece's favor.

"I think Raul wanted to add something," offered Flores.

Rodriguez looked at the wrangler without comment, as if trying to hold his impatience in check for a few brief moments.

"The -- there's a place," stammered Raul, "about a hundred miles north of here -- an old, abandoned, silver mine that's in a deep canyon high up in the mountains. There's a good spring an' some old cabins --"

"How do you know about this place -- have you seen it yourself?" asked the captain.

"My uncle was married to an Indian woman who lived in a canyon near there," Raul answered. "He worked in the mine but he got killed when the tunnels caved in many years ago. I was just a little boy. I don't even remember my uncle. None of the bodies were ever recovered. The owners left the mine and were never seen again."

"You've been there in recent years and seen the spring?" asked the captain, suddenly leaning toward the wrangler. Rodriguez sat with his mouth half opened, intently watching Raul's eyes, waiting impatiently for his answer.

"A few months ago, *Señor* Rodriguez. I take my mother there every year to visit where her brother's body lies buried under a mountain of rocks. She puts flowers by the old entrance to the mine and…"

"Tell me about the spring," Rodriguez interrupted. "How much water does it have?"

"It's the only good water for maybe twenty or thirty miles. There should be some for us to share. Several Indians live there with their children and animals. They have some goats and sheep and a few chickens and a couple of burros. They drive them up into a high basin in the mornings, where the browse is good, and bring them down in the evenings for water. They have a big garden and grow their own food with water from the spring. We could --"

"We'll try to get Reece first at the place the Swede and I have in mind for an ambush. If we don't get him there then we'll hurry and move on north and set up a camp at the springs," Rodriguez said with enthusiasm. "The place we have in mind for the ambush is a long open area with only a few hiding places, then a steep mountain slope of shale that stretches for over a mile across, starting at the base of a cliff. Anyone who dares to cross it has to move very slow or he can start a slide that'll bury him in seconds under a mountain of rock."

"That's a good plan *Capitán*. I know the place you mean. We detoured below it when we built the line," Sanchez said grinning, showing his approval of a plan he seemed to believe would succeed.

"We can set up rocks for a bench and table and lay a saddle across them for the Swede to rest his rifle on," Rodriguez said, no longer showing any of his earlier discouragement.

"Why is the Swede so afraid for Reece to reach..." Flores stopped his question, realizing it could set Rodriguez off on another fit of anger.

Rodriguez stopped for a moment as if pondering whether or not he should answer Flores' question, he then grinned and explained. "Swede knows Reece sometimes cooks for guides in hunting camps. He also knows if a newspaper reporter finds out about our sheep hunt, his company could get some embarrassing publicity and he might have to give up his exceptional trophy. Not having a permit could cause a problem. Now don't ask me any more questions about the matter and don't even discuss this among yourselves!"

After a long period of silence, Sanchez quietly asked, "If we don't catch Reece at the slide, what will we do then?"

"You and Raul will leave immediately and go and set up the base camp. He'll show you the way. I'll arrange to bring fresh horses." Rodriguez's eyes flashed with a new excitement. "We'll move maybe twenty men and our stock in by..."

"But there won't be enough water for that many more people and animals -- the families there could share with a few of us but --"

"Goddam it, Raul, just how dumb can you be? We're not going to be sharing that water with anyone," said Rodriguez smugly with another big grin spreading across his face. "This is an emergency and the Mexican government doesn't have to share that water with a bunch of dirty Indians! They don't own the land or the water. *¡Tonto! ¿No intiendes?* Can't you see that?"

Flores saw immediately the chagrin that crossed Raul's face. He had not foreseen that his attempt to assist his captain had put the lives of innocent people into immediate peril, people who knew his family. His mother might never forgive him.

"What do I do about the ones who live there?" asked Sanchez.

"Give them an hour to get their things and clear out."

"What about their animals? They'll come into camp at night and keep us awake, looking for water."

Rodriguez spurred his horse hard, reining it cruelly back toward the trucks, then turned in the saddle and yelled, "Look, can't you figure out something so simple? Drive them back up into the hills and shoot them!"

CHAPTER 31

MADDENING THIRST

It was mid-morning on the sixteenth day say since John Reece fled into the mountains. He saw a prominent boulder ahead that he remembered, leaning down-slope at the top of a finger of rock. When he reached the boulder he stopped and looked ahead at the line of wooden poles, stretching for miles across the high plateau. The vegetation was stunted along the top of the rocky slope, but farther down, where the slope steepened, he could see the tops of condalia thickets. He knew they were much taller than the shrubs growing along the rocky crest.

At dawn, he'd glimpsed men on horseback riding through an opening in the thickets. Though they were miles below him, they appeared to be riding upward at a slight angle. If they continued the same course they could eventually reach the telegraph line near where he was headed. He'd been unable to jerk the telescope from the backpack in time to view the riders or count them before they'd crossed the narrow opening. He knew who they must be but where they were headed remained an important question.

His body still quivered from the unexpected sighting.

He checked the leg wrappings of metal screens he'd cut from the windows in the doctor's office. Strips of the once-white tape on the mid-thigh to ankle protectors now hung in dirty tatters. Thorns and branches had ripped the tape as he'd plowed through countless thickets of chaparral. Without the screens he would have had to run across more open desert and through sparse stands of mesquite and cactus. He knew his chances of being caught within days would have been almost certain. Reece pressed down on the layered screens and rubbed the tender muscles and tendons lying along the inside of his shin bones. Days of running across every type of terrain had left a constant throbbing in his legs and hips. At night, sleep came in short intervals. The ground was cold and hard.

Reece added new strips of tape, tightening the leggings where the screen's edges had been pulled loose or stretched. He looked at his notes. A simple "23 sparrows flying north" was the notation he'd made to guide him to his next cache of water and a jar of peanut butter. The reference points like the rock slide he'd selected were easy to remember. But he'd carefully noted the number of poles to the hidden water and the direction, in case his memory failed him. If for any reason he'd been searched there would have been little likelihood that notes about the sighting of birds would have aroused suspicions.

The slide, as best he could recall, should be no more than five to ten miles ahead. Within less than a mile past the slide he would reach the twenty-third pole. Expecting to reach his next water jars before noon, Reece had drunk his last few swallows at dawn, emptying all of the water from both rubber canteens.

Reece moved on, slipping along through the thorny, waist-high scrub, chewing on grains of fried corn as he watched below for any signs of movement. At the last water cache the day before, he'd also dug up a jar filled with the corn. When they built the line and no one was looking, he'd fried corn in greasy skillets on top of the cooking grate. The yellow kernels, kept in burlap sacks for feeding to the mules, were tasty when cooked in grease where salt pork had been fried. But he knew now he should have buried more water jars. The heat and strain of trying to reach the border was exhausting every nerve and muscle in his body. At least the pork grease, like the tablets Alvarez gave him, contained salt that his body desperately needed.

Each day's end had left him thirsty but still anxious for the morning and another chance to get closer to the border. He'd lost track of the days but he was determined to be there for Eula Mae's graduation.

It was almost noon when Reece came out of a stand of head-high mesquite and saw the wide expanse of gray rocks, layered on the steep slope below the bluffs. The thin flakes had broken from the dark, looming cliffs over thousands of years as seasons of rain and freezing cold eroded the cliff's porous surfaces. Gravity and the flake's slick surfaces had sent them cascading onto the mountainside.

A flash of sunlight caught Reece's eye from a movement somewhere below him. He crouched and backed into the mesquite as his heart raced wildly. Taking the telescope from his backpack, he waited, unsure of whether or not he'd been seen. After several minutes, he poked the telescope through the branches of the mesquite. Slowly moving the slender tube across the lower sides and bottom of the rockslide, he watched for any signs of men or horses. After almost half an hour he'd detected no movement of any kind nor seen any men or animals.

There was little shade for him in the sparse growth of shrubs, the ground they clung to was almost solid rock and the wall of mesquite provided a scant cover, at best, from any prying eyes below. The minutes dragged into at least an hour while Reece strained to catch a glimpse of any hidden danger below.

The hours slowly passed. With his water cache hidden less than two miles away, Reece's thirst was maddening. He considered slipping back and trying to work his way around the bluffs without being seen. The western side of the Sierras, he knew, dropped steeply into Copper Canyon. Unsure of his ability to find footholds on the canyon walls, Reece decided to wait.

Something kept drawing his attention to a place where the condalia leaves seemed to be of a different shade. The area appeared screened by bushes leaning in an unnatural state, showing a slight difference in the way the leaves reflected the light. They could have been cut and placed to hide someone watching the expanse of open shale where nothing grew.

As the shadows lengthened Reece knew he had to make a decision. Waiting to cross the treacherous shale after dark could be a deadly mistake. One slip and he could be buried under an avalanche of rocks, tumbling and sliding down the mountainside.

After spending most of the day, waiting and watching for any signs of danger on the lower slopes, Reece became impatient to move on. He was convinced that no one even suspected his presence along this stretch of the Sierra's crest. There was a gentle, cooling breeze that bouyed his spirits. In the fading light he moved out onto the shale, placing his feet carefully with each step.

As he turned once more to face downslope and look through the rifle-scope for any last sign of danger, his right leg suddenly buckled, pitching him face forward onto the rocks. There was a strange numbness and a feeling that his leg was missing. The loud booming sounds of an explosion came from somewhere down below. All was quiet as the aches in his lower body ceased and his thirst no longer mattered.

CHAPTER 32

MAN WITH A PITCHFORK

Sergeant Sanchez drove the old prison truck for almost five hours, stopping only once in the town of Chihuahua, for gas and water for the steaming radiator. Raul sat in the front seat with the sergeant. Several times he'd wanted to caution Sanchez about the high speed at which they were traveling but each time thought better of it. The sergeant never tolerated the slightest criticism from guards beneath his rank.

"That was it!" Raul exclaimed, twisting around, leaning out the truck window and pointing back alongside the road.

"What do you mean, 'that was it'?" asked Sanchez, turning and glancing back in the direction Raul had pointed.

"That was the sign to the mine. We gotta go back and turn up…"

"Damn you, Raul!" Sanchez swore, braking hard and cranking the steering wheel, "you just let me drive right on past!"

"I'm sorry. I didn't know the sign had fallen down."

The truck lurched to the side and bounced across the rutted grooves in the packed dirt when Sanchez suddenly pulled off the graveled roadway and braked to a stop.

"You'd better pay attention, Raul, to what you're supposed to be doing. That's all you got to do is sit there and watch, and you can't even do that right." Sanchez continued to chastise Raul as he swung the truck around in a field of head-high weeds just off the side of the road. The stock trailer they were towing swayed from side to side as the wheels rolled over mounds of dirt pushed up by rodents that had burrowed into the low, sloping bank.

"That's it right there." Raul pointed to the weathered wooden sign with faded white letters reading, "The Silver King Mines." The sign on the rotted post had been propped against a boulder. It was barely visible among the stunted shrubs growing in the shallow roadside ditch.

"I'd better move the sign out closer to the road or the *capitán* won't see it if they come in after dark."

"Hurry up and get it done. We got work to do," Sanchez grumbled.

Sanchez turned up the lane that led to the abandoned mine. It, too, was overgrown with weeds. Only a single well-beaten pathway meandered up the old lane.

Raul glanced through the small window in the back of the truck. The two new guards sat with their backs to the cab, holding neckerchiefs over their faces to keep out the swirling dust. Sanchez finally slowed the speeding vehicle after he lost control on a stretch of loose gravel, skidding dangerously close to the edge of a gully. Carrying two squealing horses, the stock trailer barely stayed upright when its wheels on the left side slid over the edge of the gully's bank. The tall, young gray was scared. He fought to regain his footing when he momentarily slipped and his shoulder and flank slammed against the trailer's sideboard. For the next mile Raul watched the gray, pulling back on his lead rope, the whites of the gray's eyes showing his fear.

The muffler had rusted and fallen off long ago, making it impossible to carry on a conversation. It was just as well. Raul was already feeling sick. Fumes from the leaking exhaust pipe were being sucked up through the open spaces between the truck's missing floorboards. The fumes and the winding road made him feel dizzy and sick at his stomach.

Within minutes -- if Sanchez didn't wreck the noisy, ancient vehicle -- they would be arriving at the spring where the Indians lived. It was the moment Raul was dreading. If he was lucky, none of the inhabitants would recognize him, since none of them had ever seen him wearing his prison uniform. But it was the crops and especially the people's livestock that concerned Raul the most. Running them out of their home was one thing, but it would be cruel and heartless to kill their animals. Surely, he thought, there must be some way to save them.

Sanchez slowed to a more moderate speed and shouted to Raul above the din of the rattling truck. "No use in waiting for evening when the herds come down for water. It'll be too hard to drive them back up in the hills an' shoot them when they're thirsty. And the *capitán* will be furious if we leave any stinking carcasses around the camp."

"But they could be scattered for miles across the highest slopes and some of them could be out of sight down in the canyons where it'll be…"

"You just do as I tell you, Raul. You must be spending too much time daydreaming about that woman you're seeing -- missing that road sign like you did."

"I'm really sorry, *Señor*, but none of us have gotten much sleep since

Reece got away. And I don't know whether we'll ever catch up with him or not, he just…"

"Raul, you better shut up that stupid talk. If the *capitán* hears you say something like that he'll bust your ass and both you and Flores better watch your step. He has noticed that often when the two of you are talking, you lower your voices. Neither of you better make any dumb mistakes that keeps us from catching that damn Reece."

"I'll try to be more careful -- and I'm sure Flores will too." Raul said. He was concerned as to just what it was that either he or Flores had done that had upset the captain. Surely, Rodriguez hadn't learned that Raul didn't kill the pups.

Sanchez looked over at Raul briefly with a withering glance then back at the narrow winding lane. He was apparently upset about Raul's remarks about catching Reece but the sergeant made no further comment for several minutes. Raul knew, however, that Sanchez never forgot even the slightest mistake. The sergeant glanced over again at Raul with a look of reproach.

"You better keep in mind what I told you. As soon as we get rid of the Indians you go on up and shoot all of their stock that you can find. Francisco and Alonzo will clean out one of the buildings and have it ready for the *capitán*. We might be here for two or three days or even longer."

Before Raul could even collect his thoughts about this unexpected change in the previous plan, the truck rounded the last curve and the old mining shacks loomed immediately ahead.

Chickens scattered, squawking and running for the cover of the rows of tall corn in the garden, when the truck abruptly clattered into the dusty yard and slid to a stop. Two skinny dogs stood their ground, growling and showing their teeth, hair raised stiffly along their backs.

An old, white-haired Indian with a sparse beard sat dozing in a chair made from bent and peeled willow branches. The chair, partly covered with a piece of sheepskin, leaned against the wall of a gray, weathered shed that was open on two sides. A homemade crutch stood nearby. Tables made from what appeared to be planks taken from the open sides of the low, squat building were piled high with dried corn and squash.

Raul and Sanchez got out of the truck and cautiously looked around. The old man was the only person in sight. Any others that might be hidden would have heard the approaching truck's noise for the last several hundred yards. Raul then noticed that the ground had recently been wetted around the tomato vines that were growing between the corn and the hills of squash. Clothes hung on a fiber rope, stretched between the corner of one of the buildings and a dead mesquite. Drops of water still clung to the bottom edge of some of the recently washed garments. Other inhabitants were definitely still nearby.

Past the garden area, Raul saw a lone burro standing in a small corral made of slender poles. A bulky mound of blankets, small bags, and cooking pots sat against the rail fence, just outside the corral.

Smoke from a small fire drifted upward slowly swirling around a carcass that was hanging by a wire from a wooden crosspiece. There was an enticing aroma from the slowly cooking meat that looked to be either lamb or goat. A pile of dried sticks lay between the crutch and the wicker chair, no doubt left there to be added to the fire, as needed, by the man still dozing by the shed.

The thin, elderly man roused, turned his head and squinted his eyes against the bright mid morning sun. His bony and weathered hands raised abruptly above his lap and began to tremble when he noticed the two guards who stood with their rifles at their sides near the back of the truck. He watched them suspiciously, and began nervously chewing, his toothless gums allowing the tip of his nose and his chin to almost touch. One of the dogs advanced, snarling.

"Call off your dogs or we'll shoot them," yelled Sanchez.

The old man cupped a hand to his ear and appeared to be unsure of what had been said or just why armed men in uniform were suddenly standing so threateningly near. He glanced around at the garden and row of buildings with a frightened look, as if to see where others might have recently disappeared to, or maybe even deserted him while he dozed.

The cry of a baby came from the second building.

Within minutes, men and women and shy, curious children began to appear from behind the rows of corn in the garden. Some could be seen peeking out of the doorways of the other weathered buildings, on a rise farther up the canyon. The last structure leaned precariously with the slope of the land that dropped steeply where the canyon narrowed into a clump of willow trees.

Just above the leaning structure a brush-fenced enclosure contained a field of ripened hay. Then, from behind a haystack, stepped a powerful-looking man with a pitchfork in his hand.

Sanchez appeared to be concerned when he looked up and saw him. He eased over by the open window of the truck cab, and stood with his hand resting over the door frame near his rifle.

Raul couldn't help but enjoy the unexpected response of the usually overbearing sergeant. Sanchez appeared disturbed by the sudden appearance of a man holding the crude weapon -- a weapon that seemed so insignificant when compared to their four repeating rifles, three of which the guards held in plain sight.

Raul sobered, realizing they were in a vulnerable position. If any Indians that might still be hidden had firearms they would easily be able to shoot them before they could locate the source of the attack or reach any form of cover.

The man with the raised pitchfork started walking down toward them. His measured stride didn't give the appearance of a man who would be easily frightened. From the previous trips with his mother to the abandoned mineshaft, Raul knew none of the Indians was ever hostile, yet all of his earlier trips had been of a peaceful nature, carrying flowers instead of a rifle.

Only the man who was somewhat bowlegged and still carrying the pitchfork made any move toward them. All was quiet except for the growling of the dogs and the wail of a baby. There was little doubt that the one coming down toward them was the settlement's leader. He came on with a rhythmic pace, his broad shoulders swaying from side to side.

Raul noticed that Sanchez was standing with his mouth slightly open, as if uneasy. Suddenly, the sergeant reached in and pulled out his rifle and abruptly cranked a shell from the magazine of the Mauser into the firing chamber. The man coming toward them showed no emotion and made no change in his stride.

Stopping less than five feet from Sanchez, the man stood the end of the wooden handle on the homemade pitchfork near his right foot, much like a soldier standing at parade rest. Raul could see the dark hair showing gray at the man's temples. With the slightest motion from his left hand, the dogs stopped their growling and lay down.

"What you want?" he asked in a calm, dignified manner, neither haughty nor arrogant, but as fearless as if he were a general with a thousand armed soldiers behind him.

Sanchez, who was accustomed to ordering people around at the prison, hardly seemed prepared for this type of meeting with an individual who stood unblinking in the face of what appeared to be such unfavorable odds.

Sanchez nervously swallowed. "You...you'll have to leave this place immediately," he finally stammered. After a long pause and a deep breath the sergeant spoke up more forcefully. "The *capitán* from the prison at Matamoros is coming here to set up a base camp," Sanchez blustered, "and you'll have to leave within the hour."

"Why you say leave?" asked the man, his thick shaggy eyebrows lowering. Slowly a dark scowl spread across his broad handsome face. He inched his head and shoulders slightly forward, as if he might be considering impaling the sergeant on his pitchfork if he didn't like the guard's answer.

Sanchez was an effective officer when dealing with routine matters at the prison where he could call upon the captain when he ran into unexpected problems. The sergeant's loyalty and dedication to duty were without question when he was following orders. Raul could plainly see, however, this was no routine matter. The man standing unflinchingly before them was certainly a courageous one. He had no doubt assumed that the sudden appearance of armed men in uniform were an ominous threat to his people. A man of his age would have seen times where timidity and subservience had cost the scattered remnants of his tribe both their self-respect and most of their meager possessions -- and some, undoubtedly, their lives.

The sergeant backed up, ever so slightly, seemingly aware that he had better move with caution and treat this man with dignity and respect. The four sharp tines of the fork, little more than an arm's length away, were an intimidating factor that could hardly be ignored. Raul felt sure that the sergeant must now realize he'd let the man get much too close. One quick thrust and Sanchez could be fatally stabbed.

"This place many day, many mile from prison. Why you say leave homes?"

Again, Sanchez lost the expected advantage of a well armed aggressor. The slight movement backward, if only an inch or two, suggested to Raul that the sergeant was not sure of himself and perhaps trying to stall. Sanchez nervously glanced around at the other guards as if trying to better judge his next response or movement. He licked his lips and swallowed. The man facing him, apparently a master at reading an opponent's nerve, was pressing him for an answer.

"We -- we must find someone -- a man -- a man who ran away from the prison."

The Indian leader's brow wrinkled and a hateful glower showed on his face. He turned and looked up at the towering mountain range in the distance. Then he asked, "You think man who run away somewhere up there?" He made a wide sweep with his left arm extended, shaking his head in disbelief that a prisoner might be anywhere in the vast wasteland, stretching for miles both north and south. "Must be Indian." he added nodding his head up and down.

"No. He's a *gringo*, trying to make it to the border."

"No white man run this far!" he said, continuing to shake his head from side to side. "No. Not find white man up there."

The captain had emphasized to both Sanchez and Raul that he didn't want

240

them giving information to anyone who might question the need for a base camp at the spring. He was still concerned that word might spread about the *gringo* who got away and he hoped Reece could be captured without incident.

The sergeant had either become so rattled that he'd forgotten the captain's instructions or he was momentarily more fearful of the man intently watching his every move than he was of Captain Rodriguez.

When the Indian turned back toward Sanchez his dark eyes flashed with a new intensity and hatred, his knuckles whitening as he fiercely gripped the wooden handle of the pitchfork.

Seeing his opportunity, Sanchez had stepped back quietly and swung his rifle barrel up and pointed it at the middle of the man's chest.

"I told you the *capitán* from Matamoros will be here soon. You had better be using your time to move your people out," Sanchez said in a voice now laced with boastful defiance.

The tension between the two men had reached a new level of intensity. One of them would have to either back down or make a move that could only lead to bloodshed, yet both men stood their ground. Finally, the Indian leader looked at the other three guards as if to size up their commitment to the sergeant. When he looked at Raul he paused, his eyes squinted, showing a sign of curiosity and possible recognition. Raul immediately felt his gut tighten, and he nervously swallowed, then glanced away from the piercing stare. The man looked back at Sanchez and spoke calmly; this was not the time to do something foolish, he seemed to realize. He lowered the pitchfork.

"We go now. But I remember you and way you treat my people." He looked around at the sound of a door with squeaking hinges opening on the second building where the cries of a baby had ceased. An old woman stood holding a handful of bloody rags. She said something to a young girl who immediately started towards a pail sitting on a bench. Two other women smiled and stepped in front of the girl and one lightly touched the girl on the shoulder. The one closest to the pail grabbed it and ran toward the spring.

The Indian leader turned back toward Sanchez. "We get animals on mountain." He pointed toward a high basin where the land rose into a shallow bowl several miles across. Thickets of yellow-green creosote bushes grew along the steep slopes just below the lower lip of the basin. Raul could barely make out a half-dozen or so small black and white specks which, he assumed, could be both sheep and goats, grazing on the slopes above the thickets.

"No. You will take the things you can carry and leave here within half an hour," Sanchez ordered, taking out his watch and looking at it. "You are wasting the time I gave you earlier."

The woman holding the bloody rags looked directly at the two men facing each other. She frowned with a look of defiance and disgust. Speaking to a boy who looked to be five or six years old, she then nodded toward the table with the dried corn. Before the boy could move, three women reached for the corn, each grabbing several ears and ran to the corral where the burro stood, his shaggy head hanging over the top rail. Another woman fetched him a pail of water.

Raul looked at the woman standing in the doorway. She looked tired. Lines showed across her forehead and deep creases in the skin at the corners of her eyes indicated a hard life spent outdoors. Her slightly arched nose and generous mouth accentuated the perfect cheekbones and jawline of a woman who had been beautiful in earlier years. As she dropped the bloody rags in the pail of water, fetched from the spring, she nodded and smiled briefly at the young girl who stood gazing up at her. While one of the women began washing the blood from the pieces of cloth she looked again at the two men who faced each other.

"What about animals and crops?" The leader asked.

"We will take good care of them," Sanchez said. Raul looked at him sharply, knowing he was lying.

"Need burros for old ones to ride and goats have milk for children…"

Sanchez cocked the hammer on his rifle and said in a most authoritarian manner, "You'll do exactly as I told you. Now get moving!"

When Sanchez turned and walked away the leader held up his hand, rotating his wrist in a circle. The others watching hurried over. After a brief discussion in barely audible voices they moved off quickly in different directions, their faces strained with a look of bitterness.

Raul sat on the tall, gray gelding that he'd saddled, watching helplessly as the people scurried about, rolling their belongings up in their blankets, tying them with pieces of hemp and stringing blackened pots and pans together to throw over their shoulders. Some of the women hurried down to the spring carrying goatskin water bags.

Skipping the cabin with the baby, Sanchez and the two new guards began to inspect the old mine shacks. The best one would be readied for the captain. As soon as the guards were out of sight Raul rode over by the camp's leader, where the man kneeled in the dirt near the corral, tying up a roll of bedding. Raul dismounted, glanced at the burro eating the corn, then busied himself, tightening the cinch on his saddle.

"I -- I need to talk to you," he began.

The leader looked up at Raul as if he would like nothing better than to strangle him and the other guards.

"You don't recognize me, but -- I come here with my mother every year to put flowers up at the old mine shaft where my uncle was killed."

The Indian stared at Raul without comment. "I remember -- but you not have uniform," he finally responded, his angry countenance softening and his voice less hostile.

"I'm really sorry that this had to happen to your people. The prison *capitán* is going to bring in many guards and their horses and take all the water."

"Then you no let animals drink?" The scowl quickly returned.

This was the most difficult part for Raul. He hoped it would still be better to tell this man the truth -- he did not seem like one who could be easily fooled.

"I've been ordered to go up and -- and -- shoot them so they don't come down at night looking for a drink. If we fence them away from the spring they'll keep everyone awake bleating for water." Raul swallowed and waited for a response from the Indian who stared at him with a withering sneer before looking away and shaking his head in disgust.

Raul quickly continued. "But I'm going to ride up now and try to drive them a couple of miles to the north, toward that canyon over yonder." He nodded in the direction he intended to drive the herd. "You'll hear me shoot, maybe 20 times. If you circle around with some of your people, you should be able to find your stock and take them with you."

"I see." The Indian leader finished tying a knot in the rope he'd wrapped around the bedding without further comment. Raul waited anxiously. He could feel the dryness in his mouth. To even consider disobeying the sergeant's order and then revealing this intent to a total stranger could result in a lengthy prison sentence.

The leader stood and slid his knuckles up and down the side of his face as if deeply pondering Raul's comments and his obvious predicament. Finally, the man looked intently into Raul's eyes and spoke.

"You take great risk. I not forget. So, you chase white man who run away?"

Raul let out a long deep breath in a relieved sigh before he responded then he softly said, "Yes, but he's not just any man. We've been after him for days now on horseback. He runs hard and never seems to get tired."

The Indian leader made no response.

The woman, who Raul now realized must be a midwife who'd been sent for to help with the new baby, took two of the top rails from the corral fence.

She leaned them against the remaining rails, spacing them some three feet apart. She then began to weave and lash slender willow branches diagonally across the space between the rails as a woman stripped the finger-sized branches from the wicker chair. Raul realized that within minutes the midwife, whose rapid hand movements were hard to follow, would have a travois completed and ready for travel.

The old white-haired man hobbled among the rows of corn, twisting ears from the green stalks. Two girls who looked to be no more than seven years in age began filling a burlap sack with squash and tomatoes.

The bitter memory of the evening when Rodriguez and the Swede sent Raul scrambling up the loose shale would never be forgotten. Being ordered to make the treacherous climb and look for any sign Reece was wounded had ignored any concern that Raul could easily be crushed under a mountain of sliding shale and boulders. It had been the most terrifying experience of his life.

Raul looked around and lowered his voice to little more than a whisper. "But I'm afraid the *gringo* won't make it to the border. He's been shot and he's lost a lot of blood but no one else knows it."

The midwife glanced at Raul, her face, for a moment, unable to hide the unexpected news she'd heard of a *gringo* being shot. She quickly looked away, her fingers deftly lacing the edge of a piece of canvas as a covering over the woven willow branches. Raul studied her profile. He was sure he'd seen her before.

"I hope you not catch man that run so far."

The midwife led the burro from the corral and hitched him to the travois. She strapped a crude harness of canvas strips over his shoulders and neck and around his girth. She then nodded toward the cabins. The Indian leader went into the second cabin and came out carrying a young woman. He placed her gently on the travois.

When the midwife picked up the bundle leaning against the corral fence and struggled to swing it onto her back, the Indian leader took it from her and lashed it onto his own heavy load. With a loud grunt he managed to get the entire bulk onto his back and started off down the winding lane. Some 30 people, all carrying bundles on their backs, fell in single file behind him. Two of the followers carrying large bundles were boys who appeared to be no more than eight years old. One young man near the back of the line limped slightly. His left foot twisted out to the side at an angle with each step as if his leg had been broken at one time and never properly set.

Following their defiant leader, the rag-tag group made a dismal sight as it moved off down the trail toward the distant valley farms that lay some forty miles to the east.

Sanchez and the two other guards returned after inspecting all of the shacks. They stood watching the small tribe trudging away from their homes. The midwife walked behind the travois, carrying the newborn baby.

The old man hobbled along on his crutch at the back of the line. The partly cooked meat, wrapped and tied in the piece of sheepskin from the chair, was hanging from a rope looped across his narrow, hunched shoulders. When he passed the guards he stopped, shook his crutch at them, muttered a string of curses, then hurried on to catch up with the others.

Raul spurred the gray hard and raced up toward the basin, pretending he didn't hear Sanchez yelling to him.

CHAPTER 33

THE FOLLOWERS

Flores had come in with the captain and some twenty other men after midnight. Raul shook him awake two hours before daylight. They fed and watered the stock and began to saddle the horses and load the pack mules with supplies of water and food for a long day's ride.

By noon, two seven-man groups going after Reece were spread out both north and south for 20-30 miles across the eastern slopes of the Sierra Madre.

Captain Rodriguez led the group of four men who rode straight up toward the peaks on the western skyline. They would cover the middle area of the mile-high plateau where the telegraph line crossed, trying to pick up any sign of Reece, if he'd come that far. Flores and Raul rode last in line, wondering if they would ever catch sight of one wounded prisoner on the run trying to slip through such an expanse of desolation. It was likely, they agreed, that one of the groups would find Reece's body.

Straight ahead, the barren treeless crags loomed above the clouds. Pockets of white contrasted with the deep, darkened and weathered crevices where the snow still clung to the steep north face of the crags.

After a brief stop to let the horses rest they refilled their canteens. They rode on for another two hours with no sign of Reece's trail.

Shadows from the midafternoon sun were already cast by the tallest peaks and lay in darkened bands down across the light-colored sands where the line was built.

It would be another long, grueling day's ride. The higher peaks, lightly dusted with a recent snow, were at least 25 miles from the spring.

The weather was beginning to change. At times, dust devils made it difficult to see ahead for any distance. The small whirlwinds that danced across the unbroken slopes picked up debris from under the cactus and chaparral, whipping it into a blinding, whirling mass of sharp, dried needles and coarse, stinging sand.

By late afternoon a hot, searing wind from the east began to blow the sand in blinding sheets up toward the crags on the western horizon.

After they had ridden for an another hour, without seeing any sign of Reece, the winds began to subside. Almost immediately, Flores spotted bootprints, some half-filled with blown bits of dried leaves and dust, wandering across a stretch of sand. Raul and Flores dismounted and led their horses through the mesquite. Flores showed Raul where the toe on the right boot was dragging a slight furrow with each step.

Within a few hundred yards the trail showed where Reece had stopped. A few spots of dark red showed in a shallow depression on a rock that the scrub mesquite grew against. The blood was still sticky. Raul kicked sand over the spots as he turned and motioned to the Captain that they'd found Reece's trail. Nearby, a grouping of tracks between two large boulders indicated that Reece had hunkered down and waited out the worst of the sandstorm before moving on.

"Probably afraid he might get lost if he kept on going when he couldn't see more than a few feet in front of him," said Flores.

Flores knelt and called Blue over. The bitch picked up Reece's scent and moved off along the line of tracks.

"Come on, let's go!" yelled Captain Rodriguez. "We'll get the bastard now." He spurred his horse into a gallop, easily following the tracks of Reece through the scattered scrub.

Within half an hour, however, the tracks disappeared when they reached a long stretch of limestone that covered the slopes ahead as far as they could see. Flores dismounted and waited for Blue to catch up with the winded horses.

"Hurry up and get that bitch working on Reece's trail," ordered the captain when Blue shortly emerged from the chaparral they had ridden through. Flores squatted, cupped his hand and poured Blue a drink from his canteen. The panting bitch lapped cravingly at the offered water.

"Let's get moving now, Flores! She can drink all she wants after we catch that *gringo*," demanded Rodriguez.

Flores poured Blue another drink, avoiding any eye contact with the captain.

"Flores, you bastard, the *capitán* said now!" Sanchez yelled.

Flores mumbled an apology to the captain as he motioned for Blue to circle and find Reece's trail. After remounting, Flores watched closely while the bitch methodically worked the area ahead of the last visible bootprints. Her body tensed momentarily when she caught Reece's scent. She quickly swung her muzzle back and forth to pin the location of the route along which the quarry had fled.

"It's best if we don't crowd her and give her a little room to work. She may need to backtrack from time to time to pick up the scent on these rocks. Conditions aren't good, It's awful hot and windy today."

Flores liked the fact that Blue was a silent trailing dog. Even though she never barked, her stubby tail always gave him a clear indication of her progress. When she broke into a lope Flores called out. "She's got it figured out now!"

The captain spurred his horse and quickly took the lead. Flores wished the captain wouldn't ride so close to Blue, but he knew Rodriguez never listened to any advice from anyone except the sergeant. The metal shoes on the gray Flores was riding clattered on the rough, lichen-splotched surface. The gangling young mount was awkward and the footing gave him trouble but he had good stamina. He would have eagerly taken the lead if Flores had let him run.

They had traveled less than two miles when a swirling, hot, eastern wind and dust-devils began blowing again. The winds gradually increased in intensity and began blowing Reece's scent up across the slopes and into the rocks and cactus that grew along the ledges and bluffs, making it tedious and almost impossible for Blue to follow the invisible particles of spoor.

Their progress slowed while Blue worked back and forth, often in complete circles, attempting to follow the scent that had been whipped and blown in so many different directions.

Again they hit a long, sandy slope that stretched ahead for miles. They were off and running hard, the fresh tracks in the soft surface clearly showing and easy to follow. The wind that was swirling the scent up among the rocks and onto the ledges no longer mattered. Reece's tracks showed plainly in the soft footing. His wounded leg was forcing him to now flee along the easiest course.

Rodriguez yelled and spurred his horse ahead of the others, then abruptly reined his horse around and stopped. Raul and Flores urged their sweating mounts forward at a lope and soon reached the point where they'd seen Rodriguez and Sanchez rein up abruptly and dismount. As they rode alongside, Raul could see that the captain was highly agitated. He stood looking at the ground in front of him and muttering curses to Sanchez then kicking the dirt up wildly.

Tracks showed where more than twenty people had crossed Reece's trail, heading west, climbing higher into the mountains. At least two dozen head of livestock had been traveling with them. Within a short distance, Reece's lone tracks appeared again, still wandering in a northwesterly direction. His stride was much shorter now. "He's beginning to weaken," Flores whispered to Raul. He's hit in his right leg and he's barely able to lift his foot. These dark spots here coated with sand show he's bleeding again. He can't last much longer."

Once again, there was wild elation from Rodriguez and Sanchez as they whipped their mounts into a gallop.

Tracks now showed where others had come down from the higher plateau and were now following along the trail where Reece was making a desperate effort to keep going toward the border. All four guards dismounted and led their horses, following along where a profusion of tracks had obliterated most of Reece's bootprints. At first Flores thought the ones who had followed Reece's trail were just being playful. One of the followers had stepped directly into the tracks made by Reece.

Within a few hundred yards others had come down and joined them and soon people's tracks were wandering off in all directions and then coming back and mysteriously criss-crossing each other. The last ones who had joined had been traveling with a flock of sheep and possibly some goats. Tufts of wool showed on the low, brushy chaparral. The flock had bunched together, squeezing through openings where the desert vegetation grew in thorny thickets. Paw prints showed where two dogs followed the flock.

In places, some of the Indian's tracks went off for a couple of hundred yards or more then disappeared into the rocks. The sharp cloven hooves of the animals traveling with them left the soil plowed into shallow furrows.

Captain Rodriguez was becoming highly agitated, loudly cursing those who had recently obliterated any sign of Reece.

Raul showed Flores the tracks where one Indian had walked. "See how the left footprint here turns out at an angle? He's the one I told you about! There's no question, they're the same ones we ran off from the spring."

"The first bunch of tracks we came to showed that a couple of burros were traveling with them. But I don't see any burro tracks here," said Flores. "They probably took their families and belongings on up higher to safety. But it looks like some of them came back down herding the sheep and goats ahead of them just to wipe out Reece's trail. You know how they damn near worship any of their men who can run for days across the desert. Their best runners are the ones they treat with greatest respect."

"Now Reece is going to be like one of their own -- especially since we're treating them like they are little more than animals -- taking their water and homes like we did," said Raul.

"I'm glad you thought of a way to save their animals," said Flores. "That's the least they had coming."

Raul nodded. "I just couldn't bring myself to shoot them -- since it was all my fault that the people were being driven out of their homes -- if I'd only kept my mouth shut."

Raul glanced over toward Sanchez and the captain before he continued. "I know a little bit about these people. They're going to do whatever they can to slow us down."

Flores looked over again to where Rodriguez and Sanchez were still leading their horses, trying to make some sense of the many tracks that often led them in circles. Flores felt sure that the sergeant was puzzled about the tracks that were made by the flock of sheep and goats, although they were now at least fifteen miles from the spring. Sanchez had glanced over a couple of times toward Raul, his brow wrinkled into a suspicious and questioning stare, but had said nothing. Even if Sanchez was convinced the tracks were made by the people they ran off from the spring, he would be reluctant to mention it to Rodriguez. It was too late to do anything about it now. If he said anything the captain would find plenty of blame to go around for all of them -- and, after all, the sergeant had been in charge.

Rodriguez stopped and stood with his hands on his hips, breathing hard, and glowering at the trampled ground around him. His jaw was set and his face pale with anger.

He then shook his fist in the general direction where the tracks meandered on ahead of them and shouted curses until his voice was little more than a hoarse whisper.

As darkness neared the guards no longer had any idea which set of tracks to follow, the many trails began spreading out over several miles. As they repeatedly circled and rode back and forth the hoofprints of their own mounts only added to the confusion.

Flores could see that Captain Rodriguez was a badly beaten man. Flores, too, was weary with exhaustion -- but he felt a sense of euphoria like he'd never felt before. The Indians had saved their flocks and found a way to salvage their self-respect -- nullifying in such a simple and subtle manner all of the determined efforts of the mounted guards when they were so close to catching the lone desert runner: A man still struggling ahead with no knowledge of the Indians whose efforts had bought him a little more time, perhaps another half-day at the most.

When total darkness descended the pursuers gave up and rode in silence back down the mountain.

CHAPTER 34

AMBUSH

John Reece hunkered beside a boulder, while overhead a cold wind howled throughout the night. The pain in his leg made sleep near impossible. When he'd watched the sun set behind red-streaked clouds the evening before, he saw it as a bad sign, the kind some folks called an omen. Barely able to drag his foot, he'd kept going until darkness closed in around him. With little sleep, the fierce winds and the blackness of the long night had overwhelmed him. He prayed for the light and warmth the morning sun would bring.

As dawn crept across the mottled landscape, the dim outline of creosote bushes took shape. Reece closed his eyes and waited for the sun to break over the horizon and take away the chill.

The drone of buzzing insects awakened him with a start. The sun was up, warming the air currents moving up from the wide valley to the east. Flies crawled over the torn screen where blood had seeped through the woven mesh.

Reece fearfully looked around. He'd been sleeping in an area with little cover, in easy view of anyone scanning the upper slopes. When he tried to crawl to nearby shrubs, he found the night air had stiffened his injured leg. The slightest movement sent a pain shooting from his foot up into his hip joint. He was out of water and unsure of where his next jars were hidden. He'd never felt so alone and helpless.

Dragging his wounded leg, John reached a screen of sagebrush and pulled the rifle scope from his backpack. Nothing moved on the broad, arid expanse sweeping toward the north. The line of telegraph poles they'd built down from Nacozari disappeared through a notch in the hills on the horizon. Creosote bushes lined the banks of shallow arroyos that cut across the sage flats. Reece remembered running with the mules along the stretch of line on a day when the crews were spread for over ten miles. He'd been in good condition. Neither the heat nor the distance had slowed him as he led the mules at a fast trot along the line.

252

The possibility of an injured leg had not been thought of in his earlier plans. And it had been the Swede's long range shot that took away the lead he'd held since fleeing in the prison truck.

Now he had to make a decision and he knew he had few choices. Even though it felt like the bullet had only grazed the bone on the side of his knee, Reece wondered if he still had any chance of reaching the border. He knew many believed one's destiny was sealed, something no amount of effort could change. Facing what appeared to be a crushing defeat, Reece refused to believe that somehow he couldn't make it. Hoping for a lift in his spirits, he reached inside his shirt and pulled out the two letters from Eula Mae.

Since he had memorized them word for word, he didn't remove them from the well-worn envelopes. He sat, looking at Eula Mae's name neatly typed in the corners. He then pressed them against his chest and felt an immediate surge of hope.

If he could find his water jars and make some kind of a crutch he would try to cross the open plain at night. He put the letters away and took out the record of his hidden jars and picked up the rifle scope. He slowly swept the scope along the line of poles and then across the sage flats where the arroyos cut the plain. There was no way for him to know whether his greatest danger would come-from men still chasing after him or moving on ahead and lying in ambush.

A flash of movement caught Reece's eye. He quickly swept the scope back along the creosote. There was nothing in sight except the yellow-green foliage, gently waving in the morning breeze. Reece was nervous. The last time he'd thought there was movement near the bottom of the rockslide, and then ignored it, was the day he'd been shot. This time he'd wait and watch until he was sure no danger lurked along the arroyos.

After long minutes passed with no sign of movement he again studied the line of telegraph poles. He was desperate to find his buried water. Swinging the scope back toward the arroyos, he wanted to make sure he'd been mistaken when he thought he saw something move near the head-high bushes. There it was again, the same brief flash of movement, but when he focused on the same place, nothing moved.

He laid the scope on a rock and aligned it on the spot where he was sure something had moved, twice. He stared without blinking until his eyes teared -- then he saw a glimpse of movement. He kept staring until he saw it again. His legs began to tremble when he realized what he'd seen. A horse hidden behind a creosote bush had switched its tail. He knew it must be tormented by the same biting flies crawling on his leg, feasting on the drying blood and pus.

While he watched for other movement, he heard the shrill whinny of a nervous horse from off to his right. Within seconds, he heard other faint neighs, answering from scattered locations in the distant arroyos. The high-pitched neighs meant that many horses and guards were hidden in the arroyos that spread for miles across the plains. Reece knew they were all watching for a wanted man to start moving across the expanse of stunted sage.

The brief sightings of a horse's tail flicking into view and the nervous calling of the others crushed Reece's spirits. He knew now he was a beaten man. He couldn't move forward and there was no other place to go.

The wily Captain Rodriguez now held the last trump.

John Reece lay hidden, pondering his predicament. Exhausted and thirsty he found it hard to think of any remaining options. He was puzzled that Rodriguez had ridden so far ahead to set up an ambush. Didn't they know he was wounded and bleeding -- that he could no longer run at the fast pace he'd maintained since his escape?

He thought of Thompson and what it must have been like for him, lying alone in the desert, knowing death was closing in -- knowing he'd made a terrible mistake and he'd never see his wife again.

The hours slowly passed. Without water, the heat worsened. The slanting rays of the afternoon sun crept under the taller sage, stealing away the scant shade and heating the rocks and soil there, too.

Near delirious, Reece waited, wondering if his destiny was near -- wondering if all hope was lost. He closed his eyes and tried to blot out the reality he knew he had to face. His mind reeled, unfocused.

Something touched him on the shoulder. He jumped and opened his eyes, and was startled at the sight of an old Indian woman kneeling beside him. Her gaze was steady as she looked intently at his face. A dark shawl lay draped across her head. She wore a loose fitting blouse, gathered at the neck. She raised a goat-skin water bag to his lips and nodded. After a few swallows she pulled the water away and shook her head. He had to drink slowly. Somehow, she seemed to know he'd been too long without water.

Reece wondered if he was delirious or if someone had really brought him water. He'd heard of men lost and dying of thirst in the desert, convinced they could see water all around them. She raised the water bag again, and now he could see the drops of perspiration on her face and neck and smell the sweaty odor of her body. She must have traveled for a long ways in the heat to find him and bring him water. But why? Why was she giving him water? Was she going to turn him in for a reward? She must know prison guards were waiting for him, not far ahead, in the arroyos. A more puzzling question was where did she come from and how did she know where to find him? None of it made any sense to him. She sat the water bag down and disappeared into the bushes. Shortly, she returned, carrying some dried sticks. She pulled some rawhide strings from a pocket and began lashing the sticks together.

The light was beginning to fade when she helped Reece to his feet and handed him the crutch she'd fashioned. Motioning for him to stay bent low, she led the way back into the taller sage brush, away from the waiting guards and their repeating rifles. As darkness fell around them she kept going, shaking her head when Reece wanted to stop and rest.

Reece watched the moon rise over the plains and valleys to the east. He hobbled along as best he could, sometimes tripping and falling. The woman helped him up each time then led off again toward the south.

Each hour was long and tortuous as the moon moved across the heavens. It had passed overhead when they reached a brush enclosure hidden in a dark, narrow canyon. The strange old woman refilled the water bag at a spring and then helped him onto the back of her hidden burro. Leading the shaggy beast, the woman abruptly changed directions and began climbing to a higher elevation. Reece could hear the burro's hooves striking shale that made the little beast stumble when loose pieces slipped from beneath its feet. They continued on through a mountainous area. Since the moon had disappeared behind dark clouds, Reece had no idea of the direction they were going. He worried about the woman's reason for such behavior, but he didn't object. She'd supplied him with water when he was desperately thirsty and led him far away from armed men waiting to kill him.

Dawn was breaking when they reached a camp where Reece saw a circle of blackened rocks and what appeared to be two sleeping forms. A few cooking pots and some bedding and burlap sacks sat nearby. The woman unfolded a dark brown woven blanket with tassels knotted at each end. She spread it across a layer of pine boughs and motioned for him to lie down. She stoked the coals in the circle of rocks and added dry twigs and larger pieces of mesquite, then sat a blackened pot into the midst.   ·

Without any hesitation, she took a knife and cut the dirty tape, holding the screen in place on his right leg. After slowly removing the metal legging and cutting away the lower leg of his pants, she bent close to examine the bullet wound on the outside of his knee. Reece raised up on his elbows to see the area where the bullet had struck. Until the dried blood on his leg was washed away it was hard to tell the extent of the bullet's damage.

A groove in the curved screen wrapping showed where the bullet had been deflected a couple of inches before its momentum tore through the layered wire. The projectile's long flight path had slowed it, lessening the magnum cartridge's impact and preventing Reece's knee from being shattered. Who was this strange woman and what was she doing, he wondered? She moved with a confidence that made it seem she knew quite well what she was doing.

When the liquid in the pot began to steam, both sleeping forms raised their heads and looked at Reece. One appeared to be a girl of maybe twelve or thirteen and the other was a boy of about five or six. It was hard to tell since they were still lying in bed, under the covers.

When each of the children gave him a sleepy-eyed grin, he looked again at the old woman who was peeling a piece of prickly pear she'd dumped from a bag. Her quick moving fingers deftly pushed aside the sharp spines as she extracted a filleted pad.

She washed the injured area with the warmed water and placed the slab of the skinned inner flesh of the prickly pear over the open wound. Stripping long fibers from a yucca leaf, she wrapped and tied the poultice loosely into place.

Could it be, Reece wondered, he'd seen this family before, well over 100 miles to the south of where they were now? Most of the round-faced, dark-eyed children of the Indians looked much alike to him and he'd never gotten a close look at the woman who stayed back in the shadows. It wouldn't make any sense that an older woman and two children would have traveled such a distance with only one burro. There would be no reason for them to come to such a desolate mountain area where it appeared no other Indians lived. Since the woman had only pointed and shrugged when she'd found him, he assumed she spoke no English and he also assumed neither did the children. It disturbed him, when he thought of the great risk they were taking. The woman had to know something about him to have traveled so far to the place where he'd all but given up. Surely, she had to know the Mexican authorities were conducting a widespread search to find an escaped prisoner. Her interference could have severe penalties for both herself and the children.

Taking a handful of seeds from a small pouch, the woman placed them on a flat rock and pounded them with another rock. She poured the crushed bits into the boiling pot.

After the children got dressed, the girl began preparing corn-meal tortillas.

Removing the boiling pot from the coals, she slid a thin piece of metal over the fire, resting the sides on the small circle of rocks for support. The woman poured a dark brew from the pot and handed it to Reece. She motioned for him to drink it. Since the pain in his leg had eased, he took the offered cup.

The boy stood by the fire, wiping the sleep from his eyes. He watched the woman who appeared to be his grandmother, lead the burro out of sight across a steep slope of chaparral and sparse grass. He looked at Reece and grinned. *"Buenos días, Señor* John."

Reece sat upright, alarmed that the boy knew his name and had spoken to him in Spanish. He was dumbfounded. He looked at the girl who was busy cooking the tortillas. His first thoughts were that they were going to take him in and collect a reward. He was sure Rodriguez must have posted notices throughout the Sierra's range, with his name and description, and perhaps a sketch of how he looked. It was the action he'd feared the most, the offering of a little money to the widely scattered and impoverished Indians.

"How do you know my name?" Reece asked, afraid of the answer he might hear.

The boy grinned and turned his face away, as if embarrassed that a *gringo* man had spoken to him directly.

The girl looked up from where she was squatting by the fire, "*Señor* John, your name is known by many of our people." She spoke clearly and distinctly.

"So you speak English. Please tell me who you are an' how you learned my name."

"You don't remember us, do you?" The girl smiled and Reece could see a strong resemblance to the older woman.

"I'm not sure. You do look like someone I remember, but that was a long way from here -- 'bout a hundred miles or more." He looked at the blanket he was sitting on. It had two white stripes a few inches apart, running across each end above the fringe of tassels. It looked like the one the old woman's burro had worn over its back -- the woman he'd been so sure was stealing his water jars, months before.

"For a long time we were afraid that you were dead. We never saw you again after the guard beat and kicked you -- it was just a few days ago that my grandmother heard that you were still alive, but that you'd been wounded."

Reece took a deep breath and relaxed, relieved that this family hadn't looked for him because of any wanted notice posted on a tree.

"Does your grandma speak any English?"

"Not really. Her parents were driven from their home on the Babicora when she was just a little girl."

"Yeah, I heard 'bout that -- an' it wasn't right."

"The Mexican dictator sold all of our people's lands to white men with lots of money from your country. After that my grandmother began working on farms owned by the Mormons when she was no older than my brother here."

"How did you learn how to talk so good?"

"I go to a Mormon school in Casas Grandes part of the year, when I'm not helping my grandmother dig roots and gather plants for medicine." The girl slid one of the tortillas onto a dried corn shuck and brought it over to Reece. "She wants you to eat and then go to sleep until she comes back." She brought the pot over and refilled his cup.

"What's in the drink? It taste like coffee."

"It's made from the seeds of a jojoba bush. It's good for inflammation and some people do use it for coffee."

"All that workin' around the Mormons an' your grandma didn't learn any English?"

"I'm sure my grandmother knows many *americano* words but I've never heard her use even one. I think it's her way of showing her disrespect for the people who stole our lands. Some of them probably think she's just dumb. They would be insulted if they knew how she really feels about them."

"She ain't dumb. That's for sure. But how come you traveled so far to this place -- nuthin' much around here anybody could want."

"My grandmother is known and respected by our people in these mountains. She's a midwife, the only doctor they have. She goes wherever she's needed at any hour of the day or night if a runner is sent for her. Word goes out when she moves to a new location."

"You didn't tell me why she's here."

"Oh, yes. About two days walk from here there's a camp where a young woman has been living. She was going to have a baby and her mother was afraid that her daughter was so slim it would be a difficult birth. They sent for my grandmother. The day the baby was born, my grandmother overheard a guard that was looking for you say you'd escaped from the prison, but you'd been shot. They said you were coming in this direction."

"Where's your grandma now?" Even though the girl was very convincing, Reece still wanted to be sure he wasn't being set up for a reward.

"First she wanted to stake the burro where he can find some grass and then she's going to go back for maybe ten miles and take some brush and wipe out the tracks that she and the burro made last night when they brought you here.

If it isn't cloudy tonight and the moon is out she wants us to move on to another place she has in mind."

Reece could see that the boy was shy but the girl was going to be just like her grandma. She seemed to have the same self-confident attitude. Talking to an adult didn't bother her at all.

"But she must have spent a lot of time just lookin' for me. I don't understand it."

"You're the first white man she ever saw who showed any one in our family an act of kindness -- at a great risk to yourself."

"Mostly just some leftover scraps, would've been throwed away anyhow. Didn't amount to that much."

"Sharing the peaches you'd cooked -- that was so good of you. My grandmother was so upset when you were knocked down and kicked. Her heart was broken but there was nothing she could do. She had trouble sleeping for a long time. You'd better rest now. If we move on tonight it'll be a hard climb and you'll have to walk most of the way."

"Where're we going?" Reece asked.

"My father and uncle are working at a sawmill near where the trains stop for water. It's between Madera and J. Matta Ortiz. They got a few weeks work loading lumber on a train that'll be shipped north. My grandmother has an idea of how they can help you escape into Arizona."

Reece opened his eyes. He could see it was late afternoon. Steam was rising from the pot on the fire. He sat up and looked around, noticing that the pain in his leg was almost gone. The boy was kneeling in the dirt, carefully building a pyramid with pebbles, placing each one just right so as to keep the others from falling. He never turned his head in Reece's direction but his dark eyes glanced over to see whether or not Reece was watching his progress. Reece saw a slight grin spread across his round happy face.

The girl came up from the slope where the burro had been led away. She was carrying the water bag on her shoulder and an armload of wood for the fire.

A rustling sound came from higher up the slopes and a rapid movement caught Reece's eye of something moving through the mesquite. The girl stopped and looked up the slope then ran toward the camp. The grandma came running down toward them, dodging around the spiny stemmed ocotillo in a headlong race to reach the camp. She said something to the girl as she neared her and reached for the water bag and hurried toward the fire.

Reece stood, looking up toward the ridgetop. He heard what sounded like the pounding hoofbeats of several horses, breaking brush and striking rocks. He got a brief glimpse of them as they raced across an opening on the higher slopes.

They were out of sight when the old woman suddenly put the water bag down, apparently realizing the smoke had already been seen. She grabbed Reece by the shoulders and spun him around. "Down," urged the woman, pushing Reece into a kneeling position with his back toward the rapidly approaching sounds.

"Stir," she commanded shoving a pot in front of him and handing him a short piece of mesquite. She grabbed the blanket he'd been lying on and threw it over his shoulders and tucked it under his feet, hiding his boots.

"But there's nothing in…"

"Stir!" she repeated as Reece got the message and bent low over the pot, shielding its interior from view with the edge of the blanket as best he could.

The girl began casually picking up the scattered sticks where she'd dropped them moments before. The boy continued to place pebbles onto the pyramid, while glancing nervously over at his grandma and back up the slope where the sounds of running horses grew louder.

Dropping to her knees by the fire, the grandma drove her hands deep under the glowing coals into the ashes then rubbed them into Reece's tousled hair. He could feel her slapping at embers that singed his hair, giving off a pungent odor.

Reece glanced up into the woman's calm stoic face that gave no sense of urgency. She calmly placed sticks on the fire as the riders cut around the ocotillo and came thundering down upon the peaceful encampment. He watched helplessly from under the blanket as the riders slid their lathered mounts to a stop, sending a sheet of dirt over the bowls of food.

The horse on Reece's right, a dark bay with a left white foot whirled when the boy panicked, leaped up, yelling for his grandma and ran toward her. The bay's flailing hooves struck the pyramid and sent a spray of pebbles rattling against the metal pot on the fire as the boy ducked behind the woman's long skirts.

"Get over here! All of you!" The unmistakable voice of Rodriguez commanded.

"Turn around old woman when I'm talking to you!"

Reece kept stirring as he'd been instructed.

"Give me your whip!" Rodriguez ordered.

"*Sí, Capitán,*" Sanchez said, laughing.

Reece saw the braided end of a bullwhip drop by his right knee.

"I said, turn around old woman!" Rodriguez yelled.

Reece saw the shadow of an arm being raised as the end of the whip was pulled back out of his sight. His mind raced. Did he dare chance sprinting for the dense thickets that were less than one hundred yards away. If his leg held up he could be thirty yards before anyone could get off a shot or spur their horse after him. Even if he got the jump on the riders and beat the winded horses to the closest cover and the rider's hurried shots all went wild the family left behind would pay a terrible price.

"*Por favor, Capitán.* No. No whip. Sister no hear!" The grandmother pleaded, stepping between Reece and Rodriguez. "No mean no respect." Reece could see the shadows of both her hands pointing at her ears.

There was a long pause when nothing was said then, he heard the rustle of paper as if it was being drawn from a saddle bag.

"Have you seen a white man, a *gringo*, one that looks like this?" Rodriguez impatiently asked.

There was a long pause while the old woman studied the paper, even turning it over to look at the back side.

"See man? No. Just boy. This one," she said, pointing behind her.

Quiet comments were exchanged among some of the men behind him then Reece heard the crunch of boots on gravel. At least one of the men had dismounted. There was laughter. then Reece heard the gurgle of water when the man picked up the two water bags and began filling the rider's canteens. One of the goatskin bags was tossed back onto the ground where the remaining water drained onto the coarse gravel.

Rodriguez whirled his horse and whacked its rump, shouting, "We're wasting time, let's get out of here, these dumb…"

"Hold it!" he commanded, sliding his horse to a stop. The girl was kneeling, not more than ten feet away directly in front of Reece. Her face blanched, her eyes fixed in the direction of Rodriguez. Was the captain going to take her for a play thing?

When she glanced at something on the ground on Reece's right then looked back toward Rodriguez, Reece realized his crutch had aroused Rodriguez's suspicions. It was then the grandma spoke in a kind and imploring manner.

"Sister hurt leg. No walk. *Por favor, Capitán,* help find burro. It lost."

Sanchez's voice boomed, "*Capitán* Rodriguez has no time to look for your worthless burro!"

The sounds of running horses faded as the last rider in line topped the distant ridge, then dropped out of sight.

The evening shadows lengthened when the sun dropped behind the high plateau to the west.

Reece tested the strength in his much improved leg, adjusted the crutch, with its added layer of fibers from the yucca, then followed after the others down into the darkening canyon. A full moon broke above the eastern horizon.

CHAPTER 35

LOST TRAIL

A stiff breeze drifted dust into the shallow arroyo where Captain Rodriguez and Lars Neilson squatted and studied a well-worn map. Fist-sized rocks held the corners of the map in place where it lay on a slab of sandstone. Each man took turns drawing imaginary lines across the map with their fingers. Flores could hear only fragments of their animated conversation. The two men, at times, appeared highly agitated.

Raul continued carrying water from the barrels on the back of the nearby truck, pouring it into the two half-barrels that had been cut and fashioned into watering troughs. Thirsty and hungry animals milled in circles in the pole and brush enclosure -- following a well established pecking order. A cliff of weathered stone, pocketed with cavities where sparrow-sized canyon wrens nested, formed the rear wall of the temporary corral.

Each of the two dominant mules stood over a trough, their muzzles dripping water, while other mules and horses watched and waited. Since the second truck had broken an axle and was left miles away down the mountainside, there wouldn't be enough water for all of them. Even though the two pack mules had drunk their fill, they stood defiantly, flattening their ears and baring their long yellowed teeth when others ventured close. A glance by either mule would frighten the most timid animals into retreat to the farthest corner of the enclosure.

"Just like some people," Raul said as he walked over to get his whip.

Flores nodded. "It's too bad, but you're right. Really no difference at all."

Rodriguez rolled up the map. When he slid it back into the leather tube and started over toward the corral, Flores anticipated he would be giving new orders.

The captain stopped and stood the map case against a bush, brushed the tops of his sleeves, then vigorously beat away the accumulation of grit that had settled onto his shirt.

Flores was sure of one thing. None of them had expected that the chase would have taken them this far. For a day and a half, twenty men, spread for miles along the arroyos with their mounts, had hidden and watched a fifteen-mile stretch of high desert. On the afternoon of the second day they'd ridden hard into the mountains to the south, convinced that Reece had collapsed or headed west into the canyons. The two days of stifling heat with limited water and food had been especially frustrating with no visible results.

"Get over here, Raul, now! You too, Flores."

Raul hung his whip over the pole gate to the corral and hurried over to where Flores joined Rodriguez and Neilson.

"We have a new plan. We've worn ourselves out chasing all over those mountains," Rodriguez said, pointing at the highest peaks toward the south. "I want you two to take a couple of the best horses and Blue and head back up past the area we covered yesterday. We know that the last tracks we saw showed that bastard was headed into that general area. There's no trace of him on these lower slopes. I don't think he's come this far."

"I'm sure he hasn't," Neilson spoke up adamantly, his pink ears and neck reddening. "He's hit. That much I'm sure of. I've shot antelope at over seven hundred yards and that hobo wasn't even that far."

Flores glanced at the captain who started to say something but apparently thought better of it. Since Raul had told the captain it was too dark to see any blood on the rocks at the top of the slide, they couldn't be sure of Reece's condition. Later, Raul had kicked sand over the blood-spots, the last day they'd found his tracks.

Flores remembered the early morning they'd moved into position below the slide. They'd hidden and waited for Reece to move along the crest. They'd finally glimpsed him and then seen him duck back into cover. After watching for hours, they'd seen him when he came out of the mesquite, just before dark, and started across the slide.

Neilson had beamed when Reece finally reached an open area, well out onto the shale, and said, "Watch this." He'd already estimated the distance at 550 yards and calculated the bullet's trajectory. Lying prone, he wrapped the rifle's sling tightly over his left forearm and back up under his armpit. He pressed his right cheek against the breech, where it joined the walnut stock. He held the rifle steady across the padded leather seat of the saddle while he sighted through the telescopic lens.

Flores' legs were trembling as he helplessly watched one man deliberately try to cripple another man who'd done him no wrong. And now, after several days had passed, that man had disappeared without a trace.

Rodriguez looked at Flores first and then at Raul. "I want both of you to leave here at least an hour before daylight. Hopefully, taking the bitch, you'll find his trail within no more than fifteen miles. The border is still over a hundred miles from here. The Swede here and I do agree on one thing -- he's most likely trying to make it to Juarez, then across the Rio Bravo to El Paso."

Rodriguez took out the well-worn map again and turned to face north. He looked toward the horizon and then squinted at the map. "Juarez should be about there," he said, pointing toward a break on the horizon where two low mountain ranges appeared to join.

Rodriguez studied the map again then swept his finger up along a line lying east of the boundary between the states of Sonora and Chihuahua then over to a point almost directly north of the city of Chihuahua. "Here's where the Federal Pacifical crosses the Rio Bravo at Juarez."

Neilson nodded and his tone softened when he spoke again. "Just north of there at El Paso, the line joins the Southern Pacific railroad where it goes west to Tucson then northwest to Phoenix." Neilson moved his hand and pointed to another location on the map. "The tracks going north here, out of El Paso, go to Las Cruces and then on to Albuquerque. Another line, lying east of the railroad to Las Cruces, goes to Alamorgordo. There's just no way to tell what Reece'll do if he gets anywhere near the border. That hobo seems to have had plenty of experience riding freights and it's my guess he'll go with what he knows best."

"He might get a big surprise if he does try to sneak on one of the trains. Most of them, on their runs up to the border, carry plenty of armed guards. The railroad owners are not going to let any of their shipments be damaged or stolen before they reach their customers in the States," Rodriguez said.

Flores could see the men were trying to work together. Each man had spent years striving to be the best at what he did. Their common problem now was trying to capture a man who conformed to no set standard either had ever encountered. Reece was a simple man with few skills and little formal education, an average-looking man who would go out of his way to avoid any undue attention. Neither Raul or Flores had any way of knowing how badly Reece was injured, but one thing he'd shown them both, he was a man of unbelievable determination -- a man who wouldn't give up as long as he still had the strength to take one more step.

Neilson picked up the map and after studying it closely for several minutes shook his head. "I never thought that hobo would get this far…"

"We've got to get him within the next few days or the son-of-a-bitch is going to get away," Rodriguez interrupted.

Flores could hardly believe he'd heard the captain actually admit that Reece might make it to the border. Rodriguez was a man well known for his unwillingness to ever concede defeat. The captain continued, speaking slowly, vacantly staring in the general direction of the distant Sonoran desert that had taken the lives of so many men over the previous centuries.

"He could head east and catch a train running up from Chihuahua or even cut back toward the Babicora. They ship a lot of cattle to the states at this time of the…"

"A lot of Mormons and Mennonites ship fruits and vegetables in reefers to northern states up through Cases Grandes," Neilson interjected.

"Flatcars loaded with timbers come out of Madera going to Arizona and New Mexico," Rodriguez added, then shook his head. "I don't think, unless he's pressed hard and we cut off both rail lines running north, that he'd head through the canyons and try to make it to Hermosillo where he could then try to reach Nogales…"

"No. He wouldn't do that. That's over 150 miles from here -- I don't know why we're even discussing this," the Swede added irritably. "I tell you, he's hit!"

Rodriguez's brow wrinkled into a sullen scowl but he didn't respond to the Swede's adamant comments. Flores and Raul looked at each other. Neither could be sure if the renewed argument would be dropped.

Rodriguez turned his back toward the Swede and spoke directly to Flores and Raul.

"Remember, I want you well on your way before sun-up. As soon as you find Reece's trail I want you both to get your bearings. Follow the trail until you get a good idea of which direction he's headed, then stop and study the surroundings carefully. Flores, you stay put right there with the bitch and Raul, you get back here as fast as you can. Hopefully, we might be able to get hot on his trail by late afternoon tomorrow. I'd like to give that goddam reporter something different to write about next time."

Flores glanced at the Swede. The mere mention of the word reporter seemed to make him nervous and not quite so sure of himself as he usually appeared. He had to know that any reporter would be pleased to hear of him getting drunk and into a fistfight in Chihuahua over the record ram he'd poached. Flores was also sure that if Reece had been hit, Rodriguez would willingly take the credit. It was another subject that wouldn't look good in any newspaper -- allowing an American contractor to shoot another American, even an escaped prisoner, could be a front-page story on each side of the border.

"If by chance it looks like Reece might make it to the border, we'll call in the mounted unit of the state police. But that's only if we lose him or we find he's changed direction and headed into the Copper Canyon area," Rodriguez added.

The Swede shrugged his shoulders, grimacing, and shook his head with a strained look on his face. "If he heads back southwest and gets into the canyons we'll lose him for sure. Horses won't be much help. And since he's done a lot of hoboing in the past he just might try to make it to the railroad that has a weekly run up from the lumber mills at Madera. That's his best bet. He'd never make it from here across that Sonoran Desert if he's trying to reach Nogales on foot. He definitely couldn't if he's been hit."

Flores couldn't tell whether or not the captain agreed with the Swede's idea of what Reece might do next. Neilson was plenty observant and good at figuring out what wounded prey would do next and he knew a lot about the states of Chihuahua and Sonora. The problem was nobody knew much about Reece. So far, almost everything he'd done had been completely unpredictable.

Rodriguez drew the toe of his boot across the soft dirt in front of him, his brow furrowed as if in doubt as to the next move that he should make. He shifted his weight then slowly drew an intersecting line with the toe of his other boot. After a long pause he spoke.

"There is a group of almost a hundred men bivouacked at a small lake less than 50 miles from here. The *capitán* is a friend of mine but I don't want them called in except as a last resort. Do you understand?"

"*Sí, Capitán,*" both guards responded.

"Now each of you pick out a good horse. Make sure they're fed and watered and take care of that old bitch, too. Remember I want you on your way at least an hour before daylight. It'll be another hot one tomorrow."

CHAPTER 36

OLD WOMAN'S CAMP

It was still dark when Flores and Raul rode across the lower sage flats. They saw the silhouetted creosote along the arroyos where they'd hidden with their horses and waited a day and a half for Reece to start across the plain.

Climbing up toward the skyline, they rode on in single file. The creak of saddle leather, shod hooves striking rocks and the horses' labored breathing were the only sounds. Creosote mixed with mesquite now dotted the eastern slopes where rain seldom fell.

Near the top of a long barren ridge that curved westward, Flores turned his horse to the east and followed along the contour of the mountainside. The footing for the horses became more difficult where erosion had loosened the underlying strata. Pockets of layered shale gave way, sliding out from under the hooves of the tiring mounts. Both riders dismounted and took the first drink from their canteens. Flores kneeled and gave a drink to the short-haired bitch that had been trailing along behind. The success of the search would be largely up to Blue. Detecting Reece's scent after three days of dry searing heat wouldn't be easy. And, Flores realized that a night and two days of strong winds would have scattered the microscopic bits of spoor left in Reece's wake.

Flores led the gray gelding across the crumbling shale until they reached a bench of hard clay, giving the horses better footing. Within an hour they reached the telegraph line they'd built months before.

Flores reined up and turned back toward Raul. "Never thought we'd see this place again, did we?"

"Naw, and I haven't missed it at all. It was about forty miles south of here where I was sent on back to work at the prison." Raul sat on his horse looking south where the line disappeared over a ridge of broken limestone. "There's the bluffs straight ahead. You remember them, don't you?"

"Yeah. They look like they could be fifteen, maybe twenty miles from here. They're a couple of miles above the line, not far from where the Indians wiped out Reece's tracks with their sheep and goats."

Raul chuckled, "That was some day to remember. The *capitán* and Sanchez never did notice Reece was dragging the toe of his right foot."

"And you're still mad at both the *capitán* and the Swede, right?"

"Damn right I am. You'd be too if they told you to climb a mountain of sliding rock, knowing it would be dark by the time you started back down. That goddam Swede was more concerned if he'd hit Reece than he was knowing I could've been killed in a rockslide," Raul said with a sneer.

"You don't care if Reece gets away, do you?" Flores asked.

Raul shrugged and grinned and looked off to the east.

"We know he was headed in this direction when the Indians came back down and saved his ass. Who knows? That poor bastard could be lying out there anywhere, dead or dying. It's such big country that we may never even find a trace of him."

"That's possible. We're just paid to look for him -- we don't have to find him." Raul said, in a matter-of-fact voice.

"You get the silliest look on your face every time the Swede tells Rodriguez that he knows Reece was hit. Think how red his face would get if he knew you'd lied about it being too dark to see if there was any blood on the rocks."

"I told them I saw Reece's tracks in the dirt where the rocks ended. That's all they deserve."

"I suppose," Flores said dismounting. He took Reece's old boot from the saddle bag. "This looks like as good a place as any to start. We'd never spot boot tracks on this rocky ground. Who knows, he could've come right through here." He called Blue over.

The panting bitch worked a slow circle then moved off to the southwest working through a stand of mesquite. She circled back and moved higher on the slope toward the bluffs on the skyline. Riding along slowly behind, Flores watched Blue work. The slowed pace gave the horses a much needed rest. An hour had passed when Blue's stub of a tail began to wag.

Flores stopped and dismounted at the place where Blue had detected scent. After a close examination of the ground he said, "Take a look at this, Raul. This is strange, very strange, and I don't understand it." Flores moved over to a place where there was a thin layer of soil.

Raul dropped the reigns and joined Flores. After a brief glance at the ground, he looked at Flores and grinned and closed his eyes. "Let's see now. Look's to me like the Swede's right. The *gringo's* definitely dragging his right foot. Probably hit in the leg would be my guess. Am I right?"

"You figure things out real fast, Raul. I take my hat off to you, but tell me this. Why is Reece going south instead of north and whose tracks are these walking ahead of him? When you get that figured out tell me what made these little round holes along here."

Raul squatted near Reece's boot tracks and studied the ground closely. "I don't understand any of this," Raul said, in a serious tone. "That crazy *gringo* is going south and he's taking someone with him. I don't get it."

"No. Reece isn't taking someone with him -- someone is taking Reece. Someone with small feet. And it looks like that someone may have made him a crutch."

Within a few miles Blue led them to a small clearing under a stand of scrub oak and pine where a camp had been recently occupied.

"Wait a minute!" Raul suddenly exclaimed riding into the clearing. "We were here day before yesterday. Look at these tracks. The *capitán* stopped his horse right here. There were two old women, a girl about twelve and a boy no more than four or five. The *capitán* damn near rode right over the top of the boy where he was playing right here in the dirt."

"Are you sure?"

"I'm telling you this is the place. We rode down here when we saw smoke while you were working the eastern slopes with Blue."

"It does look like whoever was camped here must have left in a hurry -- didn't even take the roots and plants they'd gathered. Two old women and two children?"

"Yeah, one of them was deaf -- didn't even hear us ride up. She was facing off that way, her back covered with a blanket or a shawl -- gray hair sticking up above the wrap. She kept stirring something in a small pot. The *capitán* started to whip her when he told her to turn around and she didn't. The other old woman jumped right in between them, said her sister was deaf. She was going to defend her sister with her own body. Wait a minute! It couldn't be. No, it couldn't be," Raul repeated, shaking his head from side to side.

"What do you mean, it couldn't be?"

Raul didn't answer. He walked around in a circle, closely examining the ground. "This is unbelievable. What's this?" he asked suddenly holding up a roll of screen wire that had been lying under some bushes. He looked inside. "There's a piece of a man's pants, caked with dried blood, rolled up in this screen. Take a look at this. I can't believe it."

Flores took the roll of screen wire and turned it over.

"Dr. Alvarez reported that Reece cut the screens right out of the window frames in his office after Reece cut his throat and tied him up. That's what

270

we've got here. He made leggings out of the screens, must have wrapped them in layers around his lower legs for protection from snakes and thorns. And this is a bullet hole where it looks like he was hit alongside his knee, where the screen has been flexed. The screen probably deflected the bullet just enough to keep his leg from being blown right off."

Raul took the improvised legging back from Flores and pulled out the dirty piece of clothing. "When Reece got hit the blood was trapped inside the layers of cloth and screen until it made a clot -- that's why there wasn't much blood where he got hit."

"This means he's been right here in this camp -- now what are you grinning about, Raul? You got that silly look on you face again."

"Now it all makes sense. When we rode up one of the women -- the one who defied the *capitán* -- was putting sticks on the fire. We had seen smoke so we came on down, spurring the horses and riding hard, hoping to surprise Reece if he was around before he could run away and hide."

"Who the hell could she be?" Flores asked.

"I have no idea, but the *capitán*'s gonna shit when he finds out that the old woman he was going to whip was Reece."

CHAPTER 37

WOUNDED QUARRY

Raul traversed the upper slopes slowly as he led the bay mare toward the camp where the captain and Neilson waited. He could see smoke from their campfire, not more than two miles away. Within another mile he'd mount up and ride hard into camp, yelling and spurring the bay. He'd make sure that when he rode into camp her flanks were heaving and she was lathered in sweat. After his report he wasn't sure what the captain would do since there would be less than two hours of remaining daylight.

Captain Rodriguez would have to make a tough decision: should they go on up and make a dry camp, or wait for morning and leave before dawn on fresh mounts that had been watered and fed.

Raul had left his half-filled canteen with Flores. The young guard, he knew, would be taking a well-deserved siesta. So would Blue. The strong, gray gelding would get a good rest too, but, at best, he'd have to go the night and another long day without water.

One thing he and Flores were agreed on: the captain would delay calling in the crack, mounted unit of the state police when he learned that the elusive desert runner was wounded. Before Raul mounted the bay to return with his anxiously awaited report to the captain, both guards had discussed their best options. Raul would report tracking a man who was dragging one foot. They had further agreed that the captain would have to figure out for himself that the one squatting under the shawl and reported to be deaf was the man they'd been chasing for over twenty days.

Raul slowed the mare where the slope steepened, the second time she tripped and scrambled to regain her footing. She couldn't hold to the all-out pace when crossing loose rocks on the hillside.

When they were within 200 yards of camp, Raul could see men getting to their feet and walking toward the corral. He knew they' were watching the galloping mare's weaving descent and could hear her shod hooves, crashing through dead brush and rocks.

272

"You're late!" Rodriguez said as Raul swung down from the mare, lathered in a sweaty foam.

"*Sí, Señor* Rodriguez, I'm sorry." Raul replied, steadying himself, placing his hand against the saddle skirting. He could feel the rapid movement of the bay's breathing and smell the pungent odor from her sweat streaked flanks.

"What did you find?"

"We-we found his trail," Raul stammered, trying to catch his breath, "about a mile above where the old women were camped." Raul tried to make himself breathe deeply and appear calm, however, the guilt he felt under the steady gaze of both the captain and Sanchez caused him to skip all details and blurt out the part he wanted to delay until the end of his report.

"He's hit. He's dragging his right leg and…"

"I told you I hit that goddam hobo!" The Swede yelled loudly, shaking both fists above his head as a cheer went up from the other guards.

"Where's Flores?" Rodriguez asked, his face immediately showing his relief that the grinning Neilson was right after all.

"He's waiting, not far from where we turned back two days ago."

"Saddle up! We ride! And load them two mules at the troughs with water." Rodriguez ordered, his voice revealing a renewed confidence that Reece would soon be captured.

There was near bedlam as the guards scrambled and playfully shoved and pushed each other aside, grabbing for saddles, blankets and panniers, each wanting to be first to be mounted and ready for the impending chase.

Raul was relieved that the captain showed no interest in any details of the day that he and Flores had spent locating and trailing Reece. The fact that Flores was waiting with their best tracking dog, finally ready to close in on the now-wounded quarry, was cause for much boisterous bragging and an unusual level of excitement. The boredom of the long day of idleness and the weeks of frustration was being vented by the guards, now anxious for action.

"*Capitán*, I have your horse ready," said one of the older guards. He led a gray Arab over to the captain and waited for his answer.

"*Gracias*, Benito," Rodriguez said, giving Benito a big smile. "Hold him, Raul. You're saddled and ready to go. I need to get a few things."

CHAPTER 38

ABANDON CAMP

It was almost dark when Raul led the captain and his men down toward the camp where he'd left Flores.

"*Capitán*, we're almost there. It's right down that slope, less than a mile ahead," Raul said, pointing off to his right.

A shrill whinny echoed up across the slopes. Raul jumped, when the bay mare he was riding threw her head high and answered the gray with a long, high-pitched neigh -- a startling, primeval call, that had bonded the easily frightened prey animals to their herds since they moved out onto the grassy plains eons ago.

Within minutes, the light of a campfire showed ahead through the mesquite. Raul knew the sighting of a campfire at night would have been an equally welcome signal to nomadic hunters returning from the chase.

Flores walked out to greet them, his shadowy form silhouetted by the campfire behind him.

"That you, Flores?" Rodriguez asked.

"*Sí, Capitán.*"

"Raul tells me we have good news about Reece," Rodriguez said, stopping the Arab and reaching for his canteen.

There was a pause when Flores didn't respond. Raul knew Flores was in a difficult situation. His lack of an immediate response was covered by the tethered gray's repeated nickering an anxious·welcome to his mates.

"We did find Reece's tracks, *Capitán*. And there's no doubt he's been shot in the leg."

"In the leg?"

"*Sí, Señor*. He's dragging his foot with every step."

"How can you be sure he's not hit in the hip or the foot?"

There was a long silence when Flores again didn't respond immediately. Raul knew they could both be in trouble.

"I-I'm almost sure, *Capitán*."

274

"Good work, Flores. This calls for a celebration. Neilson brought some of his finest scotch for the occasion."

As Raul dismounted he could see that the fire Flores built was near the one where Reece had hidden under a blanket. A large pile of dead branches were piled near the fire. Flores had been busy, no doubt, scouting the area with Blue for both wood and any scent of Reece or tracks left by the ones who'd abandoned the nearby site.

As Raul removed the saddle from the bay, Flores walked over. "I think I had better show the roll of screen to the *capitán*. What do you think?"

"You're probably right, but he's gonna explode when you do -- might be better if you wait until after he's had a couple of drinks and something to eat. It'll be such a letdown after being told we found Reece's trail and we know he's been hit."

"We can talk about it some more while you give me a hand unloading the mules."

Sanchez spoke up, "Quiet everybody, the *capitán* has something to tell us."

Rodriguez turned in the saddle, facing the men who'd ridden up behind him.

"We only brought 40 gallons of water. If we don't find a good spring, the water we brought will last for two days at the most. If we're lucky we'll have all we need -- but don't let me catch anyone wasting a -- wait a minute," Rodriguez said, looking around the area as he'd started to dismount. "This is the same place where we saw the two old women with the kids. The one that had a deaf sister -- Flores, are you telling me that bitch tracked Reece to this same place?"

"*Sí, Capitán.*"

"What makes you so sure Reece was here?"

"You can see where they left camp and the end of the crutch made marks on the ground, *Señor*."

"What does that prove? Don't tell me that bitch has led us on another wasted trip!"

"Not this time, *Capitán*. Not this time."

"Maybe we should get the *capitán* and the Swede aside and show them the screen, Raul whispered to Flores."

"*Capitán*, can Raul and I speak with you and Mister Neilson in private? We have something to show you."

CHAPTER 39

DRIPPING SPRINGS

The chase after Reece led the column of guards up a dry wash of hard packed sand. Flores was in the lead. A glance to the rear showed Rodriguez lagging behind, his gaze still fixed straight ahead.

The evening before the captain had been like a wild man when Flores showed him the torn screen while the Swede had been ecstatic. Flores couldn't imagine any event that could have caused a more opposite reaction between the two men. The chagrin of Rodriguez was even greater than the day they found the wrecked truck. Being fooled by an Indian woman in front of his own men was a crushing blow.

Neilsen's face glowed, however, when he saw the deflected bullet's path. He repeatedly traced the groove from where the bullet struck to the point where it ripped through the wire. Neilson could see that his shot had struck exactly at the point where he'd aimed and, as he proudly explained, there was no way he could have adjusted the aiming point without knowledge of the protective layer.

Ahead, Flores could see another sweep of thorn thickets that stretched to the base of the lower limestone bluffs. Within a few miles the trail turned and climbed onto a long sloping shelf. When they reached the lower edge of the thickets, Flores saw that once again the trail disappeared into a dark shaded opening, barely the height of a horse's belly. It had been like this since early morning. Each time thorns had blocked their way the detour around had taken the guards an hour or more. Seldom did the trail last for more than a few hundred yards until they lost it again where a tangled wall of briers grew in profusion. After each detour Blue had to relocate the trail.

On the steepest slopes, erosion had left shards of exposed rock. Tufts of wool thread and burro hair, clinging to thorns, showed the quarry was still ahead.

One thing was certain: the one choosing the tortuous path knew the mountains well.

Flores was puzzled that Reece's flight was still heading south. After so many days of chasing the man toward the border, the reversal of direction was definitely having a dismal effect on both the captain and Sergeant Sanchez. Flores turned in the saddle and looked back. The captain and Sanchez were now lagging farther behind than they were earlier during the midday heat. The urgency of the earlier chase now seemed diminished.

Even more of a puzzle was the goal of the *gringo's* companions. Was the route in the opposite direction chosen to confuse and frustrate any who tried to follow? Did the stooped old woman have some nefarious scheme to lead them into a trap? Or, could this be the first step in some circuitous route to eventually get Reece across the border? It didn't seem possible that the grueling chase had now taken such an uncanny twist.

Flores tried to think of what other ways that the Indian woman might devise to thwart the armed, mounted riders she knew would follow. Perhaps a deadly rock slide could be triggered if other tribal members were lying in wait.

It was early afternoon when Raul moved into the lead. The procession of riders climbed on up toward the highest peaks, another ten miles in the distance. At last, the thickets of thorns appeared to be mostly behind them. At the higher elevations vegetation was sparse and stunted.

Blue had found the trail early. When the long barren ridge-top they were ascending reached another series of bluffs the trail turned abruptly and climbed up the side of a chasm. It leveled off at a point where the ledge led across the face of a sheer bluff.

Within an hour the rock ledge narrowed again where it curved out of sight around a protruding column of granite. Raul watched Blue work her way along the treacherous footing before she disappeared around the curved wall.

Raul looked down to his left. His skin tingled and his breathing became shallow. The gray inched away from the sheer drop that was at least a thousand feet. When the outer wooden curve on Raul's right stirrup scraped against the towering rock face, the gray stopped. Raul could feel the gelding trembling beneath him. He'd come too far. There was no room to dismount or turn the horse around. If he attempted to push himself back over the high cantle and get into position to slide over the horse's rump it could panic the young gelding. Raul had never before dismounted in such a manner from the recently broken horse.

Raul glanced over his shoulder. Flores had reached the point where the switch-back onto the narrow section of the ledge began.

"Stop, Flores! Don't come any farther!" Raul called out, hoping his raised voice wouldn't cause the gray to panic. When Raul called to Flores, Blue came back into view and looked at Raul.

Raul swallowed, took a deep breath and sat perfectly still as he stared ahead and tried to collect his thoughts. It was hard to believe that the ones they were after had dared cross the ledge, no more than two feet wide at a point straight ahead on the precipitous cliff where Blue was standing.

The woman, it now appeared certain, was deliberately leading them into the most inaccessible and dangerous terrain of the central Sierra range. The ones being pursued no doubt had another advantage. It was likely that the burro that had pushed and bulled his way through and under the thorny thickets below was equally adept at crossing treacherous rocky shelfs, like the one directly ahead.

"Back," Raul said quietly, easing back on the reins. The frightened gray needed no further urging. The horse shifted his body slightly and Raul felt his own racing heart pound even harder. It was then Raul realized that the young horse was lightly tamping and testing the footing under his rear hooves before he committed himself to the slightest movement backward.

"You're gonna be all right," Flore's calm voice assured Raul. "Let the gray take all the time he wants. I'll wait right here where he knows my mare is standing. It'll help calm him while he works his way back down here beside me."

Raul slackened the reins. He peered over the edge at the jagged outcroppings below. He felt helpless and knew immediately that his own fate was now hanging on the instincts of an animal totally inexperienced and in a predicament that was not of his choosing. The slightest mistake would increase the threat of both plunging to a sudden death.

"That's good. Don't try to guide him, just let him have his way," Flores cautioned.

Raul could feel beads of sweat beginning to run down over his ribs from just under his armpits. Strangely, just as quickly, his mouth felt as dry as cotton. In the quiet of the high desert air the slightest sounds were accentuated: the grit and pebbles on the ledge were being crunched and scraped under the gray's steel shod hooves.

Blue stood panting on the ledge ahead of them, seemingly unconcerned by the dizzying height. She idly watched as the tall gelding backed slowly down the narrow shelf, no more than a few inches with each cautious step.

The sweet pleasant odor of sage filled Raul's nostrils although the last of the stunted bushes they'd ridden through were miles below. It was then, Raul realized, that the intensity of the fear that gripped him had honed every nerve in his body to a feverish pitch: the strong scent of sage came from the waxy bits clinging to the horse's fetlocks.

The sounds of riders approaching from behind meant that the others were catching up.

"Just what the hell are you trying to do now, Raul?" the Captain's loud irritated voice bounced off the rock surface of the bluff.

The gray tensed and stopped, the harsh shout freezing its movements. Raul turned quickly to hold up a hand for silence.

Flores was already off the bay and hurrying back toward the point where the impatient Rodriguez waited.

Raul watched Flores stop and raise his hand as he neared the Captain.

"Goddam you Flores! Don't you ever shush me again. I am *Capitán* Rodriguez! You seem to have forgotten that!" Rodriguez sneered, driving his horse forward and forcing Flores backward.

Flores stumbled momentarily, lunging off-balance near the edge of the precipice then quickly staggered into a crouching position and spread his feet, the ring-wise wrestler quickly regaining his balance. He stood for a moment, his arms hooked outward in an automatic defensive stance. The captain had advanced again and was now leaning forward over the left shoulder of his horse, his scowling face no more than three feet from that of the startled young guard.

Without taking time to think, Flores lunged forward, grabbed the front of Rodriguez's shirt with his left hand, twisting and pulling the fabric downward and jerked the face of Rodriguez down within inches of his own. The epaulets on the shoulders and the collar of the shirt were pulled inward and down by Flores' vise-like grip.

Raul watched, spellbound, realizing the captain was now completely off-balance and unable to right himself.

It was a dramatic moment of truth for both men: Raul had never seen Flores lose his temper and attack another person. Neither had he seen Captain Rodriguez show the slightest fear. The man's eyes were now wide with fright. He no doubt realized how easy it would be for Flores to hurl him over the side of the cliff.

Flores continued to hold him while he talked to Rodriguez in a low voice. The captain's face that had been white with fear, now turned red as Flores twisted the shirt tighter and effortlessly pulled the helpless captain's head a few inches lower: the taut folds in the shirt front radiating outward from Flores' straining hand.

Raul could not distinguish the quiet words that were being spoken but the look on Rodriguez's startled face told the complete story.

The gray moved slightly and Raul turned to check on his mount. He glanced back again. Flores had returned and mounted the bay. His face was relaxed, showing no trace of his jeopardizing actions of moments before. Those waiting behind and below the captain could have neither seen nor heard but little of the events of the totally unexpected confrontation.

The arrogant nature of the captain was not a serious problem when he was working at the prison where the rules were fixed and clear. His dictatorial authority there was never questioned. But it was not the same in a chase across the desert. Raul could now see that clearly. A desert chase required a leader of a different character. One who could cope with a different set of problems each day. A man not consumed in his own ego but respectful and caring for those under his charge.

Rodriguez was not that man.

The gray kept slowly inching backward.

"That's it. You're doing fine. Remember, just let him have his way." Flores continued, his voice as calm as before.

Raul looked back to check the distance to where the shelf widened. He could see that Neilson had ridden up behind the captain's horse and dismounted to study his map.

Raul turned back and watched Blue walking down toward them. He then felt the gray relax when its rump brushed against the mare's shoulder.

The captain spoke in a moderate voice.

"We're turning back. We'll camp tonight at the river where we can all bathe and wash some clothes and get some rest."

It was almost sundown when the riders neared the Rio Santa Maria. The well-worn trail to the river they were following led back under a steeply sloping bluff that jutted outward from its base. The dark imposing bluff cast a long shadow across the trail and up onto the face of the granite precipice across the canyon. Boulders the size of small houses lay scattered among the mesquite on the slope below the trail where they had fallen from overhead and crashed among the trees. Discolored cavities in the ominous overhang, where lichens were only beginning to grow, showed the origin of boulders that now rested on the slopes. The outline of the sharp jagged shapes in the cavities above could sometimes be visually matched with the rock that had broken away and dropped for hundreds of feet to its present location. Flores thought of the seemingly insignificant and timeless ways the mountains changed over the millions of years since they were formed. The distinct and worn pathway, beaten smooth by the countless feet and hooves that had passed before, was nothing more than a slight abrasion that, too, in time, would be swept away. It was no more permanent than the flies and gnats that buzzed around the heads of both the riders and their tired mounts.

The air was still in the deep gorge leading down to the river. A damp marshy area where a gully came down from the left showed that underground seepage was working its way down from the peaks where winter snows had melted months before. Wasps busied themselves at the edge of the shallow stagnant seepage that was mottled with swirls of pale-green scum floating on the surface. Cattails grew in clumps along the sides, their long round spikes a rich brown contrast against the bright green of their leaves.

The trail ahead curved out of sight where the gorge changed directions. The gray stopped suddenly, head up and ears erect.

Flores knew immediately that the gelding had heard or smelled something that was around the bend, still not in sight.

Flores sat waiting for the other riders behind him to catch up while he watched the point where the trail vanished. A lone burro appeared coming toward them, nipping at the low brush growing below the trail. He was carrying something on his back. It was still too far to see distinctly. After a few minutes another burro appeared and after a short while two more came into view with a man following along behind the last one. When the slow-moving procession came nearer, Flores could see that the man on foot carried a tall walking stick with a crook at the top. The man wasn't much taller than the back of the burro he was following. He walked bent over and appeared to be an old man that could be anywhere between 60 and 80 years of age. He gave no notice that he was aware of the column of armed and mounted guards watching his approach.

Captain Rodriguez rode up and stopped the arab off to the side of the gray. Flores could now see a curved iron pick with a short wooden handle, lashed onto the lead burro's pack with criss-crossed pieces of different sized ropes, knotted together. The ancient and grizzled man approaching was undoubtedly a prospector, still searching for the mother lode of the Sierras. One thing for sure, he would probably know these mountains as well as the elusive Indian woman who seemed so determined to lead the fugitive to safety.

The lead burro stopped. After briefly looking at the bunched riders and their mounts blocking the trail he began browsing for forage on the slope directly in front of the gray.

"Hey, old man!" Captain Rodriguez called out, *"¿A que distancia al río Santa Maria?"*

The startled old miner stopped, and looked up, dwarfed by the tall uniformed man facing him, sitting astride a tall horse. He seemed to be at a loss for words for the moment. He then grinned and the deep wrinkles around his eyes, accentuated by his toothless gums, made him appear to be even older than he had when he first came into view.

"Buenos tardes, Capitán," the miner greeted, pushing his tattered sombrero onto the back of his head. *"Él río Santa Maria* is maybe not even one hour for the fine mount like the one you ride."

Rodriguez took a swallow from his canteen, rinsed his mouth and spat on the ground then tilted up the canteen and drank several swallows before replacing the cap.

The old prospector appeared to not notice the captain's rude greeting or lack of any cordial response.

"Do you know these mountains well?" Flores asked, feeling foolish for posing a question with such an obvious answer. He could now see drops of water oozing through the damp canvas water bags hanging across the withers of the burro grazing near the gray.

"Sí, Señor. For over sixty year now I have been looking for gold in thees mountains. It gets in the blood and nothing will make it go away. I know one day I will find it." He wiped the spittle from his lips onto his ragged sleeve then continued, grinning. "When I do I will buy a beautiful hacienda." He then chuckled and looked a trifle sheepish at his own implausible little story. "And, of course, I will find me a pretty young wife for when I am old."

All of the guards except Rodriguez laughed at the seemingly ridiculous dreams and goals of the aged prospector whose worldly possessions appeared to be worth, at most, very little.

As the laughter of the soldiers died away a wide toothless grin spread immediately across the unshaven face of the diminutive storyteller's face.

Rodriguez looked over at Flores, apparently reluctant to say anything that might cause another confrontation that others could now witness. It appeared he either wanted Flores to continue his questioning the grizzled prospector or lead on down to the river where they could at least temporarily escape the heat and flies.

"*Señor*, do you know of any nearby Indian encampments or villages?" Flores asked, trying to be as attentive and polite as he could, hoping the earlier laughter had been well received by one who appeared to immensely enjoy the lonely life he had chosen.

"*Sí, Señor*. Thees way, maybe forty, maybe fifty mile," he said turning and pointing in a southeastern direction, "the beeg lumber mill near Madera is cutting lots and lots of trees. Many poor Indians come for a job -- some come from very far since the beeg silver mines closed at Batopilas many years ago now. There is *no mucho* work there anymore."

"Batopilas? Why that's at least 300 miles south of Madera. It's down at the lower end of the barrancas There isn't even a road into that area. Just steep mountain foot-trails." Neilson spoke up.

"Ah, *sí, Señor*, but that *distancia* is nothing to a Tarahumara."

Flores knew the captain was more interested in the possibility of Indians in the area they had been searching. "*Señor*, can you tell me if you have ever seen an old Indian woman traveling with a burro in the bluffs up there?" Flores inquired, turning and pointing to the mountain range they had spent two days searching.

"I see her almost every year, sometimes maybe two, three time. I wave. She turn her back and go another way. *Mucho loco*, crazy old woman. Dig up roots like a gopher and load them on the old burro she bring with her."

"Can you tell me, is there any water up high above the granite bluffs where someone could go and stay for a few days?" Flores asked nodding at Rodriguez and pointing at the leather cylinder strapped behind the cantle on Rodriguez's saddle.

Rodriguez handed the map holder to Flores without comment. The look on his face made it obvious to Flores that his patience wouldn't last much longer.

"Why you look for thees old woman?" he asked looking around as if counting the number of rifles carried in leather saddle scabbards lashed above the horses' flanks. "She rob a bank in Chihuahua and ride away so fast on her old burro you no catch her?" the prospector asked, raising his shaggy eyebrows in mock surprise and holding out his hands palms upward, then chuckled at his own attempt to be entertaining to his unexpected audience.

The Swede laughed hard and he didn't seem to notice or care that the others were being intimidated by the hard stare of Rodriguez.

The old man, however, immediately recognized that the captain was growing impatient and waiting for an answer to Flores' question.

"*Sí, Señor*. There is only one little spring. You have a map? Here let me show you where to find it." The old man squinted his watery eyes and traced imaginary lines on the map until he got his bearings. "It is about here at the bottom of this arroyo that comes down below the highest mountain top."

"This is the highest peak here. This one?" Flores asked as Neilson stepped over and watched Flores' explanation.

"*Sí*. It is thees one here where the lines turn back," the man said, tracing the crude contour line that had been drawn on the map at the point where the canyon leveled out onto a narrow bench.

"How much water does it have?" Flores asked.

"There is only enough water for two, maybe three men and their horses. Not too many people know of thees place. Nothing up there but rock and…" the Mexican storyteller paused and grinned again, making sure his audience was listening. "And, of course, the mother lode." he added, shaking his head up and down with exaggerated enthusiasm and doing a couple of shuffling steps in a little dance, his arms circled as if holding a woman tightly against his little round belly.

"*Sí. Mucho* gold." Flores nodded, joining in with the prospector's open friendliness and gusto.

"It weel be a long hard climb for your horses but if you start when the rooster crows," the old miner grinned and cupped a hand to his ear and leaned to the side as if listening for the early morning wake-up call of the common barnyard fowl, "you can get there before the sun sets. You will not find it in the dark. It is back under a beeg rock. You must lay on your belly and reach in and dip it out with a cup."

"Do you have a name for the place? We'll put it on our map." said Neilson.

"*Sí*. It is called Dripping Springs."

The old man tipped his hat, saying, "Adiós, *amigos*. Now I must go and find my fortune. Pretty *señoritas* don't like to be kept waiting."

CHAPTER 40

HEADING SOUTH

Up to his right, Reece could see the outline of a high bluff, silhouetted by the moon sliding behind the crest. Earlier in the evening, when the terrain wasn't so steep, he'd ridden on the midwife's burro. But now his injured leg throbbed from hours of scrambling over uneven rocky surfaces.

After leaving the camp where he'd been hidden under a blanket they'd pushed hard, always toward the south. Twice, they'd stopped, to give the burro a brief rest.

As they entered a canyon between two sheer walls of granite, the midwife stopped and spread her shawl on the rocky ground. The girl kneeled and lay the sleeping boy upon it. The midwife spoke quietly to the girl, then disappeared up a darkened gorge.

"What are we gonna do here?" Reece asked anxiously.

"We'll fill our water bags from a small spring that's hidden under some boulders. Then my grandmother will change the bandage on your leg."

"What'll we do then?"

"We'll rest for a while and then move on. It'll be daylight soon. Then we can go faster in the places where you can ride again."

"I should go on by myself. Your grandma's takin' an awful chance, just to help me."

"She knows that, but she's not doing this just for you. For many years she's been very angry about how our people have been treated. To her, all Mexican officials and the white people who stole our lands, are nothing but devils. If she can help you escape it will help pay them back."

"I don't know. It worries me what could happen."

"When she overheard you'd escaped and been wounded, she couldn't wait to go looking for you."

"I don't even know your names."

"It's best you don't know. If they catch you, you can't tell them anything -- even if they torture you..." The girl's soft voice trailed off.

Reece felt the hair raise on the back of his neck. They sat in silence for several minutes, listening to the slow rhythmic breathing of the sleeping boy before the girl continued.

"I was terribly frightened when I heard the horses coming. But I was so proud of the way my grandmother quickly hid you and fooled the Mexicans when she spoke to them in English."

"My legs were shakin' but I didn't know what I could do."

"Her life has been hard. She recently told me about something that happened to her when she was about my age, now -- something she never even told her own mother."

"You must be very special to her."

"I hope I am. She wants me to be all the things she never got a chance to be. She never went to school and can't even write her own name. She doesn't even know how old she is. When she was born her parents worked on a farm for one of the Mormon owners. And every day since she was about eight years old she had to drive their small flock of sheep and goats into the mountains."

The sleeping boy began to whimper. He quieted when the girl spoke soothingly to him and began softly humming. Reece could hear her patting the boy.

"You were sayin' somethin' happened to her when she was just a girl?"

"Yes, when she was about my age. The foreman had two sons, about the same age as my grandmother. They were maybe thirteen and fourteen years old. They rode spotted ponies and often came to fish in a lake where she took the sheep and goats once a day to water. But my grandmother never let the flock go down to drink when the boys were there fishing. She was afraid of them."

"Did she have a reason to be afraid?"

"She just didn't trust them. One day they hid and waited for her to bring the animals down to the lake. They caught her in the open and roped her, then tried to make her bite the head off a green frog they'd caught. When she spat at them instead, they tore her clothes off and tried to push the frog up in..." The girl stopped her account of the event and swallowed before continuing. "She finally bit and kicked herself free then ran into the thickets where she hid for two days before..."

The girl stopped and began to sob quietly.

Sounds of the approaching burro meant the grandma was returning with their canteens filled with water. The sobbing ceased and Reece saw the outline of the girl's arm when she raised her hand to wipe her eyes.

"We have to keep ahead of the men who'll be coming after us. My grandmother will take us through the steepest part of the mountains where few springs and trails even exist. To lose the guards, we must cross a high, narrow ledge on a canyon wall that is no wider in places than our little burro."

"That sounds mighty dangerous."

"It will be. But none of the men riding horses will even try to cross it when they see it and if we make it we'll gain at least a day and maybe two."

"That sounds like a good plan but what if they send some men on foot across the ledge and they bring their tracking dog?"

"Grandmother has thought of that too but thinks they'll all turn back when they see the trail. Whenever we're passing anywhere near a spring she'll leave us miles away and take the burro to carry the water back to where we'll be waiting. If they bring dogs, they'll only be following your scent and your scent will never be within miles of any spring." Reece sat in wonder, amazed at the scheming old woman and her seemingly endless bag of tricks.

"If we can stay ahead of them for the next two or three days they'll have to turn back when they're out of water."

While the midwife wordlessly bathed and changed the dressing on the still painful gunshot wound, Reece tried to concentrate on the nearby mountains. The early light now showed the dark thickets that stretched for miles toward the south. Thanks to Al's teachings, he could now recognize the shrub-trees mottling the middle sections of the slopes below the mesa rims. Most of them were the medicinal plant, condalia, with the nasty thorn-tipped stems that often formed a tangled wall.

When the little band, with Reece astride the burro, again moved southward, he began to wonder if he was making a big mistake. He tried to remember how many days were left until Eula Mae's graduation.

Even though he'd never been there, Reece figured Wisconsin had to be at least two thousand miles to the north.

CHAPTER 41

VENGEANCE

The sun's slanting rays vanished from the highest peak while dusk settled in the canyons below.

"We'll stop here," Sanchez quietly said as he swung down from the big-footed roan gelding. Flores and Raul reined their mounts off to the side and dismounted.

"We can't be more than a mile below the spring -- two at the most -- if that old prospector wasn't lying to us," Sanchez added as he tied the roan to a clump of mesquite. Sanchez pulled the map from the holder and turned the top to his left. "North should be about there." He nodded toward a haze-covered valley, now just a darkening blur in the distance.

"The spring should be below that peak and to the right where that shelf below levels off then slopes to the south." Sanchez pointed toward an overhanging ledge. "Keep your voices down and watch where you step. We got a good chance to sneak up and catch that old bitch and Reece too. I'd like nothing better than to return to camp dragging them both in by their hair."

Flores looked up at the overhang. It was like the old prospector had described. And, like he'd cautioned, they would have to press hard to make it to the spring before dark. He was glad they had left Blue with the other guards down at the river. Her sore feet could use a couple of days of healing. He took his canteen from the saddle horn, then tied the gray a few steps past the sergeant's gelding. Sanchez poured water into his cupped palm and then rubbed it over his face and neck. He poured more water and rubbed it over his throat, wetting the front of his shirt before tilting his head back and drinking most of the remainder.

Raul finished tying the bay. "We got a ways to go yet," he said in a low voice. "I wonder if they're still there?"

"They're up there all right -- I can smell 'em. And when we get 'em -- remember, they're mine!" Sanchez held up a clenched fist.

Flores couldn't picture them sneaking up on the kind of people they were after. Both Reece and the woman would be watching their back trail.

Flores led the way at a steady pace. When they were barely halfway, the barrel-chested sergeant's plodding gait had slowed until he barely stayed in sight as the trail curved around boulders and mounds of limestone shale.

When they were no more than three hundred yards from the overhang, Flores stopped when he saw a pile of drying burro droppings. Raul joined him and said, "We better wait or we're going to embarrass the sergeant. We don't need that."

"Yeah, he's a lot like the *capitán*," Flores added in a low voice as he watched Sanchez struggling up the trail. He could see the sergeant was now in no condition to drag anyone, anywhere.

When he finally reached them, Sanchez stopped and wiped his sweaty face on his shirtsleeve and said panting, "Do you see any sign of them?" His florid complexion and bulging eyes reflected the strain from the steep climb. He turned up his canteen and drank the last of his water while some dribbled off his stubble-covered chin.

"Not yet, but it does look like someone came along here within the last day," Flores said, pointing at the pile of burro dung.

Sanchez glanced briefly at the pile of small round droppings and then held his canteen out in front of Raul. "Pour some of your water in here," he said in a hoarse whisper, his chest heaving hard from the altitude and heat. After he drained his canteen of the water Raul had poured for him, Sanchez stood, head down, staring at the pile of dung. With the toe of his boot, he finally kicked the pile of droppings aside. The little balls of dung scattered across the trail where some lodged between the shards of limestone shale. Scurrying to hide under a tuft of grass, a black dung beetle wobbled through the rock shards.

"How can they stand to eat that crap?" Sanchez asked.

"Probably taste like candy to them," Raul said, and then laughed nervously. Sanchez frowned for a moment, then his face broke into a grin.

With Sanchez, Flores knew, you had to be careful of most anything you said. It was impossible to be sure how the unpredictable sergeant would respond to any comment someone made. It usually took him a little longer to mentally process anything he heard before he reacted.

Beads of sweat continued to run down the sides of Sanchez's face and disappear into the creases under his double chin. Still, he made no attempt to head on up to the spring or urge Flores onward.

Flores realized Sanchez was stalling. He was in no condition for such a climb but he didn't want to admit it. Lowering his voice to little more than a whisper, Flores offered an explanation of the droppings, "It looks like the burro crapped here on his way up the trail as they came in. I don't see any indication that he's been staked near here or browsed on any grass."

As the shadows moved over the tallest peak Flores wanted to move on, for the old prospector had said the spring would be hard to find in the dark. Finally Sanchez grunted, "Let's go."

They crept along the sloping ledge until they could see the overhang directly ahead no more than another 200 feet. There was no sign of anyone nor any sounds coming from the direction of where the spring should be. Close-cropped, stunted bushes and grass now showed where the burro had grazed. They tiptoed quietly up to within fifty feet of the massive overhang without seeing any signs of life.

"The spring must be right back under there," Flores whispered when he eased on ahead and saw a dampened slab of sloping limestone. He kneeled, then saw where a skim of water still clung to the shallow depressions on the rock's surface.

"They've left here within the last hour or two -- no more than that. In this heat the water spilled over this rock would have evaporated," Flores said as he noticed the sergeant taking the cap from his empty canteen.

Kneeling beside Flores, Raul offered a possible explanation for the absence of the camp's recent occupants. "Maybe they saw us coming and filled their water bags. They could be hiding along the canyon rims and waiting for us to leave in a day or two. Then they could come back. There's no way to know for sure."

"I'd sure like to get my hands on 'em!" the frustrated sergeant blurted.

Flores studied the area where it appeared water had been deliberately poured over the rocks. Then he started to crawl back under the shelf above the darkened spring. "Here, fill mine first," the sergeant demanded, holding out his canteen.

Flores could hear the water dripping from overhead. He lay flat on his stomach and felt the drops splatter down onto his wrist as he reached to dip the sergeant's canteen into the basin. The water was only a couple of inches deep, however, and it felt like there was a layer of moss growing over the rocks under the water's surface. In the shaded niche it was hard to tell. Flores lay the canteen on its side and gently pressed it down onto the spongy bottom, hoping to get it to fill at least halfway. He knew Sanchez would be upset if bits of moss came loose and floated into the neck of the galvanized container. He listened to the soft gurgling sounds as the cool liquid ran into the open mouth of the canteen and thought of the old woman who continued to thwart them. She had no doubt watched them tie up their horses, then filled her own water bags before leaving. Before she left, however, she'd dipped out most of the remainder and wastefully poured it over the rocks.

When Flores handed the half-filled container to the anxious sergeant, he gulped a few swallows, stopped suddenly, then dropped the canteen. With a choking cough he sent a fine spray of water over both Raul and Flores.

"What are you trying to do, poison me?"

Flores picked up the canteen, poured some of the contents into his cupped hand and noticed pieces of a brown fibrous material. The liquid was dark and smelled foul. "What kind of moss is this," he wondered. He crawled back into the spring and pulled out a handful of the spongy material. Backing slowly from under the ledge Flores squeezed the water from the contents in his hand. It was then he realized the people they were chasing were now fleeing down some canyon and they weren't coming back. Their plan to buy a little more time and frustrate their pursuers had worked.

"Gimme that!" ordered Sanchez as Flores got to his feet.

"I'm sorry," Flores stammered, "I didn't know that...."

Sanchez rolled the darkened substance between his fingers and smelled it then flung it to the ground in disgust.

"You stupid idiot," he bellowed. "This is burro shit!"

CHAPTER 42

TRAPPED

They'd pushed hard for two days now with little water, trying to lose the pursuing guards.

As he hobbled along and tried to keep up with the others, the pain in Reece's leg returned. He'd also noticed that the dark shaggy burro walking just ahead was tiring badly. The donkey's head drooped lower and the tips of his worn hooves now dragged across the rocks with each plodding step. The wheezing sound of his breathing had become more labored. He couldn't be pushed much farther without collapsing.

Reece knew the little beast must be at least twenty years old, maybe even thirty. Gray hairs covered the upper part of his head and ears and encircled his muzzle. The old woman kept glancing back with a look of concern at both him and the burro, apparently trying to determine if either one of them could make it to the last bench below the highest mesa.

Finally the woman held up her hand to signal a stop, then spoke briefly to the girl. The exhausted pack animal immediately lay down while the woman looked back, scanning the lower slopes. Her squinting eyes widened when she spotted the dark line of mounted men advancing up the steepening incline miles below. She clenched her jaws, drawing the corners of her mouth downward in a hard look of defiance.

Reece had already seen the approaching riders but was waiting for the woman's reaction to the relentless threat that plagued them.

Reece was sure they'd have to take to the condalia thickets growing on the long sloping shelf above and just below the mesa, otherwise, their slowed pace in the open would soon allow the guards to overtake them. The thorny shrub-trees would be their only hope of escape. Taking the rifle scope from the backpack, he rested his elbows on the top of a nearby ledge to steady the metal tube, then swung the scope slowly across the lower mountainside.

When he detected movement along the top of a barren finger of rock, he stopped and held it steady. The magnified lens clearly showed that Rodriguez had moved into the lead. The Swede rode close behind. The other guards were following in single file with little space between their mounts. At the back of the line, a stocky man half-hidden under a large sombrero and riding a bony white horse, led a string of gaunt pack-mules. The captain had apparently enlisted the services of a Mexican peasant to pack their food and water.

Reece was certain that Rodriguez had decided on an all-out push to trap the fugitives near the steep redrock mesa walls looming against the skyline.

The sight of the mounted riders made Reece nervous and anxious to move on. They desperately needed to increase the slim lead they held. There was no question in his mind but that the woman and both children would be able to travel much faster if they didn't have to stop and wait for him and the tiring burro.

While he watched the advance of the threatening force below, winding its way upward through the scattered clumps of olive-drab creosote bush, he wondered if the woman didn't have thoughts of abandoning both him and the almost useless beast. Reece limped over by the girl. "Here, tell your grandmother she can take a look through the scope and see them much better," he said, handing the captain's prized gift from the Swede over to the girl. "Just be careful. It could break if it's dropped," he added, pointing to the semi-open stands Rodriguez was now riding through where the creosote bushes, shrouded under a canopy of yellow blossoms, grew taller. The captain's head and shoulders showed above the upper branches. His horse's head bobbed into sight, picking its way through the openings on the rock strewn mountainside,

The girl took the metal tube. When she tried to hand it to her grandmother, the woman drew back. Fanning her hands across in front of her, she shook her head forcefully. She wanted nothing to do with the slender dark cylinder.

Reece motioned for the girl to take a look. When she hesitated, he took the scope from her and held it up to his eye, showing her how simple it was to use.

The girl looked to her grandmother for permission but the woman's attention was still riveted on the men riding toward them. The granddaughter placed her hand on the woman's arm and then said something to her. At first the woman's deep frown and pursed lips only indicated a feeling of mistrust of the hard steel tube. Her face then softened and she nodded with a look of reluctant acceptance at her granddaughter's curiosity.

Disbelief registered on the girl's face when she first observed the magnified images that appeared in the scope's ground glass lens, her expression revealing the magic she was witnessing, all contained in the slender tube that she lightly held in her hand. When she lowered the scope into alignment with the riders below, her hands began to tremble, her eyes opening wide with fright.

The girl turned immediately, talking rapidly and pointing. She appeared to implore her grandmother in her native dialect to take a look. The woman finally took the tube and held it up to her right eye. She showed only a mild curiosity as she swept the rifle-scope across the long open expanse below them. Her body tensed when she spotted the advancing guards. Violently, she flung the scope aside. She breathed an audible sigh of relief when she saw that the distant riders really hadn't somehow suddenly overtaken them. Still, she was plainly worried. The shock startled her into immediate action. She kicked the burro's rump sharply as she spoke forcefully to her grandchildren.

Reece retrieved the scope. At a glance he saw that the lens had cracked when it struck the rocks. A distorted image could still be seen, however. He put it back into his pack.

Within two miles they reached the shelf where the possibility of hiding in the thickets gave them hope of eluding Rodriguez and his men.

They saw, however, a seemingly impenetrable wall of spiny shrubs. The tops of the condalia could be seen where the thickets stretched for another two miles or more to the cliffs that formed the supporting walls of the flat-topped mesa on the skyline.

While the old woman searched for the best place to enter the tangled growth the burro found a bit of shade and lay down.

Choosing a place to enter was a critical decision. They could easily become disoriented and entangled, unable to move in any direction.

Reece remembered looking for a missing hunter in the mountains above Gunnison, Colorado. It was late fall. Reece had been the cook for a guided party of six deer hunters. The third evening, one of the hunters didn't return to camp.

The missing hunter, Reece later learned, had shot at a deer and then followed it into a thicket. It was two days later when they found the man delirious and exhausted. He'd become lost and disoriented, barely able to speak above a whisper.

His plaintive whimpering like an abandoned pup had finally led rescuers to the thicket where he was trapped. It had taken Reece and one of the hunters half the night to cut through the chaparral and free him. Reece now watched as the midwife paced rapidly along the lower edge of the thicket. She stooped and motioned for the girl to join her, then pointed to an opening under the growth. After the woman had a brief discussion with the girl, Reece assumed a decision had been made.

Taking a stick, the diminutive midwife drove the burro under the low growing limbs of the condalia, following an opening that appeared to be barely big enough for rabbits and coyotes.

By crawling on their hands and knees over the shards of rock they were able to follow the burro under the mantle of thorns. Within a few hundred yards their way was blocked where the spine-covered limbs of the condalia grew into interlocking tangles.

The weary burro collapsed and made no attempt to rise -- even when the woman whacked him sharply on the rump.

Reece could see no avenue of escape as they lay there cramped in a small opening.

The midwife looked up at the blue sky, showing through the tops of the small trees. Shadows playing across her face accentuated the whites of her eyes. Minutes passed slowly as they hid under the thickets in the stifling heat. No words were spoken. The listless burro lay with his eyes half-closed but the wide open eyes of the children showed their concern. Waiting for something to happen was the worst part. The guards had them hopelessly trapped.

Reece looked up at the tangled web above. Clusters of blue-black berries were just overhead. He'd eaten the tasty fruit before when he and the other prisoners were building the line. Trying to appear calm, Reece reached for a cluster of berries. His sleeve caught on a dead limb that broke with a snap. He paused motionless and listened.

Voices that had been only a distant murmur became more distinct. Rising in the morning heat and moving up the mountainside, air currents carried the clamor and excitement of the men who wouldn't give up the chase.

"Here's the place they went in!" someone yelled.

Shouting men, calling out directions, tried to cover all avenues of possible escape.

They listened to the clatter of steel-shod hooves when a rider circled the thickets on their right to watch from above and look for any sign that the escaped prisoner and his escort had moved on up to the highest mesa. Within half an hour they heard him when he rode back down and yelled. "None of them made it through! There's not a track anywhere."

A shout went up. Reece could hear a new level of excitement as many voices blended into a boisterous discussion.

Pushing on the burro's rump and tugging on his shaggy mane, the midwife moved the animal's head around. She began to stroke his muzzle and rub his weary legs. The seemingly futile action annoyed Reece but he made no comment since he had no ideas himself for solving their predicament.

From the bag she always carried on her back, that gave the woman the appearance of a permanent hump, she removed a small sack and began to pluck at the cord, tied tightly at the top.

The girl had told Reece earlier it held her most prized possessions when he'd inquired about why she never let the bag out of her sight. A Tarahumara midwife, the girl had further explained to Reece, had to be ready to tend to her people, day or night, in all kinds of weather. They lived in remote canyons and on narrow ledges, scattered for two hundred miles along the Sierra's eastern slopes. For almost twenty years she'd said her grandmother led her burro, often climbing over steep mountain trails covered with snow. The arrival of newborn babies didn't follow any schedule. And it was the smaller sack that held the magic charms that she relied on.

Reece listened to the raucous sounds of the men who had them trapped, convinced they wouldn't be deterred by any magic objects carried in the goatskin bag.

Reece heard a shout, mingled among the others, a shout that chilled him to the bone.

"Let's burn 'em out!" It sounded like the Swede's voice. It was the kind of thing the burly contractor would think of first. Reece was convinced the man was capable of unspeakable cruelty.

Shouts and excited verbal exchanges continued. If the old woman heard or understood the menacing sounds she gave no indication. She instead began to sing quietly and then the song turned into a low chant as she removed a highly-polished wooden bowl from the sack. Both the girl and the small boy looked at each other. It appeared they might be glimpsing a side of their grandmother they'd never seen before. The low chant continued as the woman polished the bowl with her callused fingers, rubbing small circles on the bottom and then rubbing the tips of her fingers over the intricate carvings on the sides of the small container.

She suddenly stopped the chanting, pointed upward, and spoke quietly to the children. They both nodded their heads and immediately began to wriggle into the lower branches where small openings permitted and picked the fresh plump fruit. The woman spread a woven cloth on the ground. She motioned toward it while shaking her head and frowning when the boy started to eat the berries.

Again Reece made no comment, although he wondered if the exhaustion of endless pursuit and scarce food and water had affected the woman's mind.

Reece was sure he could hear dead branches breaking. He glanced around and overhead at the intertwined limbs of the condalia with a new sense of helplessness. The six-year drought had left many of the older trees dead or dying.

There was loud laughter from some of the guards, the distinct sounds carrying on the breeze blowing up through the thickets. The girl looked at him, her innocent dark eyes showing alarm.

From her canteen, the woman filled the bowl and took from the bag a small pouch tied with a beaded drawstring. Then she raised her hand, sprinkled a fine dark mixture over the water, and slid the container under the muzzle of the burro. The thirst-starved animal raised his floppy ears and eagerly emptied the contents. She refilled it and gave every indication she would rather die than leave her companion of so many years. She then poured the last of the water into the bowl while she continued her singsong chant.

"What does she keep in that pouch?" Reece whispered to the girl, trying to make conversation and allay their fears for the moment from the shouting and tumult. He had no real interest in some old woman's mystic chanting and practice of witchcraft but he wondered if either the girl or the woman really understood the seriousness of the Swede's shouted threat to burn 'em out!

"I think it's red root from up on the mesa," the girl said nervously while looking back over her shoulder toward the sounds of shouts and laughter. When Reece made no comment she took a few deep breaths, then continued. "In the winter time she goes down in the little valleys and gathers the seeds of the Syrian rue. In the fall she digs the roots and I help her grind them into a powder." The girl paused again and watched her brother, whose berry-stained fingers were trying to grasp a cluster of berries just out of his reach. She seemed to realize the youth had little concept of the imminent peril they faced.

"Some of the medicines are for the heart. He's getting old and she worries about him," she added, nodding toward the sleepy little beast, "just as if he were her baby."

Reece noticed that her legs began to tremble while she looked anxiously at her grandmother.

A faint odor of wood smoke drifted up through the thickets. The same air currents brought the crackling sounds of fire.

CHAPTER 43

PAMPERED BURRO

The helpless looks on the children's faces made Reece realize this was all his fault. He'd sealed the destiny of innocent people by his own refusal to serve the sentence imposed by the Mexican court. It seemed too often in this life that it was the innocent ones who suffered.

A puzzled expression showed on the girl's face as she leaned closer to the chanting woman, turning her head and listening closely to the singsong words.

"What's she keep saying, over and over? Is it some religious death chant?" Reece asked anxiously, afraid of what the answer might be.

"She's praying for the spirits to help her remember something from a long time ago when she crossed the mesa up there -- trying to remember what it looked like down here. It's not coming to her. It's been too long."

The chanting never changed when the woman reached for the square of woven hemp that contained the pile of sweet, juice-laden berries. Reece watched with a feeling of disgust while she fed them by the handfuls to the pampered, and almost useless burro -- the same food that she'd forbidden her hungry grandson to eat.

The midwife opened her eyes and looked around for the ever-present worn leather bag. She pulled out a small knife with a curved blade and began slicing the smaller limbs and thorns from the trunk of the largest condalia next to her. She pushed herself up as the opening cleared above her head until she was standing and reaching, her arms fully extended. Her tough, worn hands deftly worked through and around the needle-sharp growths. Wedging her sandal- covered feet into the crotch of the tree, she stretched almost to the topmost slender branches and cut out an opening. Layers of black smoke drifted across the darkening patch of sky.

The crackling sounds of the approaching fire grew louder. As soon as the heat increased into a furnace-like atmosphere, Reece knew, the fire would begin leaping ahead, flashing across the tops of the plants and feeding on the gases the heated vegetation released directly into its path.

The boy was now sitting trancelike, confused by the unusual events that surrounded him. He stirred and bent toward his trusted grandmother, listening closely when she whispered in his ear. The look on his cherubic face changed as he looked up at the opening where the limbs had been cut away. Without hesitation he began climbing up through the opening, jerking his hands away without a sound and quickly feeling for a new grip when he inadvertently grabbed a thorn. The uppermost strong slender limbs bent slightly but didn't break as the boy reached the topmost branches and slowly raised his head and peered through the black smoke drifting across the thickets. He coughed and rubbed at his eyes as flying embers and ash lit on the small dark green leaves.

The old woman kept repeating the same words as the boy turned his head slowly and looked in all directions.

"What could she possibly expect the boy to see?" Reece asked, unable to make any sense of using the boy as some kind of lookout.

"My grandmother thinks she remembers there were openings in the thickets when she was on the mesa, but it's been so long," the girl said. "She thinks she remembers the rock was so hard that nothing could grow in some places. Now she's asking my brother to point to any barren places he can see."

When the boy released one hand to point, Reece could see blood where he had hastily grasped a thorn in his scramble up the tree.

"Now he's being asked how far away the largest opening is. She's asking if it's the distance from our goat pen to the spring. Now she's asking if it's more like the distance from the house to the cornfield on the hillside above the spring."

The crazy old woman was unbelievable. In the path of a raging fire she still showed no fear and kept on trying to work her own brand of magic. The boy made his way down the tree and the strong stench of burning hair filled Reece's nostrils. The old woman slapped at smoking embers lying on the boy's thick dark hair. Tears filled his eyes but he still didn't make a sound while the old woman kept rapidly talking to him. They knelt to the ground and the woman swept away gravel and twigs and she and the boy drew pictures in the dirt with sticks.

Seemingly satisfied with the boy's observations, she reached into the sack of magic charms once more and withdrew a length of hemp. Reciting new incantations, she began to tie knots into one end of the fiber rope.

Now it seemed for sure the woman had completely lost her mind. Tying knots in the end of a rope while reciting her new singsong phrases made no sense at all. Reece knew the fire would engulf their hiding place within a matter of minutes. He could already feel the rush of hot winds at his back.

A crude harness was fashioned at the other end of the rope and then the harness was for some strange reason was fastened around the shoulders of the listless burro. His limp body was positioned in a new direction.

The rope was stretched down between his front legs, back under his little round belly and up between his hind legs. Grabbing the thickest blanket from the roll of bedding, the now wild-eyed old woman quickly wrapped it in a layer around the burro's neck and shoulders. A second layer of bedding was fastened over his neck and floppy ears and lashed tightly with the remaining pieces of hemp.

With the rope wrapped tightly around her wrist and skinny forearm and just ahead of the knots she'd tied, the woman took a sharp stick in her other hand and jabbed the lifeless-looking burro hard into the area of the withered scrotum where his testicles had been removed years ago.

Dragging the burro's head down under the lower branches and keeping it there with the weight of her body, the gritty old woman continued her painful assault on the hapless animal's most tender parts. The terrified animal plowed straight ahead. As his body drove like a tapered wedge under the low-lying limbs, tufts of the protective wool blankets were ripped away and left dangling onto the sharp points of the condalia spines.

Within minutes, the struggling animal, crawling on his knees, his hind legs driving hard, had reached the nearest open slab of red barren rock.

The badly frightened people, crawling close behind the burro, stayed ahead of the flames and then collapsed. Over them rolled the cloud of dense smoke that hid them from the riders watching from the mesa rim.

CHAPTER 44

FIELD OF ASHES

The fire had taken all night to reach the bluffs and consume the expanse of thickets. As dawn broke, Flores stood looking out over the wide field of ashes and blackened stumps of the charred condalia. In the early light he could see scattered flames licking at the twisted limbs of the once-green, tall, spiny shrubs. The victim's seared bodies could be hidden under any one of a thousand still smoking heaps of intertwined branches. The location and recovery of any remains could require days.

Tears came to his eyes as he thought of the innocent children and the excruciating way they would have suffered. Flores had never felt so disgusted with his own life and the part he'd played in the relentless pursuit.

As soon as the rest of the men woke up they'd leave for Madera, a little over twenty miles to the southeast. When they reached an old wagon road leading down to the rail line, the thirsty, worn-out horses and packmules would make better time. Madera would be a welcome sight with plenty of food and water and a place to rest until transportation became available.

At Madera, they'd catch the next train south on the Mexican Northwestern railway line running between El Paso, Texas and La Junta. There they would make connections with the Chihuahua al Pacifico, another rail line running east from La Junta. The al Pacifico would intersect the Mexican Central at Chihuahua where they'd change trains again and go south to a point within fifteen miles of the prison at Matamoros.

The long, tiring days of chasing an escaped prisoner were over. It had been an experience Flores would never want to repeat. Hearing steps of someone approaching from behind, Flores turned his head and nodded without comment.

"Morning," the Swede said, raising his cup of coffee in greeting. Looking out over the lifeless mounds of smoking ruins, Neilson commented. "I didn't expect it to all end like this, but it's just as well. The hobo and the old woman brought it on themselves."

"What about the children -- they never had any choice."

The Swede shrugged. "The old woman interfered in a legal government action. The meddling old fool made a mistake. Families that do that have to take the final responsibility for their own deeds."

Flores didn't respond.

It was late on the second day since Rodriguez and his search party arrived at the station in Madera. They all stood and watched the Mexico Northwestern steam engine chugging down toward them. People waiting to catch the twice-weekly run surged across the platform. Flores was as anxious as any of them to leave the ill-fated chase behind him. He stood near Rodriguez who was tall enough to see over all of the people waiting for the train to roll to a stop. The screech of steel wheels sliding on the rails and the hiss of escaping steam drowned out the voices of the excited people around him.

Flores watched as the uniformed conductor stood on the top step of the first passenger car and squinted at the people assembled on the platform. When he spotted the tall Captain Rodriguez he walked briskly toward him.

"*Capitán* Rodriguez?" he asked.

"*Sí, Señor*. What can I do for you?"

"We stopped for water just this side of J. Mata Ortiz near the sawmill. One of the men wanted me to tell you he'd seen some people cross the tracks early this morning -- said I might see you since he'd heard you were somewhere in the area."

"Why should that concern me?"

"The man said you'd want to know. He said there was a man walking with a crutch, an old woman and two children and a burro."

Flores watched for Rodriguez's reaction. The Swede and Sanchez were watching the captain too, each with a strange questioning expression on their face.

"Could have been anyone. That's not so unusual. Did he notice anything else?" Rodriguez asked, his face hardening into a scowl.

The man said, "Their clothes were black with what appeared to be soot and holes were burned in the fabric across their backs. The burro's hair was burnt away in places down to its skin."

CHAPTER 45

WOODCUTTER'S CAMP

Reece waited behind a screen of underbrush, still shaken by the narrow escape from the burning thickets two nights before. He was still baffled how the old woman had kept going, leading them to safety through the swirling smoke and flying embers.

The sounds of axes striking trees had ceased a few minutes before, at dusk. He could now see men walking along trails to brush arbors where smoke from cooking fires hung in layers above the campsites, scattered among the pines. Excited children's voices rang out in the still air as they ran to meet fathers, returning from a grueling day of cutting and carrying timbers down off the mountainsides. One man reached to pick up a toddler walking unsteadily toward him with outstretched arms. Without breaking stride he picked the boy up, tossed him in the air and in one motion, caught him and sat him on his shoulders. The child's round face beamed with pleasure.

Reece realized he'd missed so much not being there when his own daughter was just a child. He could only imagine the thrill of having had Eula Mae squealing and running to greet him after a day of exhausting labor.

The old grandma and both the girl and the boy had disappeared into an arbor on the far side of the camp where several women and children surrounded them. Reece thought of the time he'd first seen the woman, months before, in the early morning light past the corral where the children were eating the marrow from chicken bones. Feeling pity for the hungry children, he'd never even suspected the old woman waiting in the shadows was the most respected and dominate member of all the mountain people.

The girl had explained to him when they first reached the make-shift logging camp, they'd be given food and clothes and a chance to rest before the final ordeal, still ahead. Reece had stayed hidden and watched her when she brought a bucket of corn for the burro.

When Reece had asked her what they would do next, she'd told him only that it would be a long night for her father and uncle. They would go on ahead to a railroad siding near Casas Grandes. She would have to go, too. It would be up to her to distract any guard lingering near loaded railcars her father and uncle needed to inspect.

The trip up and back would take the men all night. They'd have to run hard and be back at daylight to resume their work in the woods. Two long days and one night of ceaseless effort would be a stiff test of endurance for even a Tarahumara.

Reece took out his two letters from Eula Mae. He was no longer sure of the date or how long he'd been on the run but he reckoned he had either four or five days left to make it to her graduation. If by some miracle he made it across the border without being seen, he knew he'd have to travel day and night without stopping to make it to Milwaukee, Wisconsin, somewhere north of Chicago. Being there for his daughter's graduation would be the most important thing he could ever hope to do.

CHAPTER 46

TRAIN TO EL PASO

Flores reined the bay mare across the railroad tracks when they reached the main street in Casas Grandes. At the second intersection he turned left down the street that led to the plaza at the rear of the train station. When they reached the public square Rodriguez rode his mount under the shade of an ancient wisteria. He motioned for the guards to gather around as he dismounted and waited for the stragglers to catch up. The weary, unshaven men and their tired mounts had covered over thirty miles since sundown the evening before.

Overhead, Flores could see where the wisteria's gnarled trunk branched outward, intertwining across and through the slender weathered poles, fastened into a grid. The dark, mottled shade, cast by the leaves and lavender tinted blossoms, played over the captain's strained, brooding face. Flores was sure he understood at least one of the captain's main concerns. This could be the last day of the chase. If Reece, somehow, slipped through the *federales* surrounding the city, he would be hard to find again. But if he was on any of the passenger or freight cars, as they suspected, they should have him within a couple of hours.

The former hobo, Flores figured, may have caught his last free ride on a freight car in the mixed train.

Flores listened to the yelling coming from the direction of the station. The steady din of voices was often broken by the bawling of frightened calves. Cows, nearby, bellowed an anxious response to the plaintive calls. Shouts by men grew louder, sounding angry and ready to fight. Guards standing and holding their horses glanced nervously in the direction of the noisy uproar.

When Rodriguez spoke, Flores noticed the captain's usual commanding voice sounded troubled.

"We've had a report that Reece is on this train. If the son-of-a-bitch is, we've got him this time. With the whole goddam town surrounded he won't get away again, I promise you that."

Rodriguez paused, reached up and jerked a hanging piece of vine from the wisteria. He seemed to be weighing all of his options as his gaze swept the group gathered around him. The last of the riders came into view, some leading horses that were limping, both riders and mounts looking ready to collapse. Rodriguez idly stripped off the vine's leaves and blossoms and dropped them onto the ground. When the last of the stragglers came within earshot Rodriguez continued. "I'm convinced the man seen crossing the railroad tracks near Mata Ortiz was Reece. Since this may be our last chance to catch him, I expect each one of you to make sure you do your part. And I don't want to hear any complaints about how tired you are. Is that clear?"

The men nodded and said, *"Sí, Capitán."*

The sounds of escaping steam meant the train's engine, sitting on the main line, was loaded and ready for the run up into the states through the border town of El Paso. The roofs of freight cars showed above the tops of locust trees growing along the low stone wall at the back of the plaza.

The train had been scheduled to leave the evening before but a telegraph sent by Rodriguez when they reached Ortiz had been delivered in time to the captain of the state police. He had been pleased with the opportunity to both exercise his newly-appointed authority and give his young troops some real live action: his men had become bored with their desert training and were waiting to take the train back to their base near the city of Chihuahua. Now, a manhunt after an escaped prisoner would be an exciting and fitting climax to their month of hot, dusty, field maneuvers.

The train scheduled to arrive at noon from El Paso was being held on a siding in Ciudad Juarez.

Rodriguez nervously tapped his fingers against the wisteria's rough bark, apparently absorbed in the quest that still consumed his every waking moment. "Any one of you who finds Reece will be given a two month's bonus and I'll definitely keep you in mind for future promotions, too."

A portly man wearing a white shirt and tie, short gray vest and dark wrinkled trousers hurried toward them. He wore a green shade over his glasses. His face was pale and puffy and when he reached the group he stopped and stared at the captain.

Flores could see the man was out of breath from the slight exertion. He stood with his mouth open, breathing deeply, a worried look about him, while his chin quivered. The cuffs on his shirt sleeves were pushed up near his elbows and held in place with rubber bands. Flores then noticed that the two top buttons on the gray vest were missing. The man's dress gave the impression that he worked at the railroad station. A black mustache, drooping over his upper lip, began to twitch.

Rodriguez turned to face the man who had approached in such a hurry. He waited impatiently for him to speak.

The shouts coming from the direction of the station were becoming louder and more strident. When the man still hesitated to state the purpose or his reason for joining the group of guards, Rodriguez glared at him and asked, "What the hell do you want? If you have something to say then say it! If not, then get the hell away from here!"

The portly man clumsily took a half-step backwards, intimidated by the tall glowering officer. "Please, *Capitán*," he pleaded, "all of the people are still waiting to go on their vacations to the states. This unexpected delay has gotten them upset. Some have traveled for long distances and have been sitting on the train all night." The man fidgeted with his tie then pressed the tips of his fingers against his twitching mustache. When the captain didn't make any comment he added. "The cows and calves were loaded at noon yesterday. They're very thirsty and some calves got mixed up in the loading, separated from their mothers and put in the wrong cars." The man paused to catch his breath again and appeared to be waiting for the inevitable wrath of the notorious captain's response.

Rodriguez glared at the man but said nothing, waiting for him to finish. After a long pause, he asked. "Do you have anything else to say?"

"Well yes, thank you, *Capitán*, I do. I would like to add that most all of the ice in the refrigerator cars has melted. The fruits and vegetables are going to spoil if more isn't added soon. They have plenty of ice at Juarez but we don't have any more here. There are more than twenty cars that came in just from the farms down near Los Mochis. They're filled with tomatoes, cantaloupes, lettuce…"

"I don't need to know every stinking item you've got on that train. Now tell me, is there anything of real importance you wish to add?"

"Well, yes, there is one other matter of quite some importance. The foreman responsible for the cows -- that's him you can hear yelling the loudest -- says some of the cows are down and can't get up. He says if any more get down the border inspectors will turn them all back. They'll think they're diseased. The owner's the richest Mormon in this area and these are some of his finest cattle. He's sending them to a ranch he bought in…"

"Now I have another goddam *gringo* to worry about. Is that what you're telling me -- and a rich one at that? That's really just too bad. Now get the hell away from here. I don't want to hear another word from you!"

Hearing Rodriguez's heated comments, the railroad man's eyes widened and his face lost its color. When he hurriedly turned he stumbled then regained his balance and walked as fast as he could to the station. From the sounds that continued to increase in intensity and volume, Flores knew, the man's reception at the station wouldn't be any better.

Rodriguez briefly reviewed his men's assignments. "It's now up to us. Remember, the *federales* have the town surrounded. Anyone leaving will be stopped and every vehicle will be thoroughly searched. We've got to cover every inch of this train. Check under each car. Crawl under and look up into the undercarriage. Make sure Reece isn't hiding in some dark place where it's hard to see. I'm convinced that within a few hours at the most, we'll have a prisoner to take back with us." The tired captain managed a forced grin and added. "Let's get to it."

When the captain and the 15 scruffy-looking uniformed guards marched into the station yard there was an immediate hush. Flores had never seen such an unexpected reaction. It was then he realized they certainly didn't look like the kind of armed men to be trifled with.

The captain nodded and each man hurried to his assigned duties. Rodriguez made no attempt to address the large gathering or tell them what they could expect. For the time being even the ones who had been yelling threats as they approached, stood silent and only watched.

Men assigned to search the refrigerator cars climbed quickly up the ladders and onto the roofs. They opened the hatches that covered the two ice-bunkers at the end of each car. Any one of them could be used as a place for Reece to hide. Others entered the two passengers cars at the rear of the train to search through all of the people and their luggage.

Flores followed the captain down along the tracks to where the engine crew waited for the signal that they could start the run to El Paso.

"Flores, take that bitch and start down there at the front of the engine. With the breeze blowing from the west, Reece's scent should drift along this side of the train," Rodriguez said, nodding ahead when they reached the rear of the coal car. He stopped and added, "I'm going on back and keep an eye on the other men."

As Flores and Blue neared the engine he could see the man at the controls leaning out the window, watching their approach. As they got closer Flores saw that the man's striped hat was pulled down over his eyes and his chin jutted out defiantly. The engineer's mouth was turned downward in an ugly sneer.

He appeared to be about sixty years of age, no doubt, a man with a lot of seniority. He was plainly infuriated that some prison guards were holding up his scheduled run to the border and beyond.

Steam curled outward from near the tall iron wheels, driven by the powerful engine. Blue stopped and tried to turn back, terrified of the hissing black monster. Flores had to drag Blue through the place where the slowly escaping exhaust settled along the tracks. As they reached mid-point a blast of hot steam and scalding water shot out from the side of the engine. Flores felt the force of the blast burning his lower legs as Blue yelped and disappeared under a cloud of white searing exhaust. He could hear the two men in the engine laughing. Without thinking Flores reached for his pistol and drew it as the engineer jerked his head back out of sight but not before Flores saw the man's defiance quickly turn to fear. Flores quickly emptied his canteen over Blue's head and muzzle, in an attempt to relieve the pain.

The disgusted engineer had kicked the lever to the cylinder cock open, shooting steam and hot water directly into their path.

It took the crew of guards over an hour to thoroughly search under each freight car between the engine and the last of the refrigerator cars. Blue cowered against Flores' legs, her short tail tucked down in fear and submission as they slowly moved along the long line of cars. The pink skin inside her ears had been blistered by the scalding steam. It had taken all the control that Flores could muster to keep from going back and beating the two men senseless.

Flores finally got to the cattle cars where the cows and calves continued their sporadic bawling. He heard Sanchez and the Swede talking to the men who were getting ready to climb in and search through the animals. Flores could see that a man hidden there would be difficult to find. He could keep moving, crawling under the bellies of the tightly packed animals where the guards had already checked and cleared them.

"I know quite a bit about Jerseys." Flores heard the Swede brag to the men hanging on the wooden slats, peering in at the restless cattle. "I used to work summers at my uncle's dairy. Let me tell you something. There's nothing meaner than a Jersey bull. You'd better be careful because you're going to find that some of them cows in there are really bulls." The Swede grinned and then added. "The hair along the top of a bull's neck is usually blacker than a cow's. If you're not sure which one is which, just reach under and see if you can feel tits. But if you feel balls you'd better get out of there fast or you're going to find a sharp horn up your ass," the Swede cautioned, then roared with laughter.

The guards looked at each other, rolled their eyes, and then nervously laughed at the Swede's warning. It was sometimes hard to tell whether or not Neilson was joking.

Flores and Blue moved on down the line of cars. Another half hour passed with no sign of Reece.

Flores and Blue reached the first of the twelve flat cars, loaded with rough sawn timbers. Placards stapled to the sides of the first three cars showed that some loads came from one of the mills in Madera. The others came from a small mill near Mata Ortiz. The cars loaded with twelve inch by twelve inch pine timbers, all 20 feet in length was a special order destined for a silver mine near Yuma Arizona. They had been cut and loaded on the forty-foot long flat cars by Tarahumara Indians during the last month. Some of the cars had been loaded for weeks and left setting on a spur track. Whirling saw blades had cut away the slabs of outer bark, squaring the four sides and leaving coarse grooved flat surfaces, now darkened by the relentless sun.

Hearing a commotion behind him, Flores turned to see a man standing face to face with Rodriguez. "I'm going to report your insolence to the governor at Chihuahua!" The man in a finely tailored suit and expensive looking shoes, snapped impatiently at the captain. He'd just stepped out of a shiny black Packard sedan that had arrived at the station within the last few minutes. The driver's door was standing open.

The well-dressed man turned toward the cattle cars, placed his hands on his hips and watched disdainfully as the guards continued to search for Reece through the prized dairy cows. He looked back over his shoulder at the weary and frustrated captain.

"You won't be so arrogant when you find out the governor's a personal friend of mine."

The captain didn't respond to the rancher's threats. Flores knew, however, that if the man didn't stop harassing the captain he would soon find out that Rodriguez's immediate and only concern was finding the missing prisoner. His quiet, sullen countenance in no way meant he was intimidated by either the owner of the cattle or the governor of any state in Mexico.

Rodriguez's lack of any response seemingly encouraged the rancher. He became more indignant and added another threat. "I'm tired of hearing about all of this fuss being made over some prisoner who got away and from what I hear, all you've done for the last month is chase after this one man. I don't really care if 100 of your prisoners get away. They're your responsibility, not mine. But if any of my cattle that are down get trampled to death," he said shaking his finger in Rodriguez's face, "or they all get turned back at the border by the brand inspectors, then I can assure you, you'll forget all about any prisoner you've been chasing and find your troubles haven't even started yet!"

The stationmaster carrying a dark blue-covered booklet, followed by his assistant wearing the bright-green visor, approached Rodriguez and the rancher.

Flores walked slowly along the third flat car, loaded with timber. Taking his time, he listened to the loud argument no more than 150 feet away. Only one thing was clear. There was no agreement as to who had the authority in the present situation. There was nothing in the station manual to specifically cover a prisoner being chased by guards on railroad property. There definitely wasn't any provision for guards holding a train including passenger cars overnight on the mere suspicion that an escaped prisoner might be on board.

Rodriguez and the successful rancher now stood face to face, sizing each other up, each in some ways a mirror image of the man they were looking at. One man consumed in his wealth and influential friends; the other was consumed by his authority and need to control others. The loud confrontation was being watched closely by impatient passengers who'd gathered around. With a forceful new leader some were now yelling additional threats at the prison captain.

It was the captain's turn to speak. He calmly ignored everyone else and stepped even closer to the rancher whose face was now only inches away.

"Tell your good friend the governor that a man assigned to guard prisoners for the state is doing his very best! Tell him also that the man's name is *Capitán* Mariano Rodriguez!"

With the last comment Rodriguez shoved the man aside and strode over by the cattle cars. The man made no attempt to follow. Instead, he turned to those around him and said, "I'm going to wire the governor and the warden." With the rancher's last threat, some of the weary passengers clapped briefly and walked back toward the station office.

Flores reached the last two loads of timber, just ahead of the two passenger cars on the mixed train. He noticed that Blue seemed to be losing some of her earlier fear. She no longer tried to huddle between his legs. The flatcars' undercarriages had been checked and cleared earlier, by other guards. The tightly stacked timbers with their squared sides left little room for even a mouse to hide.

A large crowd of people now milled around the station. Some were obviously enjoying the spectacle. Flores noticed the sharp contrast between the two classes of people assembled along the station platform. A few of the women wore expensive looking jewelry and fitted suits. Some wore beautiful lace dresses. The well dressed people, almost without exception, looked tired and irritated, their excitement of leaving on planned vacations abruptly squelched the day before.

Poorly dressed Indian children moved among the travelers offering bits of quartz and hand made trinkets for sale. Some of the children received coins for shinning shoes and carrying luggage for passengers still arriving for the delayed trip.

Flores noticed an old one-legged man sitting on a bench feeding scraps of bread to a flock of pigeons. He smiled as the hungry birds fluttered and dodged around the small children trying to catch them. Nearby, a woman set up the bottom half of a rusty steel barrel. She began selling tortillas as fast as she could cook them. Her two small children joined the ones trying to catch the pigeons.

Against the wall of the station, an old woman sat in the sun. Loose folds in the dingy shawl draped over her head hung down even with her eyes. She seemed oblivious to the activity surrounding her and all alone in her own little world. Taking a roll of yarn from a small bag, she began weaving threads through holes in a torn blanket. Her shoes were little more than scraps of leather wrapped and tied around her feet with strips of dirty thongs. The excitement of the affluent travelers was a world away from the simple life she reflected.

Flores couldn't help feeling sorry for someone so impoverished amid those who had so much.

A tall slender man wearing a felt hat with a curved brim and a sharp crease in the crown stood between the old woman and the steps at the front of the first passenger car. He'd repeatedly glanced toward the men arguing with Rodriguez. Flores had noticed him earlier walking up and down the station yard. He tipped his hat to all of the women he passed and nodded to the men. He occasionally took out a small note book and made an entry.

It seemed there was no reason to continue the search. All cars had been thoroughly checked both inside and out. The heavy sliding doors on the fruit and vegetable cars were all still sealed. There was no way for Reece to have climbed inside without breaking the metal security strips. All of the wire-lined cages in the ice bunkers had been inspected. Reece had not cut through any of them to gain entry into the "reefers" where the fruits and vegetables were stored.

Blue raised her head and sniffed at the next to last load of timbers. She wagged her stubby tail slightly and whined but backed away when Flores urged her forward. Flores looked at the solid wall of heavy wooden beams stacked tightly together. The rough sawn pieces were held securely in place with upright unbarked poles, tapered at the ends with an axe and driven into the steel slots, some two feet apart, bolted along the sides of the flat cars. Strong wires were twisted across the loads and tightened between the top ends of each pair of upright poles. The flat cars could be slammed together with little chance that their loads of square cut timbers would shift more than a couple of inches at the most. Flores didn't know why Blue stopped here, for this car had already been searched underneath. Perhaps Reece had tried to hide under the car. Maybe he had seen them coming and was somewhere in the area or perhaps as had been the case so many times, he had again set up a diversion and was fifty miles away by now.

The other guards had finished their assignments without finding any trace of the *gringo*. They stood in groups of three or four talking and watching the women who idled about or wandered in and out of the station and the two passenger cars. The guards were waiting for further instructions from the captain.

The man feeding the pigeons flattened and folded the paper sack and put it back in his pocket when all of the bread was gone. The woman making tortillas had finished cooking and selling the last of the ingredients she'd brought with her. Her two children were now over walking along the top of the stone wall at the edge of the plaza.

Flores was surprised when Lieutenant Juarez came out of the station and approached the slim man wearing the dark blue fedora. He smiled and shook the stranger's hand with obvious enthusiasm. Flores could hardly believe it when he heard the Lieutenant say, "Congratulations. I hear you are going to marry Maria."

The man in the felt hat nodded, smiled broadly and then said, "Thank you very much. Yes, I certainly am. She finally said yes."

Flores looked around but he saw that the captain was too far away for him to have heard the conversation between the stranger and Juarez.

The Swede and Sanchez were farther down the line talking to some men by one of the cattle cars. Raul walked up and joined them.

Juarez looked at Flores and nodded a greeting. He then motioned for Flores to join them.

Flores hesitated. None of the other guards were paying any attention to either him or the captain. They were watching a pretty dark haired girl barely in her early teens standing near the one legged man on the bench.

Flores sidled over and spoke to Juarez. "I had no idea that you were anywhere around here." He then nodded to the man who'd acknowledged that he was going to marry the nurse at the hospital -- the one that both the captain and the doctor had been feuding over. "This is *Señor* Enrique Cardenas. He's been sent by the owner of the largest newspaper in Mexico City to write a story about the *gringo* who got away."

"How do you do," the man greeted Flores. "Yes, I have been assigned the job of writing about this man John Reece -- the one you men have been chasing for quite some time now, I understand."

Flores shook the man's offered hand and said, "That's true, we have, but I'm still puzzled at all the interest this man's escape has caused."

Señor Cardenas nodded and smiled and hesitated for a bit before he offered an explanation.

"Actually, this wasn't my idea to come here and write a story about a prisoner who escaped into the desert. I've never really cared for the desert but since I work for Dr. Alvarez's father-in-law he insisted that I see if there isn't a story here somewhere. He's the one who wants the story written. After all, this is the man who supposedly cut his son-in-law's throat. If this man Reece makes it to the border you can see that could make quite a story. And he'll be the first to make it from Matamoros if he does."

The reporter smiled and tipped his hat to a middle-aged woman, wearing a large hat, when she walked past, obviously trying to get the polite man's attention. When the reporter turned to smile at the passing woman Flores noticed that Lieutenant Juarez had an amused look on his face.

The reporter continued. "I've interviewed everyone that seemed in any way able to shed any light on how the man actually escaped from the hospital." He smiled sheepishly and then added, "I guess I've interviewed some more often than others." With the last comment the newspaperman excused himself and strolled over by the station.

"What did he mean by that comment, 'some more than others'?" Flores asked.

Lieutenant Juarez looked around to see where the reporter had gone. "He's referring to Maria. I'm not sure, but it seems the doctor's father-in-law had met Maria on a visit to the hospital with his daughter. He'd noticed that the doctor couldn't keep his eyes off a certain nurse. So, he wanted his ace reporter to meet her. The man's been lonely and in need of a change of scenery since his wife died a couple of years ago. It seems his boss took a gamble: If Reece made it to the border it would make a good story. If he got the reporter interested in Maria that might keep the doctor at home with his daughter and grandchildren."

"How did you and the reporter wind up here?" Flores asked.

"The warden received a telegram saying Rodriguez had been given a report on Reece -- that he'd been seen near Ortiz. He had me catch the next train coming this way. Cardenas was already on the train when I boarded. He'd received a telegram from someone in Chihuahua. He didn't say who."

"Well, we still don't know what happened to Reece but it does look like Cardenas' boss won on his plan for keeping a doctor in the family," Flores replied. He then asked Juarez, "And I guess you're here to complete your report to the warden?"

The Lieutenant nodded and smiled. He seemed to relish that his report on Rodriguez's failure and bungled chase would soon be on the warden's desk. He never had tried to hide the fact that he wanted to be the next Captain once the warden retired. "I've been the acting *capitán* since Rodriguez started his desert chase and never returned to make a complete report to the warden. Now, I've got one more assignment to fulfill. This sealed letter in my hand is for Rodriguez. You can relax now, the chase is over. The letter is from the warden. It specifically orders Rodriguez to return for a formal disciplinary hearing. You're a good man, Flores and you take your responsibilities seriously. I'm counting on you to be one of my top men once I'm in charge. Another thing you should know about. Neilson, the superintendent of the line construction is in plenty of trouble, too. Some prominent sportsmen in Chihuahua heard about the record ram he poached in an area closed to hunting. He's going to be paying a heavy fine and he definitely won't be taking the trophy out of the country. There's also a strong possibility he won't be allowed to finish the line construction on down to Durango."

With the last comment Juarez moved through the crowd in the direction where Flores last saw the captain.

Flores was relieved that the chase was over. He had no idea how Reece had gotten through all of the guards and the state police surrounding the area if he actually had been on the train -- but he no longer cared. He was totally exhausted and anxious to return to his regular duties. The warden was right. Too much had been made of one man who got away. Flores wondered if anyone could have kept ahead of the flames and survived the fire. Besides, small families traveling with a burro was a common sight.

A runner hurried past and talked to the conductor standing by the caboose just behind the last passenger car. Flores wondered if the captain had made a decision.

A child's sudden cry caught Flores' attention. The boy still chasing after the pigeons had fallen and skinned his knee.

Two loud blasts came from the engine and a cheer went up from the people who were waiting for their trip to the states. Flores lost track of the boy as the passengers surged forward and lined up to enter the cars.

Flores looked down the line. Black smoke was pouring out of the engine's smokestack as the fireman shoveled more coal into the furnace and prepared to finally get the heavily loaded train in motion. Rodriguez stood off by himself, his face showing dejection. Flores was sure that the captain had to know the chase was over. A sudden frown indicated he'd spotted Juarez making his way toward him.

Most of the people who'd come down to see the train depart moved nearer to the tracks.

Blue stood with her attention still riveted on the next to last flat car on the train some twenty feet away. Flores watched as the cocky Juarez sauntered on down toward the captain.

A sudden sharp series of banging sounds rattled down the line of cars from the engine to the caboose.

The cows and calves just as suddenly stopped their bawling. The engine had moved forward a few feet, jerking the slack from each of the steel couplings that hitched the heavy cars together. Flores stood near the edge of the wooden station platform by Blue while another series of jolts rattled down the line. The violent reverberations of the couplings shook the ground under the station platform. Flores felt Blue push her side up close against his shins.

Only a few stragglers remained near the passenger cars where they waited until the last moment to say goodbye to friends and relatives before climbing aboard.

The conductor waited by the last step, smiling and greeting each passenger as they stepped up and reached for the hand grip.

The beaming reporter stood nearby. He'd no doubt catch the next train south that was still waiting on a siding in Juarez. He gave the appearance of a man who'd found the great romance of his life.

Flores could now see that the small boy who skinned his knee was snuggled into the old woman's lap that sat over against the wall. The boy stopped crying when the woman hugged and kissed him. He jumped up and skipped over to where the pretty girl was feeding an old shaggy burro a discarded half-eaten apple and took hold of her hand.

The train inched ahead and then stopped. For some reason Blue kept watching the back end of the flatcar.

Thick black smoke billowed back over the coal car as the engine strained against the weight of so many cars. The springs and axles under the cars squeaked and popped as they compressed and twisted, adjusting to the weight of the loads that each floor supported.

The boy pointed to the same spot that had riveted Blue's attention. He suddenly giggled then waved and called, "Adiós Sen..." just as the girl reached down and clamped her hand tightly over his mouth.

Flores stared at the place where the boy pointed. Some of the timber's sides showed saw cuts that were still like new in the last stack of timbers at the back of the flatcar. The newly exposed cuts contrasted sharply against the dullness of the timber's sides that had been exposed for weeks to the sun. He looked at the other beams on the front half of the car and then on down the line to the next load of timbers and then the one after that. All of the exposed timber's surfaces showed the same dullness.

The girl glanced around nervously while the boy tried to hide his face against her skirt.

Flores saw that the reporter was closely watching both Blue and the girl, then glancing back at the contrasting wood surfaces.

The girl was standing off to their left where she could see the ends of the timbers above the steel coupling.

When the train inched ahead the timbers at the back end of the car now came into the view of Flores and the reporter. Flores could hardly believe it. The bright cuts on the ends of nine timbers showed in a grid at the bottom of the load, starting at the floor of the flat car, three across and three high. Flores was now convinced they had been cut and made into a perfect wooden escape door. The entire section of lumber on the rear half of the car had to have been taken off and restacked. A dark slot cut across the top of the three timbers, an inch or so wide, provided for ventilation and a chance to watch behind.

Flores felt a sudden and overpowering surge of emotion. He wasn't sure what he should do.

But there was no doubt now. The hidden cavity behind the door had been cut out at night somewhere along a siding where the cars were held for shipment. Timbers had been shortened and the cut off pieces discarded.

The reporter looked at Flores. He showed no expression nor made any comment. He was no doubt waiting for Flores to make the first move. A young guard in Flores' position could make a name for himself. A bright future could be his with only a word to the conductor to signal the engineer to stop the train. An escaped prisoner was going to get away. He had to stop the train even though he'd come to admire the man whose determination to reach the border, against unbelievable odds, could become legend.

The first passenger car was now almost even with them. Within a few seconds it would pass.

Blue and the boy had both been right.

The girl's anxious eyes watched both men closely.

Flores looked back again in complete awe at the old woman with scraps of leather wrapped around her feet. He now realized that she was the one who had led the flight across the treacherous mountain trails. She showed no notice of the train's progress. She continued to weave threads through the holes in her blanket. Then Flores saw her steal a brief glance at the train from under the folds of her shawl.

It was too much for Flores. The events of the last two minutes had been overwhelming. An almost unbelievable story was being played out right in front of Flores and the reporter -- a story that no one else in Casas Grandes except the Indian family and the man hidden from view even suspected.

No words were spoken.

Each man knew what the other was thinking. So did the girl who intently watched them both and waited.

Flores opened his mouth to call out to the conductor to stop the train. He was unable to make even the slightest sound. He drew his pistol to fire a warning but found his finger wouldn't close around the trigger. He reholstered the pistol, paused for a moment in confusion, then gave a slight salute toward the hidden prisoner. Slowly he backed away, tugging on the rope to Blue's collar.

The man assigned to write a story smiled at Flores and tipped his hat then grabbed for the grip and jumped on the step at the back of the caboose as it passed.

The hobo was going home.

EPILOGUE

GRADUATION

At a hand signal from the stage, the young usher flipped a switch as he'd been instructed. The lights in the small auditorium dimmed for a moment, signaling the graduation program was ready to begin. Stragglers began taking their seats. The students waiting for their diplomas sat in the first three rows in front of the stage, their white caps and uniforms clearly visible to relatives and friends seated in the rows behind them. The assembled audience looked to be dressed in their finest clothes.

A tall slender man wearing a dark suit, and who looked to be in his sixties, rose and walked to the podium. He was the Milwaukee Nursing College's president. After his brief remarks and offers of congratulations, two other speakers followed him, each delivering a similar brief message. It was a happy yet solemn occasion. The last speaker, a dignified woman in a fitted blue suit, put on her glasses. She would read the names of the graduates and give out the diplomas.

The usher heard the door open behind him. He turned as a man entered the vestibule. The usher stepped forward to intercept him, for this man obviously didn't belong at the ceremony. His tousled hair and bloodshot eyes accentuated his gaunt and unshaven face. The dirty, wrinkled clothes he wore made it highly unlikely he'd even know any of the graduates. Perhaps he was hoping some food would be served at the end of the ceremony.

Yet something about the determination reflected in the man's eyes made the usher step back as the man tiptoed past and into the auditorium, taking a seat in the last row.

The stranger sat quietly without entering into the polite applause following the introduction of each graduate. Only three of the young nurse candidates remained to be introduced. When the speaker called out the name Eula Mae Reece, the man stood and continued applauding after all other sounds had ceased. While the audience turned and watched he wiped his eyes on his tattered sleeves.

The startled young honor graduate turned and looked out over the audience after taking her diploma. She stared for a moment at the ragged-looking man then visibly shaken she reached out to the podium to steady herself. After the final two graduates walked across the stage Miss Reece ran down the aisle and into the arms of the stranger.

Printed in the United States
777500003B